GRIP ON THE CITY

GRIP ON THE CITY

Liberating Harlem Heights

U.S. HICKS

Order this book online at www.trafford.com
or email orders@trafford.com

Most Trafford titles are also available at major online book retailers.

Printed in the United States of America.

ISBN: 978-1-4269-2309-8 (sc)

Trafford rev. 04/04/2011

 www.trafford.com

North America & International
toll-free: 1 888 232 4444 (USA & Canada)
phone: 250 383 6864 ♦ fax: 812 355 4082

For we wrestle not against flesh and blood, but against principalities, against powers, against the rulers of darkness of this world, against spiritual wickedness in high places.
(Ephesians 6:12, KJV)

Prologue

Good Confronts Evil

A conversation takes place in the spiritual realm between two individuals who were once brothers, now eternal enemies.

One, Solomon, represents the glory of Heaven; the other, Fratricide, reflects the fury of Hell. As both spirits hover above the city known as Harlem Heights, the big demon dominates the conversation. "Hmm, I will never surrender my domain to the Tyrant. I'm happy being the ruler of this piss pot city rather than a servant in that place you angels call Paradise—Empyreal, blah."

Not bothered by the filthy language, Solomon responds to the evil overlord. "Remember, I made the effort to warn you. If this is the path you choose to take, then so be it. We have a directive from the Savior to win this city. We shall take it as commanded."

"Go ahead, do the Tyrant's bidding like the good choir boys you are. I take orders from no one! Fratricide does what pleases Fratricide—that's why I left you slaves in that so-called utopia. I'd rather rule in Hades than serve in Heaven, hmm."

The cordial conservation becomes intense as the big demon draws his sword to further emphasize his point. "And how dare you venture into my domain threatening to take what's rightfully mine? Take this city if you dare. Be advised, you must come through me first, which I doubt you can do; you wimpy guardians have always failed miserably trying to overcome me. What makes you think you can succeed now?"

Without warning, a band of demon warriors suddenly appears, surrounding Solomon like a pack of ravenous wolves on the kill. The faces of the wicked spirits reflect menacing glares while the pungent smell of swamp gas pollutes the air. With yellow sulfur smoke puffing from their gaping mouths, the rabid-crazed demon dogs move in close, eager to rip the angel apart.

Fratricide watches with amusement to see how Solomon reacts. The angel plays it cool.

The demon is disappointed. "Hmm, does the servant of Empyreal dare not flee to save his puny life?" the evil one inquires. "Surely you know we mean business."

Solomon prefers a better course of action. "Why flee when *we* can fight?"

"We?" Fratricide is a bit puzzled. "Who are we? There are none but us."

"Correct you are … none but us."

"Halt!" shouts the overlord to his warriors. "Cease with these riddles! I've ruled long enough to know when a snare has been laid. Where are they?"

"To whom do you refer?"

"Don't play dumb with me, Bethlehem Boy. There's no way a single spirit like you would dare confront me without reinforcements. Where are the guardians hiding?"

"It was agreed that we would meet to discuss this matter in peace, don't you remember, William?"

"You will not refer to me by that slave name! I am Fratricide the Conqueror—don't you forget it."

"Whatever, Billy," is Solomon flippant reply.

Pushed to the point of anger, Fratricide lunges, attempting to lock a strangling choke hold on Solomon's neck. The big demon is quicker than expected, but not quick enough as the angel slips his grip. However, the evil one is rather crafty himself, and his attempt to bind the messenger is nothing but a mere ploy to draw a reaction from those who remain hidden out of sight. As Fratricide pretends to pursue the Empyrean, his eyes look about, searching for signs of enemy activity. Noticing nothing, he speaks. "Hmm, the Carpenter's slave wishes to play games, yes? Seize him!" the wicked spirit commands.

The demons are more than eager to follow orders, and just as they draw near to rip the angel to pieces, a trumpet blares. Empyreal warriors suddenly appear to wage a battle with the hellions.

"There you all are, just as I figured," croons the overlord. "What happened to coming in peace?"

Solomon justifies the actions of the guardians. "We came in peace; you didn't. And let today's event be a warning. The Lord has plans for this city that will not be hindered. Leave freely while you can."

Fratricide, amused, takes the threat as a challenge. "The Shepard has sent His crazed lambs to the slaughter; surely your minds are not right. I own this city. You will not enter my domain without paying the price. Hmm, I dare you to come before me, let's see how bad you want this."

There's much at stake if the guardians want to win Harlem Heights for the Lord. Evil's threads are deeply woven into the garments of society, and the cloth doesn't wash easily. To defeat the dark side, the forces of good must conquer the source of evil in the city of Harlem Heights. Willie Mo' is the key.

1

How it All Started

In the early 1970s, I am just a boy when I find myself standing inside a five-point star—a pentagram—drawn on the floor with chalk. Black candles burn on every point of the star, the room lights are dim, and a faint smell of sulfur hangs in the air. The foul scent grows thicker … stronger by the passing second.

The séance begins. Chanting witches and warlocks begin humming louder when the presence of Hell enters the room. What appear to be large, slow-rolling cotton balls are really thick, tumbling white waves of fog creeping along the floor, making a trail toward a throne where someone of high rank would only dare to sit.

I'm offered an object that resembles a blade to cut my finger with, so I can sign my name to a satanic contract in blood. The ceremony is going smoothly until I show reluctance to pierce my skin with the dagger's sharp edge. A swift, harsh slap across the face motivates me to pierce my skin—the contract is signed.

My life would be comprised of sadistic ceremonies and hideous crimes until the day I would meet the true Lord and Savior.

They call me Willie Mo', but my real name is Willie James Moore. I was born from a mother whose addiction to drugs caused me problems in my early life. At birth, I was an underweight baby who suffered withdrawal symptoms. I cried all the time as an infant and never sat still as a toddler. My mother's drug use led to my attention deficit disorder as a preschool child.

Thanks to a certain spirit, I became a really naughty kid. I was so aggravating that my own momma rejected me at an early age. Instinctively, I knew she didn't like me, so I would purposely do things to piss her off. Even though she whipped my butt good, I would still lash back at my momma the best way I could. At that young age, I could do nothing but cry for endless hours while constantly getting into mischief. My mother could get no rest unless I was asleep. I knew it and exploited every opportunity to pester my no-good mammy. This was pretty good progress considering I was just an innocent child. Little did I know there was an evil force behind the scene *molding* my character.

Maybe if I had known better, I would have treated my mother better. To her defense, she was a victim of the streets too. I don't know much about her life, but I heard she, Cynthia was her name, fell in love with a man who deceived her. The so-called lover was nothing but a pimping wolf pretending to be a devoted lover. That hustler played his hand smoothly using drugs to turn my mother into a prostitute that stalked the streets day and night searching for the next opportunity to get high. Like any young, naive female hustling the streets for drugs, she eventually gave birth to an unwanted baby boy, me.

I grew up in the city where most people believe witchcraft and voodoo is something those southern folks like to practice. You know, people in the city are too smart to mess around with that Johnny-the-conqueror-root stuff. That's a big mistake! Such ignorance is the reason the craft flourishes so well in the city—it's the same reason why I thrived in darkness.

Due to the circumstances in which I was born, I became an unusual child. Oftentimes, I could be found all alone playing without supervision, and naturally so, a child left alone is a child in trouble.

Trouble came to me in the form of an old man, Mr. Levy. There was something within me that attracted him, a hidden power that scratched at the surface of my soul yearning to be released, crying to the one who could draw it out. Levy was the ideal man for the job; the job was ideal for the old man.

I can't ever recall a time of being without Mr. Levy; it seems that he has always been in my life. I believe he got in good with my mother by providing all the money needed to buy drugs without her having to sell her body on the streets on a daily basis. Whatever he did, Levy won my mother's favor and even gained legal custody of me, which kept other family members from interfering in my life. Cynthia neither knew what was going on behind closed doors with me, nor allowed it to concern her. My mother had drugs, and the old man had me—a fair exchange is no robbery, I suppose.

All my memories of Mr. Levy are the same. He was always a quiet man who kept himself busy with cooking and chanting. As a kid, I never knew why he cooked so much food, nor did I understand why we almost *never* ate the things he prepared. Visitors would always come by the house to pick up the concoctions he created. Some of these dishes emanated a savoring aroma that would rouse my appetite. Other dishes smelled horribly foul and took several days, sometimes a week or so, before the odor finally cleared the kitchen.

Though he seldom left the house, Mr. Levy worked for someone, but he never discussed his business with me, and I instinctively knew better than to ask.

As I mentioned before, my memories of the old man are mostly the same. He's always been that skinny old guy of average height for a man with no hair on his shiny bald head. His smutty black skin and hazel eyes makes for an exotic look. I never knew how old this toothless man was, for none of us ever celebrated birthdays. From the little bit of time I did spend in public school, I learned from the other kids and parents that my Levy was a weird man. For instance, no matter how cold the temperature, the old man was always sweating. He also carried on conversations with himself too, but I always referred to it as chanting. Though his behavior seemed odd to others, it was normal to me. I suppose that both of us were a bit detached from mainstream society, which explains why I never got along with my peers and school teachers.

What most people didn't know is that Mr. Levy is into the craft. The old man is a teacher of the dark arts, and I was his superb student. The elder exposed me to things that brought me spiritual powers. He took me to special places and introduced me to people who also took interest in my development. Some of these places were located in the affluent parts of town while others were deep in the slums where cops seldom went. I saw all races and religions of people at the occult gatherings. It's astonishing to see how evil occupies every level of society.

Mr. Levy oversaw every aspect of my training which, for the most part, always went fine except for one thing: I didn't like human sacrifices. From where this distaste for killing came, I never knew. According to Levy, it was the prayers of my Christian grandmother that caused me to be stubborn. He said the woman's prayers to the Heavenly Father would hinder the rituals, making it impossible for me to participate in the sacrifices. This angered the old man to the point of wanting to rid the Earth of my grandmother, but somehow he was always powerless in his efforts to outright harm the woman. Still, this never stopped Levy from attacking the church she attended—he even taught me how to do it.

I hardly ever spoke to my grandmother. I would visit on some holidays as directed by the State social work office when they appointed Mr. Levy to be my legal guardian. Still my relationship with my grandma, Mattie Moore, is distant, and we barely exchange words when we do see each other.

Getting back to my education, I was schooled very well, just not in the typical manner as most other kids were taught. My childhood experiences exposed me to supernatural wonders that no classroom could ever match, unless, of course, it was an occult classroom. I quickly mastered the three R's: reading, writing and arithmetic—even excelled at chemistry, my favorite subject. More importantly, I learned to be very intuitive when interacting with others.

Manipulating and influencing other people's emotions became my specialty. I quickly learned the benefits of using someone else to do my dirty work: Take credit for everything good; pass the blame when things go bad. I also learned the power of persuasion is the most effective and powerful tool to wield on the masses who seek leadership—it matters little if the leader is good or bad, people just like to be led.

Mr. Levy and I developed a unique bond. He helped me to discover the power of the craft which led me to do the evil that I did. Honestly though, I can't blame everything on him. I only needed a little persuasion to commit the sins I did; just lead me to the water, and I would gulp more than my fair share. At times, my thirst for violence and self-gratification was unquenchable. Vengeance became my obsession. I had to strike back at society for being black and poor. The kids who made fun of me had to pay too. My mother was in need of punishment for being the drug addict who brought me into this wretched world. Mr. Levy helped me to achieve the things that no one else could provide in my life.

You may wonder why I mention so much about Levy rather than myself. I do so because the old man was the lens through which I viewed the world—in essence, he was an extension of my life; a liaison between me and the spirit realm. Still, this didn't pacify my curiosity to know why my inner guide never manifested himself to me. I eventually learned that evil spirits work through a medium because it's difficult to steer a human vessel, or they are not permitted to do so until the mortal reaches a certain point of maturity, thus the reason for the old man in my life.

As a medium, Mr. Levy's primary job was to mentor and train me while a certain spirit monitored my progress closely. It was necessary to cut all means of love and affection from me, which caused my heart to become cold and callous ... a place where no compassion could be found. In the absence of love, I fed on the bittersweet taste of hatred. I became a reflection of Hell and the demon waiting to occupy my soul. This served to make me the evil menace that I am today: Willie Mo', king of the Black Pharaohs.

Little did I know that Mr. Levy's job as my teacher would someday end, causing our role as student and teacher to be reversed. I would become the master; he would be my slave. It was all setup by that spirit, Molder, who in turn, enslaved me.

2

Enter Molder, Exit Levy

Having reached the age of young adulthood, the time has come for Willie James Moore to cut ties with Levy and lead a life of his own. The student must undergo one last ceremony to acquire a personal guide who will lead him on the dark spiritual journey where danger will be constantly lurking.

When the day arrives, the barefoot apprentice is dressed in a black silk robe that does little to conceal his naked silhouette. Led to a dimly lit room, Willie assumes a kneeling position inside a chalk-drawn pentacle on the cold concrete floor. As Mo' meditates, a satanic priest approaches to bless the young man with desecrated holy water. The droplets of liquid burns Willie's skin, but he resists the urge to flinch. Once again, Mo' is offered a knife to cut his finger, so he can sign with his own blood. Years ago this would have been a difficult task; today he is older and eager.

The moment he signs the contract, a bolt of energy surges through Willie Mo's body causing him to jerk about as if having a seizure. A frenzy of wicked jubilation erupts within the room that causes Willie Mo's gyrating hips and flapping arms to move in cadence to the chanting on-lookers. The festive mood fades away and the mortal relaxes.

The apprentice remains on his hands and knees within the center of the chalk-drawn star, still recuperating, still waiting for the next series of events to take place. With his head hanging downward, Mo' catches a glimpse of a slim flickering flame from the corner of his eye. Another small flame appears in front of him, then on his other side, and he assumes lights are flickering behind his back as well. The black candles on each point of the pentacle have mysteriously come to light without any mortal providing a flame.

The same priest that sprinkled Willie with the desecrated holy water now holds, in hand, a small silver goblet containing special herbs soaked in animal's blood. He speaks an incantation and the contents of the goblet begin boiling until the liquid turns to a fine white powder. The priest pours the magic dust in Willie Mo's cupped hands, watching as the young one utters a chant and throws the powder to the air, which drifts down upon the candles causing them to explode with large, blinding flames that bear no heat—ice flames. Plumes of smoke engulf the immediate area where Willie and the priest stand and the scent of a sulfuric acid is strong within the air.

As soon as the smoke clears, there stands a tall, slim figure with a look of supreme intelligence radiating from his eyes. "I am Molder, your wisdom and guide. Trust in me, and I will lead you to places that you have never been."

Molder walks into Willie's body taking possession of the mortal's soul. The entrance causes a burning sensation that's worse than any pain he's felt before. The mortal is compelled to scream out in agony.

In Willie's mind, he hears a voice. *"If you ever disobey me, this is the price you'll pay; if you ever dare to betray me, this will be the pain you'll feel. I, and I alone, am your master. I am a jealous god, and you'll put no one before me,"* declares Molder with his blasphemous tongue.

All spiritual guides have a sidekick, a crazed warrior to watch their backs during times of trouble, or a bully who can deliver a clear message that leaves little room for confusion. Molder is accompanied by the warrior, Wrath, who stands guard outside Willie's body with his sword drawn. The horrid creature's eyes are inferno red and glower with a menacing look. The warrior's vicious claws can shred human flesh with the slightest touch. Serving as Willie's personal guard, he will fight many battles on the mortal's behalf. Times will also come when this very same spirit will punish Willie for disobedience.

Molder and Wrath now have full control of their mortal vessel. He will serve the demons well as they seek to rule the city of Harlem Heights, and already the young man is set to execute his first task as a warlock.

Since Molder is in Willie's life now, there is no need for Mr. Levy's teachings. The old man is well advanced in age, which means his value in the dark kingdom has dwindled, and so it comes as no surprise when the orders are given for Willie to face the old man in combat. The confrontation takes place in Mr. Levy's shack.

Standing across the room from one another, they stare each other down. More than usual, the old man is sweating profusely. From the beginning, Levy knew this day would come. Willie is too young and ambitious to realize he will eventually share the same fate if he remains in the occult.

Mr. Levy looks Willie up and down while his mind goes back to the times when the young man was just a poor boy. Mo' was just another fatherless black kid, neglected and unloved. If it were not for the old man, he probably would have died early or ended up in prison like so many other young minority males—just another statistic. Yet his life took on a drastic change under the supervision of Levy. Now the old man, talking in his Southern Black dialect, attempts to delay his fate by taunting his heir.

"Boy, do ya dare come 'gainst me? Everythang you know, I teached you; I made you what you is today and dis how you seek ta repay me?"

Though Willie is the best student Levy ever taught, all pupils have a shortcoming or two. The old man is well aware of Mo's reluctance to kill. Taunting his pupil, the teacher takes a chance, hoping that has not changed.

"To take my place, you must be willin' ta do certain thangs. Do you think you ready to walk in my shoes? You bettah think again if you can't get yo' hands bloody, boy."

Willie stands before Levy with a blank expression on his face. Deep within his cold, dark heart, he bears no animosity toward the old man. Mo' could use some motivation; it's hard to kill just for the hell of it.

Without making a physical move, Mr. Levy uses his spiritual powers to lift Willie to the air and slam him into the wall. Attempting to try again, the elder is not able. The old man strains with all the power he can muster, yet his efforts are useless. For extra strength, he tries to summon the demons from Willie's body, but the spirits won't leave a younger, stronger vessel for an older, weaker one.

On the contrary, one spirit after another abandons Mr. Levy's body making him weaker. Soon he finds himself lying in middle of the floor in a fetal position moaning ... gasping for air as his dark skin, once sweaty and shiny, becomes bone dry. Levy's bright hazel eyes are dull, and his tongue is cotton white. The old man waits patiently for the next blow to strike his physical body. It never comes. The young one can't bring himself to destroy the old teacher. Mo' simply walks away with the intention of never coming back again.

3

Fratricide, the Visit & Truce

The Black Pharaohs and the Latin Reds are rival gangs that occupy the east and west sides of town. These gangs formed back in the 1970s after the civil rights movement of the '60s ended.

It was the loss of leaders like Martin L. King, Jr., and Malcolm X that gave rise to the dangerous inner city gangs throughout America. The ideals of nonviolence gave way to murder, drug dealing, and violent crimes. In Harlem Heights, Fratricide is the evil overlord who employs this devious scheme to keep the city in bondage.

Fratricide is an obese spirit whose blubbery carcass is wider than a king-size mattress. The rolls of his big belly jiggle with the slightest movement of his body. The mammoth's leathery skin is dull gray in color and wrinkled rough like an elephant's hide. A fat face makes his round eyes appear to be two yellow slits. When sitting, Fratricide resembles a plump Buddha statue. When standing, the behemoth's height is towering; he dwarfs most spirits who stand in his presence. Despite his grotesque appearance, the large one is an awesome sight to behold when he spreads his massive wings that expand the width of a city street.

Though the big one is heavy, the demonic dinosaur is quick on the draw, handy with a sword, and possesses strength beyond measure. Being a control freak, the quick-tempered Fratricide rules with an iron fist and has little tolerance for failure.

At the moment, Fratricide's army stands upon the rooftop of the 8th Street warehouse waiting anxiously for the Prince of the world to arrive. As the demons stand motionless on the rooftop, a mild breeze begins to stir. Gradually it becomes stronger, bringing with it a scent of sulfur that clings to the air; the evil forces can smell the arrival of Hell.

The chopping sound of leathery wings flapping in the wind can be heard over the distance. Like a squadron of attack helicopters on a wartime mission, the Prince and his entourage of Sheol's most deadly spirits come into sight, causing a frenzy of cheers to erupt from Fratricide's forces.

When the command is signaled, every spirit stands deathly still—like a statue—at the position of attention. A group of naughty imps stand as quietly as possible with smirks plastered on their faces. Very few are above five feet in height; most are less than three feet tall. As with all spirits, their wings remain invisible while grounded. The small ones, even to their detriment, are irresistibly curious by nature and prone to mischief. Dozens of eyeballs are rolling in every direction; none dare move their heads.

Like children in the classroom, the rascal imps snicker and snivel, belch and fart quietly among themselves. Despite their efforts to be serious, stone-faced warriors, they look comical and mischievous. Their swords are small like children's toys in comparison to the larger spirits' weapons. The imps are harassers, pranksters, doorkeepers, and troublemakers—pests sent out to keep mortals focused on anything but God.

Nearby the smaller spirits are the ministers. They stand much taller than their fellow pranksters. Disciplined enough to remain silent with their bodies perfectly straight, heads tilted slightly back with pride, the ministers differ greatly from the little ones. There's an aura of intelligence radiating from the ministers. None smiles, yet cunning and amusing expressions shape their faces. Having the ability to remain focused—which is a challenging task for the imps—the ministers can easily separate business from pleasure. These fallen angels relish the fact that it takes superior skills to be deceivers, artists of all sorts, spirits of infirmities, infiltrators, and guides. They don't specialize in fighting, but, when cornered, they can raise hell too. This is Molder's class of demon.

The warriors comprise the last group of evil spirits. They are the most intimidating and largest. Many are eight feet in height, others even taller. Some resemble giant men, while others appear to be ogres and hunch-backed werewolves. Jet black scales averaging three inches in diameter cover their bodies. It would take a mighty powerful blow to penetrate this armor. Claws on their hands, talons on their feet, yellow fangs, and a sword comprise the warriors' weapon system. These demons are skilled in all forms of fighting. They introduced mankind to martial arts many centuries ago.

As the Prince and his horrid motley crew arrive, harsh winds cause the imps to bend over clawing the ground with their hands and feet. Some, despite their efforts, manage to anchor their hands into the ground while their legs and feet sway in the spiritual wind like flags. The other unfortunate scoundrels roll across the roof like billiard balls scattered about a pool table on the first break. The ministers and warriors are not fazed by the wind at all.

The Prince of the world along with his group of evil angels has arrived to Harlem Heights. As their clawed feet touch the warehouse roof, all the subordinates render forth their honors: *"All hail Lucifer; all hail to Apollyon; all praise to Satan, the Prince of the world."*

The fallen star takes his time looking about the horde before he utters a word. Content with conditions, the Prince hisses the order for everyone to rise, and then he summons Fratricide. The mammoth's big body glides effortlessly before the former archangel, Lucifer.

The Prince, forever concerned about the mission, has no interest in exchanging pleasantries. "What good news do you have for me?"

Fratricide is accustomed to his demanding lord and tries to give an appeasing answer. "Hmm, the city has been won. It's completely under our control."

"What became of those troubling saints? Are they still a hindrance?"

"Your Highness, the church is no more. We put forth extra effort to destroy it by setting fire to the building, which scattered the saints to the winds. There is no light in this city, Harlem Heights belongs to us."

"Splendid. Make sure it stays this way. Much has been invested to transform this place into a refuge for demons to dwell. I expect this city to thrive in darkness, growing until we own this whole nation." The Prince speaks as though visions of ruling the Earth dance in his eyes. "To make this happen, you must ensure a certain delivery makes its way here to Harlem Heights without interference from above. Your orders are to dispatch your best warriors to guard the shipment."

Surprisingly, spiritual beings are subject to the same shortcomings as mortals. While the Prince and Fratricide discuss operation plans, a little spirit becomes restless.

Seeing the chance to have fun, a gremlin quietly draws his sword to poke the imp in front of him. The victimized spirit, knowing full well the consequences of moving or yelling out in pain, withstands the torture. Not content with the results, the mischievous one pokes a different victim. The results are great. The suffering imp jumps to the air screaming, "Someone struck me!" Drawing a sword, the victim rolls his eyeballs in a frantic search of the perpetrator. The hunt is on.

The guilty one pretends to be unaware of what is going on, yet his mischievous nature can't resist the pleasure of relishing the moment. Trying hard to hide a sheepish grin with quivering lips, the gremlin lets out a grunting laugh like one trying to hold back an unwanted sneeze. Too bad now, his cover is blown.

The victim, knowing he's doomed for moving without permission, zeroes in on the culprit to get revenge. Both are oblivious to the warriors headed their way. Just as the victim raises his sword to initiate an attack, his head is suddenly sliced from its neck. The headless body charges forward a few paces before it evaporates into thick dust particles like a vampire in sunlight.

The troublemaker, already regretting his mistake, attempts to flee but meets his fate just a split second later. A red flash slices his body from the crown of his head down through the bottom of his crotch.

The action is over. Still several warriors run about the battalion on all four legs like wild dogs looking for signs of disobedience among Fratricide's forces. Not one imp or gremlin dares to move.

The master is not pleased. "My brother-killer, the discipline here is lacking. I hope for your sake this is not indicative of your leadership."

"No, my Lord, it will never happen again."

The Prince takes a moment of silence as he contemplates something in the back of his mind. "You still have yet to tell me about the woman."

Fratricide's mind draws a blank, then he suddenly remembers—or so he pretends. "Hmm … yes, the old woman. She's the only true saint whose prayers gave us trouble. Our efforts to kill her have been partially effective. As I speak, the woman is in the intensive care unit due to cardiac arrest."

"Why is she not gone?" the angry Prince demands to know.

"My Lord, the enemy has placed a hedge around her. We have scouts at the hospital to make sure she does not live much longer once that protection is gone," answers Fratricide.

"She'd better not be alive when I return. I don't handle failure too well."

With the news just provided to him, the Prince takes off toward the sky with a black cloud in tow, yet one spirit is left behind—Informer. This little runt remains to provide details on the shipment. He's also there to keep an eye on things for the master.

No one cares for Informer and his big mouth. Despite how bothersome he is, Informer is untouchable, and he makes sure everyone knows it.

The 8th Street warehouse is an abandoned building that serves as the headquarters of the Black Pharaohs. No longer the industrial factory it once was, it's used as a meeting place, shelter, and a processing plant for illegal drugs. Gang members stand guard 24/7 to keep unwanted visitors away. This same warehouse also serves as a roosting place for Fratricide's minions.

The Black Pharaohs are gathering within the warehouse, waiting for their leader, Willie Mo', to appear. Normally, the Pharaohs would gather for such an occasion after a battle or to execute a major distribution of drugs. However, they come here tonight for another special reason.

The gang leader arrives to the warehouse with his personal band of gangsters. No longer an aggravating little boy whom anyone can slap around, Willie James Moore is well over six feet tall with sinewy muscles bulging all over his body. His beige linen suit is loose fitting and does little to hide his well-built frame. Willie's presence demands immediate attention when he enters the room.

Ready to reveal the news, Mo' brings the crowd to silence and begins to tell all. The Pharaohs are in awe when they learn of the shocking news. How can the gang profit from a truce with the Latin Reds? This goes against all the rules.

The Pharaohs and Reds were once bitter enemies who have now come together for one common cause: money. With a shipment of narcotics on its way to the city worth millions of dollars, every gang member will be rich for a season.

Willie Mo' and his gang have just finished the business part of their meeting. Everyone is eager to hear more of the plans that Mo' has, but they'll have to wait. The Pharaoh makes it a habit to give his crew just enough information at any given time. He's learned from the past that too much information can be just as bad for his plans as too little.

The music is blaring loud with plenty of scantily dressed females dancing to the groove. Reefer and cigarette smoke clouds the air while spilled beer dampens the floor.

Loud cursing and coarse joking is a delight to the demons hovering above. One spirit after another begins descending into the bodies of the gang members to take part in the festivities. Being a human and demonic orgy, every creature is fulfilling its craving for whatever it desires.

Spirits of addiction whet the appetites of those experimenting with drugs. They sit among the humans talking and manipulating their senses. While the mortals snort coke, the spirits squeeze the users' hearts with a sinister pinch watching the suffocating organ palpitate. The youth are ignorant of the physical effects of cocaine.

With inhibitions drowned in beer and liquor, sneaky hands creep up someone's blouse or dress. Intoxication opens the doorway for lust to slip in. Spirits of lust are on the prowl seeking whom they can seduce. Demons of infirmities travel alongside the lustful ones in search of opportunities to pass on sexually transmitted diseases to those willing to expose their bodies for a few moments of pleasure.

Lust also uses the more seasoned humans to prey on the younger, less experienced mortals for pleasure. Females are not the only victims of choice; teenage boys are targeted too. Some men like young males who are not fully aware of their manhood and are easily persuaded to try an alternate lifestyle.

Even though he is evil, Willie Mo' never hangs around for the wild parties at the warehouse. He learned to never let his guard down by getting intoxicated. The gang leader is also trained not to get emotionally close to women. Mo' is cold as ice.

Jermaine Trotter, also known as JT, is Willie's closest associate. In the Pharaohs' army, he's the platoon sergeant of the gang. He makes sure everybody follows all of Mo's orders.

Jermaine doesn't mind doing the dirty work and relishes his reputation as a true gangster. He never revealed his wish to be the leader of the Pharaohs, but his ambition does show when Willie Mo' is not around. Murder is in JT's heart, and he craves ruination.

4

Murder in His Heart

JT and Mo' leave the party early, going their separate ways. JT feels an urge to pay a visit to the hospital, so he can finish the job with the old lady. A companion travels with JT—it's Murder.

Since Jermaine Trotter was a fetus in his mother's womb, Murder was there in his heart. He first entered JT when his mom attempted an abortion. She didn't have the heart to go all the way through with it, but her initial actions opened the doorway for Murder to occupy Jermaine's soul. Ever since then, the spirit has influenced the mortal in doing a countless number of devious things.

As a young boy, JT loved to play with fire. The naughty kid required close supervision and could never be left alone with matches or a lighter in his hands—turn your back and the pyromaniac would set the house on fire. His mother, along with other adults in his life, could never figure out why Jermaine Trotter was so fascinated by fire.

Trotter also grew up without a father figure to guide him, so he quickly became an unruly kid that would grow to be an adult hoodlum. The lack of proper discipline in JT's life led to his unusual pleasure in killing things. As a youngster, he started with little bugs and rodents, which led to bigger things such as mutilating kittens and puppies. But, before this young killer realized it, he was about to put his talent to work for the first time—big time—when he joined a gang.

As a part of his initiation, Jermaine had to kill someone. According to gang rules, it's too easy to snuff the life of the enemy; taking the life of an innocent was the requirement. This is how Murder sealed a grip on JT's heart. The mortal can remember the incident as if it were yesterday.

"C'mon man, don't be scared now," says an older gang member wanting to initiate JT. "That's what's wrong with you young bloods today: ya'll want everything for free. You wanna be down with us, you gotta earn it. Take this heat and burn somebody with it." Though he's eager to be part of something big, JT is scared to commit. "Whatcha need, lil' man, huh? Come get some of this courage; take a sniff ... yeah, feelin' like a big man now? C'mon, dog, get this gun and put in some work. We can't hang together unless you get dirt on your hands too."

The cocaine makes JT feel more courageous than ever. Taking the gun, he stocks the streets seeking someone to take out. Murder walks with him screaming obscenities into the boy's mind, enticing him even more.

"Oh, oh, who should I chose?" sings Murder with childlike glee. "So many to pick from, which one is the best? There's a woman—that child would be better. No, bad choice, let's pick another, hmm ... let's see ... him, yes, *him*," yells Murder with an accusing finger pointed at an elderly man. "Take him out—he offends me!"

The old man isn't a preacher, but he is a Christian. A Jesus-freak like him is outspoken and tolerates no disrespect from children. The Holy Roller calls the cops anytime he spots a dope dealer hanging around the neighborhood. He also quotes scriptures aloud. The old fool is John the Baptist incarnate: brazen and troublesome to those up to no good. For these reasons, Murder hates the old man.

JT pulls out the pistol and blasts away. Lying prone, dead in the street, the old fool bleeds profusely from a gunshot wound to the head. The young killer quickly flees the scene without being apprehended by the law. His first experience with Murder is scary but exciting.

Gang initiation took place a long time ago when JT was just a teenager looking to fit in with his peers. Now he's a grown, seasoned killer with another mission on his mind.

Jermaine Trotter is on his way to the hospital to take care of unfinished business. He intends to visit the old woman, Mattie Moore, who survived the church burning. During the chaotic event, she inhaled a lot of hot smoke that caused her to suffer cardiac arrest. The old woman's recollection of the event isn't clear, but she does have a faint memory of large men carrying her out of the church and for some strange reason, they carried swords. Could they have been angels? Whoever they were, Mattie is thankful to God to be alive. Now she's hoping to recover soon and return to the comfort of her home. However, the visitor has different plans for the old lady.

With flowers in hand, JT approaches the hospital information desk to politely inquire on the whereabouts of Mattie Moore's room. His spiritual companions are with him: Murder, Hatred and Anger whisper obscenities into JT's mind, encouraging him to follow-through with the plan to take the old woman's life. Just the thought of killing makes the adrenaline rush through the man's veins.

Exiting the elevator, Jermaine steps out on the seventh floor heading towards room 726. Upon entering the doorway to Mattie's room, Trotter suddenly stops. He sees the woman sleeping peacefully on her bed, but the killer can't move; something is stopping him from going any farther.

What the mortal can't see are two guardians standing before him blocking the entrance with their swords. These angels have been assigned to guard the life of Mattie at all cost.

The demons that accompany JT are paralyzed with fear. They never expected to find guardians in the old lady's room. All three spit blasphemies toward the Empyreans.

Heaven's warrior gives an order. "Flee from here, the Lord forbids any harm to this woman!"

"You have no right to interfere; her life belongs to us," hisses Murder. "Your Savior gave us permission to burn the church down—now let us finish our business!"

"Burning the church was enough. You filthy denizens have run this city ragged. Your season of destruction is coming to an end, and it brings joy to our hearts to know the Father above has given us permission to fight back."

The evil doers are enraged. Murder swears that he is going to kill the old lady and the guardians. Anger throws a tantrum, waving his sword back and forth through the air, cursing. All the while he's careful enough not to get too close to the angelic warriors who are guarding Mattie. Hatred does his usual routine of yelling how much he hates the situation.

All three devils protest, but none initiates an attack. As they leave, the demons threaten to inform the overlord, Fratricide.

Of course, JT cannot see what just happened in the spiritual realm, but he can sense something has changed. Feeling empty, he stands in the doorway fully aware of why he came to the hospital, yet the motivation to kill is no longer within him. Still hating the old woman, the killer is not able go through with his plans for now.

Murder, Anger, and Hatred scurry through the evening air with demon speed, wanting to get away from the guardians before more trouble starts. Finding themselves a safe distance from the hospital, they stop to argue things over.

Anger hisses with all the venom his voice can muster, "Who's going to tell Fratricide we failed?"

The foul spirits look around as if someone might magically appear to answer the question. None of them has the heart to approach Fratricide with bad news. Murder is the strongest of the three, so he pulls out his sword to make the decision.

"Hatred, go tell the overseer we suffered an attack at the hospital."

"I hate it when you do this. It's not my fault that you couldn't stand before the enemy. Hades' curses upon you, I don't want to do it," whines the loathsome spirit.

Murder holds his sword to the coward's throat threatening, "You will do as I command—or die."

Hatred flies off in a flash, whining all the way to Fratricide's domain. There's nothing he dislikes more—besides thinking of judgment day—than bringing bad news to the behemoth.

At Fratricide's lair stand guards who question the imp's reason to see the overlord. It's bad news, so the lonely spirit is allowed to inform the big one himself.

Approached by the underling, the mammoth gives Hatred a look of suspicion. "What business do you have here, spirit?"

"Master, something unexpected happened at the hospital. We were nearly destroyed by the enemy's ambush; we never had a chance—it's all a disaster!"

"What are you talking about, fool?" roars the overlord.

"Our orders were to kill the woman at the hospital, but we were attacked by Heaven's warriors." Hatred tries his best to look worn and distraught. "There were many of them protecting the old woman. It took everything we could muster just to escape with our lives."

The big one makes a visual inspection of the imp. "You surely don't look as though you've been in a battle. Where are your wounds, hmm?"

Oops, Hatred didn't even think about battle wounds before he made up his lie.

"I ... I don't have any because ... I managed to evade the enemy before ..." Hatred's mind goes blank, and now he fears what could happen next.

Highly upset, Fratricide renders the lowly spirit a dazing blow to the head that sends the imp sliding on his back.

The large one sits forward on his throne to issue an order. His Buddha belly jiggles as he barks out demands. "Listen, you rascal. Your job is to watch that saint; don't let her out of your sight. Find out what's so important about that woman, then report back to me. Hmm ... if the sons of Empyreal are protecting her, I must know the reason why."

Having struggled to his feet and regained his bearing, Hatred assumes a kneeling position before Fratricide—at a distance beyond the ruler's reach. However, with a weapon in hand, the big one easily overcomes the space using the hot sword tip that prompts Hatred to stand.

As the loathsome spirit stands, the large one's sword slowly makes a trail down the spirit's throat, along the sternum and down a quivering stomach. The mammoth slowly slips the sword between the spirit's thighs until the blade is resting sharply underneath its rump. The upward pressure of the sword causes Hatred to rise on his little imp wings—like a kid riding a seesaw—until he is eye level to the overlord. The rascal's wings flutter frantically to reduce the body weight sitting on the blade. Fratricide draws him in face to face.

Hatred is scared to breathe in his master's face ... petrified to look into his yellow, beady eyes. The big one bounces the imp into the air and swats Hatred's rump, using the flat side of his sword the way a Major League slugger swings a bat. The gremlin flies like a baseball to center field. If this is a sign for him to leave, the spirit doesn't need another clue.

5

The Guardians Find a Shepard

Several blocks from the warehouse stand two angels observing the night's activities. One spirit, Solomon, is a high-ranking spirit who serves as a messenger of God. His voice brings the good news of the Lord ... encouragement to the world. A golden trumpet has been placed in his hands. With this instrument, he heralds the gospel to mankind.

The messenger stands well over seven feet tall with broad shoulders. If just a mortal man, Solomon would definitely be of African descent. Wide nostrils, wooly hair, and high cheekbones give him the appearance of a tribal leader.

Solomon's light brown eyes reflect peace and wisdom. It doesn't take much for his thick lips to draw thin, revealing a smile that is as warm as the morning sunrise. Due to the present condition of the city, his brown eyes are just like Lee's.

Lee is the comrade of Solomon. These brothers have been given the assignment of breaking Fratricide's grip on the inner city. Lee's somber blue eyes bear a deep concern for the moral state of mankind. And, even though the two angels are in agreement with their goals, Lee plays a different role in this game. Lee is an Empyrean warrior. He stands just as tall as Solomon, but he has golden blond hair, bronze tanned skin, and a frame that is thicker, more massive than that of his companion.

Serving as the fury of Heaven, Lee holds protection in one hand and destruction in the other. With one swipe of a sword, a plague, famine, or natural disaster can take out generations of people. Besides worshipping the almighty Lord, there's nothing more fulfilling to him than engaging the enemy in battle. Lee was created for this purpose.

Solomon and Lee wait patiently for the scout, Siron, to arrive with the news. Siron is also a warrior, but his mission differs from that of Lee. Unlike the captain warrior, Siron has a slight athletic build. About six feet in height, the scout bears the looks of a Native American. A powerful demon would never fear a fight with Siron. The only thing the kingdom of Sheol fears about Siron is his crafty nature in the conduct of reconnaissance. He has a way of finding out information by getting into places where even Heaven's sons fear to go.

The scout is returning from the warehouse with some important news to tell Solomon and Lee. The information confirms the uneasy feelings the two captains were experiencing within their spirits. It's the same feeling they felt over two thousand years ago after witnessing the scene at the cross. The fallen star, Lucifer, has made a visit to the city.

Siron explains the intentions of the gangs to form an alliance as a means of getting drugs into the city. Such clandestine activities have kept Harlem Heights in bondage for decades. This strangling grasp of evil has been a stumbling block for the Empyrean's forces, and repeated attempts to break this grip have continually failed. They all know the reasons why.

The American industrial revolution brought people of various backgrounds into one large place, all seeking economic opportunities. The great migration of European immigrants and Southern Blacks into Harlem Heights caused the city to become a powder keg of dynamite fused with low wages and a limited number of jobs.

Hell's brilliant scheme to exploit ethnicity and race led to violent rivalries among the Irish, Czechs, Italians, Germans, Polish, and Blacks. Factory owners deceitfully used each ethnic group as scabs to undermine the other if any dared to protest against unfair working conditions by striking.

Fratricide kept the business owners thriving as long as they agreed to sign a pact in blood for prosperity. Those who couldn't afford a business resorted to underground trades like bootlegging alcohol and selling drugs, which proved to be profitable as well.

As times changed, living standards for most of the ethnic groups improved for the better except for the people of color. For some reason, they failed to fully assimilate into mainstream society, and this shortcoming has led to the difficult position they hold this very day.

Still, the overall situation for Harlem Heights is not good. The city's history will not go away until the saints deal accordingly with the issues of the past. This is the reason why the angels seek a mortal who can lead the citizens of Harlem Heights to make a change for the better.

Randy Robinson and his wife are new arrivals to Harlem Heights. He's come to the city as a replacement pastor, but he is unaware that the church he has come to serve has burned down.

Pastor Robinson isn't too impressed with his first sight of the city. Wind-blown trash is scattered along the streets. Some parts of town teem with life while others places are vacant and condemned.

The most prominent color in Harlem Heights is gray; whatever isn't gray is a dull brown. Even on a clear, sunny day, the atmosphere appears dim. The west side has been like this for quite a while and seems to be getting dimmer.

As Randy drives his red minivan, packed with the couple's few possessions, slowly down Market Street, Louise Robinson leans out the passenger-side window looking for the address of the church, 1220 Market Street. At her hand signal, Randy slows the vehicle to a crawl as it approaches building 1216 then 1218 ... The next place should be 1220. Instead it's an empty lot bearing the scars of a fire. By the smell, the Robinsons can tell the fire must have been recent.

Louise is shocked. "How come no one called to tell us the church burned down?"

Randy is beginning to have doubts. "I had a strange feeling about this assignment," he admits. "The sight of a burned-out lot where a church once stood doesn't make me feel any better."

"This isn't what I had in mind either."

"Yeah, I know. I just wish I had done more research about this city. Had I known, I would have asked for a different mission." Still disappointed, the pastor tries to think positively. "But who am I to accept only the good? Perhaps better things will come in the near future."

Siron rides along in the minivan with the couple. Cool as always, he sits back talking to the two mortals as if they know he is there. While

Randy Robinson gazes at the torched ruins, the scout places his hands on the pastor's shoulders to minister words of encouragement. The mortal reacts to Siron's influence. "This place is no longer what it used to be. It won't ever be the same. We shall rebuild on this foundation to establish a sanctuary for the King of Kings."

Louise gently reaches for her husband's hand, letting Randy know that she supports what seems to be a dead-end assignment. The reason for mission remains unknown for now, yet the couple has enough faith in the Lord to place the matter in His hands.

Pastor Robinson puts the minivan in drive and slowly pulls off to find the house in which they will stay. The mortals leave behind Solomon and Lee who stand on the church grounds. They have identified the pastor who will lead the saints to rebuild the church. It's time to implement the next phase of the plans.

6

Reaching For the Lost

Mattie Moore has recovered well enough from smoke inhalation to leave the hospital. When the old woman arrives home, she finds a message taped to her door. It's from the pastor and his wife:

Dear Ms. Moore,

Hope this note finds you doing well. After a few phone calls, we finally got in touch with an old acquaintance of yours. He told us a lot about the struggles of the church and about the fire. It seems the enemy is really busy on the west side. Whenever you get a chance, please give us a call at the number below. We will be praying for you.

Randy and Louise Robinson

The message brings joy to the old woman's heart. She's always prayed that God would bring a change to the church and the city. Maybe this pastor will be the one to make a difference.

For years, Mattie watched the church struggle with all sorts of problems that eventually led to its ruin. First it was the issue of being charismatic. Some members didn't appreciate the saints jumping around shouting praises to the Lord; it just wasn't a dignified thing to do. That issue led to another conflict about speaking in tongues. Some members believed it wasn't necessary, while other insisted everyone must practice it. These little matters became major problems that divided the church. What really hurt the congregation, however, was the fact that the saints stopped praying.

The lack of prayer took a toll on the church because its leader, Reverend Brown, was rendered ineffective. He had started out as a good preacher with a heart totally dedicated to the Lord. As a concerned citizen, Brown took an active role in the community, ministering to troubled teens and helping to meet the needs of the poor. The reverend was also known for his dynamic deliverance ministry. One could feel God's glory emanating from Rev Brown's hands. But his ministry went to Hell when the church stopped praying.

To be honest, it wasn't the saints alone that ruined Brown. The reverend, himself, contributed equally to his own downfall, and this he did by being prideful—the greatest of the seven deadly sins. Pride gripped Brown's heart leading him to do the unthinkable. He changed from a tolerant man to a person who no longer had the patience to work with people in constant need of help. Becoming a self-serving pastor, Brown expected the congregation to cater to his demands. He also preached a gospel that brought him glory; everything about the preacher became a show and mankind were not the only ones watching.

Pride was there all the time with Rev Brown. This vain spirit massaged the preacher's ego and whispered to Brown's heart telling him how good he was. Perhaps a year or so went by as Brown's vanity increased. The man finally went too far when he fell victim to the temptation of a woman.

Sister May, a fine-looking woman whose beauty none could deny, became the downfall of the reverend. Where she came from nobody knew, but her presence caused quite a stir at the church. Like wildfire on dry grass, imps ran about the church spreading rumors of Rev Brown and Sister May having a sexual relationship. Many of the saints refused to believe the gossip until reverend's peculiar behavior proved otherwise.

The pastor soon delegated his duties to others while he spent most of his time and church salary on hotels, clothes, and expensive dinners at fancy restaurants. Reverend Brown got to the point where he just didn't care who knew what was going on with his personal life. Eventually, he was banned from the church.

The lack of trust in leadership made it hard for the next few preachers to stay. Pastor after pastor came to lead the church. Somehow, with each one, the congregation would rise up in rebellion, driving the preacher away. The Light of Hope Church focused more on manly doctrine than Biblical principles; it became a spiritual cesspool in the eyes of the angels and a den for demons to dwell in.

Mattie Moore has gotten well acquainted with the Robinsons and even offered to hold Bible studies at her house since the church has been burnt down. As the saints gather at Mattie's place this evening, they are joined by the guardians who attend the meeting for reasons of their own.

Solomon, seeming optimistic, gladly tells his brother, "The Almighty has honored our request to provide a way to resurrect the church. When the prayers of the saints are firmly established, we can begin the attack on Fratricide's forces."

"Let the scouts go searching the city for those saints who are dedicated to the Father," responds Lee. "These loyal ones can be used to carry the burden of prayer for the city."

As the command is given, Siron takes flight through the city leading his fellow comrades to spread the good news about the gathering of the saints. Like shooting stars through the evening sky, they streak through the night air leaving trails of light in their wake.

Darting between buildings, whisking around corners, they spread the good news. Every time a worthy saint is found, an Empyreal messenger rushes by touching that person's heart.

This is a pleasurable task for Siron, and it brings him joy to know the gates of Heaven will prevail in the very end. While he relishes the thought of victory, he suddenly comes across Reverend Brown.

The reverend is by himself just staring off into space. He wears a bathrobe with food stains on it, dingy white socks, and slippers. He looks depressed. On Brown's shoulder sits Depression massaging the reverend's brain, whispering to his mind, *"Nobody likes me … I'm a complete failure. I had it all, and it all slipped away because of me."*

Suicide is watching too. Finding the situation amusing, he decides to add his comments. *"I'm not worthy to be alive."*

Both spirits hold their bellies giggling as tears quietly roll down Brown's face. Rejection lies at the man's feet yelling, *"Stop the crying—nobody cares about a loser."*

Now all three spirits are having a good time poking fun at the fallen reverend. Having reached his limit, Brown suddenly bursts out in loud, convulsing sobs, "Oh, Jesus, please help me, Lord!"

The sound of that name causes all three imps to pounce on the reverend's head in effort to shut his mouth. They hate that name.

"Look what you made him do, stupid," cries Rejection.

Suicide whines, "It kills me just to hear that name."

The harassers do their best to soothe the mortal, but it's to no avail. It will take better efforts to stop the man from calling the name above all names.

"Pity, get up here and do your job," demands Rejection.

The little wimpy spirit comes up from the reverend's belly, whispering to his mind. *"Oh, Lord, why me? I don't deserve this; have mercy on me."*

Suicide gives Pity a nudge with his elbow indicating that he wants to join in too. *"Please, God, bring this pain to an end. I don't want to live anymore."*

The tactics of the devilish imps seem to be working; the mortal is quiet. As the spirits find their folly amusing, they cover their mouths as if to keep the mortal from hearing them cackle. Once again, they've succeeded in bringing the man down emotionally, and they have kept Brown from calling on that holy name.

Siron watches the show from outside the apartment window. Having to move on with his work, the scout makes a mental note of Brown's condition. The recon will tell his brothers about the situation when his duty is done.

The designated saints have been touched in the spirit, and a seed to rebuild the church has been planted in their hearts. Solomon and Lee are content for now. However, a twinkle of concern lights both their eyes as Siron brings them the news about Revered Brown. They know the tormenting of Brown is necessary to compel the man to repent for the error of his ways. If he can survive the trial, Brown will be a stronger man than he was before.

As the meeting at Mattie's is brought to an end, a vow is made before the Lord to pray for the city. All present join hands, closing their eyes. Even the sons of Heaven join the saints in prayer.

More so than usual, Pastor Robinson's prayer is passionate. He doesn't know exactly what to say, but when the words come out, it's perfect.

The pastor first prays for the city—that God would bind the overseer and allow the urban community a chance to see the light. He then prays for the church, the Light of Hope. His words ask that the Lord see fit to resurrect the building. Finally, the prayer comes to the subject of Willie. All the saints petition the Holy One to open the gang leader's heart and eyes to the gospel.

The amazing thing about prayer is that time and distance cannot hinder it. As the saints pray, the Mighty One begins to work on Willie's heart. The gangster feels something being stirred up inside him. Molder and Wrath occupy his soul, and they, too, feel it. The nauseating feeling of sickness is so intense that Willie is doubled over, coughing.

"What in Heaven is going on?" cries Molder.

"It has to be the prayer," Wrath assumes, "the saints are praying again."

Both demons step outside Willie's body to avoid the torment.

"This is the work of that old woman. She should have been destroyed at the hospital—why wasn't it done? How dare she come directly against me. She will pay for this," howls Molder.

Suddenly, Molder and Wrath are struck to the floor, overpowered by loud voices that seem to emanate from invisible speakers. *"Lord, we come before you on the behalf of Willie James Moore,"* pray the saints. *"Jesus, he's been a lost soul since the day he was born; he's never had an opportunity to see things from your perspective. So Lord, we pray and faithfully hope for the day that you'll reveal Yourself to Willie. We also pray that You will use him to help clean the streets in Harlem Heights of gang violence."*

Suddenly a bright light appears, shining about the room in which Willie stands. Like a beacon on the shore, the wide beam of light sweeps about the place as if searching for something, illuminating every crack and crevice, it cuts through the darkness like a dust mop along the gym floor. The beam, radiating with the power of the Most High, forces

Molder and Wrath to flee their mortal home or suffer the glory of Empyreal.

Pastor Robinson has been in a pensive mood ever since the last Bible study. Thoughts of the fallen Reverend Brown weigh heavily on his mind and the pastor just can't shake away the concerns. Is it a crime for a new pastor to meet his predecessor? Perhaps the fallen preacher can provide the new guy some insight on church matters. So Randy decides to pay the lost reverend a visit.

Robinson makes his way up the steps of a musty-smelling stairway. Maybe the source was deposited a day or two ago, yet the ripe urine odor is pungent as ever.

Besides the sound of bass bumping from a loud stereo, the apartment complex is rather quiet. It's not a large housing project, but the place is ghetto fabulous.

Two males sit along the staircase casually talking, smoking cigarettes. Giving their attention to the lone man headed up the stairs, the two squatters become silent as they read the pastor's behavior for an indication of what he's doing there. Does he intend to buy or sell something? Strangers always come by to deliver or receive some type of goods or service at this housing area. This visitor is different. He carries a Bible in his hand.

Robinson gives a few loud knocks at Reverend Brown's door. Not wanting to be bothered, the reverend remains steadfast on the couch, wrapped tightly in his dingy bathrobe watching a TV evangelist preach.

The knocking continues. Sighing, the reluctant reverend answers the door.

"Hey, Reverend Brown, my name is Randy Robinson, how are you?"

There's a long pause before Brown responds. He doesn't extend his hand, neither does he smile. "I don't care to buy anything, thanks anyway."

"No, brother, I didn't come to sell you anything. I'm not here to criticize you either. I just want to know how you're doing," replies Robinson.

"Isn't obvious how I'm doing? Can't you see—" While talking, Brown notices the Bible in the visitor's hand, and it sets him off. "What are you doing here with that book? If you came here to witness to me, you got another thing coming! Look here, I've traveled the very same path you're trying to walk. I can tell you everything there is to know about that book. I don't need you preaching religion to me."

Randy Robinson remains humble as Brown showers him with spit and loud words. The fallen reverend's spiritual tormentors take jabs at the visiting pastor as well, not to mention the two individuals sitting on the stairway laughing aloud as Robinson is humiliated. The demon spirits are the ones who have Brown upset, talking with anger. Pity, Suicide, Depression, and Rejection are agitated and determined to turn the visitor away. It doesn't work though; Randy becomes more patient. The rascals can sense the Holy Spirit within him. They can also see something else that causes them all to quiet down.

While Brown is busy giving the visitor a piece of his mind, Robinson is praying under his breath. *"Lord, in the name of Jesus, let the peace in here be still. Whatever manner of evil this is, let it be bound by the blood of Jesus."*

Brown suddenly ceases to talk and, for a second, his mind blanks out. Quickly his thoughts clear and he finds himself shaking hands with Randy. The men go inside the apartment to have a civilized conversation.

Meanwhile, the guardian spirits that accompany Randy hold the imps in check with their swords. Rejection, Pity, Suicide, and Depression are forced to sit at the reverend's feet, listening to Robinson talk about Christ. "Reverend Brown, I know times have been rough for you lately. You feel ashamed ... forsaken because of what has happened in your personal life. What I have for you is a word of encouragement." Robinson pauses to see how receptive Brown is to the message. The reverend is all ears. "You can go back to the one who loves you unconditionally. My brother, God is still waiting on you. I had to do the same thing when I slipped and fell. I stood back up. What are you going to do?"

Brown knows that everything said to him at that moment is true. All he has to do is repent of his shortcomings, but sometimes a task such as this is easier said than done. The reverend still has issues within himself to address—the biggest concern being his pride. The spirit of pride dwells quietly within Brown. The man's current condition doesn't warrant much of a role for the haughty spirit. Pride's main purpose is to keep Brown from admitting his mistakes.

Before leaving, Randy Robinson has prayer with Brown. The words pertaining to the blood of Christ, the resurrection, and spending eternity in Heaven while Satan will be eternally bound in Hades makes the imps in the room sick to their stomachs. All four of the demons are doubled over in pain from the tormenting words of Christ. Being too much for the evil spirits to bear, they all flee hoping to return when Robinson is gone.

The prayer brings a period of relief for Brown. Later on that evening, he reads his Bible until he falls into a peaceful sleep.

The devious imps return the next day only to find their fallen preacher praying to the Lord. Immediately, Depression jumps on the mortal hoping to bring his spirit down. Usually his claws would go easily into the brain of Brown; they barely scrape the surface now. Rejection, trying his hand at influencing the reverend's emotions, does no better than his conspirator. Pity and Suicide know better than to try, so they all wait a comfortable distance from the praying fool until he stops.

7

Things Get Better & Worse

The day of traveling south to bring a shipment of dope to the city is quickly approaching. As the Pharaohs and Reds prepare for their mission, members of both gangs become anxious. Arguments and fights are breaking out among the gangsters; for some unknown reason, confusion has settled among the thugs.

The sudden rush of confusion at the warehouse disturbs Willie. His stomach is aching again. Molder and Wrath also notice the atmosphere in the warehouse has changed for the worse. They suspect the saints' prayers are causing all the havoc.

Molder tries to soothe Willie Mo' by ministering to his soul. *"It's all right; things are going good. Everyone is feeling the pressure of getting the shipment here safely. Conditions will become better once we get the plan started,"* Molder whispers to Willie's mind. *"Go somewhere private to meditate,"* urges the spirit guide.

Mounting a motorcycle, Willie Mo' leaves the warehouse and speeds through the city streets, the buildings become a blur to his eyes. Going nowhere in particular, Mo' happens to approach old man Levy's shack. Willie has not seen his elder since the last time they had battled a few weeks ago. Out of curiosity, he decides to make a stop. The young gangster finds the old man sitting in a chair either dead or in a deep sleep. A closer look reveals the faint breathing of the teacher who waits upon death to take him from the world.

Mo' takes action to revive the old man, making him feel invigorated. As he admires his handiwork, a thought comes to Willie's mind, and so he poses a question to his former teacher. "Despite the past, I still believe that you and I have a bond, do you agree?"

The old man looks Willie in his eyes and says nothing at all. His mind races back to the time when he first laid eyes on a dirty little boy whom no one loved. Mr. Levy, for the most part, treated Willie rather well. He never spanked the child excessively, just enough to discipline the boy which kept him out of mischief. It was seldom that either one would smile or laugh, yet they became close as they learned the nature of the spiritual world together. In essence, they are like father and son.

Mr. Levy nods his head in agreement that a bond exists between the two.

"Then let's work together. You can provide me assistance, and I will give you protection, deal?"

With a raspy voice, the old one asks, "Whatcha want, Willie?"

"I need your wisdom and prayers. There's strange trouble at the warehouse that could mess up the operation. Need you to find out what's going on."

Within a moment's time, Mr. Levy is sitting upon the floor in a dark room, chanting and staring at a single lit candle that causes him to sink into a deep meditation. His body becomes lighter and lighter until it begins to float.

Opening his eyes, Mr. Levy can see his physical body sitting on the floor, locked in a trance. Still floating, his spiritual body now hovers above the roof of his shack. The old man achieves astral projection. An elastic silver cord stretches from Levy's spiritual body and connects to the physical one: his lifeline. Maneuvering through the air takes the slightest effort; he only has to think a direction and his body moves that way. As a predator, his instincts tell him to search Market Street. He recalls hearing that Willie's grandmother is still alive. She has always been a praying woman, and such a person is a threat to the kingdom of Sheol. So Levy heads to her place of residence.

In all his years of witchcraft, Mr. Levy has never seen an angel. His experience with the spiritual realm has been limited to interactions with demons only. This is normal for people who choose to live the occult lifestyle. Evil can only show them the works and creatures of Hades' kingdom and imitations of Heaven.

Just as Mr. Levy enters the airspace of Market Street, he is suddenly snatched to the ground. He attempts this time to walk along the street only to be knocked to the ground again. Now Levy hears voices laughing at him. Astonished, his eyes behold a wall of angels watching him. The old man doesn't know whether to stay or flee.

Of all the spirits, the old man's attention is drawn to the dark one who smiles at him. The angel's eyes are passionate, and he has a peaceful aura about him. "Samuel Levy, haven't you grown tired of this life you're living? For years you've worked evil, cursing and leading others astray. You've hurt many people, broken up many families, and all that for a master who really doesn't love you."

Levy, in awe, can only reply, "Who are ya?"

"I am Solomon, the messenger of Jesus Christ, who is the Son of God that was crucified and resurrected three days later from the dead in order to save the lives of all mankind. The Savior told us all about you. Indeed, you have been misled. Your remaining time on Earth is short, and you need to repent for the error of your ways. Repent while you can."

This is a shocking encounter for the old man. He wants out of the life he is living, but how does he escape? He's seen what happens when one tries to leave the occult—it's not pretty. It's common to be skinned alive. Some individuals are forced to watch while their loved ones are tortured to death. Others are afflicted with diseases that no doctor can diagnose.

Levy knows there is no place he can hide from the hand of Satan. At the same time, he knows once the occult sees no need for his services, he's good as dead. Whether he chooses to leave or stay, Levy will be in for a fight to save his life.

The old man stares intently at Solomon, who reflects the peace and beauty of Empyreal. Though it was long ago, the mortal remembers his days of youth attending camp meetings on the plantation. He knows enough to realize this messenger speaks the truth.

"Please, tell me how I can be saved," begs Mr. Levy.

"I can guide you in the right direction, but it is the task of mankind to show you the way. You know Mattie, Willie Moore's grandmother. Seek her. She can show you how to be saved."

Instantly, Levy is sucked back to his physical body. Gaining consciousness, the teacher finds himself lying face down on the floor, sobbing loudly, "I wanna be saved." Realizing he's back in his physical body, Levy quickly hushes his mouth. Perhaps Willie Mo' is there?

The old man takes a cautious look around to see if anyone is present. He calls out, but no one answers. Mr. Levy lets out a sigh of relief as he replays the words of Solomon in his mind. He wants to be saved.

After a night of fitful sleep, the old man decides to venture outside his shack to see if he can recapture just a bit of yesterday's experience. Having reached the stop at Market Street, Mr. Levy exits the bus slowly being careful not to fall as his elderly legs are not the strong limbs they once were. Safely on ground, the elderly one takes a long look at the street sign which reassures him that his conversation with Solomon was real. It was exactly at that corner where he encountered the angels and maybe the guardians will provide him with another experience, he hopes.

It is broad daylight, people are walking about and the old man is starting to have big doubts about seeing the angels again. Determined to make sense of his encounter with Solomon, Levy walks further down Market Street, stopping only to take a closer look at the burnt church. Feeling the urge to go closer, he walks upon the ruins just for a better look.

If Willie Mo' catches Levy on Market Street, the old man better be able to explain his actions. But getting caught is the least concern on the old man's mind. If he couldn't penetrate the angels guarding this street, then neither should any other forces of evil do so. Unlike his shack, the church ground provides him a sense of safety and freedom. It brings a little something extra as well. The old man finds a worn Bible that somehow survived the fire.

Reading the good book is a struggle at first; something inside him is resistant to the gospel. Being desperate to know exactly who Jesus Christ is before his time on Earth expires compels Mr. Levy to plow on with the reading.

Unknown to the mortal, two angels stand beside the old man, surrounding the loner with their celestial wings as he wrestles with the message the Bible has to offer. Demetri, a guardian, looks over Levy's shoulder encouraging the elder as he flips back and forth through the pages. The spirit also knows the old man is here for more than just the gospel.

Samuel Levy has a directive to join Pastor Robinson's prayer group with the intent to destroy it; however, his personal mission is to learn firsthand about Jesus Christ: Why the name is so hated, feared, and even praised? The old man really wants to give his life to Christ before someone else takes it. He must play a smooth hand to keep his true intentions hidden.

Levy is now at the warehouse meeting with Willie Mo'. The gang leader wants to know what hinders his operations. "Old man, did you find the source of our problems?"

"The problem's on Market Street," the elder reveals. "I couldn't get down the street ta see what happenin' dere."

Molder is curious to know why Mr. Levy could go no farther. He speaks through Willie. *"What stopped you from entering the street?"*

"I don't know. T'was somethin' stronga den me and maybe you, too."

Molder points a wicked finger at the old man. *"Strike him for insulting me,"* the demon demands.

Willie slaps the old man to the ground.

"Dang it, go easy now, Mo'! I try doin' like you say, but I wasn't allowed."

The foul spirit continues to speak through his mortal, *"Who stopped you? Who would dare come between me and my desires?"*

Levy is still on the ground struggling to recover from the blow that nearly rendered him senseless. Gathering his wits, the old man rises to one knee, lays a hand to his ringing forehead to collect his thoughts. Thinking back to his encounter with Solomon, the old man allows a slight smile to show on his face. Molder notices the smirk, which causes Hell's fury to burn within the demon.

"When I got to Market Street, I was snatched to de ground. I tried to keep goin' on my way; I couldn't move though. I was gettin' mad... ready ta give up, when all of sudden I saw somethin' I nevah see'd in my life—angels. Dey was standin' close togetha, side by side, holdin' hands. None of 'em spoke or moved, 'cept for one who called his self, Solomon."

The warrior, Wrath, loses his cool after hearing this. Drawing his sword, Wrath slices straight down Levy's left shoulder, through his heart. The old man falls prostrate to the ground, showing signs of a stroke.

"What happened next?" yells Molder.

"Why you hurtin' me like dis? I did everythang you tell'd me."

"We ask the questions, you give the answers, fool!"

The old man resumes the story. "Solomon said fo' me to repent … serve a new master," the frightened elder confesses. "He says I was fightin' a lost war; Jesus won the war at da cross."

The mention of that name causes Molder and Wrath to drop to the ground. The grimace on Mo's face indicates he's in pain too. The elderly one is tempted to say it again, but the effect is too sickening for him to withstand as well.

"Old man, your days are numbered. We're watching you closely. You will infiltrate that prayer group and bring it down. If you fail, I will kill you myself. And, one more thing—don't ever say that name again. Now get out of my sight," curses Molder.

Levy struggles to his feet, shuffling toward the doorway. The left side of his body is still numb. Despite the physical discomfort, Levy is more focused on getting involved with the church. He has a personal mission of his own to pursue.

The Pharaohs and Reds are ready to take their trip south. A caravan of cars slithers slowly out of Harlem Heights, making its way to the Interstate. The vehicles travel within the posted speed limit, doing their best not to draw unwanted attention from the law. With four armed passengers in each vehicle, there is enough firepower to protect the cargo should any trouble arise.

Mo' and the Reds' gang leader, Mingo, remain in Harlem Heights making phone calls to crooked accomplices in various federal and state law agencies to ensure their backs are covered. A big operation such as this requires major inside support. Waiting in a Mexican town are several kilos of cocaine and opium poppy used to make heroin.

After a few days of driving, the Pharaohs and Reds arrive at their destination. The caravan drives along a dusty country road leading to a farm hidden by heavy vegetation. Once they are past the thick bush, a clearing reveals a field littered with bright orange poppy plants. The locals who cultivate this cash crop watch it closely. Armed guards are posted in towers placed strategically throughout the ranch. Trespassers will quickly know they're unwanted. The gang members see the riflemen but feel comfortable enough to drive toward a structure that resembles a horse stable.

As JT steps out of the dust-coated black SUV, the bright Mexican sunshine penetrates his dark sunglasses causing his eyes to squint. Jermaine Trotter's arrogant demeanor makes a bad first impression on the *campesinos*, the farmers. "*Que pasa*, amigo? What's going on around here?" he asks.

The Mexican dealers return the gangster's greeting with silent contempt. The message is clear to JT—don't fool around with these drug lords.

Instinctively, JT steps aside gesturing for his partner, Miguel, to start the transaction with the Mexicans. The Latin Red begins a conversation in Spanish by apologizing for Mr. Trotter's behavior.

Getting business underway, the gang members open their briefcases revealing hundreds of thousands of U.S. dollars to be exchanged for Mexican dope that will bring millions on the American streets.

The campesinos bring forth their goods. The sweet sight of dope brings a smile to everybody's face. JT digs in his pants for a pocketknife. Cutting a slit in a plastic bag of powder, he takes a small sniff of coke that brings a cool burning sensation to his left nostril. A light rush of euphoria causes his heart to flutter just a bit. Using a gesture of bravado, JT shows his approval of the product by pounding his chest like a gorilla.

The buyers make a brief inspection of all the goods. JT and Miguel are pleased with the high quality of dope. It can be cut several times and still remain strong. The cocaine will draw crackheads from all over to buy the potent product, while the heroin will keep the junkies hooked on the main line.

The gangbangers' only worry now is getting back across the border. To ensure a successful crossing, the cars are disassembled so large quantities of dope can be hidden within its hollow parts to avoid detection by the police. The reassembled parts will need touch-up paint jobs that requires time for drying, so the American thugs will stay a few nights on the Mexican ranch before traveling back to the States.

The gangsters are wise to take such drastic precautions. They've been under surveillance throughout the duration of their trip; guardians have been watching from afar. The ideal time to make their presence known will come once the shipment reaches the border.

The vehicle lines at the border patrol are long and slow moving. This provides a window of opportunity for Empyreal forces to alert the local authorities of the gang's attempt to smuggle drugs.

Deciding to travel underground, Siron takes to the sewer system hoping to move without being detected. Flying a few feet underground like a shark in water, the scout rises to the surface to hide within the hood of a five-ton truck hauling cantaloupes. Now Siron can see the vehicle in front without drawing attention from the enemy.

So far, everything looks clear. There are no demon guards around except for the regulars assigned to the border patrol, which is a cause for concern—the shipment should be heavily guarded.

Still concerned about a surprise attack, Siron attempts to cut the brake lines of the old five-ton truck, hoping it will ram the back bumper of JT's SUV to expose the drugs. Busy tampering with the brake lines, the scout doesn't notice the demon headed his way. The denizen warrior swings a sword at the angel's neck, missing by mere inches. Siron tries to block the following blows with his own sword, yet the warrior's strength is too much to bear.

The other guardians see the skirmish, yet they remain hidden waiting for the right moment to launch an attack.

No way can Siron defeat the aggressor, so he lets off a war cry summoning his fellow warriors to battle.

Heaven's forces appear in abundance to assist their comrade. The show of defiance draws a similar response from Sheol's combatants, who are more than eager to engage the enemy in a fight.

The wicked spirits exude confidence mainly because their numbers are far greater than the Empyreal angels. This compels Siron's fighters to remain at bay. The only action that takes place is among a couple of guardians who assist Siron in evading the wrath of the fierce demon.

Wisely, the Empyreans retreat from battle as Hades' forces are far too powerful to be dealt with at this time. The Harlem Heights caravan will make it safely back to the city with a band of warriors protecting its precious cargo. Evil has prevailed again, but the war still looms with more battles to follow.

8

A Brewing Storm

Louise has a premonition. "There's a burden lying heavy on my heart," she tells her husband as the unforeseen worries weigh on her mind. "I just can't figure it out. Something horrible is on its way to the city, like a bad storm in the forecast."

Randy empathizes with his wife. "The same feeling is bothering me too."

"Sounds like we're in for some intercessory prayer, honey."

"Yeah, let's call the members so we can schedule a time to get together," Randy suggests. "Perhaps we can meet within a day or so to talk about it."

Solomon stands within the presence of Louise and Randy. He knows the shipment is on its way to the city, and it will take a lot of prayer and human intervention to deal with the trouble it brings.

As Pastor Robinson and the prayer group meet at Mattie's house as usual, the same people are there in addition to a few newcomers. The Lord is drawing new members to the group causing it to grow quickly.

Prayer meetings always start with praise and worship. Pastor Robinson has a bit of musical talent, so he plays chords on his portable keyboard. The passionate music opens the saints' hearts to the Lord as the atmosphere within the room begins to lighten. One by one, each saint stops singing only to begin praying.

Eyes from afar are watching Mattie Moore's house. The dark forces can easily see the glory of Heaven emanating from her residence. The same can be said of the stranger who walks toward Mattie's place now.

The slow moving figure creeps along the sidewalk dragging its foot. Sometimes it limps, other times it hobbles as if injured. Panting, it heaves for air like a motor running on fumes, and it mumbles something in a deep guttural voice as it gets closer and closer to the house.

At last it reaches the front steps of Mattie's door. Stopping short, it appears to be making an effort to catch its breath or to confirm it has the right location. Slowly it takes one step, then another up the stairs only to stop and mysteriously go down on all fours attempting to crawl. A sudden change of mind brings it back on two legs as this creature continues toward the door. Seeming to be in pain, one hand holds its belly while the other hand knocks at the door.

At first, the knocking is so faint that no one hears it. Solomon stands within the midst of the praying saints knowing what's at the door. Eager to get things started, the angel places a hand on Pastor Robinson's shoulder, whispering to his soul, *"Answer the door."*

The pastor is still playing a slow melody on the keyboard. Opening his eyes, he takes a long look at the door feeling the urge to check it out. He plays another minute or so longer before rising from his chair to see what's at the door. Robinson thinks to himself, *Lord, I have a funny feeling about this. Whatever it may be, please protect us all from harm.*

The pastor slowly reaches for the doorknob, turns the handle, and pulls the door back cautiously only to see a bald, elderly black man with hazel eyes who is sweating profusely.

With a raspy voice the stranger inquires, "Is dis da Light of Hope Church?"

"Yes, sir, it is," Randy answers. "You came at a good time; it's prayer service tonight."

"Oh, I can feel it." The visitor is obviously in some type of discomfort.

"C'mon in and make yourself comfortable. We're a small church with big aspirations. We believe Jesus Christ to be our Lord and Savior."

The mentioning of that *name* brings sharp pains to the stranger's belly. He clutches his stomach, resisting the urge to double over, for any sudden movement will cause a massive slip of the bowels. If the torture doesn't stop anytime soon, he will have to leave immediately.

The pastor can sense the visitor's uneasiness, so he silently prays for mercy, which seems to bring a bit of relief.

While the visitor sits with his head between his knees recuperating, Robinson notices the saints have stopped to watch the show. Not wanting to make a spectacle of the old man, the pastor quickly tells everyone to resume praying.

Most go back to praying except for Mattie Moore. There is something familiar about the old man; she just can't figure it out just yet.

The visitor, seeming to have recovered a bit, is sitting upright. "Sir, are you feeling better," inquires Robinson.

"Yes, son, I is."

"What exactly can we help you with? I can sense that you're having trouble, sir."

"Young man, can you hep me find what I'm lookin' fo'?"

Robinson is unsure of what the stranger is asking, yet it's clear to see that something is irritating him. "Sir, in our church, we don't believe in wasting time. You want help, let's start right now; c'mon let's pray. This is the first step to a good relationship with God," declares the pastor as he motions for the saints to join hands.

The stranger is reluctant at first. He can barely stand to hear the name of Christ. Every time Jesus is mentioned, he can feel his guts twisting inside his belly. Remembering the purpose of his visit, the stranger agrees to pray.

As Randy Robinson approaches the visitor to hold his hands in prayer, the stranger suddenly feels hot. The closer the pastor gets, the hotter his flesh becomes. The visitor can't stand it any longer. *Don't come closa, else I'll holla,* he thinks to himself.

Pastor Robinson reaches for his hands again causing the stranger to quickly jerk back as if his flesh is burning. Smiling, with his hands still extended, Pastor Robinson teases, "Is this how friends treat each other? C'mon, sir, I promise not to hurt you; I just want to help. You ain't afraid of prayer are you?"

Louise reprimands her husband using the sweetest tone she can muster. "Honey, don't patronize the man. Can't you see he's scared?"

"Everything is good, baby. The Lord allowed him to be here tonight, so we're going to deal with him as God sees fit."

"Great day, don't touch me. Yo' hands is hot. An' stop sayin' dat name all the time."

The tone of Pastor Robinson's voice reveals a hint of playfulness. "What name are you referring to, sir?"

The visitor, still sweating profusely, is getting antsy. "You know dat name, don't say it no mo', you makin' me sick to my stomach—and back up from me ... pray widout sayin' it again."

The last thing Randy wants is for the visitor to think he's being harassed. To prevent the situation from escalating, Robinson asks a question. "You have something to tell us, don't you?"

"Yessum, I do. But furst, I need a drank of water for my dry throat."

A cold glass of water is brought to the old man who gulps it down quickly, making him feel better.

The visitor has another request. "Can I use da commode? My bladda ain't what it use ta be."

The old man's dialect is sometimes hard to understand.

"...Oh, you mean the toilet?" the pastor clarifies while eyeing the stranger as if uncertain of the old man's intention. "Now all of sudden you have to use the bathroom—or is it that *they* have to use the bathroom? Well then, right this way please."

Robinson escorts the man down the hallway to the bathroom and then reminds the guest of his reason for the visit. "We'll be awaiting your return. There's some business we must take care of."

The stranger hurries into the bathroom to relieve himself. An empty bladder reduces the stress he was feeling. With his thoughts clear, the voice in his mind gives instructions. *"Stand on the toilet seat and take out the bottle."* The mortal reaches into his pants pocket to retrieve an object that resembles an aspirin bottle. *"Yes... that's it. Now dab your finger in the brine and draw that picture on the ceiling. Make us a nice pentagram right above this toilet, a great place for a doorway,"* says the spirit within the stranger.

It's a quick job. The brine is nothing more than urine and blood mixed together and cursed by a wizard. It blends in well with the paint. Now the enemy has an entrance into Mattie's house and the right to interfere with prayer meetings.

The visitor returns from the bathroom to find the pastor waiting on him. For now, Robinson is unaware of the old man's deceit. Wanting to know more about the stranger, Randy asks a simple question. "So sir, what did you say your name was?"

"Stanley, but you can call me Stan."

9

The Spider's Web

"Hughes, it's me," says the caller on his cell.

"What's up, Diggs?"

"The boys are back in town."

"Did they bring anything?"

"Yep, we'll check it later on to see what they got," says Diggs, and he snaps his cell phone shut.

Detectives Patrick Diggs and Hank Hughes are officers with many years of experience on the police force. They started out being decent policemen with the intentions of doing good things for society—at least one of them did. But somewhere along way, they managed to stray.

Diggs became hopeless when all his efforts to do the right thing came to no avail. Disappointment with judges who put the love of money and a successful career before true justice discouraged him mostly. Perhaps crime does pay? Working in a corrupt system finally broke down his moral immune system, causing him to give into the temptation of taking the law into his own hands.

Hughes had been a dirty officer from the start. He grew up in family of corrupt policemen. As a youngster, he listened to his father's wild cop stories of crime fighting and soaked in the violent tales of bashing the bad guys' heads. A childhood fantasy of his was becoming a slick detective who would go undercover to foil major drug deals. When his mother wasn't around, Hughes' father would school him on how to obtain free service from prostitutes without getting static from their pimps. He became a cop for all the wrong reasons.

Both Hughes and Diggs are deeply involved in the gang culture that dominates the inner city. They are well acquainted with leaders of the Pharaohs and Reds. For a fee, they allow these gang leaders to operate freely without the threat of major police interference. The benefits are great. Only God knows how much money they have received from gang activities.

Hughes and Diggs do a great job of covering their clandestine activities. Periodically they plot with both gangs to have an aspiring dope dealer arrested. They call it a sacrifice, but really it's a scheme to keep anyone at the precinct from becoming suspicious of their underhanded dealings. Unaware of the plot, a dealer is allowed to grow big-time in the dope game. As the chosen one creates a name for himself, his actions are monitored. Finally, when the hustler reaches the top of the world, the rug is pulled from underneath his feet when he's arrested. This is how the game is played; it's a give-and-take relationship that benefits those at the top.

Hughes and Diggs believe themselves to be the only ones with knowledge of the shipment. Of course, they're wrong. The police commissioner, who is subject to the mayor, who in turn is directly under occult leadership, is also aware of the delivery—they all know.

Everyone is tangled in Fratricide's web and if anyone of these guys step out of line, his career, and quite possibly his life will be ruined too. Evil spins a terrible web that entraps all who dare to walk its path.

JT and his cohorts travel the Interstate wearing looks of confidence on their faces. Above them flies a mob of Hell's warriors with their swords drawn for battle. A daring attempt to attack the horde would be a foolish move by Empyreal forces.

As the flock of demons soar above the Harlem Heights suburbs, a gigantic spiritual shadow mirrors their movement on the ground. The silhouette chases cats under cars, frightens birds from the trees, and sets dogs to barking wildly at what seems to be thin air to human eyes.

A messenger is sent to inform the big one. "Master, it is here; the shipment has arrived to the city."

Fratricide is pleased for the moment. "Hmm, the Tyrant has permitted the shipment, that's good news indeed. I've waited so long for an opportunity like this."

Fantasies of ruling the nation flash rapidly through Fratricide's mind. Quickly, he puts his imagination in check. The big one didn't make it this far with wishful thinking. Rather, hard work has won the faith of the prince.

As the moment of celebration is brought to an end, focus is shifted to the processing of dope for distribution. Ever mindful of failure, Fratricide makes a mental evaluation of things that could undermine his plans; namely, the prayers of the saints. And one must not forget the two meddlesome demons, Molder and Wrath.

Wanting to make Harlem Heights their own kingdom, the renegade demons plot a way to use the drugs to their own benefit too. Disposing of Mingo and putting Willie Mo' in place to rule both gangs is the ultimate goal. Unsure of how the Reds would respond to a new leader is reason enough to proceed cautiously with the plan. Success for the conspirators depends on precise timing and gentle persuasion.

Willie Mo' stands in the window gazing at an empty roadway. Like a lonesome dog awaiting the arrival of his schoolboy master, Willie eagerly waits for the vehicles to appear around the corner bringing the treats his heart desires. He thinks to himself, *any moment now that shipment will be here with the goods.*

Mingo sits back on a plush leather chair with his feet resting on a coffee table, hands and fingers interlocked behind his head, just chilling. Though his intentions are innocent, he utters the most inappropriate statement to Mo': "My Reds made it happen for you this time."

Molder uses the comment to stir anger within the Pharaoh's soul. The spirit whispers, *"How dare he take credit for the shipment?"* in Willie's mind.

All comments are put aside when a caravan of vehicles appears on the street. It's led by JT's black SUV.

Orders are given at once to raise the doors and allow the vehicles to enter without stopping. The shipment enters the warehouse to the applause of excited gangsters eager to become rich.

Mingo steps out of Mo's office to get a better view of the rejoicing. The office is on the second floor and opens onto an indoor balcony, so the Reds' leader stands above everyone else chanting loudly for all to hear, "Where my Reds at?" The gangsters respond with their motto, "Here in the blood". Even the Pharaohs get caught up in the celebration and begin chanting the slogan too.

Willie Mo' glares at Mingo wondering why he's calling out signs. Now it's time for Mo' to make his presence known. The chief Pharaoh steps onto the balcony with his arms folded across his chest. His presence alone quiets the crowd by drawing the attention of everyone present in the warehouse. Mingo is overshadowed.

Willie doesn't smile or say a word. Molder and Wrath are beside him. The warrior has his sword drawn while Molder leans on Mo's shoulder speaking to his mind. *"Look at how they respond to your presence. You're the man, not him. He's not worthy to stand on the same stage as you. In due time, you will deal harshly with him."*

Informer is present and watches with great interest the rivalry brewing between Willie Mo' and Mingo. The runt clearly sees who's fueling the fire. He'll report back to Fratricide with all the details.

The processing is going well. Around the clock, there's someone working in the warehouse preparing the drugs for distribution.

Some workers boil freebase into crack while others cut the coke. The high quality cuts are for the customers uptown; the low grade is for customers who can't afford such fine quality.

Mo' is running the operation smoothly.

The first load, already prepared for distribution, awaits a blessing from a satanic priest who's present in the dark abyss of the warehouse with many other interesting individuals. To conceal their identity, the members hide their faces underneath hooded robes as they chant cultic hymns. They're all gathered to pray for "prosperity in the blood."

The priest recites a curse from a book that binds an imp to every ounce of dope. The thick smell of sulfur once again fills the air and the dark energy causes a frenzy of spirits to swarm about the warehouse like sharks.

A few city blocks from the warehouse are Solomon and Lee. The two angels stand upon the rooftop of the local television network station shielded by satellite dishes that serve as cover as they watch the festivities taking place at the warehouse.

"We have to confront the enemy soon. If we don't, those drugs will wreak havoc on the city. Now is time to set the stage for battle," Lee says to Solomon.

10

Trouble in the House

Recovering from unconsciousness, Mattie has no idea as to how she ended up lying face down on the floor. This isn't the first time either. Several times throughout the day she's found herself waking up with no recollection of ever blacking-out. Now Mattie walks about the house in a slight stupor. She's conscious of her surroundings, but her body is numb. This is a new experience for Mattie. The old woman must take action quickly to remedy the situation before something tragic happens. The only option she can think of is to call the Robinsons.

The elder manages to get to the phone. Taking much effort, she struggles to dial the correct numbers. It seems like an eternity passes before she can hear the ring tones. One ring, two rings ... now the fifth ring. If it rings one more time, the voice mail may pick up the line—that's the last thing Mattie wants. "Please, Lord, allow somebody to answer the phone," pleads the desperate woman.

Just as she about to give up, a voice answers the call, "Hello?"

Overcome with relief, Mattie lets out a loud sigh as if a heavy load has been lifted from her back. "Oh, Louise, something strange is happening in this house!"

Mrs. Robinson is caught off guard. "Mother Mattie, what's the matter?"

"Ever since the last prayer meeting, there's been a presence in the house, and it's trying to smother me. I can't ..." the gasping old woman is struggling again, "... get my mind together to make a decent prayer."

Louise is forced to concentrate in order to follow the older woman's jumbled words. "Mother Mattie, slow down a bit, so I can understand you better."

Again, Mattie makes the effort to tell the story, speaking more slowly ... deliberately.

Listening intently, Louise arrives to her own conclusion. "I had a funny feeling about that stranger who visited the other night, what did he say his name was?"

"Stan," answers Mattie.

"Yeah, that's it. I wonder who that rascal really is. He stayed in your bathroom for a long time, and I bet he wasn't using the toilet. I believe he may have created a doorway for a spiritual attack. Mother Mattie, you gotta anoint your house to get rid of that presence."

"Oh, can you help me cleanse this house?" pleads the elder. "I'm so discouraged ... too weak. I can feel that same presence coming against me now. C'mon, Louise, let's pray together."

Having the gift of discernment, Mrs. Robinson can sense what's going on. Right away, both ladies commence to pray for deliverance. It brings temporary relief, but the spiritual torment won't stop for good until the house is cleansed and blessed.

As the prayer ends, Mattie retreats to the couch with Louise still on the line. As soon as she begins to relax, the old woman suddenly feels something sitting at her feet ... it feels almost like a dog. Nothing visible to her human eyes, yet there is an eerie presence in the room with her. It does no harm, but it won't go away either.

Mattie continues her conversation on the phone. "Things are better now. The tormenting has stopped, except for this presence in the room with me. I can feel it. Help me get it out of here."

"Plead the blood of Jesus over yourself; command that evil presence to stand still. We're coming to your house right now to find the root to your problem and get rid of it."

Randy enters the house just in time to catch the tail end of the conversation. Without saying a word, he reaches back into his pants pocket to retrieve his car keys. They head to Mattie's house.

"So how long has this been going on?" Randy asks his wife as he drives. "And why hasn't she simply cleansed the house?"

Louise shrugs her shoulders, "I don't know, and I didn't ask." Mrs. Robinson can sense her husband's frustration with the matter. There must be something else on his mind.

"I'm sorry, baby," Randy apologizes. "I shouldn't be so uptight. I just learned something new about this city and its police department. The corruption around here is outrageous. Even worse, the community doesn't seem to care at all about the condition of their neighborhoods. How can anyone stand by just letting the community go to Hell?"

"I understand your feelings about this community, but a friend of ours is in desperate need of help. Let's take care of Mother Mattie's problem and talk about the other issues later," suggests Louise.

The Robinsons arrive at Mattie's house. As soon as they step through the door, the battle is on. The same evil presence seeking to squeeze the life out of Mattie attempts to smother the couple too. The pastor and his wife have foolishly walked into a spiritual ambush without preparing first. Now all three mortals are struggling to keep their minds in focus.

Mattie is on her hands and knees. Already weakened, the evil presence within the house has forced her to the ground. Louise and Randy feel the urge to submit to the force as well, yet they instinctively resist by remaining in standing positions.

Joining hands, the Robinsons concentrate their efforts in prayer to loosen the grip of evil within the house. As they intercede for strength to fight, they walk toward Mattie with their hands and arms intertwined to form a bridge of shelter over the weak elder.

Pastor Robinson says aloud: "Lord, we come before you requesting the strength to withstand the attack of the enemy. Jesus, we plead your blood all over this house, asking that you reveal the source of this trouble. God, we also request that you shield and protect Mattie, and let us stand in the gap on her behalf, so she can recover from this assault on her life."

This is just the beginning. Randy directs his words toward the enemy within Mattie's home. "We now take back dominion of this house proclaiming it to be a dwelling place for our Lord and Savior, Jesus Christ. You have no place here. How you got in this house, we don't know, but the time has come for you to leave."

As the three pray, Pastor Robinson walks about the house. He goes to every room with a bottle of olive oil in his hands. The oil represents the blood of Christ. Pouring just a bit on the palm of his hand, the pastor anoints each room by touching the walls, doors, and windows with his oily hand. All the while, Robinson pleads the blood of Christ, by proclaiming the house to be the holy ground of God. Not until the pastor reaches the bathroom does he notice something strange. *What's so different about the bathroom?* he thinks to himself.

Suddenly, the answer comes to mind. This is the same bathroom that Stan used. As he examines the bathroom for clues, a noxious feeling comes to his stomach. There's nothing in the trashcan or behind the toilet. The pastor even lifts the lid of the toilet tank in search of a hint. Still nothing. Inside the medicine cabinet is clear too. As Robinson closes the door, he immediately notices a faint hand print on the wall, just above the toilet. It looks as though someone used the wall to balance themselves while standing on the toilet seat. In search of more clues, the pastor look towards the ceiling, and what do his eyes behold? He spies a design that resembles a star—a pentagram to be exact.

Randy calls for his wife and Mattie, and they confirm what he suspected all the time.

With the anointing oil in hand, Robinson is ready to close the spiritual doorway. He lowers the toilet seat cover to stand upon it. Reaching to the ceiling, he cleans and anoints the area where the pentacle appears. The hellions must leave now.

Lee, the warrior, is present. Since the source of the problem has been found, he can legally force the enemy to leave.

The evil spirits are reluctant to go. Lee persuades them with the flat side of his blade as he swings away at an imp who is slapped silly. Dazed, the imp floats in mid air looking dizzy. His companions get the message and flee quickly before the warrior resumes batting practice.

As they leave, one spirit comments to another that he is happy to be leaving such an uncomfortable environment.

"I believe there is more to Stan than what he told us," says Mattie. "He's the only stranger who has used this bathroom as of lately. This trouble didn't start until he visited us that night."

"Yes, ma'am, we are going to be more careful in the future when it comes to strangers. We just can't let anyone come freely in the house to set up snares," declares Robinson.

Louise is always analytical and poses questions that cause everyone to think deeply. "I wonder how he found out about us? Why would he want to bother us? I believe this proves we have a definite reason for being here in Harlem Heights."

After helping Mattie to cleanse her house, the Robinsons make a quick stop by the grocery store, and then they head for home.

Louise rips open a bag of chips as Randy explains the corruption plaguing the city. "I've been researching the history of this rough city. I just discovered why this place never seems to progress past a certain point—especially the churches. According to the police officer that joined our prayer group, there's a history of mysterious crimes that take place around here all the time."

Louise's attention is more on the bag of chips in which she's buried her hand. She laughs, shrugging off the idea of another city myth. "Oh great, another urban legend."

"Really, baby, check this out. For instance, in the 1930s, sometime during the Great Depression, factory owners made a pact with the devil for riches."

Randy's wife interrupts his story again with sarcasm. "Whoa, a boogey man story?"

"Baby, stop playing and listen to me for a minute," says the slightly frustrated pastor. "As I was saying, they all came together and signed their names to a contract with their very own blood. The promise made to them was for financial security as long they honored the obligation of the contract."

Louise, satisfied with her share of the chips, rolls the bag closed and wipes her mouth clean with the sleeve of her arm. "What were the conditions of the contract?" she asks, now developing somewhat of an interest in the story.

"The requirements of the contract demanded a human sacrifice to be made at the time of the full moon each month. There would be additional sacrifices for each holiday celebrated by Christians too. That's a lot of murders each year."

Mrs. Robinson is not surprised. "Yeah, but it's nothing compared to today's murder rate."

The pastor goes on to describe the horrors that took place in the city. It was publicly known by many that a full moon meant death for someone.

Normally, it would be a visiting stranger with no clue as to what goes on in Harlem Heights. In total ignorance, that person would stop to have a drink at some innocent-looking bar where the local patrons would treat him with special kindness. Drink after drink would be provided for free; one mug of beer after another would bring the fool closer to his death like a powerless raft drifting toward a steep waterfall. Intoxicated and ignorant of his deadly fate, the drunken victim would stumble from the bar into the streets where death awaited around the corner.

The bartender, knowing the victim's fate, would take a drink in honor of the sacrificial lamb whose death would keep their city's economy thriving.

The local patrons would raise their glasses too, making a toast in honor of the victim. It was never a happy moment, and the relief was only temporary. Everyone was just glad the unknown person was not a friend or family member. So, with beer mugs and shot glasses raised in the air, a chorus of *"prosperity is in the blood"* would fall from the lips of the men who had bought the drinks that led the lamb to slaughter.

Through fear and intimidation, everyone in the town—from the mayor down to the barber—participated in the sacrifices that took place on the land where a certain warehouse was built and still exists to this day.

11

Levy Tries Again

Old man Levy is feeling more miserable than ever since he stumbled upon his newfound dilemma. He has orders to destroy the prayer group, yet he doesn't want to hurt the people who can help him escape the occult. Fortunately for him, the Lord is answering his secret prayer for divine intervention.

Willie Mo' and Levy sit alone in an office that probably belonged to the top manager when the warehouse was a thriving, legitimate business. Willie is giving his instruction on how to destroy a church that just won't go away. "Get into that prayer group and stay this time," he urges. "Block their progress in every way possible; make 'em quit. Aim for the pastor by coming between him and that woman of his. If a conflict can be established there, it will roll downhill onto the saints. Find out what their plans are and lead the prayers astray. Keep them preoccupied with feeding the hungry, rebuilding the church, or starting a media ministry. Just keep their minds off of seeking the word of … well, you know who."

Levy nods his head slowly in acknowledgment. He knows exactly what to do. This is the opportunity he's been waiting for.

As the old man finds himself back at the prayer group again, it comes as no surprise that his welcome is not as warm this time.

"Well, looks who's back," says Louise with sarcasm in her voice. "I thought we saw the last of you, Mr. Stan, after you pulled that stunt. Are you back to cause more trouble?"

Caught off guard by the rough greeting, he's unsure of how to react. Stan stares down at the ground like a scolded child, and then he turns to Robinson hoping he'll be more reasonable. "I know'd I cause much troubles," he confesses to the pastor. "Believe me, I had no otha choice but ta do it; had ta see if y'all is real Christians. I got some good in me, jus' get to know me bettah, y'all see den."

Randy Robinson responds with a couple of questions. "Why didn't you just say so at first? That trouble you caused wasn't necessary. Besides, why do you need our help?"

"I seek some deliverance. Dat's all I can say fo' now. If you's true saints of God, y'all know da rest afta while."

Louise is in no mood for games. "Randy, you should kick this man out of here this instant. You know he's up to no good. The last time we saw him, he was sweating up a storm like he is now, and he also has that smell."

As Mrs. Robinson continues ranting, the pastor tries to hide his concerns but it's obvious he feels embarrassed for the old man.

Louise continues, relentlessly, "We couldn't get rid of that smell until we spiritually cleansed Mother Mattie's house. This old rascal has the devil in him."

"Baby, take it easy," pleads the pastor. "These are the people we're supposed to help. Jesus loves this man too—even if he's up to no good." The pastor cuts his eyes back at Stan to emphasize his point.

Louise reluctantly agrees to Stan coming back. "I'll be watching him."

"Honey, we're definitely gonna watch as well as pray," Randy cautions. "What happened last time will not happen again."

Pastor Robinson and the group form a circle about the old man, holding hands. Before he can ask what's going on, the saints begin praying.

Instantly, Stan feels sharp pains throbbing within his stomach as he is overwhelmed with nausea. The power of Christ can be overpowering. Sweating more profusely than ever, he seriously considers that he might have to abandon the plan to infiltrate the church if the torment continues.

While the saints pray silently among themselves, Pastor Robinson gently places his hand on the old man's back. Stan flinches as if being branded with a hot cattle prod. Robinson, noticing how his touch irritates the man, removes his hand to prevent stirring up Stan's flesh. Then the pastor speaks, "The one whom you've been serving for quite some time—the great enemy—was defeated when Jesus gave his life for the sins of mankind at the cross. If you come to the Lord, He can protect you from the occult." Robinson's tone changes from prayerful to straight talk. "As servants of Christ, we have only one thing to offer: the gift of salvation. If you've come for salvation, then please speak up so we can get you what you're seeking."

This is the opportunity Stan's been looking for—a chance to safely escape the brotherhood and live. Does he dare take a chance?

"Yessum, I seeks a way out, I confesses so. I needs a safe place to stay. I cain't go back ta where I's come from. The people dere is mighty powerful and dangerous. They run dis city. How's can you protect me from da bruthahood?"

Pastor Robinson is taken back. He has suspected something like this all the time, yet it surprises the pastor to hear it. "What exactly does the man mean by the word *brotherhood*?"

Randy doesn't realize he's thinking aloud until the old man responds to the question. "Da bruthahood has been in dis city befo' you and I's ever lived heah." The elderly one confirms the story that Robinson has already heard.

The pastor poses a few daring questions. "Stan, do you want a change in your life? Are you willing to let go of all the things you learned in the occult?" Robinson challenges the old man. "Finally, are you ready to worship the King of kings and Lord of lords?"

Stan wants to say yes, but he can only nod his head in agreement, which seems to be a big struggle. Then the old man suddenly goes unconscious.

Pastor Robinson has seen this act before and takes immediate action to deal with the matter. He points across the room at his Bible, Louise grabs for it. "Read aloud from the book of Revelation, chapter eighteen, until I say stop," he commands. She flips quickly through the pages as Robinson continues with instructions. "Now I need everyone else to quietly sing some praise and worship songs. If this is the game the enemy wants to play, we'll wait patiently on the Lord to handle this problem."

Louise reads with fervor from the book of Revelations. In the background one person starts humming a worshipful song which compels the others to join in.

Robinson calls upon the Lord. "Jesus, we ask that you will seal this room; let this place be a holy place … a sanctuary where we can do your work without interference from the enemy. Lord, we come before you asking that every word being read from your Bible is loud and clear in the ears of the enemy."

Suddenly, the old man sits up with his sweaty forehead glaring in the light. In some sort of a trance, he reaches for the Bible that Louise is holding. With a deep guttural voice that is not his own, he says, *"Stop reading, I hate that book!"* Stan loses consciousness again.

Startled by the monster's voice, Louise jumps back saying, "No, I will not stop reading." She continues to do so with even more passion.

Pastor Robinson now intervenes. "By the power of Jesus Christ, I bind you, evil spirit, and command you to hold your peace and be silent until the time comes for you to leave."

As the old man comes to again, the pastor quickly gets his attention. "Stan, you've got to control that spirit. Don't allow it to take over your mind. Fight back."

Stan looks at the pastor as if he's crazy. "How I'm s'posed ta do dat?"

"First, you must make a decision as to who you will serve: Jesus Christ or Satan. You can't serve two masters at once."

It's evident to see the old man is struggling with his choices. He likes the power of the dark side, yet still yearns for the safety and freedom found in Christ.

"Mr. Stan this is serious business; you can't straddle the fence with indecision—it will destroy your soul. Either you continue with this occult lifestyle or you let it go. You gotta make a choice and stick to it."

"How can I do it, pastor?"

"If you're serious then confess your sins—come clean with everything you done. After that you must plead your allegiance to the only God there is by acknowledging that Christ gave his life on the cross for your sins and rose from the dead. Can you do that?"

"It seems easy."

"Great, Mr. Stan. Let's try it."

The old man attempts to make a confession, but once again he goes unconscious, forcing the pastor to intervene yet another time.

With the precision of a seasoned cleric, Robinson calmly speaks in an easy but authoritative tone as if reprimanding a child. "By the power in the blood of Jesus Christ, I command you evil spirits to be still and hold your peace." He places a gently hand on the old man's forehead hoping the caring touch will rouse him from the demonically induced sleep.

Stan wakes up again, giving Pastor Robinson an opportunity to question the recurring phenomenon. "This spirit, that knocks you out every time you try to commit yourself to Christ, how did it get into your life?"

The old man struggles for an answer, which requires Randy to help him along. "Well, when did you have your first encounter with the spiritual realm?"

The question brings the old man's memories into perspective. Going back to his younger years, Stan starts with his life as a farm hand. "It happened down South on da plantation when de conjure-man hep me escape da sharecroppin' life. He teached me how ta get a personal guide dat would show me da way up Norf."

"So that was your start in the occult?"

"Well, yeah and no."

"So how did you get involved in the occult here in Harlem Heights?"

"Dere was no jobs when I fust git heah. Ya had to know da right peoples ta finds work. I wash dishes awhile only 'til business went bad. I even gathers firewood ta sell which everyone else was doin'. I could do carpentar and butchar work that I learn't on de plantation, but dem jobs was save mostly fo' de white folks."

The saints, fascinated by the visitor's storytelling, have given their undivided attention to the man whose mannerisms reflect the character of a plantation field hand.

Stan explains how he found other means of work in the big city in the most unusual place. "Somehow's I came cross work at da breedin' house—a place dem men folks would go ta lay up wit womens, an' when da womens get knocked up dey babies was gave ta da bruthahood ta use as dey saw fit."

Louise is appalled by Stan's story. "That's an outright shame. Who in their right minds would do such foul things?"

The old man intends to answer Mrs. Robinson's question, but he continues with his story first. "Surprisingly, t'was a woman who ran de breedin' house an' she was deep in de craft too. Dough we never married each udders, everyone thought us ta be man an' wife. Dat woman taught me a lot 'bout da craft. From her I got a spirit ta hep me draw young womens ta work in da breedin' house. The power I got made my life so much bettah that I 'came a member of da bruthahood myself. I could finally say I made it in da big city as Pimp Slim."

Pastor Robinson feels skeptical about the story. "So what happened? Why aren't you dressed all fancy and looking good?"

"Believe me, in my younga days, I was a handsome man … hard ta resist. For da longest times, I ran the streets in Harlem Heights. I had a stable of ho's—excuse me … didn't mean ta offen' da ladies." Stan looks like a sheepish child caught with his hand in the cookie jar.

As the old man talks, his behavior becomes animated; his gestures get lively while the volume of his voice rises with passion. Stan is revealing a side of his character the saints have never seen. "I always had da latest fashion of clothes, and kep me a bankroll in my pocket. I even went ta night school an' got rid of my plantation accent."

Pastor Robinson fights back the urge to laugh at the old man's last statement.

"The mo' I tried to leave da bruthahood, the mo' money an' fame came my way. My beaut'ful hazel eyes and dis slick tongue could sell anythang on da streets."

Both Randy and Louise are getting disgusted with the old man's conversation; Stan is running off at the mouth something awful now and getting out of control. Having heard enough, Robinson demands silence. "Sir, all that boasting isn't necessary and please spare us the details of your life as Pimp Slim. Obviously the lifestyle didn't do you any good just look at yourself now."

Stan suddenly looks heartbroken, sad, as if a flood of bad memories have come to his mind. "I wasn't always old an' ugly like you see me now. It's his fault dat I look da way I do; t'was all a setup."

"What are talking about?" inquires Robinson.

"T'was a long time ago when da bruthahood had a secret meetin' one night. For some reason or 'nother, a man called Brutha Devine was bein' punished for disobedience. I's nevah seen a high rankin' member bein' punish for failin'. Normally da top folks avoid troubles by puttin' blames on da the bottom peoples; da weak ones. But dis time, Devine couldn't pass da blame, an' so he was punished—he didn't get da regular kind of chastise."

The pastor is eager to know the details. "Well, what did he get?"

"Dey punish his daughter. Devine sho' nuff loved dat gurl, and he tried mighty hard to protect her. It didn't hep none 'cause she was brutal raped while he was force to watch it all. Dat's right, he had to watch 'cause if he dare looked away, Devine would haf been tortured an' kilt himself."

This was not the end of Brother Devine's punishment. Stan explains how matters became worse for the man. His beautiful daughter was ordered to work for Pimp Slim at the breeder house. More specifically, she was to be hustled hard outside on the street corner like a field-hand slave on the plantation. Stan didn't want to do it, but his options were limited. It was work the girl like a mule or risk being punished for disobedience himself. Within a few months, the young lady looked as though she had aged twenty years.

Following the rules still didn't help Stan either. The old man goes on to say, "In da 'cult, if ya cain't get back at dose who harm ya, den harm dose who can't touch ya. Dat's why Brutha Devine tried to get afta me. He'd come at night time in his spirit form attackin' me at home. Dat no good hammer-knocka would conja up ways ta make me fail at my job. Finally, when's I no longer had the patience left to tolerate it anymo', I struck back."

Stan goes on to tell how he fought back. The pimp got together with the women at the breeder house to retaliate against Devine. Still, the adversary was too strong; Brother Devine forced Stan's women to abandon him, leaving the man to suffer alone. Pimp Slim was severely beaten and raped in the same manner that Devine's daughter had been assaulted. Last of all, the pimp was forbidden to attend any of the brotherhood meetings.

"I loss everythang," Stan confesses. "Den I was made ta join dem low-life gangs dat didn't care anythang about spiritual powers. 'Long as dey had dope and guns, dey had no udder inklin' ta do better wit dey lives—dat's what I fust thought." Stan reveals what he eventually learned from the gangs. "Furtha dealin's wit dese thugs proofed udderwise. Many of dem is educated, dey blends in good wit society, and dey seeks to conquer the city. Dey use money from the fast life to draw chillrens to join dey gangs."

The pastor is fascinated. "So this is where our youth are headed. They're on a pathway to Hell, and society can't see it."

Stan nods his head in agreement, responding, "Soon y'all see a time when Harlem Heights will be ruled by dese gangs. Dere's a man by the name of Mo' who will take control of dis city sometime soon." The old man changes subjects. "By de way, I nevah finish my story 'bout Brutha Devine who finally got his jus' due."

"What happened?"

"Da man kilt his self."

There's something Randy doesn't understand. "Why would a strong man like Devine take his own life?"

"We attacked da man by cagin' him. Mo' personally came 'gainst Devine and snatched away all of his demons. He forced Devine ta sign ovah da deed to the warehouse where da Pharaohs live now. Den he went into a bad depression an' took his life jus' like his daughter did a yeah befo'."

"What do you mean by caging'?" asks Louise.

"It's a curse used ta control 'nother person's mind. Mo' was able to capture Devine's mind when he started showin' a weakness."

Mrs. Robinson seeks clarity. "What was his weakness?"

"He showed too much love fo' his daughter. Devine had dat girl on a pedestal. Once dis love was discovered, t'was used as a way ta undo da man. Da 'cult has no mercy on anyone—it don't mattah what position ya got."

Stan's story keeps leading to more questions. "Why would this Mo' want to do such a thing to Devine?" Pastor Robinson is curious to know.

"Devine offend him one day widout knowin' it. He called da street gangs society's trash—an' anyone dat mixed wit the gangs as scum of de Earth. In da bruthahood, you gotta be careful whatchu say. You nevah know who be listenin'."

"How did Mo' become so strong in the occult?" asks Randy.

"Dat boy was fortunate he 'herited two strong devils, dat's all."

"How? Why would they want Mo'?"

"I don't know what dey saw in him, but dat boy caught on quickly ta the workin's of da devil. He grow'd up tough and was eager ta learn. I was given da job of keepin' da boy goin' in the right darection."

Pastor Robinson makes another inquiry. "So this is the guy who is, right now, trying to gain control of Harlem Heights. How long will it be before he takes full control?"

"It won't be long now, 'long as no one meddles wit his business."

"What are you talking about?"

"Somehow, what y'all do heah messes wit thangs at the warehouse. Da name dat y'all mention causes a ruckus on dem gangs," Levy reveals.

The old man doesn't know it, but Randy's been working on a pet project that he's never shared with anyone. Among the few treasures he possesses, the pastor has a map of the city which he has mounted to the wall in the basement. On that map is a display of the various neighborhoods in Harlem Heights. A red thumb tack marks the location of the warehouse, which is centered directly in the middle of map.

As the guardians build their forces to break the evil's grip on the city, surely they must be pleased with their efforts to bring a young Hispanic police officer to the prayer group. Hector Perez has eleven years of service on the force. The officer keeps keen eye on gang activity, and he knows drugs and crime run deeper than just the streets.

Also new to the group is a couple, the Evans, whose parents were European immigrants. They know the origins of the curse that settled on Harlem Heights and have already told their story to the Robinsons.

Stan's revelation, along with the expertise of the police officer and the Evan's couple, has the wheels turning Pastor Robinson's mind; he's beginning to see the source of trouble in Harlem Heights.

The pastor, eager to bring the meeting to an end, beckons everyone to one last prayer. "Tonight's events have revealed how much work is required to clean up the city of Harlem Heights. So please everyone, let's join in prayer and ask the Lord for his insight on this matter."

All heads are bowed and all eyes are closed. The first few seconds are pure silence; the pastor seems to be at lost for words. As he searches his heart for the right things to say, a light begins to shine down upon him. Instantly, Solomon and Lee fall to their faces as the presence of the Lord pays the loyal prayer group a visit.

The holy presence of the Lord is a sweet fragrance, warm … bright. It calms the atmosphere. Before Robinson can form his lips to say the first word, he quietly chuckles to himself. "Yes, Lord, my Savior. We welcome this visit; it's so good to be in your presence. Oh, Jesus, thank you for sacrificing yourself on the cross to save all of mankind, so we can enjoy a simple moment like this. Please stay, Lord, please stay," prays the pastor.

Randy is so busy relishing the moment that he almost forgets the reason for the prayer. As he begins to get lost in the Lord, the Holy Spirit leads him back on task. The pastor begins, "Almighty Father, we present to you the city of Harlem Heights. This city is under attack. It has been under assault for decades, and now the attack has intensified."

Solomon and Lee raise their arms in holy reverence as they agree with the mortal's prayer.

"Lord, the enemy has a plan so devastating that it could possibly affect the welfare of this nation, and we now pray that you will somehow intervene. Don't let the enemy prevail in its attempt to destroy the city with violence, racism, and—most of all—drugs. We now ask that your people come together to bind the enemy who sees fit to keep your people in bondage."

The prayer group makes a vow before Heaven to fight until a breakthrough for the city is achieved. They hope to see a judicial system that stands for true justice, and a police department that can clean the streets.

Lee, feeling motivated from the visit of the Lord, is eager for a battle with the enemy. Before he and his warriors can lead an attack, however, they need to clear up a few administrative issues. In preparation for the big fight, information must find its way to federal agents about drug trafficking and the ritual killings in Harlem Heights. So far, an inquiry from the FBI has been made, but the bureau has yet to conduct an official investigation. There is still something lacking, but Solomon is working on that part

12

The Mayor's Boy

Mayor Thomas J. Hurt has been the top man of Harlem Heights for over fifteen years now. He's always managed to stay in office despite tough competition looking to dethrone him every reelection year.

Hurt is a man people either love or hate. Some despise the mayor because he's so self-serving. Programs to help the poor or improve education are secondary concerns for him unless it's reelection time. The mayor's priority is big business and this is why other people love him. He brings big bucks to the city by specializing in manufacturing industries, major sporting events, and underhanded deals.

The man is successful as mayor for another primary reason: He keeps his foot on the enemy's neck at all times. No one dares to openly challenge him on issues they know will bring trouble. Talking about these matters could result in a sudden loss of life.

The mayor rules the city through intimidation. Hurt's only weakness is his son, Tommy Hurt Jr., a spoiled kid who learned early in life that his father has clout throughout the city. If he wants something, Tommy needs only to mention his father's name and the wish is granted. Perhaps this is why the son lacks the driving work ethic of his father.

Tommy is also an impulsive, spoiled punk who refuses to accept responsibility for anything he does wrong. Several times he's wrecked his car while drinking and driving. He even took the life of an entire family while driving under the influence of alcohol. Of course, his father got him out of trouble by paying the surviving family members off, but his son's repeated mistakes in breaking the law are thorns in Mayor Hurt's side.

The young man has dropped out of high school, and the father, wanting to take care of his son, has started Tommy a lucrative business.

The mayor's boy has his own nightclub. A multitude of people throughout the city are drawn to this business establishment. It's the hottest spot in Harlem Heights attracting local celebrities and popular sport figures. Inside the club, patrons can do whatever they wish; the law doesn't exist inside.

The mayor didn't want the club to be a cesspool. What he had in mind was a classy place where businessmen could sit down, have a drink, and still maintain an image of decency. The father would have voiced his opinion a long time ago; however, Tommy is finally doing something he's good at, so Mayor Hurt lets him run the club as he sees fit.

Tommy puts on the appearance that he is running the club; he isn't. JT is the main operator. Jermaine and Tommy met during their brief time at high school. JT is the thug who bullied everyone around. When he learned Tommy was the mayor's son—and that he liked to smoke dope—they became good friends. When the concerned father found his son a business, he really started a business for JT.

Tommy's friend, JT, had all the great ideas. He's the one who got the word out to the community about the club and found the hottest DJs to keep the place hopping with music. Now that the club is firmly established, the Pharaohs have a place to sell dope and launder money. Tommy has the luxury of getting high on whatever drug he chooses free of charge—a fair exchange is no robbery.

The club is kept under the protection of the dark side. Anyone can visit the place and do whatever they please. Drugs and sexual favors are in full abundance.

Detectives Hughes and Diggs are busy with their schemes again. They have Mingo sitting in the backseat of their unmark vehicle, trying to convince him to play a role in their devious plot. The Latin Red doesn't have much say-so in this matter. Being the snakes they are, the detectives will simply blackmail the gang leader if he refuses to play ball with the cops.

Hughes gets straight to business. "Mingo, you made a special batch of that smack, right?"

"Yep, it's potent, man."

"That Tommy boy's a smack addict, he might as well put a loaded gun to his head if he shoots up with that stuff," says Diggs.

Hughes continues with another question. "You also got another shipment coming in, right?"

"Yeah, there's another one due in a few days," Mingo confirms.

"Let the clowns have it all. Let 'em get it all in their possession and we'll catch 'em red-handed with the goods," Hughes advises. "When the mayor's boy overdoses we'll connect Tommy's death to the Pharaohs."

Diggs promises an incentive for Mingo's cooperation. "When we catch the Pharaohs with the stash, we gotta keep half of the product for evidence, but you'll get the rest to sell. Like always you'll pay us a percentage and then ride off in the sunset. Do us dirty, you'll pay the price."

Mingo has his doubts. "All this sounds good, but how can I trust you?"

"Trust is not an issue. You will do as we say or find yourself in the same predicament as your buddy. All you wannabe kingpins are fortunate to be walking the block. One phone call is all it takes to sweep these streets clean. This is your opportunity to make some money—don't mess it up. Chances like these don't come often."

Why can't life be simpler? It's hard enough dealing with the mysterious Willie Mo' who never wants to cooperate unless matters are to his own liking. Mingo also has to deal with detectives Hughes and Diggs, two undercover dirty cops with bad intentions. No one is trustworthy. Mingo wishes he could just leave the game ... be done with the fast life, but it's not so easy to get out once you're in.

The Latin Red doesn't have a good feeling about the situation. "C'mon man, we need a better plan than this. Who's gonna take the blame when bodies start dropping like dead flies all over the city? If the wrong person dies, this plan is gonna backfire on all of us."

Hughes isn't worried about failure. "It's too easy, just put the package where it belongs. When bodies start turning cold, we'll get involved and clean up the mess. All we need is for you to make the first move."

"I don't want any piece of this plan. It's gonna spill over on innocent people and bring mad heat on the streets," Mingo warns. "When that happens, anyone suspected of having a hand in this mess is gonna get fried—including you two."

"Nothing bad is gonna happen to you; we got it all under control," says Hughes. "Just deliver the goods as planned. When the dogs go hunting, they'll be tracking the Pharaohs' scent, not yours. Believe me, I got your back on this."

"Yeah, that's what you say now. Whose gonna watch your back if this situation gets bigger than you?"

"Mingo, you worry too much. Let us do the officer stuff; you handle business on the streets. I promise it'll be all right."

The tall Hispanic male exits the vehicle, leaving the detectives to their own thoughts. After he takes a few steps away from the car, the engine roars to life, the lights flick on, and Hughes pulls off with a lit cigarette hanging from the corner of his mouth. Diggs sticks his arm out the passenger window and throws a peace sign to the air. The detectives go their own way.

Molder's spies rise from the street gutter. They have been ease-dropping on the whole conservation between Mingo and the detectives. With the inside information they just acquired, they can make plans to double cross the detectives.

Easing out from the blue mail-drop box is Siron. He, too, knows of the plan, which he will report to Solomon and Lee—spirits stay busy.

Mingo walks back to his car which is parked a few blocks away, a measure he felt necessary to take so as to avoid being seen with cops. A ten minute stroll and he can now see José sitting on the driver's side of a plain looking sedan with a fading paint job. The driver cranks the engine, as he's ready to roll out as soon as Mingo gets inside.

"Where we headed to now?" asks José.

"Go to the club, I got a special delivery to make."

Upstairs in the club is the manager's office. Willie Mo' and JT are there counting stacks of money made from dope sales. Profits from the last shipment have yielded great returns and the gangsters needed a slow night, like tonight, to catch up on a few loose ends. Molder and

Wrath stand among the mortals watching intently as the humans count money. Every bill that hits the table brings warmth to the demons' cold hearts.

The mayor's son, Tommy, is feigning for a hit of smack and is getting agitated as he waits for Mingo to arrive with the goods. Pacing back and forth in the same office with the Pharaohs, he hasn't sat down once since his last phone call to Mingo.

The Latin Reds finally enter the club to flashing strobe lights and loud music pounding in the air. José stops to admire the strippers dancing nonchalantly on stage. They suddenly come to life when he displays a twenty-dollar bill for a special dance.

Mingo, the more focused of the two, eases upstairs to talk with Willie Mo'. The Reds' gang leader isn't alone. Fratricide has sent rogue warriors to accompany the mortal.

Before Mingo can knock, Tommy intercepts him at the door—the mayor's son wants the goods. With the dope in hand, Tommy retreats to the couch and preps his arm for the sweet hit of smack. In a few moments he'll be sprawled out on the sofa, feeling the rush of heroin coursing through his veins.

Mingo greets everyone in the office, "What's up, fellas?"

JT, the more outspoken, replies first. Mo' continues to count money, leaving the conversation for JT to handle. The cold treatment by Willie Mo' makes Mingo more resolved to set the Pharaoh up for a big fall.

What the humans can't see is the standoff between the spirits. Molder and Wrath stand nearby their mortal, Willie, exuding arrogance, which infuriates the demons that have arrived with Mingo.

Molder, using all the scorn his voice can muster, demands an explanation, "What business do you have here?"

"Who are you to question us?" the guard snaps back.

Molder steps quickly to his rival, standing face to face, "If you wish to see your chubby master again, you'd better give some respect or suffer the *wrath*."

On cue, Wrath quickly draws his sword. Puffing thick billows of sulfur from his flared nostrils, the warrior locks eyes with the visitors. "Since when does the big one send guards with a mortal messenger? It seems somebody's plotting war."

"Why all the aggression? We go everywhere this mortal goes. It should not matter unless you all have something to hide," the visitor retorts.

Wrath is no mood for a debate. The demon gives one last warning for the unwanted spirits to leave. Though courageous, the spiritual visitors are not in the ideal situation for a fight. Outnumbered and surrounded by a confident adversary, Fratricide's forces wisely retreat to the safety of the streets, which the big one still controls. They will save the battle for another day when the odds might be more even.

The threat is now gone, leaving Molder to continue his mischievous ways. As he focuses his attention back to the physical realm, the evil spirit is attracted to the mayor's son. Heavily intoxicated, Tommy begins moaning and fidgeting on the couch. He could be having a bad trip from the heroin. The drug-induced state has been known to draw back the veil that separates the spiritual realm from the physical world, revealing spiritual beings of the most horrid sort.

Molder senses that Tommy is able to see and hear him. The spirit approaches the mortal to touch the hypodermic needle still hanging from the man's forearm. The demon's wicked touch seems to enhance the power of the dope. The mayor's son is floating in the clouds; the heroin is feeling too good.

"You are the key to the city," Molder teases. *"You will open the door, won't you?"*

Tommy is scared, but too high to do anything besides beg for mercy. "Please don't kill me!"

JT looks at Tommy with bewilderment. "Who are you talking to?"

The mayor's son continues his panicky mumbling.

"You need to go light on that stuff, man. You gonna lose your mind one day," JT warns.

Molder is laughing and saying aloud, "The man is talking with me, can't you see? I have something for him. Come Suicide, Insanity, and Fear—do your worst to the mayor's son."

The naughty spirits rush to Tommy with pleasure. They have been promised a vessel, and Molder stays true to his word. With glee, the three thank their master.

"Truly, you are the great one, my lord. Your blessings drive me crazy," says Insanity.

"I'm afraid this is too good to be true. Say it's not so, master," exclaims Fear.

"It's real ... so real, my friends," hisses Suicide. "This is what I die for ... a new home to dwell in."

The scoundrels leap into Tommy's soul and the heat of the possession burns his body. The infiltrators circle Tommy's head, dive through his brain, causing the mortal to blink his heavy eyes while his head repeatedly falls back. The heroin addict looks like a defenseless boxer suffering an onslaught of invisible blows.

Insanity rakes his claws through the young man's brain, telling Tommy he's crazy. Fear and Suicide tag team the mortal by placing absurd thoughts in his mind: *I'm afraid I'm going to die.*

Molder, feeling cocky, playfully scold the imps, "No, no, no, kids. You mustn't be so rough with your new toy. You just got 'im. Take it easy on the man or else he'll break."

Remembering that Mingo is still in the office, Molder enters Willie's body to give a verbal warning. *"Woe unto you if you're plotting against me. Nothing shall get in the way of my desire to rule this city, so let's play the game fair—no tricks."*

Mingo is surprised and curious to know how Mo' knew about the plan to betray him. The situation is starting to get a bit hairy now. Mingo will have to watch how he operates.

There sits Fratricide on his throne, pissed off about the recent events taking place in the city. The wayward actions of Molder and Wrath are undermining the big one's authority and jeopardizing efforts to accomplish the mission. Fuming with anger, the mammoth vents his frustration by slapping Informer upside the head. The runt sails through the air, bounces off the chest of a warrior who stands guard at his post, and then tumbles to the ground. The incident draws hysterical laughter from the other guards as Informer struggles to his feet, gathering his wits.

The runt has a look of shock on his face. "Why, master, do you strike me? What wrong have I done?"

"Who are you to question me?" retorts Fratricide. "Have you forgotten who asks the questions around here? A loose tongue will cause your head to roll. That's all you need to know."

Embarrassed and too weak to defend himself, Informer bows low like a cowardly dog saying, "Yes, master."

"That's more like it, my runt. You shall serve me well. Come here so I can see you better, Fratricide wants to talk."

Not knowing the big one's intentions, Informer approaches with caution, looking for one of Fratricide's mammoth arms to come swooping down with a fist to smash him into the ground. The imp is so nervous, he urinates; pee runs down his leg and puddles to the ground. The soft chuckles in the background are growing into loud howls. The demon warriors are amused and loving the fun Fratricide is having with Informer.

The runt's wet, knobby knees rub together as he creeps toward his master. "My lord, you beckoned me. Here I am."

Taking his time before speaking, the big one gets lost in his thoughts and his face reflects a distant stare. Without warning, the large one pulls out his sword with cat-like quickness. Raising the weapon over his head, he slices it downward. Informer defecates this time as the tip of the sword drives into the ground very close to his feet. A loud metallic ring sounds as the blade tip pierces the concrete floor causing bits of grit to sprout like a geyser.

The laughing ceases. The room is suddenly quiet as the wicked guards snap to attention. The mortals on the level below look to the ceiling wondering what the commotion could possibly be. "What in the world is that noise?" asks the mayor.

"Sir, I haven't the slightest clue," says the secretary.

The humans' conversation below catches the attention of the spirits above. They all pause to see how the people will react. As usual, the mortals blow it off thinking an air conditioner is malfunctioning or something of that nature.

Informer's attention is brought back to the matter at hand. Beckoned by the big one to come even closer, the runt closes his eyes while stepping a few more feet forward.

"Yes, master?" he barely whispers.

Sulfur smoke seeps from Fratricide's large mouth. A devious smile uncovers the big one's tobacco brown teeth.

Informer is a disgusting creature himself, but his filth is nothing compared to that of Fratricide. Smothered by the monster's hot rancid breath in his face, the runt finds it hard to breathe. "You will do something special for me, hmm? I want you to be my spy. That's what you do best, isn't it?"

The little one is not sure how to respond. Is this a trick question or a sincere request? Stuttering, he gives a halfhearted response, "Master … uh … I—I don't understand."

The mammoth clarifies, "You will go to the Robinsons' place to find out what they have planned. See if the enemy is attempting to direct their attacks at us. Go learn everything you can about the enemy."

The expression on Informer's face drastically changes. The look of fear gives way to a devious image that reflects the true nature of this foul imp. The excited runt quickly forgets the danger he felt in the presence of the behemoth. Ever mindful of his lowly position; however, he backs away slowly, bowing and eager to get on with the mission. Before the imp makes a clean getaway, a giant hand pulls him back even closer to Fratricide's ugly face. The hot vapor puffing from the big one's mouth causes the imp's ear to quiver. "One more thing before you leave, my dearest one," Fratricide whispers to Informer. "Watch out for those who may try to deceive me. Let me know who my enemies are within this camp."

The runt feels privileged. With a smile plastered to his gremlin face, Informer flies from the building with his leather wings snapping through the air. He's glad to be free and still in good health. Now he gets to see what's going on outside the headquarters.

13

Getting the Media Involved

Heaven's sons are seeing the results of the saints' prayer efforts. The latest benefit of the prayer cover is division within Fratricide's ranks.

Lee shares the good news with his brother, Solomon. "There's a conflict between the gang leaders; it appears that Fratricide and Molder are not getting along well. Division among the leaders makes it easier for us to uproot the enemy."

Solomon is ready for the next step in the plan. "Well, let's stir the pot a bit more at the police department to see if we can expose the corruption within the ranks of the law."

"Has contact with the woman been made?" Lee inquires.

The war angel is referring to a newspaper reporter who seeks to make a mark in the world of journalism. She's the ideal one for the covert operation.

Solomon feels optimistic about the new journalist. "It's not the most glamorous assignment, but the reporter's responsibility will be the faith section of the paper. With guidance, she will start the fire needed to smoke out the moles and every other creature wallowing in the dark corruption that eats away at Harlem Heights."

Pastor Robinson and the prayer group meet at Mattie's house as usual. Having learned their lesson with Stan, Randy always arrives early to bless and seal the house from any spiritual attack.

Attending tonight's meeting is someone special—a young, attractive reporter who is new to the city. Angela Williams is from a small town in the South where she attended college. Growing up in a Christian household where church was a priority, Angela had to abide by her parents' rules. This oftentimes conflicted with her wishes to hang out and party with her secular high school friends whose parents were way cooler than hers.

Feeling bitter about her treatment as a teenager, Angela vowed she would leave her home at the first opportunity and abandon the dumb religious beliefs of her parents. For the next few years at college, that's exactly what she did. The daughter never did anything outrageous; the aspiring journalist just laid her Bible down, choosing to live a life not centered on church. Though she can't stand religious zealots, a portion of her upbringing still remains within her.

Since being hired as a journalist for the *Harlem Heights Times*, Ms. Williams finds herself searching anxiously for a story that will put her name on the map. With a little divine assistance, she comes upon Pastor Robinson and the prayer group by accident.

While in the library researching the history of the city, Angela meets an off-duty police officer, Sergeant Hector Perez. He's conducting a bit of research himself. Both are in search of demographic information of the past.

The officer has use of the available reference material first, so Ms. Williams has to wait for her turn. Patience has never been the reporter's strongest virtue, so she approaches Perez about hurrying with the books. "Hey, when are you gonna finish with these books? You've been here for hours doing nothing but talking to yourself," Angela complains.

Perez is offended. "First of all, I'm not talking to myself; I'm singing praise songs to God. Next of all, don't rush me. I was here first. Besides, your work can't be any more important than mine."

What a Jesus freak, Angela thinks to herself. Knowing she can be rude at times, the journalist takes a different tone with the off-duty officer. "I apologize for coming across a bit pushy, but could you at least share the books you're finished with? I'm on a deadline—I don't have much time to write my story."

Perez is curious. "Well, what's it all about?"

Resisting the urge to say, *it's none of your business,* the reporter keeps her attitude in check. "I want to write an article about the religious history of this city. You know, what role did the church play in the founding of Harlem Heights?"

"That's easy. I can help you with that information. Perhaps, if you treat me nicely, I'll tell you something even more interesting than these books have to say."

Angela takes a few seconds to consider the offer. This is her first solo project, and she can use all the outside help available for such a dry subject, so the reporter accepts the help. Besides, if things don't work out as planned, she can always dump the guy.

"You never told me your name," says the officer. "I'm Hector Perez and you're …?"

"Angela Williams is my name. It's nice to meet you."

They shake hands, both smiling warmly.

Perez loves a good conversation. "The religious history of Harlem Heights is real juicy. Did you know the founding fathers of this city made a pact with the devil for guaranteed wealth?"

"No," says Angela, not sounding too enthused, "I never had a clue." The start of this conversation is already turning her off. Use of the word *devil* reminds the reporter of her strict religious childhood. A formal college education has taught her that the devil doesn't exist, and those who believe in such fairytales are religious nuts with limited education.

Unaware of what Angela is thinking, Perez goes on with the story of the sacrifices and the current murder rate in the city.

Though she wasn't interested at first, the boogeyman story has captured Angela's attention. She listens as Perez continues, "If you really want to know more, you should come with me to church sometime. We're working on a spiritual mapping project. It involves extensive research of the church history in Harlem Heights. I believe it will provide a different perspective on Christianity that many people seldom see."

Ms. Williams puts her guard up quickly. "You don't waste much time, do you?"

"What?" the officer seems clueless.

"I get the feeling you're trying to recruit me. I don't want to join your church."

"No, that's not my—"

Angela cuts him off in mid sentence, "'Cause I know all about the church and how they operate—I was raised in it. So, just in case the thought crosses your mind, I don't want to be evangelized; you will not make a disciple of me."

Perez is taken by surprise. He needs a few seconds to gather his thoughts. "I see that church is a sensitive subject for you."

Ms. Williams talks tough to get her point across, "Damn right."

Hector is speechless … Finally he manages a response. "If you already know Christ as you say you do, there should be no problems. I thought you might want to see the past from a different perspective. No pressure, just call me when you're ready to learn something new. Here's my card. Hope to hear from you soon. By the way, I apologize if I offended you."

Perez walks off disappointed. He's a bit disturbed by Angela's reaction. *Why is she so hostile toward God?* he wonders. *Or was it just my demeanor?*

Ms. Walker hopes she wasn't too rude. If so, it's no big deal. She has to be stern with religious zealots. They love to brainwash anyone willing to fall for their crap.

The reporter still visits the Light of Hope church group for business purposes only. Angela's presence at the prayer meeting surprises Perez—the angels are elated too.

Siron the scout reminds Solomon about the journalist's beliefs. "The reporter has no concern for her personal salvation; she's here for the story only."

Solomon is amused. "Well, imagine that—another human who frowns upon religion. You know what? I totally agree with her. Religion has gotten to be a circus. There's so much of man's doctrine involved, it blocks one's way to the Father. All we want for Angela's sake is a personal relationship with Heaven's creator. Let's show her the difference between religion and a personal relationship with the Savior."

14

Smack Kills & Prayers Can Save

JT and Tommy carry an unconscious dancer to the back of the club. There's no sign of a pulse, but the body is still warm and limp. It's been minutes since she passed out, never to return to life again. For such a slim woman, the stripper is heavier than the two men expected.

Tommy, feeling responsible for the incident, is frantic. The first thought in his mind is to throw the body in the dumpster. Thankfully, JT is there to handle the situation with more competence than the mayor's son. "Tommy, get over there," he says, pointing to a chair. "Sit down and stop acting so stupid. I don't know what you're panickin' for, ain't nothin' bad gonna happen."

"JT, I don't want to go to jail, man. I didn't mean to kill her."

"Shut up, man, she ain't dead. Go get a drink—I got this."

"Whatcha gonna do with her?"

"Drink, be quiet, and let me handle this. It's all under control," JT states with confidence. "We didn't do anything wrong; she did it to herself. We just gonna clean up the little mess she made."

The Pharaoh pulls out his cell phone and calls a couple of friends. Minutes later, two teenage males arrive outside the club in a nice-looking sports car. One's tall and gangly; the other shorter but stocky. They exit the car curious to know what JT wants with them. Neither one is pleased to hear the task. They're instructed to dump the girl at the hospital emergency room and keep on driving.

The tall, skinny kid makes a bold stance, "She ain't getting in my car." His face bears a frown further conveying his intentions not to comply.

Gritting his teeth, JT quickly slaps the boy upside the head. "You'll do like I tell ya!"

"C'mon, man, I just got this new car. I don't want no dead body in my car."

"Who said she's dead?" the gangster demands to know.

"She ain't moving, man."

"You better get over here and get this ..." JT pauses as he catches himself about to refer to the stripper as a *dead body*. " ...take her to the hospital for help befo' you find yourself lyin' next to her."

The short, stocky kid laughs at his skinny friend who's still rubbing his head in the same spot where JT slapped him. The slim one turns to his partner. "Hey, man, that ain't funny. I don't wanna mess with no dead person. The girl don't have no clothes on either, and look at her ... she peed on herself."

The stocky kid laughs again, "She's dead, but she still looks good though."

JT pulls a trick from his psychology bag. "Well, gimmie the keys to *my* car then. All I ask you for is a small favor and you can't do that."

Slim is feeling guilty already.

JT continues, "I bought this brand new car for you, and this how you show your appreciation? That's all right. I'll find someone else to drive it. You can walk around like you been doin'. You don't wanna help me out—then screw you."

Slim doesn't want to lose his most prized possession. If JT were to take away that car, it would crush his heart. Imagine life without a nice ride. No more picking up the boys to cruise; no more driving around slow so everyone can see him. The more Slim thinks about the losing the car, the more he figures he can do JT this one small favor.

The two young males dress the girl. Before they place her in the car, Slim hurries to cover the backseat of the vehicle with newspaper first. His actions makes JT laugh.

As the young gangsters drive off, Jermaine watches the vehicle disappear around the corner. Smiling to himself, JT goes back inside the club to check on Tommy who is halfway finished with a drink and appears to be relieved.

The issue is resolved for now, but there is another problem to address: Where's the poisonous dope coming from?

Randy and Louise talk casually in their kitchen to pass the time. They're expecting company at any moment. The news reporter, Angela, and the police officer, Perez, arrive on time to share their findings on the history of the city.

Angela greets Mrs. Robinson. "Hi, Louise, how are things going?"

Perez, entering the room right behind the reporter, yells a greeting before Louise can respond to Angela. Skipping the formalities, everyone gets straight to business.

"Harlem Heights has an interesting history," the journalist reveals. "There's so much I didn't know about this place ... things that explain a lot of mysterious deaths. I was looking through some periodicals and discovered an urban legend involving a satanic pact for riches. If the story about the city's founding businessmen is true, a lot of innocent blood has been spilled ... sacrificed ... in Harlem Heights."

"Yeah, and, if it's all true, then who's doing the sacrificing now?" Louise inquires.

Perez has an answer. "That's easy. With all the crime taking place in the city, there's more than enough sacrificing to meet the requirements for that pact."

The policeman's response is alarming. No one had thought of it in such a way. There's always a murder taking place in the city. Though not every day, at least once a month somebody's life is snuffed out for one reason or another. Now the mortals are beginning to understand the extent of evil hanging over Harlem Heights.

The prayer group has recognized a common theme throughout all the news reports: everything leads to death. The latest spell of drug overdoses ... the political and education systems ... all lead to death in some way or another. Every thread woven into the social fabric of Harlem Heights is a strand of death. This is Fratricide's tailor shop.

The pastor, now seeing the whole picture, escorts his wife and their two visitors downstairs to view his map of the city. "Up here on the wall is a map of the city," he explains. "You see the places with the red thumb tacks? These are the trouble spots in Harlem Heights ... the areas plagued by some type of serious crime. We can attack the enemy directly in the heart by aiming our prayers at these areas."

Solomon ministers to Randy's heart, *"Now you're talking good. Tell the people what they must do. Start with the mayor and work your way down to the streets."*

The pastor continues, "I think we should direct our prayers straight at the mayor's office. He's the head of Harlem Heights and can make changes that will affect the whole city. From there, we can aim for the police department and the judicial system."

Angela, being the keen reporter she is, has a question. "How do you know to start with the mayor?"

"That's a good question," replies the Pastor, "and I base my decision on this belief: always start at the top when you don't know where else to begin."

Sergeant Perez can't resist, so he adds his input. "This may be a coincidence, but do you remember the incident involving the death of the stripper who overdosed on heroin?" The policeman's question is met with silence, so he continues with his findings. "Well, her body was delivered to the hospital by two young gangbangers. When apprehended, those boys said they were doing a favor for a nightclub owner. Guess who the owner is? The mayor's son. They also said he's a heroin addict. If this is true, I think the mayor could use some spiritual help."

"So what did you do with the information you got from those gang members?" asks Pastor Robinson.

"In that circumstance, those boys were innocent, so nothing was done. But it leads me to think the mayor's son has something to do with all of the heroin overdoses. I was even able to connect Tommy Hurt to the Pharaohs but then someone from higher ran interference—somebody's trying to hide something."

Robinson is compelled to ask more. "Is there anyone in particular with special interest in this case? That's probably where the trouble lies."

"Now that you mention it, there are two detectives working this case who happen to be very secretive about the whole matter. I once offered to help out with some details, and they quickly rejected my assistance. They made it clear to stay away."

"Are they good officers?"

"As far as I know, yes. They've been on the force for years and have reputations for doing good work. I can think of no other reason to doubt them."

Randy makes a comment. "That's all the more reason to question them. Sometimes those who seem perfect are the ones to be wary of. It wouldn't hurt to check them out."

"Well, there we have it," says Angela. "There's a mayor whose son we suspect of having ties to the dead stripper. There are also two detectives who may be working their own agenda behind closed doors. That's a great place to start for your strategic prayers."

Robinson feels content enough to bring the meeting to an end. "We now have a game plan to follow. The targeted prayers should bring the results we're seeking. At the next meeting, we gotta talk about forgiveness. The people of the city must repent for the pact made by the founding fathers of Harlem Heights. If we can accomplish this, then we can win the city back."

15

The Ice Cream Man's Treats

There goes Baby Cake driving the ice cream truck slowly down the street with his chimes blaring loudly. The tunes cover the noise of the tired, sputtering truck engine. When the kids hear chimes, they know it's time for ice cream; all the rascals run wild in the street for ice cream.

The dingy white ice cream truck crawls along the road weaving through crowds of children. The youngsters are too busy laughing to realize they're also coughing from the fumes that are pouring out of the exhaust pipe.

Baby Cake sits behind the wheel grinning like a mischievous kid himself as he looks for a place to park. He slowly pulls the rusty truck aside, climbing the sidewalk curb like a lazy iguana.

The driver kills the engine and turns off the chimes only to click on the radio. A rap song takes over the speakers, which set the kids to dancing. Baby Cake heads to the back of the truck and slides the service window open. He's greeted by a mass of children pushing and shoving one another for a place in line. "All right now, stop all that pushing. Everybody's gonna get Baby Cake's treats," declares the ice cream man.

The kids settle down enough to conduct themselves in an orderly fashion.

Baby Cake is cool and quick with the orders. His hands automatically snatch the treats before the kids can finish pointing at the pictures on the faded menu board which is painted on the side of the truck. And, before his hands lay the items on the service counter, Baby Cake hollers out the price: "One snow cone, a chocolate bar, and sour strips—that'll be $3.50 my little friend."

As the line dwindles down and kids scatter about to enjoy their sweets, Baby Cake flips the radio channel from hip-hop to Motown. It seems the rap music was just a ploy to attract the youth.

Waiting on last-minute stragglers, Baby Cake pulls a menthol cigarette from behind his ear and lights up. Leaning back to relax, he exhales the white smoke while Marvin Gaye croons on the radio.

The ice cream man is feeling the vibe while his mind goes back to his younger years before he ever entered the military to fight a war. The Vietnam veteran is a wild-eyed, middle-aged, single man with a medium-size afro that could use a good combing, if not a cut. He's detached himself far enough from society so he doesn't have to care about his appearance. Yet Baby Cake is still concerned enough to work for a living—only on his terms though.

Earl Rawlins is his real name. For the most part, he's a law-abiding citizen whose aspiration to be somebody special went out the window during the Vietnam conflict.

Baby Cake watches from the service window as a group of Pharaohs approach his ice cream truck. After several years of working the streets of Harlem Heights, he's learned to identify the different gangs throughout the neighborhoods. A lot of the gangsters grew up buying ice cream from his truck. Due to his war experience and run-in's with the law, Baby Cake can relate to the thugs. As a matter of fact, ice cream is not the only thing he sells from his truck.

Willie Mo' and JT have been planning for weeks to bring another shipment to the city. Being aware of the Reds' scheme to frame the Pharaohs with the dope, Mo' takes counter measures.

"Hey, Mo', it's that time again, are you ready?" asks Mingo.

"Yeah, we're ready," Willie confirms. "When are the goods expected to arrive?"

"Sometime this afternoon. I'll call you when the shipment gets here."

That last statement rings through Willie's mind: *I'll call you when the shipment gets here.* No way do you leave Mo' in the dark, who does Mingo think he is? The Pharaoh smiles to himself, marveling at the beautiful plan brewing in the back of his mind.

Back at the police department, Hughes and Diggs conspire with a SWAT team on how to execute a sting operation. The goal is to catch the Pharaohs red-handed with dope and pin the whole operation on Willie James Moore.

Undercover officers posing as Reds have the goods in their possession. Following a directive from higher, Mingo makes a call to Willie.

"Mo', what's up, man?"

"You tell me. Is it that time?"

"Yeah, my people are headed to your place now. You can expect us at—"

Before Mingo can finish his statement, Mo' interrupts. "I'll tell you where we'll meet at. You ain't coming nowhere near here. I'll call you back when it's time." The Pharaoh snaps his cell phone shut.

Mingo is frustrated. "Who does this punk think he is? He's making things more difficult than it has to be."

Detective Hughes sits by Mingo laughing quietly to himself. "Well, well, I heard the conversation. Either Mo' is smarter than I thought, or you've been telling our plans. Which one is it?"

Mingo can't believe it. Things were supposed to go smoother than this. Frustrated and ready to give up, Mingo's hope comes to life when his phone suddenly rings.

"Is this the Mingo man?" says the playful caller.

The Red recognizes JT's voice immediately. "Hey, man, what's up with Mo'? I'm trying to do business, and he won't play ball."

"You know the man's unpredictable."

"Yeah that's exactly what I hate about 'im. Anyways, I'm trying to get y'all straight. Where you wanna meet?"

"Glad you asked. Let's do 5th and Dupree Street."

Mingo is confused. "Dupree ... man, where in the world is Dupree at?"

"You know the liquor store where your cousin, Juan, got shot at? That's Dupree."

"Oh, yeah, I remember."

"Be there in one hour." JT ends the call.

Looking to Mo' for a response, Jermaine finds his leader locked in a blank trance staring at the wall. JT is accustomed to the behavior and waits patiently for Willie to reply.

Molder whispers to his human vessel, *The big one can't fool Molder. He doesn't know tricks like I do. We'll follow his mortals from one place to another until we're sure of who rides with them. When the time is right, we'll meet where they least expect it."*

"I'm tired of the games," Hughes directs his anger at Mingo. "First he cancels the meeting at the warehouse. Then 5th and Dupree was just a hoax, and now he wants to meet on the other side of town. You better hope this goes down as planned, or your boys are going down for drug trafficking."

Mingo explodes, "How you gonna pin traffickin' on us when you arranged the whole setup? You can't expect Mo' to walk blindly into a trap; he's been in the game too long to fall for an easy trick. If this doesn't work out, it's your fault and not mine."

"Oh great, now this happens," exclaims detective Diggs as he throws his cell phone to the car floor.

Hughes hollers, "What now?"

"The trail we had just lost sight of the shipment."

"How hard can it be to follow a car?" inquires Hughes.

"Apparently it's not that simple. Somehow the Pharaohs figured out the dope car and hijacked it at the light."

Hughes can't believe it. "No way! How does somehow hijack a heavily guarded vehicle?"

"While the dope car is waiting at the light, a truck breaks down in the intersection blocking all traffic."

"A truck?"

"Yeah, an ice cream truck," Diggs repeats.

Hughes is beyond frustration, "You gotta be kidding."

"Nope, I'm serious as a heart attack. While stuck at the light, the dope car is rammed in the side by another vehicle. The same thing happens to the trail cars guarding the goods. Gunfire breaks out, and all occupants are taken out."

Hughes can't believe what he's hearing. "They took out cops?"

"Yes, and that's not all. The Pharaohs made a clean getaway with the dope."

For the moment, Fratricide has been out maneuvered by his rival. This isn't the only problem. Cops have been killed and there isn't a justified reason for the loss of the life.

16

The Shooting

A few weeks have passed and things appear to have cooled off. Willie, still wary of the police on the prowl, resorts to a crafty strategy to sell drugs. Who would have ever known Mo' had a relationship with Baby Cake? Right under the noses of the cops, Baby Cake goes about his business on a daily basis selling ice cream and dope from his truck. No one seems to notice the long lines of kids along with adult junkies seeking Baby Cake's treat. It's no longer a menu of chocolate bars, ice cream cups, and candy; an assortment of drugs can be purchased too.

Best thing about it for Baby Cake, he knows all the customers and he has the protection of the Pharaohs on every street on which he sells the goods. This tactic won't last forever, but it's good enough for the time being.

Fratricide gets wind of Molder's scheme involving the ice cream truck, so he plots to ruin business for Mo'. It's not long before the police are suspicious of Baby Cake's operation. Keen to the heat, Molder makes it a bit more difficult to track the ice cream truck. He arranges for several trucks to be put on the streets to pedal the goods. The police now have to guess which truck is the hot one.

The big one finds himself frustrated. Getting desperate, the mammoth begins to undermine his own efforts to crush Molder. The cops go from legal searches with probable cause to searches without warrants causing tension between the police and the black community to rise. This is the ideal opportunity for Molder, who resorts to a tactic often used by Fratricide.

A squad car pulls up to Baby Cake as he's parked selling ice cream to the public. The officers confront the vendor. "We need to see your business and drivers licenses along with the vehicle registration."

Baby Cake complies.

One policeman goes back to the squad car to run a background check on the licenses and registration while the other suspiciously eyes the inside of the ice cream truck. Maybe five minutes pass before both cops are back at the service window with another issue. "Okay Mr. Earl Rawlins ..."

The ice cream man confirms his identity, "Yeah, that's me."

"Get out of the truck, we're searching this vehicle," demands the policeman.

"Why you wanna search my truck? I got nothin' but treats for the kids."

"Yeah, that's what you say. I betcha have more than ice cream in that freezer of yours. Watch out now, we're coming in."

"Man, you ain't comin' in here," declares Baby Cake. "You gotta show me a warrant first."

Avoiding the legal niceties, the officer justifies his actions. "We got reports of you pushing dope. That's our probable cause—now open up this raggedy old door before I bust it in," the policeman bangs a fist on the side of the truck to emphasize his point.

Baby Cake has a freezer full of drugs, and he doesn't want to get caught riding dirty. Determined to keep the cops at bay, Cake eyes a friend in the crowd, giving the cue. All of a sudden gun shots are fired in the air. The crowd disperses like a startled herd of buffalo on a wild stampede. The two policemen instinctively take cover between the ice cream truck and the squad car, drawing their pistols in defense.

The commotion of people panicking, along with more gunshots ripping through the air, brings confusion. Neither cop can tell the difference between innocent civilians and thugs with bad intentions. Then a sudden blanket of silence falls upon the scene. Is it safe to come out? The cops remain kneeling as they take a peek from behind their vehicles to see if all is clear.

Surveying the area, the officers spot a small child lying unconscious in a pool of blood. This means big trouble for the police department.

At about the same time, the crowd emerges to check the scene. It doesn't look good to see a couple of white cops standing over a downed black child.

Seizing the moment, imps suddenly appear to instigate trouble between the policemen and the bystanders.

"Hey, who's that lying on the sidewalk over there?" says a teenage male.

"Where?" replies an unknown voice.

"There's a kid right there on the sidewalk—and he's bleeding too!"

Instantly, all the mothers lock eyes on the lifeless body lying on the sidewalk. Some begin to cry in agony at the sight of the wounded child while others frantically call their kids' names.

"Kendra, LaTonya, Reggie, where are you?"

Somehow the actual mother of the wounded child gets word of the incident and rushes over to confirm the identity of the slain kid.

"My baby, oh Lord, my baby's been shot! Please don't die; don't you go away, Kenny. Oh God, please don't take him away," pleads the mother as she falls to her knees to pick up the boy, holding the limp child to her breast.

At times, the boy seems to be alive, moving as the mother rocks back and forth cradling him. Kenny's free arm hangs down far enough for one hand to barely touch the ground. Then his fingertips sweep the sidewalk as mother rocks him like the baby he once was. The free hand flicks speckles of blood along the cement.

At other times, the boy appears dead, especially when his head falls back when there is no hand to provide support. The mother wants so badly to hold the boy closely, but his body won't respond. Out of frustration, momma screams. Her arms are wrapped firmly around the child, yet his head bobbles every time she gasps for air in between her mournful cries.

"Not my son, Lord; please, not my boy."

"Those cops just shot that innocent kid," yells one man.

Another hollers, "Yeah, they just shot that boy for no reason at all."

This is all it takes. The spirits are busy hopping from one mortal to the other defecating slander and spitting scandalous slime.

"*This is racist!*" declares an imp.

"Two cops came into our neighborhood and just shot a child. This is unheard of in the white community. Why do the cops continue to persecute our people?" exclaims another demonic agitator.

The rascality is just beginning. The evil spirits are doing a great job of inciting the crowd into believing that racism is the reason for the shooting. No one saw the Pharaoh easing around the corner with a gun tucked away in his pants resting warm against his groin. This is the person who killed the boy.

As the moment ripens, violent spirits join the party. Getting aggressive, the angry mob begins to approach the policemen. In their own defense, the cops keep their guns pointed at the crowd to prevent the mob from closing in.

"Look, we're in serious need of back up," pleads the officer into his radio. "We can't even get to our car to get out of here! It's urgent, send backup right away!"

More and more rogue creatures are drawn to the site. Like vultures, they perch themselves on the telephone lines and watch with great interest. Their big, round eyes follow all the action as drool drips from their fangs and bile falls from their bodies like pigeon poop upon the crowd below. The spirits are eager to see how the feces affect the riotous humans below—it works wonders.

The mortals, once touched by the demonic gunk, manifest the nature of the imps that afflict them. A group of boys hoot like apes as they psyche themselves up for a clash with the police. Anger settles upon the mothers as they begin cursing and criticizing the cops. Racism spreads its poison, and now the mob feels justified in taking the law into its own hands.

Two evil spirits, so caught up in their mischief, abandon the mission to bicker among themselves. "This one's mine, I saw him first," argues an imp wanting to enter the soul of a young boy holding a Molotov cocktail bomb in his hand.

"No, get away, I was here first. Go find another soul," gripes the other imp.

Like two kids fighting over a toy, they draw swords to engage one another in a duel. While they are preoccupied with fighting, another rascal slips up from behind and takes possession of the young bomber's soul. By the time the dueling imps realize what just happened, it's too late. Now the occupying spirit is the doorkeeper who refuses others entrance to the boy's soul.

Siron the scout is hidden away in an upstairs air conditioner vent watching the action below. *The sharks are in a feeding frenzy,* he thinks to himself. With each passing second, more and more bug-eyed imps come to feast on the emotions of the angry mob.

The boy with the liquor bottle in hand stares directly at the officers, watching as fear dances in their eyes. With a malicious intent, he adds flame to a strip of cloth that hangs from the mouth of a bottle and throws the Molotov through the air. Spinning like a meteorite from outer space, the bottle smashes into the forehead of a cop before shattering to the ground spreading flames. The officer's lights go out and he falls unconscious to the ground bleeding from the head. The standing cop scrambles for his partner's loose pistol before the crowd can get it. He secures the weapon only to notice blazing flames burning close to his downed buddy. Feeling overwhelmed with desperation, the lone cop tries to stomp the raging flames. The situation is getting hectic.

Siron the scout can see that the situation is getting hectic; a sense of urgency compels him to take action. Far from being the mightiest of spirits, the crafty Siron must rely on speed to hold the mob at bay. Moving with the swiftness of a falcon, he flies with his sword drawn leaving a silver streak following in his wake. Suddenly a white light smacks stars from the heads of the imps standing in Siron's path. The little devils are knocked senseless as they spin like bowling pins on the ground.

The fortunate few, who are spared the blow, draw their swords and frantically search the air for the stealth enemy. Nothing appears. Unsure of what to expect next, the imps withdraw to safety.

The mortals, too, are blinded by the sudden flash of bright light and halt their pursuit of the cops to rub their burning eyes.

Siron's tactic is a temporary fix that buys the policemen a bit more time to respond to the operator's voice that miraculously comes across the radio. "Is there anyone there, over?"

Immediately, the standing officer grabs the receiver. "We're in desperate need of backup. Please send help, over!"

"What's your situation, over?"

"An officer is down, and a child is critically wounded, over."

"Reinforcements and medical assistance are on the way. Expect several units to arrive momentarily. Radio control, out," the operator ends communication.

The officer hadn't noticed before that the front passenger door of the squad car is open. That's unusual. Seizing the moment, the able cop drags his injured partner to the vehicle and gets him safely inside. While the angry mob struggles to regain their sight, the officer has time to slip into his vehicle and drive a safe distance from the crowd. An eternity seems to pass before the sirens of reinforcements are heard wailing in the distance.

Flying above the squad cars, with swords drawn, are Lee and a band of angelic warriors. Their hardened faces reflect a look of seriousness. Determined to defend the law at any cost, they hardly resemble the peace-loving guardians they appear to be when not in action.

Molder and Wrath watch from afar as Lee and his warriors diffuse the situation.

A black officer exits the squad car to addresses the crowd. "All right, people, calm down and let us help you out."

Kenny's mother jumps to her feet pleading to the officer, "My child needs help. I have to get him to the hospital before it's too late!"

The crowd seems to trust the officer who appears to be sympathetic. He checks the vital signs of the boy. There's no indication of life. Still, he radios for medical assistance. Then he asks, "What happened here?"

Racism seizes the moment with his propaganda, *"This is a shame. The cops are attacking our community. Look at the mess they're making. Would such things happen in the white community?"*

"No," barks a scandalous imp.

"Only because were black," yells Racism.

The scoundrels use two young males to vocalize their slanderous words.

Neither one saw the shooting; they only heard the shot and presumed the white officers did it. No one questions the Pharaoh who snuck in the shot when it was least expected.

Lee points his sword at Racism, telling him, "Spare us your lies." The imp swallows his tongue as the needle-sharp tip pokes his throat.

"The time to put you all to flight has not yet come. But you all will behave yourselves and not touch these officers," orders Heaven's warrior. "Is there anyone else with something to say?" Lee is looking for a reason to deal blows to the enemy.

Though the hellions outnumber the guardians, they dare not test the strength of their adversaries. Peace settles among the mortals as more reinforcements arrive. Yet, enough damage has occurred to worsen racial condition in the city.

17

Reverend Brown is Back

Pastor Randy Robinson sits at the kitchen table, head buried in the morning newspaper. Little Kenny's death is front-page news. "Weezy," says Randy to his wife, "it looks like more trouble is brewing in the city again. Yesterday a little kid was shot and killed. The facts are not clear, but it appears the shooting involved misconduct on the part of the police."

Louise stands at the kitchen counter pouring a cup of coffee. She seems a bit puzzled. "Where's the motive for the shooting? You just don't shoot someone without a good reason."

"Witnesses say the cops stopped an ice cream truck to harass the driver. An argument started, shots were fired into a crowd of bystanders, and that's when a kid was killed."

Louise gives her husband a courteous response. "Well, that definitely calls for a full investigation."

No other words are mentioned about the shooting. The Robinsons go about their morning in routine fashion.

Solomon and Lee are present with the couple as if waiting for something significant to happen. To pass time, the messenger resorts to playing with the Robinson's pet canary that chirps loudly in its cage. The bird begins to fly wildly back and forth chasing the angel's finger. Her wings slap the cage bars causing the water to spill from its bowl and seeds to jump from the feed dish.

Solomon stops teasing the canary and allows his fingers to gently stroke the bird's chest and belly. The contented creature spreads its wings in pure delight and sings at the top of her voice, relishing the attention from Solomon.

"What's up with that crazy bird?" Louise asks her husband.

"I haven't the slightest clue. Whatever it is, she seems to be very happy this morning."

As the Robinsons enjoy the canary's antics, their attention is suddenly drawn to the crowd of people outside their house.

Louise makes the first inquiry. "Is this a parade of some sort?"

"I don't know. Today's not a holiday. Perhaps it's just a bunch of kids waiting on the school bus to arrive," Randy guesses.

"No, honey, it's still summer; the kids won't start school until fall."

Robinson goes to the living room window to get a better look. Outside he sees people fist pumping picket signs over their heads. He can't make out what the crowd is chanting, but it seems to be some type of protest. As the people get closer, Randy is able to hear the chanting more clearly. "We want justice, control the police. We want justice, down with the beast. "

At first, Robinson can't believe what he's hearing and seeing. The parade of people is not just a few protesters making a lot of noise. There seem to be thousands of minorities on this train. The pastor thinks to himself, *I didn't know so many people lived here in neighborhood.*

Louise runs to the living room to get a closer look too. She's blown away by the sight. "Is this all because of yesterday's shooting?"

"I guess so. I can't imagine any other reason. I wonder who could have gotten all these people together to organize such an event?" inquires Randy. The answer immediately appears: Reverend Brown is the ringleader. He's marching at the front of the protesters, accompanied by some other distinguished-looking men.

For a man who was just down and out, Brown is looking really good now. The contemporary, two-piece suit and shiny leather shoes make him look all the more important for his role as a savior. Randy can't believe his eyes. He has to resist the urge to stop the parade to question Brown. "Honey, take a look at this!"

"Randy, you don't have to yell so loud, I'm standing right next to you."

"Oh, sorry … didn't see you. Remember that guy I told you about when we first got here? He was the preacher at our church before it burned down."

Louise is all ears. "Yeah, I remember."

"Well, when I first met him, he was a total mess. The man was seriously depressed. When I tried to tell him about the forgiving love of Jesus, he nearly put his hands on me. All of sudden he's doing fine now."

Louise listens with great interest. She's intrigued by this mysterious figure that somehow managed to bring himself back on top. "I guess in due time you'll find out what he's all about, honey."

As the parade passes, more people join the ranks. Molder's minions march alongside to ensure the protest gains momentum.

"Racism is the cause of the black plight in America. All of our troubles and shortcomings are due to a system that puts us at a disadvantage." The speaker is Reverend Brown, but it's the spirit of Propaganda using the mortal's voice.

Already a natural orator, Brown is the ideal puppet to use for this event. "The time has come for the playing field to be made even. We can even the odds by taking justice into our hands. We must go to that police station and demand they hand over the officer who killed Kenny Collins."

The crowd goes crazy over the outrageous demands. There's no way the police department is going to hand the officer over to the angry mob—someone must put a stop to the madness.

Brown is relentless. "That innocent little boy was no threat to the police. He was shot in cold blood by an officer with no regard for human life." The crowd clings to every word coming from the reverend's mouth. "The barbaric act of that bloodthirsty officer is considered acceptable by the police department, the mayor, and every other white official living outside Harlem Heights. They don't know what it's like to be persecuted." The charismatic Brown charms the masses. The people eat and swallow every lie he utters; they drink in the hate and become intoxicated.

No jobs will be created for the masses. Drugs will continue to exist in the Harlem Heights community. The children will still grow up thinking the world owes them something for the past sins of slavery. Who's going to address these issues? No, not Propaganda; definitely not Reverend Brown, the hustler.

The sons of Empyreal know the true intentions of this rally. It's only a tactic to benefit a select few while the majority of people will be left in the same situation they were in before.

* * *

Fratricide is in a bind. His rival, Molder, has flipped the script by using the big one's tactic to his own advantage. The shooting of Kenny has rendered a devastating blow to Fratricide's power base, leaving the mammoth no choice but to rely on the efforts of that little pastor who recently moved to the city. "How's our church friend doing, hmm?" questions Fratricide with a bit of sarcasm in his voice. "Did I ever tell how much I like, uh …" The big one looks at Informer to finish his thought.

"Pastor Robinson, master."

"Yes, that's it, Robinson. He's the man." The overlord sits back with a look of satisfaction in his eyes. While his tree-trunk legs are extended forward, feet resting on meaty heels, the mammoth folds his hands across his big belly like a fat man at the dinner table. Flashing a wicked grin, the behemoth reveals his clever scheme. "Hmm, I like that Pastor Robinson. He's going to be our savior. We shall use him for his services. Correction, we will not use him; he shall work without hindrance. Who are we to intervene with his ministry?"

The conference room at city hall is a large room where briefings and other important meetings are held by mortals. Within this room is where Fratricide and his subordinates take counsel as well. As he explores the idea of using Pastor Robinson as a pawn to beat back Molder's forces, the big one drags in his feet and rises from his throne to roam about the room freely.

Talking as if he's strolling through the park, the big one makes light of Robinson. "That man and his church have a mission to complete. We must ensure no one from within our camp does him any harm." Fratricide approaches his chief warrior, stopping a few feet short of the captain—still his plump belly presses against the warrior's chest.

The chief leans his weight forward pressing back on Fratricide. "What do you command of me, master?" questions the warrior who seems not to mind the close contact with the overlord.

"You just heard all that I said, Chief Warrior, hmm?"

The chief pauses to ensure nothing else follows. "I did, my lord?"

"Go and make the passageway for the Light of Hope Church to be rebuilt. Let no other creature hinder their plans. Let them pray and sing praises to …" Not wanting to say that name, Fratricide is at a loss for words. "Let them serve the Tyrant in Heaven as they wish to do."

Fratricide turns from the warrior but still continues to speak. "Their prayers will stop the enemy that has forgotten where its loyalty lies. Molder and his guard dog will learn their lesson the hard way. And, at their most vulnerable moment, we will snuff them out of this realm, back to the abyss where they belong. Do you understand, Chief?"

The chief warrior is thrilled to get some action outside the confines of city hall. His orders are clear, but the chief has one more inquiry. "Master, do I have the liberty to touch the saints?"

"Hmm, if there's no hedge around any of them, then by all means toy with their lives. Just don't hinder the plans"

"Yes, master."

Pointing at a platoon of evil spirits, the large one gives a final order. "I shall equip you to do your worst. Let me introduce you to your reinforcements, which you'll command as you see fit. Come hither, my children, present yourself."

As the overlord calls their names, the spirits stand erect at the position of attention with cheesy grins creasing their faces. Unable to resist the urge, the miracle workers prance about with joy doing little magic tricks. One imp makes a flame of fire appear in his hand. He blows on the flame, causing it to explode. The smoke clears to reveal a vibrant red rose. The pretty flower is laid upon the ground where it transforms into a snake.

Wanting to join the fun, a different gremlin pulls a yellow rose from behind its back and lays it upon the ground. His rose, too, becomes a serpent that swallows the snake already on the ground. The imps play Moses and Pharaoh like kids playing cowboys and Indians.

The tricks entertain the overlord who watches with amusement. The imps are motivated by Fratricide's interest, so they commence to perform more tricks of greater skill. The mood becomes more festive as the musicians join in. Seductive melodies and hypnotic beats set the demons to dancing jigs. Even the big one, sitting on his throne, starts bouncing his load around to the catchy beat. Informer, sitting cross-legged at the foot of the throne, enjoys the scene until he's suddenly stepped on by Fratricide's massive foot. "Ouch! Master, my hand—get off!"

"Quiet, runt. I do as I please, whenever I please."

Informer's face bears a look of pain. The runt dares not make a fuss, for he may lose his entire hand to the sword.

Being a wise leader, Fratricide grows tired of the celebration quickly. "Go now, get. Flee from here and do your worst. Help the Light of Hope defeat Molder, yet keep it blind to its own weakness. Prove yourselves worthy of this task, and I will reward you greatly."

The pranksters, harassers, and divisive spirits evacuate city hall like bats fleeing from Hell, squealing and screeching as they take flight. Their claws grip at the air while their leathery wings bend and pop like spring-loaded umbrellas.

One special spirit remains behind, Deceiver. This spirit has a different mission. Seemingly more mature than the devious imps, he stands humbly before Fratricide awaiting his command. There is no smile creasing the corner of his lips; he shows no interest in playing petty games. With a book tucked in his arm, snuggled warmly to his chest, Deceiver resembles a wicked grade school teacher who delights in torturing his pupils. As things quiet down, all eyes focus on the spirit who is standing center stage. If Deceiver is a fallen spirit, he still looks angelic … almost human-like.

Fratricide takes the time to examine the slight, but tall spirit, marveling at the idea that such a pretty-looking fiend can wield power beyond one's expectations. "Are you prepared for your mission, my servant?"

"My lord, I am … with pleasure I might add."

Deceiver listens patiently as the big one reveals his expectations. "Hmm, remember who you work for; you answer to none but me. You are charged to fix the situation at the police department. Keep me informed of everything. Most of all, don't forget where you come from. If you get out of control, I shall make your skull a foot stool."

Obviously accustomed to rough talk, Deceiver takes the threat with ease. The foul spirit bows low in reverence, breathes a long nasty hiss and then erects himself like a king cobra as he assumes his true form. Fratricide is amazed to see the spirit is even taller than before. A long tail unravels from beneath Deceiver's robe causing the rogues standing nearby to clear a space for the slimy, massive coils to unfold. The serpent's transformation brings stinking sulfur that pollutes the air and loud cheers erupt from all the wicked spirits. "I will redeem the police department by pacifying the people. Your city will be restored," the snake declares.

Though every creature present in city hall is a gruesome devil, all the spirits are repulsed at the ugliness of Deceiver. His slithery body leaves a slimy trail like that of a slug, and his foul odor even hastens the big one to rid the room of serpent's presence. "Go and do your worst. Don't come back here until the job is complete," commands the big one.

Informer resurfaces as the snake leaves.

"My runt, where have you been all this time?"

Informer, fluttering in the air at shoulder height to the mammoth, looks at the Fratricide with a sigh of relief. "Deceiver is a foul spirit, and I'm glad he's gone now."

The runt's concern is a non-issue for Fratricide who silently takes his place at the throne to continue business as usual.

18

Revealing the Truth

Sergeant Hector Perez and Angela meet at a coffee shop for a casual talk. After a few weeks of getting to know one another, the two are starting to get close—at least the policeman thinks so. Not feeling confident enough to ask her out on a date, Perez plays it safe by sticking to topics of conversation that he feels more secure with such as work at the department. The reporter does likewise. "How are things going?" asks Angela. She takes a sip of her French vanilla coffee while Hector responds.

"Things are going okay, still trying to deal with the issues surrounding Kenny's death."

Speaking of Kenny, Angela's been itching to ask a certain question for the longest time. She tries to go about it nonchalantly. "Monitoring an ice cream truck … how effective was that tactic?" The reporter diverts her attention to the coffee cup, taking a slow sip, trying to appear only slightly curious.

Sergeant Perez is suspicious of the question and reluctant to respond, yet he concedes an answer. "Yeah, I know it sounds funny, but there was a legit reason for it. The guy had all kinds of customers you normally don't—"

Angela shows her inexperience by cutting him off in mid sentence with a humorous laugh. "You've got to be kidding. You all pulled over an ice cream truck … for what?"

"If you let me finish, you'll see why."

"So how did you all know what the customers were buying?" The journalist gets aggressive. "Did you personally go there and buy some drugs?"

The reporter's attitude is loaded with skepticism. Perez begins to think it's perhaps a mistake to talk about work with Ms. Williams. Too late now; he feels compelled to explain. "That's exactly what we did. We had undercover agents go to his truck and buy drugs to confirm our suspicions. The problem with the situation was that the driver wouldn't cooperate, and just when we were about to search the truck, a shot is fired into the crowd."

Angela is silent, obviously reloading her mind with another question to fire at Perez. "So," she quizzes, "if you all had probable cause and this guy was not willing to allow you to conduct a search, then why would shoot into the crowd?"

"Now hold it right there," Hector doesn't like the grilling session he's getting. "Who said we shot into the crowd? Where did you get that idea?"

Not realizing her slip of the tongue, the journalist looks upward as if searching her mind for a quick answer. Her efforts are useless, and now their roles are reversed; the reporter feels the pressure as Sergeant Perez lectures her. "Wait a minute, Angela. I see you already have your mind made up about what really happened. You could at least be fair and consider what we did as justified."

The reporter is rendered speechless by the assertive officer, who makes a deliberate effort to get his point across. Seeing she's not getting off the hook too easily, Angela sits back taking several slow sips of coffee.

Perez continues, "Just a few minutes ago I told you the officers were about to search the vehicle when someone from the crowd fired a shot. What part of that did you not understand?" Now having the upper hand, Hector mimics Angela's action by sitting back and slurping his coffee loudly, indicating that he wants a response.

Angela surrenders. "Okay, here's the deal—word has it the police department shot first into the crowd, killing the little boy. After hearing your side of the story, I'm not totally convinced about the accusation. Yet the perpetrator remains unknown, which doesn't reflect well on the police department. Now, if what you say is true, can it be proven to the public? Can your story stand up to the beliefs of Reverend Brown and all the members of the Harlem Heights community who are protesting the incident?"

Being a kind gentleman, Perez allows a warm smile to reappear upon his face. "All right, now I understand where *you* are coming from. It's all the protesting that's swaying your view on this situation." Hector makes a bold move by reaching across the table and grabbing hold of Angela's hands. Normally he wouldn't do such a thing, but it feels so natural at that moment. "I probably would think the same way if confronted by a charismatic preacher and an angry community. I can only advise you to be patient. The forensic report will clear up a lot of confusion. Besides, I've learned, in my years as a police officer, that there is always someone who saw something. It's just a matter of finding that person and getting him or her to tell the truth."

Siron, the scout, is present at the café, listening to the mortals' conversation. His mission is to get the truth exposed. So far, the media is broadcasting reports against the police department. Angela is the ideal person to change the media's perspective by making the truth known.

As the reporter chats with Perez, Siron places his hands on both of her shoulders to pray. "Dear Lord, who art in Heaven, I pray this woman will be the vessel you see fit to use. You know her heart and what she's capable of doing. Please prepare her for this mission; guide her and make ready the path that she will have to travel." Siron lifts one hand from Angela's shoulder to place it upon the officer. "And please, Lord, bless this man to assist her. Prepare him to be the foundation on which this woman can stand. Let their relationship be founded on truth; it is the truth, Wonderful Counselor, which we seek. The truth, Lord, will heal and redeem this city, restoring it to the state that will reflect favorably in your eyes."

With the prayer finished, Siron launches from the coffee shop like a shooting star. Two guardians remain to guide the mortals whose conversation, by this time, has gone on to other topics besides the shooting of little Kenny.

19

Mayor Hurt Has an Issue

"**W**hat in the world is going on in this city?" asks the mayor, who is disgusted by the protesting in the Harlem Heights.

"Sir, it's all because of that shooting this past weekend that resulted in the death of that little boy, Kenny. It's the police misconduct that has upset the people."

"Now wait a minute, Dudley. Where did you get that information?"

"Sir," says the Mayor's aide, "it's been in the papers for days now."

The mayor cuts a dirty look at his trusty aide—the skinny, annoying weasel named Wes Dudley. "Watch your tone of voice when you talk to me. Save the sarcasm for your peers. Is there any more news?"

"No, sir, there's nothing else." Dudley doesn't care too much for the mayor's scorn and his tendency to be out of touch with current events, but he's in no position to demand mutual respect.

"I still don't see why they wanted to search an ice cream truck and why did they shoot a little boy? It doesn't make sense," exclaims the mayor. "I'll have a little talk with the chief about this one. I'm surprised he hasn't called by now."

"Well, sir, I can guess why he hasn't called yet."

"Why, Dudley?"

"He's been busy with all the protesting going on in the streets. Your old friend Reverend Brown is back at it again."

The mayor's blood pressure rises instantly upon hearing that name. "Reverend Brown, what does he want now? We agreed there would be no other issues. That's why we paid his organization the settlement from the last lawsuit."

"Sir, this is what happens when you deal with the devil."

Dudley's comment draws hysterical laughter from Fratricide and his demons who are observing the conversation between the two mortals. "Yeah, Dudley, that's my boy. You tell him what it's like to play with the devil," laughs Fratricide.

"The reverend hasn't made any demands yet," Dudley confirms. "But, it's just a matter of time before he calls with some ridiculous scheme. Like always, he'll want something good if he's to remain silent."

Mayor Hurt seldom agrees with Dudley, but the aide is right this time. The rhyme-and-dime preacher will want something big. Last time, the holy hustler won a big lawsuit against the local grocery chains.

A few years ago, Reverend Brown and his cohorts made it their business to go around town checking out stores where minorities shopped. The Harlem Heights Grocery chain was one of those establishments. Their stores could be found throughout the city.

Brown discovered that a negatively disproportionate number of black employees—especially managers—were working in the Heights stores. Lots of minorities were spending their money in the stores, but very few were working for the chain.

The reverend addressed this issue with the ghetto community and caused the people to rise up in a revolt that led to a boycott. The lack of business had a crippling effect on the Harlem Heights Grocery chain. It was so devastating that the CEO of the company went to Brown demanding to know what it would take to stop the boycott.

The religious wolf capitalized on a settlement that benefited him and the few associated with his organization. The tactic also increased the number of minority employees in the grocery chain.

There was a negative repercussion too—the boycott drove a deeper wedge between the black and white races in Harlem Heights.

Never once has Brown boycotted minority businesses, or even criticized them for their lack of diversity. Never has he confronted the black dope dealers who sell poison to their own people. The reverend always manages to avoid the unpopular issues that undermine dignity and respect in the Harlem Heights community. Instead, the vulture circles above white establishments searching for opportunities to exploit the slightest injustice perpetrated against minorities. This is why the mayor's anger burns so fervently against reverend Brown.

"We must put a stop to this man. He's more of a problem than a solution. If we could somehow catch him in the act of doing something wrong, that would be a blessing from above," says the mayor with look of disgust on his face.

A devilish grin appears on Dudley's face as a revelation comes to mind. "Well, sir, the reverend has a child out of wedlock."

"How do you know such a thing, Dudley?"

"Oh, sir, I have my ways."

"Can you verify that he really has a child?"

Dudley is devious as ever, "Sure can."

"Before we go any further, I need proof that he's a fornicator. We have to get our facts straight before we go public with the news. This should sweep away the faith the people have for this womanizing hypocrite."

"Consider it done, sir"

Fratricide listens intently, his eyes lighting up with enthusiasm. "Propaganda," he orders, "go with Dudley. Ensure he gets what he's looking for. Let's expose Reverend Brown which will undermine the efforts of Molder."

The mayor sinks back into his reclining office chair. Placing the tips of his fingers together as if he were praying, the mayor closes his eyes to meditate. Fratricide does likewise; their actions mirror one another. The big one ministers cursed assurances to the mortal's mind. The mammoth is confident that he'll expose Brown and outwit Molder, who threatens to take over a city that he worked so hard to possess.

The Light of Hope congregation gathers as they always do to conduct their weekly prayer meeting. This particular evening is not the usual crowd; there are a lot of new faces in attendance.

Some of the people are not totally new but, rather, old members who are revisiting after a long absence. Having heard about a few good things happening at the church, they want to see the progress for themselves. This alone is not the only reason for their presence; the protest plays a role as well.

The prayer portion of the meeting starts slowly; it takes a deliberate effort by Pastor Robinson to get the saints focused on why they came to tonight's meeting. "People, if I could have your attention please," pleads the pastor. "I know there's a lot going on, but times like these require us to stick to our priorities. The first thing we must do is pray. This is why we meet, and this we shall always do regardless of what is going on in the world."

The crowd isn't too crazy about the idea of praying right now. But, like children reprimanded by their mother, the saints settle down.

The messenger angel, Solomon, is pleased with Robinson's wisdom to remain steadfast with prayer.

As the saints pray, they first ask the Lord to have His way in the Harlem Heights. They continue to seek His guidance on matters involving the community. Sweet prayers fill the house with a heavenly fragrance. This attracts one angel after another, and soon the guardians outnumber the mortals. In the spiritual realm, it's clear to see from anywhere in the city, the Lord is smiling down on the Light of Hope.

As the saints speak to the Lord, more reinforcements are sent to join the effort in winning back Harlem Heights. Solomon and Lee are pleased to see their request for more help being answered. They are greeted by peace-loving war angels whose eyes reveal an itch to mix things up in battle. Taking one look at Lee, the new warriors instinctively report to their captain.

Other guardians accompany the warriors too. They are ministering angels that go before the saints preparing the way for battle and the peace that will soon follow. They report to Solomon.

Together, the warriors and ministering angels plan to expose the devious work of the dark side to bring redemption to Harlem Heights.

Someone has a question. "Now that we have prayed, Pastor Robinson, what are we going to do about the protest?"

Randy was wondering when the topic would arise again. The congregation couldn't go a whole session without mentioning something about the protest. "To answer your question honestly, I don't know. That being said, I believe we should do nothing until the investigation is completed."

Another person, not satisfied with such an answer, makes his opinion on the matter known. "How can we just sit back not supporting our people? We should be out there supporting the cause. Besides, how would it look for our group to sit on the sidelines while every other church puts forth the effort to win justice for our community?"

"Yeah, what about us?" gripes another. "How's it gonna look when people see us sitting by ourselves while everyone else supports the protest?"

The saints are chiming in with their opinions. Louise is clearly getting agitated, yet remains quiet. Her husband, if frustrated at all, maintains his patience by responding calmly. "First of all, let's get a few things straight here. We don't know if every church in the city is participating. If they are, that's fine; and if they're not, that's fine too." Silence falls upon the saints as the pastor continues. "Next of all, was anyone here present at the time of the shooting? Did anyone here see with their very own eyes the person who shot little Kenny? At this very moment, the police department is still investigating the case, and they have yet to come up with an answer."

The saints have no interest in the pastor's questions; they want to see the green light to participate in the protest as a group and Robinson is not making it easy for them. The pastor must be careful not to allow the attitude of the old church to rear its ugly head again as it done in the past.

"I don't mean to be rude, Pastor," says one man with an angry tone in his voice, "but what can be more important than standing up for our rights?"

Content with the statement just made by the mortal, the imp that influenced the thought sits back with his arms and legs folded, smirking. "Watch this now. Let's see how Brother Robinson responds to this."

All the little devils cackle, watching with interest as Robinson replies to the saints.

"Brothers and sisters, isn't there enough help with the protest already? Besides, we're only a few, and our numbers hardly make a difference." Another idea comes to Robinson's mind as he talks. "If we want to make a difference, we have to do more than just protest. This means going beyond the surface to deal with the underlying issues that affect our community. Are we willing to go that far?"

The instigating imp makes another snide comment. "All right now, pastor, go on with your bad self."

The little trolls and imps are getting a kick out of the spirit making fun of the pastor.

"Little Kenny's death is just a symptom of our problems," continues the pastor. "Now is the time for Harlem Heights to address the social ills that affect the neighborhood—not just to criticize the police department. It's my hope that someone will stand up and tell the black community to take responsibility for itself."

The pastor gets a few weird looks from the congregation. The glares convince him that he must explain himself even more. "Let me put it this way: Historically speaking, I know life for our race hasn't been fair. We have dealt with circumstances that have limited our access to equal opportunity. And so there were times when we had to work twice as hard as the white man just to make it. This may be the case in some aspects of life today, but I think times have changed for the better."

The saints have heard this sermon before. What they want to hear is a good reason for not participating in the protest. "I hear what you saying but what's that got to do with little Kenny getting killed?" is the question from the congregation. "A child's been murdered by police and justice needs to be served."

Pastor Robinson comes back strong. "Why don't we protest when our black youth kill each other with gang violence? How come it takes a white cop to kill one of us before we holler injustice? Why don't we raise a ruckus when black dope dealers sell drugs to our people? Robinson adds a bit of parody to his speech. "C'mon somebody, raise your hands and explain why we hate each other so much."

If the pastor is trying to get the congregation's attention, he surely has it now. It would be wise for him to hurry with his argument before he finds himself in a hole that he can't climb out of.

"People, do you know that nearly forty-five percent of all murders in America happen to black people? What's so shocking is that black people comprise only fourteen percent of the country's population. Do you know what kinds of people are killing us? It's not the Klan, guess again—black folks are killing us."

The saints listen quietly without interrupting.

The imps don't like the speech at all and wish to put a halt to it, they're helpless though. All they can do is listen as the rambling pastor talks for an eternity about how to make the community better.

"I believe it's time for the black community to address the issues of teenage pregnancies and the outrageous number of abortions that take away innocent lives on a daily basis. Yeah, I understand the reasons for abortion, but it shouldn't be used as a means of birth control either. Let's protest about our black youth who are most likely to possess a gun before they ever get a driver license. Let's protest about the negative attitude we have towards the police which we need to change. The police are here to help us, yet they can't do their job if we constantly assist criminals in their efforts to wreck our community. We have to bring back the morals that our people lost a long time ago." Robinson makes his ultimatum known. "So if we're going to protest, let's stand against everything that affects our community in a negative way."

As Pastor Robinson completes his beliefs on the protest, the saints sit with their eyes wide open. The pastor has spoken honestly and even captivated the attention of the imps who momentarily forgot to the hinder the service.

There's something special about the truth—it can stand on its own.

20

Pour Out a Little Liquor

The Pharaohs have benefited greatly from the protest. They now have the luxury of selling drugs without interference from the police. The killing of little Kenny has paid big dividends. As Mo' and JT sit upstairs at Tommy's strip club where all the money is being kept, one man takes exceptional pride in their devious handiwork.

"That was a good idea to follow the police around the 'hood," says JT. Though he is not alone, Jermaine speaks to no one in particular. "As soon as we got the first chance, we smoked that little boy. Too bad lil' homie had to die. I'll remember him for what he did, pour out a little liquor."

The sick Pharaoh pours a bit of liquor to the floor in memory of Kenny. This is common practice in the 'hood.

Trotter becomes so obsessed with the notion of paying tribute to the fallen boy that he repeatedly recites the lyrics of the late rapper, Tupac Shakur, aka 2Pac, "Pour out a little liquor." Becoming animated, he flings his arms about in the air as he sings louder, "Pour out a little liquor."

Mo' pays him no mind as JT raps to himself. To ordinary eyes, JT appears to be crazy. In reality, the gangster's spirit is under attack. Drunk and howling like a sick dog, he floods the floor with liquor.

"Hey man, what's your problem," yells Tommy as he walks in on JT's craziness.

"Pour out a little liquor," sings the crazed killer.

"Who's gonna clean up the mess you're making on the floor?"

JT dances over to Tommy, confronting him face to face; wild-eyed, sweaty, and breathing heavily, he tries to dance with Tommy. The whole time he sings the same verse, breath reeking of alcohol. The skin on killer's sweaty arms looks like slimy snakeskin. His wide eyes resemble those of a zombie, which freaks Tommy out.

What the mayor's son doesn't see is that Murder and Hate are joining in the fun and dancing around the room with glee. The demons believe they have sealed Jermaine's fate since he killed Kenny. The murderous act has opened the doorway for them to have their way with JT's soul; his flesh is now a captive of the devil.

While the two villains delight in their mischief, Insanity sits upon JT's shoulder with his claws dug deep into the mortal's brain. He's the culprit that has Trotter singing, "Pour out a little liquor."

The bizarre behavior compels Tommy to try talking some sense into JT. "Whatever you've been doing has got to stop. Man, you're mind ain't right ... snap out of it!" Tommy's desperate effort to bring JT back to his senses seems to work. The thug ceases to sing. "Gimmie that bottle." Tommy snatches the liquor from his hand. "Man, you can't drink heavy and carry on like you do. You just ain't your normal self when you get drunk like this."

JT is quiet. He could criticize Tommy for being a heroin addict, but the mayor's son quit shooting-up shortly after the death of the stripper. That tragedy had been a wake-up call for him. Tommy now prefers the milder effects of weed and alcohol—and that, too, he doesn't use on regular basis anymore. The fast life is losing its appeal. The mayor's son is starting to see the club scene as a dead-end road. Selling the place and moving out of town is an appealing idea. His private thoughts must remain unknown for the time being. There would be a great deal of trouble if Mo' and JT caught wind of Tommy's secret feelings. Somehow, he has to find an exit out the business.

Violence and crime have never been big concerns for the Pharaohs until little Kenny's death. The killing has been a dividing issue causing many to question why the shooting was ordered. Had the incident been collateral damage, Kenny's death would be an easier pill to swallow; an intentional death is unacceptable.

The Pharaohs are not alone in their thinking. The Latinos are grumbling among themselves as well, and it's quite noticeable how the Reds have distanced themselves from the Pharaohs.

A few thugs gather at a corner store in Pharaoh territory. Among them are the two teenagers who delivered the dead stripper to the hospital. They talk secretly among themselves. "Man, you seen the people out there in the streets?" one gang member questions to another.

"Yeah, I seen 'em out there today. All those fools crying about Kenny and the police. None of 'em knows what really happened last weekend, but I do," claims the tall slender kid who drives the car purchased by JT.

A gang member finds Slim's comment to be ridiculous. "Shut up, man, you don't know what happened."

"Whatcha talkin' 'bout? I do know. You see, I was there when the word went out."

"Man, you lyin'. You must be the one who shot that boy."

The short stocky kid comes to his friend's defense. "Hold up, now, don't get it twisted. I was there, too, when the order came from the top."

The two friends are criticized by the others. "Y'all hear these clowns?" says one of them.

The stocky one continues. "Shut ya mouth for a minute, let me explain. You see, I overheard Mo' when he gave the orders to set the fire. You don't know what the fire is, do you?"

Everyone is eager to know what it means.

"The fire is this: come first chance, do somethin' to turn the people against the police. This could've been anything … it just happened to be Kenny." The stocky kid still has the crowd's attention as he continues. "Just look at all those nuts protesting in the streets now, all for the wrong reasons. The person they should be protesting against is the one who calls himself the top dog."

The story convinces one individual who complains about 'Mo. "That joker's always chillin' while we do all the dirty work. It's about time somebody dealt with him. He's never done anything for me."

Another homie, with a grudge against JT, jumps on board. "I remember what he did to my cousin. I couldn't say anything because the same thing would have happened to me."

"What happened, man?"

"My cousin was selling rocks for JT. One day, a crackhead stopped him for some business. They made the exchange, the junkie flashed a badge, and then three or four more pigs jumped out of nowhere. Eddie dropped his dope and jetted; the man had to run."

A quick comment is made. "You gotta watch out for those undercovers, man."

"Anyways, Eddie got away clean, went back to JT to tell his story. My cousin showed his money, and JT got mad because the cash was short. He didn't care that Eddie had to drop the rest to run. JT just smoked the man right there on the spot for being short, and then he started laughing when Eddie's body went to jerking on the ground. I wanted to kill that fool for doing my cousin like that."

"Don't worry, someday he'll be alone. Both of 'em will be alone, and somebody will deal with 'em," the slim one predicts.

The stocky kid reiterates his friend's point. "Yeah, it's about time someone dealt with them two. They've forgotten where they came from."

"Especially JT," says Slim, "He made me carry a dead girl in my new car. She was stank and dirty. We dropped her off at the hospital. Next thing we know the police are looking for us. They questioned us all night long. I got so tired of the mess that I told them everything they wanted to know."

"Yeah, I remember that, and guess what? JT never found out we dropped the dime on him," chuckles the short, stocky one. "And that's why those two detectives are after them."

"I bet that's the reason Kenny was shot. They're trying to flip the script and put heat back on the police."

Fratricide's imps are busy on the streets. They've got the gossip going with the gangsters. It's the intentions of Fratricide to divide Molder's humans, turning them against one another. The tactic seems to be working so far.

On the street corner in a plain, undercover car sit Hughes and Diggs. Their buddy Mingo sits, as usual, in the backseat listening as the detectives talk. "Your man is causing the city a whole lot of trouble," says Hughes. "A kid has been killed, and the police department is seen as the culprit. That ain't right. All officers know not to shoot into a crowd. Nobody wants a Rodney King fiasco in Harlem Heights."

"I told you that plan wasn't gonna work. Somebody innocent got killed and now all the cops are in hot water."

Hughes grabs the steering wheel and pulls himself straight in the driver's seat, yelling into the rearview mirror at the Latin Red. "Keep the preaching to yourself. I don't wanna hear none of that Monday morning quarterback stuff from you."

Mingo remains quiet, gloating inside because he was right about the risk of trying to trap the Pharaohs. Cops and a kid were killed and it all could have been avoided.

Silence falls upon the detectives, which allows Mingo an opportunity to make known his personal philosophy on street life. "I know drugs are not the most honorable business to be in, but you gotta operate by the code. You don't sell to children and pregnant women. Never start a beef with someone else unless it's absolutely necessary, and you keep that issue between yourself and the enemy. The shooting of Kenny was a violation of the code. There's more to this business than just a dollar. That's what a lot of these young ganstas fail to understand."

The officers know Mingo's words make plenty of good sense. If the detectives have a comment to make, they keep their opinions to themselves.

Now it's time for Mingo to drop the bomb on the detectives. "We know exactly who shot Kenny."

Hughes snatches his cigarette from his mouth, flips around in his seat, "Who did it?"

"I know somebody who seen the whole thing."

"Mingo, you need to start talking, so we can get this case resolved."

The Reds' gang leader, sensing he has the upper hand, slouches in the backseat and takes a long drag on his cigarette. "First you gotta do me a favor, *mi amigo*," Mingo cleverly figures.

"First of all, we're not your friends. Don't play games with us, 'cause we'll fry your butt. Secondly, we make the deals, not you. Now, since you mentioned it, what's your proposal? And don't think you may have a deal, I'm just curious to know what you're thinking," says the high-strung Hughes.

The Latin Red responds, "Well, I'm just thinking how we both can benefit from this situation …"

"Keep talking."

"I want out the game."

The detective doesn't understand. "Mingo, why would you want to do such a thing? I mean, look at all you have. You make more money in a day than me and my partner make working for a week. Why would you want to get out?"

Mingo's face bares a look of disgust. He's disappointed with the detective, who is obviously more ignorant than he appears. How can Hughes not understand why someone would want out of the fast life?

Not too often does Mingo show his emotions, but he's been offended this time. "Look, man, I've been running these streets since I was kid. No one took the time to show me a better way of life. These streets have been hard on me and everyone else this lifestyle draws into the game." Mingo sits up straight to further emphasize his point. "Don't think I started on top. I didn't. It all began on the corner with that nickel-and-dime hustlin'. I just recently hit the big time—that wasn't easy. I've been shot several times … hospitalized … and been to prison too." The gang leader reveals his greatest fear and the reason for wanting out of the street life. "I can't relax for a minute, not on the streets. Someone is always plotting behind my back. The moment I let my guard down is the very time I'm taken out permanently. Now I have a chance to leave this game behind for good. I can take the money I've earned and leave. There's a better life somewhere outside Harlem Heights, and I'm gonna find it."

Diggs seems to be getting the point. He knows the dope game is played 24/7. The detective has a family; he can escape the rigors of the street by simply going home to the sanctity of the suburbs.

Hughes is not so sympathetic. How can he fail to understand Mingo's situation? Yeah, he can let the Latin Red go, but there's one more thing he'll have to do first before he gets out of the game.

"Okay, I get your point; your argument is legit. I just need you to do one more job for us. You're the one with access to Mo'. You help us get him, then you can get your freedom, deal?" says Hughes.

Mingo is disgusted, "You just don't get it. I want out of the game *now*. I've done everything possible to help you; there's nothing more I can do."

Hughes is angry. "Watch your tone of voice, son."

"Son? Man, I'm probably older than you—I'm outta here!" Mingo exits the vehicle slamming the car door behind him which surprises the detective.

"No, he didn't just walk out here without being excused." Hughes has no sympathy, "He's gonna pay for that."

21

The Devil Stays Busy

The protesting in the streets has gained momentum. Many are surprised the demonstration has continued for so long, and the so-called Reverend Brown continues to lead the way. The saints are still clueless as to where Brown suddenly came from. These topics, among other issues, are the highlights of tonight's Bible study meeting.

Eager to get a good conversation started, a saint named Thomas poses a question. "Brother Williams, have you heard the latest news regarding the protest?"

"If you're talking about the demands that ol' Reverend Brown made to the police department, then I heard the news."

Thomas is more than willing to explain. "He wants the chief of police to be fired. Not only that, he wants the replacement to be someone black or a person of color. Brother Will, man, I'm not too sure about that idea. Ain't no telling what kind of fool we'll get if someone else replaces the chief."

Sister Betty sits by listening until she can no longer resist being silent. "Well, if you ask me, it's not a bad idea," she comments. "The police department is just as corrupt as them dope dealers on the streets. I've seen how they operate—take dope from one kid, lock 'im up, then turn around and give that same stash to another hoodlum to sell. There ought to be a change at the police department, and it needs to start at the top."

A fourth person, Brother Johnson, jumps into the conversation. Understanding Betty's point of view, he shares his own perspective on the matter. "Yeah, you're right about some cops. That's why I'm glad to know of some good policemen who will flush drugs down the toilet whenever they find them. They don't always arrest the young drug dealers and send them off to jail. They try to work with the kids and make them better. No one ever mentions these good guys."

The saints aren't feeling what Johnson just said; none has a response for him. Instead, attention is given to Brother Thomas who has a few more remarks of his own. "Reverend Brown may have a questionable history, but I think he's doing something good for the community. I think we should support him," declares the middle-age man who slides his Bible aside to pound a fist on the table.

"Are you crazy?" Johnson questions. "That man is a thief and a pimp. He has no business using the Lord's name for his own agenda."

The statement angers a few of the saints, compelling them to take the offensive. Williams, Thomas, and Sister Betty join forces to attack the lonesome Johnson.

"Well, he's better than all the other preachers around here," claims Williams. "I don't see anyone else standing up for the cause. This is why our black youth run to the mosque converting to Islam. We Christians refuse to fight for our rights as tax-paying citizens."

Johnson makes a feeble attempt to redeem himself. "I'm just saying there's gotta be a better way."

"What other way is there?" retorts Williams. "The church has sat back for too long doing nothing. Bible studies and prayer ain't enough—we need action."

The conversation is getting heated; tempers are flaring.

"Hold it now, Williams. That's no way to talk about the church; we're not as weak and helpless as you make us out to—"

Sister Betty cuts Johnson off. "That is the reason why the church is weak—weak like you!"

Bible study has taken a backseat to a heated debate on Rev Brown. Robinson and his wife have yet to arrive, so the imps that accompany the saints jump around the place like mice on the kitchen table when the lights go out. The gossip-mongering spirits sling slime around the room that splatters on the heads of the saints. Every person touched by the demonic gunk suddenly has an opinion of his or her own to express.

The gremlins are having a great time. "Look at them. Look at Sister Betty go after Brother Johnson. It's wonderful, isn't it? I love it. That's right, girl, you give that dummy a piece of your mind. He doesn't know what he's talking about, that fool. Remember when he voted republican? You know black folks vote for democrats only."

Gossip hops on Betty's shoulder and slaps a handful of slime upside her head, drenching her face. Her soul absorbs it all, taking only a few seconds before an intoxicating reaction occurs; the woman pauses as if in a trance, then snaps back to reality, ready to dig into Brother Johnson again. "Do ya'll remember during the last election who this man voted for?" She holds in a big laugh.

"Where you going with this?" Johnson believes the incriminating question to be a personal attack. "Why you gotta bring this up?"

"Ain't nobody talking to you, Bro. J," she cackles. "I asked Brothers Williams and Thomas who they voted for during the last election."

"No you didn't. You asked them who *I* voted for."

The woman knows she has the upper hand. "Just mind your business; let me talk without interruptions. Now back to my question: since when do black folks vote republican like Johnson did?" Betty explodes with laughter and her antics draw a few chuckles from the crowd.

It's the spirit of malice who's busy at work kicking up dust now. The imp holds within his hand a number of darts dripping with spite, which he tosses about the room. Three or four darts already hang from Sister Betty's back. They fail to stick to Brother Johnson, but he's clearly wounded, bleeding from the insults of the other saints. The man's spiritual condition is ideal for Pity.

In an infant-like manner, Pity heads for the lonesome Johnson and his wounded ego like a toddler crawling toward its momma wishing to be held. The imp clumsily reaches for Johnson's leg then suddenly scampers like a nimble monkey up and about the mortal's body. What seemed like a feeble toddler with no more coordination than a baby is really a slick rascal with centuries of experience in manipulating human emotions.

Pity sits on the shoulder of Johnson whispering in his ear. *"Poor me. Why is everybody turned against me? I did nothing wrong to these people, and now they want to point the finger at me. All I said was that Reverend Brown shouldn't be so easily trusted. It's not fair to blame me for ... "*

Pity has to pause for a moment to figure out what Johnson is being blamed for. The rascal doesn't recall. What is Brother Johnson being blamed for?

Pity suddenly remembers, *"They're blaming me for being a sellout. I do care for my people. All I meant was we should be careful about who we place our trust in. That's all."* Johnson is now clearly frustrated.

The spirit of Malice makes sure Sister Betty has more words for the suffering brother. "Look here, Johnson," she says, "Reverend Brown is trying to do something good. The man needs all the support he can get. Why must we always pull each other down? We should be happy for one another and hope for the best? It's enough trouble already in the world with the white man bringing us down."

"Oh, Sister Betty, why do you have to go there with the conversation?" counters Johnson. "The white man has nothing to do with what's happening in Harlem Heights."

"Johnson, that's what I'm talking about: You're one of those compromising Booker-T Negroes that hate to see things change. Those racist cops need to be dealt with, and Reverend Brown is the man to do it."

Betty's outrageous attitude is even too much for Brothers Williams and Thomas to deal with. Only to an extent do they agree with the woman. Playing the race card is a bit to the extreme.

A divisive spirit throws more into the battle: *"Who's mad? Who's mad at Sister Betty? Look what she said about white people: she hates them!"* The demon's goal, as is the goal of all the evil spirits, is to break the unity of the Light of Hope congregation.

Before the situation can get any worse, Pastor Robinson and his wife enter the room. It's not so much what they see that shocks the couple but, rather, the heavy atmosphere of strife they can't help but feel as they walk into the room.

Evil's efforts to cause conflict among the saints are working well. The Robinsons are about to discover Hell in the congregation. As the pastor and his wife make their entrance, a strange silence blankets the room. Not saying a word, Williams and Thomas eyeball one another. Instinctively, they both cut their eyes in direction of Sister Betty who is trying her best to look innocent. One can imagine her behavior as a child. It would be no surprise to learn, when still a kid that she oftentimes hit her brother first and then ran to momma crying that he had been bothering her.

Louise tries to break the awkward silence. "Praise the Lord, saints. How's everything going?"

A few individuals make a reluctant reply, but there's no prompt response, which leads the pastor to discern that something isn't right. Not wanting to handle the situation in the wrong manner, Robinson immediately beckons everyone to pray along with him before starting anything else. "Lord, I don't know what it is that hinders us today, yet we know it's not of your nature. We ask that you'll reveal to us the problem within this congregation, so we can address the issue."

Robinson comes to the conclusion the saints must reexamine their hearts, confess their shortcomings, and then forgive one another for their wrongdoings. The Lord cannot dwell in an unclean vessel. "Is there something we need to talk about tonight?" he asks. "I know we came for Bible study, but how can we concentrate on things of the Spirit when issues of the flesh are pressing hard on our minds?"

There's a lot sighing and one sassy individual has the audacity to suck *her* teeth which the pastor chooses to ignore. Still, no one dares to make eye contact with Randy. The loud silence has never felt so awkward.

Robinson has an idea of what the problem may be. "I feel that some of us are harboring bitterness in our hearts and it just didn't start tonight. These issues have been festering ever since the shooting of Kenny." The saints still remain quiet, which leaves Randy no choice but to keep talking. "Now that the people are protesting, and a certain person has resurfaced into the light, I get the feeling some of us feel slighted in some kind of way. Will someone tell us as a group what's really eating away at our congregation?" the pastor asks.

Again, thick silence. Can the saints be anymore pathetic? Robinson is working with a tough crowd tonight. Ditching his original plan to study the full armor of the Lord in the book of Ephesians, the pastor realizes this situation calls for scriptures more fitting. "Let's turn to the fifth chapter of Matthew, verses twenty-three and twenty-four. Sister Betty, will you please read it for us?"

Betty rolls her big eyes indicating she rather not be bothered. But since the pastor singled her out, she feels obligated to open her Bible and read, yet her tone of voice makes it clear she isn't pleased with the task. "'Therefore, if you are offering your gift at the altar and there remember that your brother has something against you, leave your gift there in front of the altar. First go and be reconciled to your brother; then come and offer your gift.'"

Robinson expresses his gratitude. "Thank you, Sister Betty, for the reading."

"Um hmm," is Betty's barely audible response.

Despite the woman's flippant attitude, the Pastor continues as if he doesn't notice. "The verse we just heard deals with how we should handle personal relationship in our lives. Are we doing our best to be at peace with each other? Do we feel justified in abusing others for something we consider an important cause?" Robinson takes a look around to see how the saints respond to his message. Everyone is paying attention, so he continues. "Before we can offer ourselves to be used by the Lord, we need to reconcile some issues with one another. Now I'm going to ask again, who would like to go first?"

Pastor Robinson must have struck a nerve. The saints are quieter than ever, and some even fidget in their seats. They eyeball one another thinking who's going to be the first one to speak up.

The imps that instigated the harsh debate try to remain hidden below the floor and inside the walls. Heaven's guardians, having grown tired of the stalling, use their swords to force the scoundrels out in the open. "Get out there and be noticed," demands one of the angelic warriors. "Gossip, the time has come for you to be dealt with. You may have the right to be here, but the saints will know your nature and how to react when you raise your ugly head again."

"We're going, we're going. You don't have to push us," says a pouting imp acting as a child being forced to bed earlier than he desires. The demon and his companions reluctantly take center stage. One or two spirits pace about in small circles as if in search for a place to hide. None dares attempt an escape … too dangerous.

The efforts of the pastor are effective. The congregation is coming to terms with their personal problems—except for Betty; she's as stubborn as ever.

Solomon directs a subordinate to investigate the reason for the woman's behavior. The angel reports, "I know he's there, but I can't see him. The woman is hiding the foul spirit and it has a rightful place to dwell until she repents of her sin."

Solomon reacts coolly, asking in a calm manner, "Do we know his nature, so he can be identified later?"

The guardian reveals the culprit. "Yes, it's Malice hiding in her. There's no telling who else may be in there with him. The bitter woman is holding on tightly to this particular spirit."

"Understood. She'll come around eventually to expose that spirit. In the meantime, we have other problems to resolve," says Solomon with his hands resting on the shoulders of Randy Robinson.

Trying to make communication easier, Randy takes the initiative to start some conversation. "Brother Johnson, when I entered the room, you had a look of concern all over your face. Please tell us what's bothering you."

The heavy-burdened brother takes a deep breath, sighing. "I first want to apologize for upsetting everyone. I said a few things that really rubbed some of us the wrong way ... I'm sorry."

Williams and Thomas are receptive of the apology. Sister Betty is a stone.

Johnson continues, "You see, I resent the fact that Reverend Brown is back in the spotlight again. Despite what others think, I believe Brown is a hypocrite who benefits from using the name of the Lord for his own purposes. I've seen him in action when he was pastor of this church—that's one manipulating and self-serving joker. Whatever his hand touches always goes bad. Things just always turn out to benefit him; never the people. Mark my words, you'll soon see for yourself."

Pastor Robinson nods his head. "Okay, this is a start. What's so bad about Johnson's comment?" he inquires of the group.

"It's not the comment that's so bad," Thomas volunteers, "it's just his refusal to forgive and let the guy have another chance. Reverend Brown is a gifted man who has made a positive impact on many of us. How can you ignore that?"

"I used to think the same way as you until Brown got my sister pregnant," reveals Johnson. His comment causes the saints' eyes to light up and their backs to straighten. He continues with his story. "When that happened, the church talked about her like she was a dog. The gossip became so bad she had to leave the church. Love and forgiveness were nowhere to be found then—just dirty looks."

"Well, what did you expect? She had sex without being married first," Brother Williams shoots back.

Johnson is starting to get angry again, yet he controls his emotions. "Yeah, I know it; she did wrong and got pregnant. My problem with the situation is this—everyone knows who the father of the child is. Why didn't they talk about him the same way they did about my sister?"

The conversation is getting juicy now. Pastor Robinson, who considers himself one not to get caught up in gossip, is suddenly aroused by this revelation. His wife, Louise, is sitting on the edge of her seat too.

"Why you gotta broadcast the man's business like that?" Brother Williams demands to know.

"Hey, Will, everybody knows Brown and my sister had an affair. They both were wrong. But the church had a double standard, and that's not fair. Why didn't anyone question the preacher who was in a leadership position—a position that comes with responsibility. Reverend Brown should have been held accountable for his actions just like my sister was."

Williams is quiet now. Pastor Robinson is unsure of how to continue until Betty speaks up. "Why the church gotta question Reverend Brown? It ain't our business. If you're a man, you should have confronted the reverend yourself."

Immediately the imps on the table join the revelry. "That's right, you tell 'em, sister, how to handle business."

Betty allows the spirit of Malice to use her. "It's nobody's business but the woman's. The church didn't help her lie down with that man; she did it on her own."

The venom in her voice poisons the atmosphere in the room causing Johnson's temper to flare. "You see, Pastor, that's what I'm talking about. It's not so much that my sister got pregnant by Brown; she did agree to lie down with the man. What's irritating me are attitudes like Sister Betty's." The disgruntled brother points an accusing finger at Betty. She, in turn, springs to her feet as if she's going to come across the table at him. Undaunted, Johnson continues, "How can anyone who claims to be a Christian not see the biased feelings she has toward my sister?

And, of all people, why is Betty refusing to see my point of view? I feel as though she's jealous or something."

Brother Johnson doesn't realize that his words just struck a nerve with Betty. She narrows her eyes and points a finger back at her accuser. "Your sister knew better than to mess with Reverend Brown. He was *my* man! I told her several times to stay away from him, she wouldn't listen. I watched that affair go on for months—that heifer deserved to get pregnant and ran out the church."

The conversation can't get any juicer. The mortals and spirits hang on every word spewing from Betty's mouth. "His innocent compliments about how well she sang in the choir started all this mess," she shrieks. "Your sister read into it thinking it meant more. Next thing I know, she's seeing him for counseling. What was so important that she couldn't talk to her brother? Where were you then *Brother* Johnson?" Betty is baring it all, holding nothing back. Everyone's attention is held captive. "That hot hen used any excuse she could find to hang around him. After a while, Reverend Brown was no longer interested in me. All his time was spent with the choirgirl who sang as sweet as the angels above—he would always say." Bitterness seethes from Betty's mouth as she talks through clinched teeth. "Brown made promises to me that your sister took away. When that bottom-feedin' catfish got pregnant and tried to tear down that man, I wouldn't allow it. It was obvious to see that your sister had preyed upon him. That's how she got knocked up, and then she wanted sympathy from the church. No way was she going to get it. I made sure of it."

Sister Betty has said a mouthful. The group finds the idea of Betty and Brown having a relationship shocking. What would the reverend want with an older woman? Not that older is all that bad, but Betty is far from being the best-looking woman in church. She's educated, hardworking, and extremely stubborn, but nothing close to a beauty queen. She does have money though. Perhaps this was Brown's interest?

Pastor Robinson takes the floor again. "All right, we've got a few issues out in the open. We now understand why Brother Johnson feels the way he does. We understand Sister Betty. Regardless of who's right or wrong, we must forgive one another and let it all go." Robinson can think of nothing else to say that could remedy the situation, so he keeps focused on forgiveness. "If you keep the anger and resentment as baggage, it will weigh you down. Does everyone understand what I'm saying? Don't be a slave to your hard feelings," concludes Pastor Robinson.

Brother Johnson shakes his head in agreement. "Pastor, I totally agree with you."

"Good."

The pastor turns to Betty. "We have to let go of the past."

Silently, Sister Betty conveys that she understands, still it's obvious that she's hanging on to hard feelings.

Thinking the matter has been settled, the pastor attempts to lead the saints in prayer. He hopes to bring a final end to the internal rivalries and make some progress with the church mission. As he bows his head in prayer, Robinson is interrupted by one of the saints. "Pastor, I have another issue I would like to address," says Brother Thomas.

"Of course, please make it known."

"There's something that's been eating away at us since the protesting started. I noticed the community has come together and made an effort to fight against police brutality and corruption in the government. All the churches, the people on the streets, and even the Muslims have gathered in unity for a greater cause ..." Here comes the hard part, Thomas struggles for words. "I'm sorry if I hurt your feelings, but I'm not here just to sit back, pray, and watch while everyone else does all the work. And I'm not the only one who feels this way, right saints?"

Robinson takes a look around the room to see if Thomas' words are true.

"Yes, he's right," says Sister Betty. "Our church is weak because we only talk a good fight. This is contrary to the word of God." The woman takes full advantage of the opportunity to get sassy. "In James chapter two; verse seventeen, the Bible says 'In the same way, faith by itself, if it is not accompanied by action, is dead.' I don't believe in a dead church. It's about time we made something happen."

Brother Williams jumps on the bandwagon too. Having grown so tired of Bible studies and prayer meetings, he's considering joining a new church.

One by one, the saints express their wishes to be part of the demonstration that's changing the city of Harlem Heights. There's a mutiny aboard the ship; momentum has switched to the other side. One of the imps, emboldened by the conversation, speaks up. "Let's see how well your puppet responds to this. I hope he says the wrong thing that provokes the saints to rip him apart."

Another spirit chimes in with more criticism. "He's no man of God. What can he do for the community? I bet he'll sit back and watch the rest of the churches have all the fun. You coward, show us what you got."

Solomon, in reaction to the enemies' taunts, yells with a big booming voice, *"Silence!* Now hear a message from the most high!"

The messenger's thundering voice sends the imps rolling across the floor only to be slapped steady by Empyreal swords. While the gremlins rub their hot rumps, Pastor Robinson makes a declaration. "We have a reason to protest, and I don't mind as long as we protest the truth unlike those misguided people who are out there now." The group issues a few groans, but Robinson speaks on. "That's right, misled. When they begin to stand up for the truth, I will then say let's go and support them. You may believe otherwise, but I'm not stepping one foot into anybody's picket line until we address the truth." The saints are caught off guard by the pastor's fiery statement.

"Well, what's the truth?" Sister Betty demands to know.

"The community is out there blaming the wrong people for their shortcomings," the pastor answers. "They're pointing the finger at the white man when they should be looking at themselves."

"Oh no, that nigga didn't go there," whispers the flippant Betty under her breath. She has her hands up in the air as if praising God. "Jesus, we need ya, Lawd," she says a bit louder. Her cry to the Lord is an attempt to cover her slip of the tongue.

Brother Williams, sitting quite close to Betty, takes a quick look at her to see if he's imaging what she just said. *I know this heifer didn't say what I think she just said—the doggone woman done lost her mind,* Williams thinks to himself.

Robinson justifies his beliefs. "Far too long we've placed blame for our problems on everyone else. The white man hasn't forced any of us to drink ourselves to death with alcohol, to do drugs and destroy our families, and to resort to violence rather than effective communication. Many of us have no character. We'd rather tolerate a thug than embrace a snitch who makes a feeble attempt to address the social ills in our community."

The saints are quiet. They see the logic in what the pastor is saying—except for Sister Betty. "I don't believe what you're saying," she retorts. "How can you blame all of this on our people? The drugs and lack of government funding is not our fault. The corruption and police brutality is not our fault. The giving out of loans to foreign immigrants but not Black Americans is not our fault. You better go and come again with that mess you're talking, pastor, 'cause I ain't buying it."

"Lord, have mercy," the saints all say in unison. Sassy Betty is just too much.

22

Reverend Brown Makes an Impression

Feeling the need to keep a low profile, Mo' and JT remain out of sight at the strip club while issuing orders to their subordinate Pharaohs on the streets. Not wanting to lose the people's support, Mo' concentrates all his efforts behind Rev Brown to keep the protesting alive. The Pharaohs are providing the so-called reverend with all the money, vehicles, and clothes he needs to ensure his success.

At the moment, Brown is updating JT with his plan of action. "I'm gonna meet with the lawyers today to discuss our option with the police department."

"Hurry with them results," JT says. "Mo' wants to see a change real soon or you'll be cut off again." Then JT abruptly changes the subject to inquire about a personal interest. "By the way, I need some info from you."

Brown talks to JT as if they're childhood siblings. "I'm not doing anything for you. I work for Willie Mo', not JT. If I was Mo', I wouldn't have you working for me at all with your nasty self."

"Well, you ain't Mo'. You will do as I say or else I'll tell Mo' you blowin' him off—how 'bout that? Is that what you want? Don't forget what happened last time you got so high and mighty." Acting as if everything is all right, JT switches the conversation back to his personal question. "Look here, Rev, you gonna do me that favor? It's nothing big."

"What do you want, JT?" asks the frustrated Brown who wants to get rid of his nuisance as quickly as possible.

"Who's that reporter I saw you talking with?"

"Man, I've spoken to so many reporters, I can't remember them all. Who are you talking about exactly?"

"Naw man, this one here is different. I've never seen her before," the gangster says. "She's not on television; she must work for the news press, and she did an interview with you last Tuesday."

"How do you know my business?" questions Brown.

"I've told you, we put some eyes on you. A slick joker like you needs a short leash. We watch you all the time, man. You can fool the people all you want, but you'll never trick us with that lying tongue of yours."

Reverend Brown grows tired of fussing with JT. He tells the thug who Angela is. "Don't think she's gonna give you any play," he advises. "I tried to get with her already, and she wasn't interested. She definitely won't have any interest in a knucklehead like you," laughs Reverend Brown as he leaves JT for more important matters.

There's no time to play matchmaker. Brown has a schedule to keep with the lawyers. The next task is to see how to go about forcing a change of leadership at the police department.

Willie Mo' demands a new chief of police; Molder wants to control the law. Stripping Fratricide of his power base will tighten the Pharaoh's grip on the city.

Rev Brown and a lawyer meet downtown at a local hotel for an early dinner and business meeting. Greetings are exchanged, drinks are poured, and dinner comes soon thereafter. With food, comes a serious conversation.

The lawyer wants to know about the past. "Mr. Brown, before we can make known your demands for the police department, there are a few things we need to discuss about you. Our sources say you have an interesting history. Is it true that you were banned from serving at a church you once led?"

The cool Rev Brown expected such a question. Clearing his voice, the sly one replies with a smooth baritone, "Yes, we had some trouble at that church. It's what I call a conflict of doctrine that caused me to resign as pastor."

"You weren't kicked out of the church as the allegations suggest?"

"Not at all. I have standards and refuse to compromise my personal beliefs on how a church should operate in accordance to the good book," replies the savvy Rev Brown. "If a congregation disagrees with the word of the Lord, then one of two things must happen—they accept my belief, which is the Bible, or I leave. In this case, the people refused to see things my way, so I left. Simple isn't it?"

"Well, sir, some of the background information we have also reflects the fact that you fathered a child out of wedlock. Is this true?"

Still cool and composed, Brown answers the question with no difficulty. "As you can see for yourself, I have shortcomings. It was an unfortunate situation, but something beautiful was the result of that mistake. I have a wonderful son who looks just like me. His mother is a wonderful person whom I met and fell in love with. As much as I want to be with her now, she doesn't want the same level of commitment I desire."

The lawyer's not buying the story. "But, sir, you're a preacher. Your actions with that woman do not reflect well on your part."

"None of us is perfect," declares the smug reverend. "We all have sinned … fallen short of glory. I'm no different than King David; he had his Bathsheba. The manager who runs off with his secretary is just like me too. What I did is happening right now at every level of society. The only difference is that my sin is public knowledge. Now I said all that just to emphasize this: Don't judge me because I had a child out of wedlock. I'm only human."

The so-called Rev Brown is quite pleased with himself for that answer. As he takes a drink from a glass of cola, he finds it difficult to sip and smile at the same time. A trickle of soda slips from the corner of his lips.

Silently, the lawyer watches the pompous Brown dab at his mouth with a cloth napkin. The reverend can tell that the attorney is considering another line of questioning.

"Money. Word has it that you took a lot of money from the church. You drove around in nice cars, wore expensive clothes, and could frequently be seen in fancy restaurants. What's the deal with that?"

"You're right about everything. I drove around in nice cars provided by the church. Keep this in mind though—I never owned any of those cars. The vehicles belonged to certain members of the church who would drive them too. I just simply drove whatever car was available. There were even times when no cars were available except for the church van. Who wants to be seen rolling in a vehicle like that? I didn't mind, so I drove that ugly van around too. Did your sources reveal that?" inquires Brown. "As for my clothes, what I wear is my business. The church paid me a monthly salary. Some of that money went toward clothes. Even though my threads look expensive, they're not. You see, I'm resourceful when it comes to shopping; I look for bargains. I also know people who make nice suits for a fraction of the price charged by the department stores. So, if someone has a problem with me looking good, I can't help it. Is it a sin to dress nice?"

Reverend Brown has an answer for everything. He even has some additional comments about the eating out. "People can be really nasty when they want to be. There's no need to answer this question, but I will for you. If I was ever seen eating out, then I was fellowshipping with those wishing to know more about the Lord. Is there any harm in that?" Brown is on a roll and has even more to say about dining out. "Remember this—Jesus ate with a tax collector and other sinners, and the people talked bad about Him. John the Baptist ate wild locust and honey, and the people criticized him too. If people spoke badly about them, what can you expect them to say about me? Gossip comes with the position of being a pastor. I've learned it's not what people say about me that matters, but rather, how I react to what is being said about me. By the way, would you like a refill on that drink?"

Brown signals the waiter, and both men order another round of drinks. This time, the reverend orders whiskey with his coke. The lawyer gives him a peculiar look, which prompts another slick response from Brown. "It's all in moderation, my friend … all in moderation. Besides, didn't Jesus turn water into wine?"

The lawyer, not being a religious man, is puzzled by Brown's openness. The reverend has an explanation for every accusation. Whether he's guilty or just misunderstood, the reverend is worth representing. His slick talking could win the lawyers, and a few fortunate others, a great sum of money in court.

For Mo', a victory in the courtroom would pave his way to ruling the streets, but will it get rid of that nuisance on Market Street?

* * *

Willie Mo's focus has switched primarily from the church to the demonstration. He wants to ensure that everyone of significance does their part to get the chief of police fired, yet he can't forget about the Light of Hope Church. Levy reports to the warehouse to give an update to Willie who's in a foul mood. He demands to know, "What's taken you so long to get back to me?"

The old man replies graciously, "I's been tryin' to operate widout bein' found out."

The Pharaoh bombards Mr. Levy with questions that cause the old man to fidget. "Not trying to raise suspicion, huh? Old man, you're not doing a good job—I'm suspicious. What's up with the division strategy? When are you going to tear that raggedy congregation apart? Why is it that we can't communicate when you're gone?"

Levy struggles to answer and now the sight of Mo' headed his direction causes the old man to panic.

Willie approaches with both hands clenched as fists. When he gets to within arm's reach of Levy, Mo' pops the old man upside his bald head with an open-handed slap that burns like a hornet's sting. The elder grabs his bald head with both hands and arms as if his scalp is on fire. Doubled over in pain, he kneels to the ground begging for mercy. "No, boss, please stop! No need to worryin', da plan took lotta time, but it's workin' now. Dat's why it took so long fo' me ta get back ta ya."

"You're a liar, old man," retorts Willie Mo'.

"Da saints are wise folks. Dey pray so nothin' hinders dem. Dis why it take so long, but I founds a weakness in da congregation: I appeals to dey pride," whispers Levy with desperation in his voice.

The last phrase did the trick. Willie turns his ear, in a parrot-like gesture, to the old man to ensure he hears well. "Say again?"

"Da saints are bickerin' wit one 'nother. Dey even attacked dey own pastor," reveals the old one with wicked glee.

Permitting himself to make a sly smile, the Pharaoh is obviously pleased. "Yes, is this so? Tell me more. What exactly is happening at the church?"

136

"Some saints are angry 'cause Brown is leading da protest. Dey don't trust 'im an' believe he up to his tricks again—"

The quiet, calculating Mo' interrupts Levy to express his pleasure, "Yes, he's up to more of my tricks indeed."

The old servant remains on his knees as he resumes the story. "A whole lotta fussin' den started 'mong de saints. Dere are dose who stand fo' Rev Brown an' some who o-pose him. Masta, you shoulda been dere. The saints rip into each udder as dey argue dey sides." The old man gives a toothless, guttural laugh which pleases Mo'. "Dey talked 'bout each udder's mamas, even criticizes one 'nother for votin' republican. Den da saints turn de argument on da pastor. Dey call him an Uncle Tom an' house nigga for not allowin' da church ta do dey part in da protest."

The old man has captivated the Pharaoh's attention. Mo' rubs his hands together as if he's trying to keep them warm.

Mr. Levy continues, "Pastor Robinson bettah get his peoples unda control. It ain't gonna be easy 'less he gib de saints what dey want: a spotlight in dat demonstration. Compromisin' will make his congregation weak. If he do different, it's gonna cause a fight 'mong de saints dat will rip da church 'part. Masta, da plan ta tear up da church and scattah da saints is workin'."

Feeling a little more content, Mo' allows his anger with Levy to subside. The old man remains kneeling waiting to be excused. "Go, get out of my sight. Continue to do your worst to the church. When it's time for you to report back, I'll send for you. Just remember who you work for, *Stan*. If you betray me, you'll pay dearly for it."

Mr. Levy gets up slowly and proceeds to limp toward the door. He told the gangster a good story, but not the full truth. Yet the story will buy him more time to learn about Jesus Christ. The thought of being a true Christian makes him feel warm inside.

23

The Interview

A few days have passed since the debate with the saints occurred. The pastor worries that his efforts to rebuild the church may be all in vain. Saving Harlem Heights will surely be a spiritual battle, but getting the saints to see past the physical realm is difficult. The lure of the media is not helping either. So what can he do to get the saints to realize the fight is a spiritual battle, not a fight with man?

Louise walks into the kitchen followed by Angela. The reporter's arms are full of books and a few folders containing documents, all of which she spills on the table. Getting situated, Ms. Walker pulls from the stack of books a small paperback, which is for the pensive pastor who speaks a greeting but never looks up to make eye contact.

Angela holds out the book, and Robinson slowly reaches out to grasp it. He reads the title, *Up From Slavery,* by Booker T. Washington.

The reporter smiles to herself, happy that Randy took the bait.

"Angela, I've read this book and know a lot about this man. He's definitely an odd figure in history."

"Please share your thoughts about him."

Robinson looks at journalist trying to figure out her motive. "Washington was a former slave who lived as a child during the American Civil War. He helped to establish the Tuskegee Institute in Alabama. He's famous for a quote that won applause from many whites but drew heavy criticism from his black peers."

Angela and Louise listen intently as the Pastor gives his history lesson. "Washington said before a mostly white audience, 'In all things that are purely social we can be as separate as the fingers, yet one as the hand in all things essential to mutual progress.' Washington's attitude toward social equality rubbed many of his folks the wrong way."

Seeming to be on to something, the reporter asks more questions. "If he was so concerned about the welfare of the race, why didn't he just cooperate with his peers in achieving social equality? Tell me about his vision," the reporters demands.

"Washington had a simple idea on improving race relations. It was so simple that many of his critics failed to comprehend the brilliance of his approach. He believed black people should pull themselves up by their bootstraps by establishing their own businesses to conduct trade and commerce within their own communities. Washington emphasized self-empowerment over equal rights; he thought self-empowerment would eventually lead to social equality. However, it's easier said than done."

The reporter continues with a new series of questions. "Does he remind you of someone you know?"

The pastor seems a bit cynical as he makes a confession. "I'll take that question as a compliment even if you intended otherwise. And, yes, it does remind me of someone I know—myself."

"So what's the problem with being like Booker T. Washington? He was a great man who accomplished a lot for his race."

Shaking his head, Robinson laughs quietly to himself. "Yeah, he was a great man, but far from perfect. Some say he was a big compromiser. Others consider him a manipulating man who captured the sentiments of white America at the expense of black social progress."

"Do you recall the person who gave ole Booker T. the greatest challenge in his life?"

"As a matter of fact, I do. That would be none other than W.E.B. DuBois. He, too, was a smart but radical man. I think in today's times many minorities would embrace DuBois' beliefs over Washington's. I don't understand why though. Who would want to follow someone whose only means to racial equality was centered mostly on political agitation and protest? Don't get me wrong, DuBois did have an important role to play in the pursuit of civil rights. His intentions were good, but his approach to equality was easier said than done just like Washington's." Robinson has one more thing to say. "If both men could have met somewhere in the middle with their ideals, they would have seen more success."

The reporter drops the big question. "What lessons can we take from both men, and how would it apply to our situation today?"

"Personally, I believe the Harlem Heights community should reevaluate itself. Many of the problems we face are self-inflicted wounds. We can't possibly expect to see progress if we continue to misuse the resources we already have."

"Pastor, please be more direct. What do you mean by resources?"

"It means the way in which we use education, talent, money, and taking responsibility for our own actions. The question we should ask each other is in what ways do our actions affect the community, positively or negatively?"

"Is that it?"

"That's all," replies Randy.

With thoughts running wildly through her mind, the pastor's wife suddenly turns around from the kitchen sink to make a statement. "Why don't you print this interview in the paper for the community to read? This would be a great way to get a point across."

Angela thinks Louise has telepathic powers. "You must be reading my mind. It's my every intention to make this a submission for Sunday's paper. I think a lot of people will be interested in reading a different view on matters concerning Harlem Heights."

Solomon and Lee also listen in on the conversation. The messenger angel nods his head in approval for the decision to submit the interview in Sunday's edition of the newspaper.

"We'll need Siron to make sure that the mayor reads the paper on Sunday. This should give him a good idea on how to respond to the protest," Solomon advises.

Lee is already ahead of his brother. "Afterwards, we'll get the pastor to speak at a public forum. If the people can hear the truth as we know it, they will demand more from the people within their own community."

It's early Sunday morning, and Mayor Hurt is reading the newspaper in the comfort of his home. Nothing of interest is on the front page. Flipping steadily through the paper, he stops only when something catches his attention. The sports section does the trick for a moment. None of his favorite teams won last night, so he searches the comics for a bit of humor. Before he can read about Calvin and Hobbs' antics, the mayor comes across the faith section of the paper. *Mmm, what's this about?* Mayor Hurt thinks to himself. What he sees is a headline: "The Untold Truth in Harlem Heights." Pushing his glasses higher on the bridge of his nose, the mayor digs in for a good read.

The message quoted within the article really intrigues the mayor. "The protest is a good movement with bad intentions. What the people expect to gain from the demonstration will only disappoint them for one important reason: the leaders have failed to address the real problem in the black community. What is this problem you ask? It's the lack of love for our own people, and the failure to accept responsibility for our own shortcomings."

Thomas Hurt is pleased with the message. It's the answer he's been searching for since the death of little Kenny. He can now refute the notion that the police department and local government are the sole cause of Harlem Height's social ills.

Now if he could only contact the person quoted in this article, Pastor Randy Robinson. The mayor thinks to himself, *I wonder if he'd be willing to make a public appearance and speak before the people about the statements he made?* Hurt springs from his couch excited about an opportunity to undermine the protest. Heading for the telephone, he nearly bumps into his sleepy-looking wife who's making her way to the kitchen for a cup of coffee.

"Well ... good morning to you, Thomas," she says with a drowsy voice.

Ignoring his wife, the mayor grabs the cordless phone from the wall and dials a number. Using his shoulder to hold the receiver to his ear, he listens for the ring tones while reopening the newspaper to the article.

The phone rings several times before it's answered by a groggy-voiced man, "...Hello?" It's obvious the person is still in bed on this early Sunday morning.

"Dudley, it's me. What are you doing in bed at this time of the day? Stop being lazy and get up!" says the mayor with all seriousness.

Sitting straight up in bed, Dudley immediately recognizes his boss's voice on the other end of the line. "Sir, it's six in the morning. Why are you calling so early, can't it wait until tomorrow?"

"No *Dud*, it cannot," snaps Hurt, intentionally cutting his subordinate's name short to emphasize an idea other than just the name. "Have you read today's paper yet?"

"No, sir, I haven't. I've been sleeping, remember?"

"Yeah, right. Anyways, get out of bed and grab a newspaper. I want you to read an article in the faith section. It's called, 'The Untold Truth in Harlem Heights'. The person responsible for the statements in this article is a pastor Randy Robinson. We can use him for propaganda purposes." The mayor, hearing only silence, continues, "Dud, are you following me?"

"I will be as soon as I get a newspaper," says the assistant who seems to be more interested in getting back to sleep.

The mayor isn't feeling too confident about Dudley. "Get your butt out of that bed and read the paper! You got one hour to find a contact and arrange for a town hall meeting where this Robinson can make a public speech—we need 'im."

"Sir, can't this wait until tomorrow when we all come to work? It's Sunday morning, you know?"

"No, it cannot. If you want to have a job come tomorrow morning, you'd better make this happen. You got one hour to get it done." The mayor slams down the phone smirking.

"Poor Dudley, why must you talk so harshly to him all the time?" asks Mrs. Hurt.

The Mayor is surprised to hear his wife in the same room. He thought she was still in the kitchen. Pretending to be aware of her presence all along, Hurt stretches out on the couch trying to hold back a smile. Then he responds with a simple answer. "Honey, it's only business. I'm doing what's necessary to keep you in your position as the first lady of the city."

The flattering response is enough to satisfy the mayor's wife. She goes about her business in some other part of the house.

The mayor, still tired from being up early, waits patiently for Dudley to return his call. Not even an hour passes before his assistant calls back.

"Sir, this is Dudley. The arrangements have been made. The pastor will be there Wednesday night to speak at the town hall meeting."

"Dudley, you did a great job. One more thing before I hang up."

"Yes, sir?"

"Don't call my house so early in the morning again, it's Sunday!" Click goes the phone and the line is dead.

Dudley stares at the wall with a look of disbelief on his face. "I can't believe the mayor just said that," he whines. "I'm going back to bed."

24

The Robinsons Make a Resolution

Back at the Robinson's place, things are kind of tense. Louise isn't too happy about her husband's plan to speak publicly on issues the community may not want to face at this time. She fears the backlash may endanger her husband's life. It may even break up a church that's already weak and barely standing.

"I can't believe you volunteered to speak at this town hall meeting. Allowing yourself to be quoted in that article was enough by itself. Making a public appearance is gonna get your butt in hot water with the congregation especially since you refused to participate in the protest."

Robinson is not surprised by his wife's reaction. "I had a feeling you wouldn't take this too well. Look baby, I promise not to get deeply involved; there will be no name-calling and no finger-pointing. Simply put, we the black community, must take better care of ourselves. How hard can that be?"

"Randy, it's not that simple. Some people are not going to hear things the way you intend them to be heard. Someone's going to take your speech out of context and make a big deal out of nothing."

"Guess what, Weezy?" he quizzes.

"What, Randy?"

"You're the first one to do so."

Louise tries to remain calm, but that last comment pushes her over the edge. She yanks a chair from underneath the kitchen table and takes a seat. Sliding Randy's notes to the side, she reaches across the table grabbing hold of both his hands, pleading, "Can't you see I'm trying to protect you? This racial issue can get really deep. The mayor? He doesn't care about you. He's just trying save his own butt for the upcoming election—I can see right through him. Mayor Hurt wants to shift the blame for the social injustices back onto the Harlem Heights community."

Though the moment is not a pleasant one, Randy smiles at his wife. He always admired her will to protect him from harm. Memories of Louise standing beside him during times of trouble run through his mind. Like when she first introduced Randy to her parents. Louise's mother was totally against interracial relationships, and she made it known the moment he walked through the door. The memory is still fresh in his mind.

"Mom, this is Randy, my boyfriend—the one I've been telling you all about."

"Yes dear, you told me everything except this," replies the mother with disappointment.

"What, Mom?"

"Don't play dumb with me; you understand perfectly well what I'm talking about. Your boyfriend is colored, and that's not acceptable in this family. You two can be friends. Anything outside of that will not exist."

Louise was shocked by her mother's rejection. She has always been a respectable, caring woman. She gives to the poor, no matter the color of the recipient, and even has some good friends who are black. The daughter hadn't been totally sure how her mother would react, but never had she imagined this. "Is this how you really feel about us? Mom, you don't even know him yet. At least let him prove himself to be a bad guy before you judge him."

"Louise, no one said he's a bad guy. It's just that those people's values are different from ours," said her mother as if Randy wasn't even standing there. "They don't think like we do. He's probably a Muslim or some athlete who'll play professional ball and become rich someday like O.J. Simpson. What good would you be to him then?"

Randy could hold his silence no longer. "Ma'am, my parents worked hard to pay for my education—and, by the way, I'm Christian. Now you may be right about one thing: I do think differently from you. I think it's good to get to know people before you judge them."

"That's right, Mom—he's no different from us. He may not look the same, but he has all the qualities you told me a good man should have. I'm sorry that I brought him here; he's too good to be treated like this by you!" Louise grabbed her boyfriend's hand and stormed out the door. What Randy experienced with Louise's parents was similar to the treatment she would get from some of Randy's friends.

He was a young adult back then, just a few years beyond his teenage days—they both were. Now Randy is a mature man in his early thirties. He looks across the table at his wife, a white woman, and notices once again the beauty that first attracted him to her. They first met at a Bible study group held on campus. Immediately he was drawn to her physical beauty, but it was Louise's insight on scripture that captured Randy's attention. The tactic he used to approach Louise was to engage her with philosophical discussions about the Bible. In doing so, he soon discovered she was even more beautiful inside than she was on the outside. Randy's actions were a bit more obvious than Louise's, yet it was clear she enjoyed his attention. The interracial couple developed a connection ... a good vibe. Long talks and study sessions at the library led to a deeper relationship. Many times, they came close to having premarital sex, yet they managed to resist the temptation by deciding not to put themselves in a situation where they were alone talking intimately.

Suddenly, while daydreaming of the past, Randy is brought back to the present by Louise's voice. "You're not even paying attention to me."

"Baby, I'm thinking about you right now," he pleasantly replies.

That comment takes the fire out of Louise's attitude. "About what?"

"How we first met; our experience with your parents and my so-called friends. We've been through some trying times and now this happens."

Louise's anger has completely subsided. Randy continues with his thoughts. "You're right; this won't be as simple as I would like it to be. Some people are going to be upset with me. This may even split the congregation, but I believe this is necessary if we want to improve the community. I just don't like being the one who has to tell it. This is probably how the prophets in the Old Testament felt when they were sent to deliver a message from God. Just the fear of backlash is enough to make a person turn back and run."

Louise conveys her understanding. "It's kind of like reliving history, huh? I guess people from Abraham Lincoln to Martin Luther King went through the same thing. Rejection from your own people is probably the greatest pain in situations like this."

"Yes, baby, it is. This is something I don't look forward to. I just feel led by a higher calling to make this community a better place. If at least some people can embrace what I'm about to say, then a change can happen."

"Randy, even though I don't like the idea of you speaking, I'm at peace with your decision now. Go ahead and do it. Don't expect a miracle. No matter what, I'll be by your side. Let's just pray the people will be receptive to your message."

The couple comes together in prayer, spilling their hearts to Jesus Christ in return for the courage, peace of mind, and guidance they'll need in the coming days.

As they pray, angels from Heaven flood the kitchen, spreading their wings, reaching their hands toward Randy and Louise. Empyreal servants minister the courage, serenity, and guidance the mortals have requested.

As the people gather in city hall, a panel of participants sits center stage. A microphone and a nameplate is placed before each member—Frank Rizzo, the chief of police; Reverend Brown; Pastor Robinson; Belinda Harrington, the superintendent of schools; and Mayor Hurt. Tonight they will all have a chance to speak before the crowd that is much larger than usual.

Tracey Smith, the hostess for tonight's event, walks center stage to the podium. She's in her mid forties and has the demeanor of a librarian or perhaps a nun who works a part-time job outside the church. This evening is a special occasion, and the nervousness shows on her face.

The people in attendance make for a hostile crowd comprised of unemployed men, single mothers, and discouraged minorities with a bit of hope in their hearts. Along with the mortals are imps and larger, more evil demons, awaiting an opportunity to raise Hell tonight.

The timid hostess takes a deep breath, taps the microphone to ensure it's hot, and officially begins the event. "Good evening, we would like to welcome everyone to the town hall—"

A rude critic from the crowd cuts the hostess off. "It's about time you got started! And what's so good about this evening?" says a middle-aged man with a beer gut bulging from his T-shirt that's tucked in tight. The heckler's comment draws some laughter from the audience.

The mayor thinks to himself, *this is great. We haven't started yet and the people are acting up already.*

Maintaining her composure, Ms. Smith continues with a brief introduction of the panel members. "Gathered across the stage are individuals who have some insight on how to best resolve the issues in Harlem Heights. With no further ado, let's bypass the usual formalities and go straight to the panel for their opinions on how to improve the city."

The mayor is first to take the podium. Hurt speaks, clarifying that he is just a mediator who'll keep tonight's debate headed in the right direction. By no means does he agree or disagree with the ideas of the panel members. Then he hands the microphone to Frank Rizzo, chief of police.

The chief is not so diplomatic. "Ladies and gentlemen, I respect the people's right to protest. But let me tell you this: My men have been given strict orders to squash any violence on the streets. So you people better be careful. There's absolutely no reason for all the looting and destruction going on in the city." Rizzo pounds his fist on the podium as he makes one last statement, "No more foolishness, I say, no more!"

The mayor holds back the urge to choke the life out of Rizzo. How could he make such statements at a time like this?

The people react immediately. "Get rid of the bum! He's the reason for the police brutality in the streets!" is one of many similar comments being hurled from the audience. In no time, the people are standing on their feet booing and cursing the police chief.

The mayor attempts to calm the crowd but his efforts are useless. Again, Thomas Hurt wishes he could choke the stupidity from the chief's brain. Just when the mayor is about to give up and let the audience have its way, the people suddenly quiet down. The mayor turns to see Reverend Brown standing with his arm in the air like the Statue of Liberty. Head tilted slightly back with pride, eyes closed, he takes his time before saying a word. "My brothers and sisters, forgive the chief, for he knows not what he does—he's a cop." That last statement draws roaring laughter from the crowd. "My people, as you can see, this man has lost touch with the community. He doesn't understand your pain and the issues that concern you. His lack of knowledge has caused us much trouble. As much as I hate to say it, the chief has failed us, and it's our responsibility to ensure the next chief of police will be someone who represents *us*."

The audience jumps to its feet. The thunderous applause is deafening. Frank Rizzo sits in his chair, face turning red, humiliated by the not-so-subtle threats of Rev Brown to have him replaced.

The mayor, taking a look at the chief, no longer feels anger toward him; Hurt feels sorry for the old cop. However, what concerns the mayor most is the influence that Brown has on the people. If, by chance, the Reverend dares to turn on the mayor, Hurt's political career could be in jeopardy too.

In an attempt to take the pressure off the chief, the mayor cuts in. "Thank you, Rev Brown, for your words." Hurt looks to Ms. Smith to see who is next to speak. She's nowhere to be found, and the mayor suspects that her absence is intentional. Doesn't matter, the mayor continues on his own. "Now, ladies and gentlemen, we'll hear from Belinda Harrington, our superintendent of schools, regarding the standard of education in Harlem Heights." Maybe she'll make the people happy?

"We get a lot of questions asking why our students lag behind the other students throughout the state. If the truth be told, there's no reason that our city can't compete on the same level as other schools. We have all the resources needed to score higher on standardized testing. In my opinion, the low test scores are a result of a lack of interest in education by the people. I'm sorry, but it's true."

The mayor looks at the superintendent with disgust on his face. As much as he would like to be angry with her comments, he knows it's the truth. Now he has to endure the reaction from the crowd again.

"Get rid of her; she's no good! We need someone to replace her too," says a heckler from the audience.

Unlike the police chief, the superintendent has something to say about the comments. "This is the abuse we face every day in our schools. We deal with kids who bring their problems such as drugs and violence from home to the classroom."

The negative comments keep coming from the audience, but the superintendent stands firm in the face of criticism. "I intend to make it known how the parents take no interest in their kids' education. I don't care if you vote me out; I can find another job. How about your kids? Will they be able to find employment with their poor education? They don't speak proper English, they dress like thugs, and, worst of all, they believe the world owes them something."

If the superintendent was hoping to bring down the house, she's got her wish. Both applause and booing echoes throughout the building. The mayor agrees with the superintendent 100 percent. Chief Rizzo is too angry to care, and Rev Brown seems indifferent; he's just enjoying the show. Pastor Robinson just nods his head in approval, giving a nervous smile to Louise, who is sitting in the front row.

The mayor, feeling the pressure more than ever to somehow appease the crowd, announces Pastor Robinson's name to the rowdy audience. "Ladies and gentlemen, you've heard remarks from every panel member on the board except for this man here. Some of you may already be familiar with his beliefs, for he's the one who was interviewed for the article in Sunday's paper entitled, *The Untold Truth in Harlem Heights*." Thomas Hurt projects his voice like a late-night-show announcer, "Here's ... Pastor Randy Robinson." The mayor flashes a devious smile, obviously happy to place the burden of ridicule on someone else's shoulders other than his own.

Robinson slides his chair back and slowly stands up to make his way center stage. He feels nervous inside but manages to keep a lid on butterflies fluttering in his stomach.

The imps notice the power of the Holy Spirit within the pastor's soul. As the hellions attempt an onslaught of verbal harassment, a host of guardians suddenly appear with swords in hand, standing at the ready. The appearance of angels causes a hush to fall among the evil spirits. In turn, the humans in the audience become silent; all eyes are on the pastor.

"What I have to say tonight is no big secret. If you read the article printed in Sunday's paper, then you know what the problem is with Harlem Heights. As much as I hate to say it, the white man is not the

main problem in our community. Neither are drugs, nor the police."
The audience is hanging on every word Robinson says. "What we suffer
from is the failure to accept responsibility for our actions. The time
has now come for us to take charge of our children and communities.
No one else can fix the problems but us; and as we have seen, when
other people try to fix our problems, it doesn't work too well because
outsiders don't totally understand our issues. Their assistance is okay,
but we, as the black community, must be the main effort in making
things better."

So far the crowd has been receptive of the message. There's a few
boos and negative remarks coming from the audience but nothing to
the extent that the police chief and superintendent had to endure.

Pastor Robinson doesn't want to be negative, so he puts a positive spin
on his speech. "You may ask yourself, what can I do to make a change?
Let's start with our children. Tell our sons to pursue an education instead
of pushing dope. And tell our daughters that the greatest beauty is the
mind, not the physical body." The people are becoming receptive to his
message. There's a bit of applause in the audience. "As for role models,
entertainers and athletes shouldn't be the only ones that kids admire.
There's nothing shameful about working ordinary jobs and living a
simple life. Look at us. Most of us will never be big-ballers with bling, so
let's keep it real by setting realistic goals with our kids."

Mayor Hurt is surprised by the silence of the audience. The people
have dedicated their full attention to the speaker who's telling them
what they need to hear without being overly critical

"One last thing, people: We have to take back control of our
community. If you continue to tolerate drugs and violence in your
neighborhood, there will always be black-on-black crime, which far
exceeds the rate of police brutality in our communities. No other racial
group commits more acts of violence against blacks than us. See, it's
not so much the white man we should be worried about, but rather,
ourselves."

This is not what the enemy wants to hear. Getting bolder by the
second, one rogue spirit after another begins rising to the air. All have
drawn their swords.

"I believe the enemy is looking for a fight," says Solomon with a
tone of concern in his voice.

Lee reassures his comrade, "No worry, my brother, it's under control. We can get you a few more minutes, and then your man will have to bring his speech to a close. A way has been prepared for the Robinsons to escape this building if things get hectic."

"What about the mayor and rest of the panel members? Have you accounted for their safety as well?"

Lee is more than prepared for an attack. "We have that covered too. I refuse to allow these demons to wreck this city any further. Our warriors will keep the adversary at bay."

As soon as Randy concludes his speech, a fight erupts among a few in the audience causing the people to panic.

Robinson feels an urge to exit the stage immediately. Louise, sensing something bad is about to happen, leaves her seat to join Randy. "Baby, I think it's about time we got out of here," she says in desperation.

"Yeah, I agree. I don't think the crowd is feeling too good right about now."

Before Lee gives the signal, Siron, the scout, goes to help the couple get out of the building. Ushering them toward the back, he spreads his wings to block the sight of a young male aiming to throw a Molotov cocktail in their direction. A turn down a short, narrow hallway reveals a fire exit at the end of the hall. Siron makes haste to get the Robinsons through the door. Randy pushes the door lever but it won't budge. "This is strange. A fire exit shouldn't be blocked; it's supposed to be for emergencies."

With urgency, Louise tells Randy, "Honey, try again, it can't be locked!" Panic sets in as she sees a tall muscular figure headed in their direction.

Siron suspects something foul is behind the blocked door. Being careful, he attempts to take a look outside. For some reason, he's not comfortable with this idea, yet the scout must take the chance. Stepping into the wall just to sneak a peek outside, the scout eases to the outer surface of the wall. Before he can get a view of the situation, Siron is suddenly seized by the neck and held in a vice-like grip.

"Hey! We caught him peeking," says a devious warrior with joy. He holds Siron in a chokehold as the scout struggles like a fish on a hook. The dark spirit laughs wildly, showing the prize catch to his cohorts just as a school kid would display a personal treasure at show-and-tell.

"Look what we have here—one of Heaven's finest. You didn't think this was an easy way out, did you?"

"That loud-mouth preacher and his wife aren't getting away from us," threatens another one of Sheol's warrior.

Wrapping both hands around the villain's wrist, Siron continues to struggle to free himself. It's no use; the grasp is too strong to be broken. Still the captive makes one final attempt at freedom. Reaching for a dagger hidden within his belt, Siron continues kicking and squirming in effort to cover his actions. Quickly, he draws the weapon and stabs the blade in the demon's wrist. The effort sets him free. Resisting the urge to flee the scene, Siron rushes through the wall, back into the building to see how the Robinsons are faring. Hot on his tail are the hellions who ambushed him just moments before. Up to the ceiling, through the building rafters, they chase the scout angel.

While Siron evades the warriors, the Robinsons have their hands full with trouble of their own. As Randy struggles to free the door, Louise screams in horror as she sees the mysterious male figure approaching closer. "Randy, someone is coming, and he doesn't look friendly! You have to do something before he hurts us!"

"Just hold on … I can get the door open if it would only—"

Louise is screaming. What she sees is a tall Hispanic male with a weapon in hand. As the gunman draws closer, Randy turns around to see what his wife is dreading. It's the first time Robinson has ever looked down the open end of a gun barrel. The pastor makes a conscious effort to catch his breath and compose himself. Instinctively, he steps in front of Louise to shield her from harm. She holds him around the waist squeezing tight. Robinson points a defiant finger at the man and demands, "What do you want with us?"

The stranger remains silent, looking around as if he's more concerned about someone else seeing him. Before breaking his silence, he tucks away the gun to walk even closer. "If you want to live, follow me."

Louise utters a sigh of relief. "Oh, thank you, God."

Randy is taken by surprise. He wants to know what's going on. "Where do you plan on taking us?"

"There's no time to talk right now. I can get y'all to safety, but you have to follow me. Now c'mon before someone else sees us."

"Why don't we just go out this door?"

Louise is frustrated with Randy's stubbornness to go out the blocked door. "You tried to open it a million times already; it's still locked. Let's follow him and get out of here before it's too late."

Convinced by his wife, Randy agrees. "Okay, lead the way."

The stranger wastes no time. He takes them back through the hallway from which they came, but stops halfway down. He pulls back a curtain to reveal a door that only those familiar with city hall would notice. Behind the closed door is a staircase that leads to a fire escape on the side of the building. Descending the fire escape, Robinson is surprised to see his van is parked close by. "Great," he says, "this is where we parked. Do you need a ride?"

"Yeah, we can talk while you drive," replies the stranger with a Spanish accent.

As the Robinson and the stranger drive out of the parking lot, screams of terror fill the air as people rush out of the building. Inside the auditorium, Lee has given the signal to cut the lights, bring the stage curtain down on the crowd, and activate the fire alarms. This is the reason for all the panicking.

The gang members with Molotovs in hand hold their fire in fear of getting stuck inside.

The mayor and his assistant also escape the auditorium. Safe inside their vehicle, the mayor relaxes, letting out a loud sigh. "Whew, I'm glad that's over. The people in Harlem Heights are crazy."

"You can say that again," replies Dudley.

The mayor takes a cautious look to his left and right to ensure no one from the media is around to hear his comments. "Next time we bring more security to deal with these savages. I don't know what else it takes to reach these people—unless maybe a whip and a gun."

Getting comfortable, Hurt loosens his tie while slouching in his seat. Forever thinking of political schemes, he replays the night's event in his mind. What Robinson said really struck home with him. Finally someone else had the guts to say the truth, and, of all people, it was somebody who's black.

Talking to his assistant, Mayor Hurt makes more demands. "Dudley, we have to find out who that guy is. He gave a wonderful speech. I couldn't have said it better myself. What's his name again?"

"Randy Robinson, sir."

"Yeah, that's it, Robinson. There's so many churches in the 'hood, it's hard to keep up with all the religious homies," says the sarcastic mayor.

Dudley chuckles over the mayor's attempt to use slang. "Sir, are you thinking what I'm thinking?"

"And what's that, Dudley?"

"Robinson can be the ally we need to undermine the efforts of Brown. We can put the blame back on the Harlem Heights community, taking most of the heat—if not all—off the police department and local government," reveals Dudley.

"Splendid idea. We can kill two birds with one stone. First, uncover the shortcomings of the Harlem Heights community and present them as self-inflicted wounds. Second, we can get rid of Brown once and for all. He's been a thorn in my side for the longest time."

Dudley's mind is already at work on how to network with Robinson. "Any suggestion on how we should approach Pastor Robinson, sir?"

"He seems to be a sincere guy, so, whatever you do, take precaution not to offend him. Find out what his church needs are. Do they need financial assistance? Or perhaps they desire some political spotlight? We have to get him to eat from our hands so that we can put a halt to this protest."

"I'm right on it, sir."

25

Secrets Revealed

Randy and Louise ride up front; the stranger sits in the backseat. Everyone is quiet, so Randy breaks the silence with simple talk. "I'm headed to the Interstate. We can drive a while and do a lot of talking."

From above, the minivan can be seen driving about the streets headed toward the city limits. There it enters the freeway to coast along for miles before turning back to the heart of the beast, Harlem Heights.

Feeling a bit relaxed, Robinson starts asking questions. "So what's this all about?"

"Whether you know it or not, there's a war on the streets. The Reds and the Pharaohs are involved in this war. It's not only the gangs; the police department and the mayor have their hands in the mix too."

Louise wants to get to the point. "Well, what does that have to do with us? My husband speaks at a rally, and next thing we know our lives are threatened."

"That's not true," snaps the stranger.

"Then why are you carrying a gun?"

He can't answer Louise's question. "Like I said before, there's a war going on. Many people are involved, and that includes you two."

Randy jumps in, "How did we get involved with this war?"

"Ever since you came to the city, things haven't been going right. First, you start a ministry that takes our customers off the streets. Next, Mo' loses his puppet to your church. Then we turn around and your ideas are appearing in the newspaper and you're making speeches about self empowerment," explains the stranger.

Randy shrugs his shoulders, chuckling, "What's wrong with that? We don't personally interfere with your business."

"In a way you do. You may not know it, but people are starting to respond to your message. That's bad for business. The people are starting to believe they don't need drugs. There's pressure on the kids now to turn away from the hustler's life—all because of your outreach ministries."

Robinson is still not content with the man's answers. "So what does that have to do with you being here now?"

Realizing it's time he stopped delaying matters, Mingo speaks his mind. "I know who killed Kenny."

Louise flips around in her seat surprised to hear such news. She and Randy have an idea of who did the shooting.

"We know it wasn't the cops like everyone thinks it is," concludes Randy as he recalls his conversation with Perez.

"Okay, you're on to it but do you have a name?"

"No, we don't have a name yet."

"JT. Ask your connections about a man named JT. And, while you're at it, ask about a Willie Mo'. The more you find out about those two, the more you'll learn about this city."

All talking ceases as everyone retreats to the thoughts of their own minds. Randy breaks the silence. "Anything else we need to know?"

"Yeah, there is. There's two dirty cops that rule the streets with Mo' and JT. They're in every major drug deal that takes place in the city. If you get to them, you can reach anybody."

"Can you give us names?"

"Detectives Hughes and Diggs. They know all about Mo' and the mayor's secret life."

Louise is puzzled. "What secret life are you talking about?"

"As Christians, you should know about the dark side of life. I don't mess with that voodoo stuff, so don't ask me. The only thing I know for sure is Harlem Heights is cursed. I've seen preachers come into city with the hope of cleaning up the place. Most are run out of town with their tails between their legs. The others are just swallowed up by the city."

"So that's what happened to Rev Brown," Randy surmises.

"This city brings out the dirt from your soul. Whatever power these people are messing with is real. Since ya'll are in the spiritual business, I figure you two should be the ones to know about the secret life."

The Robinsons are in awe. They don't know what to say. Randy's mind immediately goes to the Bible, the tenth chapter of II Corinthian, verses three and four: "For though we live in the world, we do not wage war as the world does. The weapons we fight with are not the weapons of the world. On the contrary, they have divine power to demolish strongholds."

If the Robinsons are looking to make a difference, they will have to take down strongholds. This task will be of great difficulty if they want to defeat Fratricide and Molder, who are quite capable of defending their own interests.

Mingo has completed his mission and is ready to leave the Robinsons. "This is good, I can get out here."

Randy is confused. "We're in the middle of nowhere; the city is miles back the other way."

The stranger takes a look through the back window of minivan just for a confirmation. "That's okay; I'll get home. My boys have been following you since we left city hall."

The pastor takes a peek in the rearview mirror. It's dark outside; all he can see are a few headlights. If one of those cars was following him, he never knew it.

As directed, Randy pulls over and notices a vehicle behind him doing the same thing. Before getting out, the Hispanic male has one more thing to say. "If you want to know more about the secret society in the city, just ask that old man with the bald head who's in your group. We call him Mr. Levy. Who knows what you call him."

With that last statement, the stranger exits the minivan. The pastor asks one more question as the man is trying to leave. "By the way, what's your name?"

"I'm just a concerned citizen ... that's all you need to know." He slides the van door shut, heading back to his own vehicle.

"Wow, that's weird. I wonder why he went through all that effort just to say that baffling stuff. Things are getting mysterious around here," comments Louise.

"Baby, I think he's trying to tell us something without exactly saying it. Whatever it is, the mayor, the gangs, and the police department are involved. We just have to figure it all out somehow."

"Randy, where do we start with all of this?"

"I'm thinking we need to ask Perez about those two detectives at the police station."

Louise jumps in with her idea. "We need to ask Stan what he's involved in too—or should we say Mr. Levy?"

"Yep, Perez and Stan will be a good start. With prayer, the good Lord will guide us on to other leads."

"Honey, what we're about to do is scaring me. I hope we'll be able to handle this battle."

Randy grabs his wife's hand. "Remember baby, this battle is not ours; it's the Lord's."

The minivan takes the next exit heading for home. Above the vehicle, flying under the cover of the night, is Siron and a few guardians. Seeing that the mission has been completed, the scout redirects his course to inform Solomon and Lee that Mingo has made contact with the Robinsons.

Standing chest to chest, JT and Mo' are huffing and puffing in each other's face. "How can you fail to snuff two weak Christians?" shrieks Mo'.

"Mo', it ain't as easy as you think it is, man. The place was crowded and dark. People started runnin' and bumpin' us from all around. Some of the guys dropped their bottles and started a fire right where they stood. We almost burned ourselves up. When I finally got free, that preacher was gone."

"You couldn't find 'im?"

"Naw, man, there were hundreds of people in that place. I couldn't tell one person from another. Besides, you failed to keep your side of the deal."

How dare he accuse me of failure. Mo thinks to himself. The anger inside Willie Mo' swells like a giant tidal wave ready to pound the shore. "I failed?" he yells out loud.

Not wanting to make the situation any worse, JT gives a cautious response. "Look, man, I don't know what it's gonna take to get rid of that pastor. I want 'im bad, but somethin' keeps gettin' in the way."

Willie Mo' knows the force that hinders his effort to do away with Robinson, yet his pride and anger won't let him admit it.

JT is more humble. "It's all right, we'll get 'im next time."

Mo' turns around. He is so angry he's crossed-eyed. "Forget next time, I want him right now!"

What else can JT do to calm the top Pharaoh who's determine to see Robinson fall? Having no idea of what to do, Jermaine takes a seat to think for a moment.

The gang leader sees JT's action as a gesture of disrespect. Again Willie is up in JT's face with two clenched fists gripping his partner's shirt.

"Hey man, what's your problem?" exclaims JT. "What did I do to you?"

Mo' says nothing.

What JT sees in Willie Mo's eyes is mystifying. The almond-shape eyes suddenly become slimmer … they look like serpent's eyes. Locked in a trance, Mo' flicks his tongue in a serpentine gesture, breathing rancid breath in JT's face. The two thugs resort to pushing and shoving each other—sounds like furniture is being moved around. The loud noise attracts the attention of the younger gang members who creep as quietly as possible toward the office trying to sneak a peek through the windows.

Finally, Jermaine can stand it no longer. "Look, man, I'm tryin' to be patient with you. If you keep on actin' like this, we gonna fight. What in the Hell has gotten into you?"

The question makes Willie Mo' laugh. It starts as a light chuckle, and then changes to a gut-wrenching cackle. His behavior becomes even more bizarre. Laughing while holding his groin with both hands, Mo' resembles a child fighting the urge to pee in his pants.

JT is bewildered by the display of behavior. "Calm down, man."

"Don't tell me what to do," orders Wrath, the demon within Willie Mo'. *"I give the orders around here; you are to listen and obey me, got it?"* The spirit uses Mo's eyes to look about the room, then yells, through

Mo', to the spectators watching the show, *"And what are you all looking at? You want some of this?"*

The gang members standing by answer with fear, "Naw, not us," says the bravest of them.

"Go mind your business then!"

Everyone clears the area except for JT. He and Mo' have some unfinished business to discuss.

Willie Mo' approaches his long-time friend slowly; his face bears a grin.

JT doesn't know what to expect, so he slowly reaches behind his back for the pistol he keeps tucked away in his pants.

The demon within Mo' attempts to ease JT's fears. *"Relax, I just want to talk. We still have work to do. It's not you that angers me, but rather those meddling saints."*

"Then why are you goin' off on me like that?" replies JT.

"It's the saints. They haven't learned their lesson by now, and it's obvious they never will. This is why I need you. I can trust no one other than you to do this task for me the right way."

Jermaine Trotter stares in Willie Mo's face still mystified by his friend's eyes. He gives Willie a reluctant reply, "Yeah, I can do it for you." Uncomfortable, JT attempts to walk away, yet the hand on his shoulder quickly tightens, forcing him to stay.

"Don't walk away from me when I'm talking to you," demands Molder. *"You have yet to hear my instructions. The gun behind your back is there for a reason."*

Jermaine's face reflects surprise like a child caught in a mischievous act. He told no one about the weapon, and was careful not to indicate his possession of it too. How could Mo' have known?

"That's all right, my friend, you meant no harm," continues Molder. *"What you have is there for a purpose."*

"I wasn't going to shoot you, man. I just had it on me just in case …"

Relishing the game, Molder goes into his psychology bag to play with Trotter's mind. *"Why are you acting so guilty? Is there something I should know?"*

JT is clearly nervous. "No, I'm not going to shoot you—that's not what I meant."

Having the upper hand, Molder exploits the situation. *"Hush, my friend, I know you would never hurt me, right?"*

JT shakes his head up and down like a sorry little boy.

"As I was saying, you were not going to use that gun on me, but for me."

"Yeah, I get it. I get it," says JT laughing, breathing heavily. He is relieved to know Mo' didn't take his actions the wrong way. "Whatcha want me to do?"

"Finally, we start to see eye to eye," says Molder through Mo's mouth. *"This is what I want from you: Kill Robinson for me. You, personally, are to kill the pastor with that gun of yours ... understand?"*

"Yeah, man, I do."

"Good. And when you finish that, you will kill old man Levy too. For some reason, Levy has forgotten who he works for. Take care of them all."

JT remains in place, a bit shaken, not moving. Mo' is amused and makes a comment to his longtime friend. *"Oh, JT, you flatter me. Are you waiting for permission to leave?"*

JT nods his head yes.

"By all means, go."

JT is glad to be out of Willie Mo's freaky presence. Whatever has gotten into the Pharaoh King has really shaken up his friend.

On the way out, Jermaine grabs a bottle of liquor from the bar. He takes a big swallow before he even hits the door.

Willie Mo' stands in his office staring at the wall while Molder and Wrath watch the mortal make his way from the club to the car where he continues to take more swigs from the bottle.

The spirits communicate with one another. "It's time to get rid of him before he becomes a liability," says Molder.

Wrath replies, "Just a little bit longer and we will do so. When he completes the mission, our friends will finish him off."

Both demons smile when they see Insanity, Alcoholism, and Murder sitting in the car with JT.

The underlings will ensure the mortal follows through with his orders. Eventually, the spirits will take JT's life into their own hands to do as they please. Until that time comes, the evil spirits stab at the man's heart and mind and suck away at his soul.

26

Little Bit the Great

Little Bit mumbles to himself as he gets closer to Fratricide's domain. He is eager to take on more responsibility; a rare chance at a promotion is his only desire. Now the opportunity has made itself available, but this is not the ideal situation. *Why must I be the one to go and tell it to Fratricide?* he thinks to himself. Little Bit is a low-ranking spirit. The foul imp knows as well as anyone that bad news doesn't go well with any overlord. This should be the job of Herod the Great, as he likes to call himself—the chief baal in charge of the police department. Instead, the aspiring Little Bit gets the honor of bearing bad news to the big one.

The feeble one approaches the guards at Fratricide's lair trying his best to sound confident as he demands entry. "It is I, Little Bit. I want to speak with the master about an urgent issue."

"You will tell us the manner of this news or else," demands the warrior with a sword pointed at the tiny one's neck.

Making another attempt to appear tough and fearless, the imp takes a long hard gulp. "It is important that I see the master now, and you will not—"

The sword, this time pressing deeper into his lumpy throat, causes the small one to swallow the last word. Now his voice changes to a more sorrowful tone. "I have bad news to tell. There are agents at the police department investigating the mortals that work for us. Our hold on the law is at stake."

With that news, the sword is withdrawn. Little Bit will be allowed to tell Fratricide this news himself. Had it been a good report, the imp would never have made it past the guards.

Wishing he never came, Little Bit creeps slowly toward Fratricide, instinctively bowing as he introduces himself. Realizing how ridiculous his name sounds, the small one tries to think of something grander. *Maybe "Little Bit the Great" or "Little Bit the Horrible" would sound better?* he wonders. But, nothing could make a gremlin with such a ridiculous name sound like a fierce spirit, especially in the presence of the overlord who is bigger than he ever imagined.

At first, Fratricide appears not the least bit interested in what this underling has to say. He doesn't even bother to look into Little Bit's face, but the behemoth's lack of concern suddenly takes a different course. From experience, he's learned to be suspicious of bad news reported by any lowly spirit. "What business do you have here?" roars the overlord who looks like an elephant in Little Bit's eyes.

Feeling petrified, the imp quickly spills the news. "Master, there are reports of an investigation going on at the police department. Nothing has been discovered and things are still operating as usual." Without wasting a second, the small one turns away to leave. As he heads for the exit, his imp ears twitch as he anticipates being called back.

"Hold it," shouts the big one. The guards standing before the entrance cross their swords to ensure the messenger doesn't attempt an escape. "Come back. Tell me again what happened."

Little Bit is scared … frustrated at having to repeat himself. He wants to scream back, *didn't you hear me the first time?* But fear, more so than wisdom, dictates he had best be patient.

"Master," he explains quietly, "federal agents are at the police department asking questions."

"What?" A gushing wind from the big one's gut nearly blows the imp off his feet. Peeking from one eyeball, Little Bit looks down to see if his feet are still planted on the ground. More than just his feet are touching the ground. The little one finds himself crouching, head between his knees. The guards snicker. Even Fratricide cracks a smile, amused by the gremlin's silly display of fear.

"FBI agents are investigating two detectives for corruption." Oops, the imp didn't mean to tell that much.

"And what are you going to do about it?" demands the big one.

"Herod the Great will fix it, master."

"How?"

"I don't know, but he will," says Little Bit, curling smaller into a ball on the ground. At this point, he'll say anything to be out of the big one's presence. Waiting to be dismissed, the tiny one remains curled in a fetal position hoping for an order to flee. His wait seems to take an eternity.

Taking his sword from its sheath, Fratricide makes his favorite move. He raises the runt's head by tapping underneath his chin with the sword's tip. Little Bit slowly rises to his feet. The sword now pats the runt on the side of his buttocks prompting the elf to face sideways. Sizing him up, the mammoth seems to be up to something. Like a batter at home plate, the big one makes a check swing. The little rascal can already see it coming. He narrows his eyes and tightens his rump. Squeezing his knobby knees together as if it would ease the pain, the little one braces for the blow … the sword whistle as it cuts through the air.

"*Yyeeooww!*" yells Little Bit as he runs in circles holding his hot butt with both hands. He prances as if his hide is on fire.

The guards laugh so hard they drop their swords. Fratricide leans back holding his big belly, howling with glee as waves of blubber shudder along the surface of his stomach. Even Informer gets a kick out of seeing someone else, besides himself, being tortured.

Still high stepping like a parade horse, Little Bit continues to cool his burning rump. Embarrassed, he suddenly gathers himself and tries to stand tall and noble. There's no redeeming himself though. The jester has done a superb job of entertaining the king and the royal subjects. Disappointed and wanting to disappear from the scene as soon as possible, the tiny one makes his way to the exit only to be stopped again.

"Did I dismiss you?" says Fratricide with laughter still ringing in his voice.

"No, Master".

"You pass this message along to Herod—"

Little Bit accidentally interrupts the ruler. "He demands we call him Herod the Great."

Seeming not to take offense, the overlord replies, "Oh, he does, hmm?"

Little Bit takes a long hard swallow as he realizes he has just made a grand mistake in correcting Fratricide.

"Well, you pass this message along to Herod the *Imbecile*. If he doesn't fix the mess at the police department, I will have his head. I will also have yours. Go tell him that."

No one has to tell Little Bit twice to get out of sight. He turns his back to hurry away. And just as he takes flight, a loud smack heats the imp's rump again, blasting him like a rocket ship from the big one's lair. He goes quite a distance before gaining control of his flight. Still on fire, he screams like a baby all the way back to the precinct.

A servant reports to inform Herod the Great. "My Lord, Little Bit brings word from the overseer."

The jail keeper is eager to hear the news. "Send him in."

The imp enters looking distraught. Trying to seem concerned, Herod talks softly, wanting to know every detail of his visit with Fratricide. "How goes it, my loyal one?"

"It was terrible ... so terrible. He says that your head will roll if you don't fix the mess around here. This kingdom will be taken from you and given to someone more competent if you fail."

Little Bit notices the effect the bad news has on his master. Wanting to see Herod worried, the underling tells more than he has been instructed to do. After enduring the embarrassment and pain of dealing with Fratricide, the imp feels justified in handling Herod this way. With his lying tongue, Little Bit claims, "I have special orders to be by your side to ensure you do a good job. Then, when beckoned, I will report the status of our progress to Fratricide. From here on out, I will have no other job but to stay by your side, guiding you through this circumstance."

Herod is skeptical of the imp. He doesn't know what to believe, yet Fratricide can be unpredictable at times. If that's all the behemoth requested, then Herod figures he can tolerate Little Bit hanging around until things change for the better. It shouldn't take long.

"Okay then, you will remain here. But you will not report a thing without my consent. Is that clear?"

The imp bows graciously, "Yes, my Lord." *Finally, I'm on my way to the top*, Little Bit thinks to himself.

27

Planning a Change

Randy has a great idea that requires the expertise of a reporter. Knowing no one else to depend upon, he calls on Angela for assistance. Ms. Walker is on duty at the Harlem Heights Times when her cell phone rings. "Hey, Angela, it's me, Pastor Robinson, how's it going?"

"Hi, I was just thinking about you. Wondering if you would be interested in doing another interview for the paper?"

"You must be reading my mind."

The reporter laughs, "How so?"

"Considering the results we got from the last interview," figures Randy, "odds are the next one would do just as well."

"Let me guess again. You want to discuss some pending issues at the police department, right?"

"You got it, Angela. It's time for our law officials and the Harlem Heights community to work together. Besides, Chief Rizzo could use a bit of love after the criticism he suffered at the town hall meeting."

"Let's meet in a few days, I'll need some time to plan questions."

Robinson agrees. "Me, too; I have some notes to organize."

The two hang up their phones, setting off to do their respective tasks. Randy goes to the basement to view the map of Harlem Heights. He has pinned colored tacks in certain areas of the map where crime is the highest. Most of these crimes are committed by minorities who victimize other minorities. There has to be a way to stop it.

As the pastor stares at the map, he's surprised to hear his wife's voice in the room. "What's the point of sharing your views in an article about the police department? What's that going to solve?"

"Oh, baby, I didn't hear you come downstairs. What I have in mind is breaking the curse that hinders this city."

"How do you plan on doing that, Mr. Man?"

"Simple. We get the people in the community and the police department to apologize and forgive one another for their past sins. When that's accomplished, we'll move on to the government. Forgiveness will break the curse."

Mrs. Robinson still doesn't get it. How does her husband plan on persuading thousands of grown, prideful adults to apologize and forgive each other—especially if they have no clue that they've been doing anything wrong?

"Who in their right minds would want to participate in what you're doing?" asks Louise.

"I really don't know how it's going to be done. I hope to get a few people together to discuss the idea of making the neighborhood better. The rest, I'll leave in the hands of the Lord."

News about the town hall meeting spreads like wildfire on dry grass. Pastor Robinson's speech, along with the brief riot, sparked a burning interest among the churches. The congregations, both black and white, are now eager to help improve social conditions in Harlem Heights.

An older priest talks with a young deacon over coffee. They discuss, in theory, the benefits of working with others outside their denomination. "I heard about this Pastor Robinson. I don't know much about him, but he seems to be genuine," says the elder.

The deacon replies with skepticism. "They all seem that way at first, until they get what they want."

The priest takes the comment for granted. "Yeah, yeah, that is true for some—and I know precisely who you are talking about—yet this guy is definitely different. I can't exactly put my finger on it though."

"What makes you so sure of this man whom you barely even know?" inquires the younger one.

"For starters, I heard him speak at the town hall meeting. He's eloquent ..."

The deacon slips in another sly remark. "They all are eloquent and charismatic. It comes natural to them ... like basketball."

The priest is caught off guard by the comment which he finds to be disturbing. "See, that's the attitude that keeps the church divided. Was that comment necessary?"

"Don't take it out of context. I'm just making a comparison to emphasize my point of view."

Still patient with the young man, the elder sighs while gathering his thoughts. "You know what? Whether it was intended or not, that statement had racial overtones. I can see someone other than us taking offense to what you just said."

The deacon has an explanation for everything. "It was nothing big, just a simple way of explaining my point of view."

"To you, yes, it was a simple comparison. To others it may be more than just that. Your attitude is a reflection of our religious institutions, which means we have yet to put aside our cultural and denominational differences to see one another as brothers and sisters in Christ."

The young clergyman is surprised by the elder's passion on the subject. This has never been an issue before in the past. "Wait a minute," he exclaims. "Where are you coming from with all this? I can recall times when similar comments came from your mouth. Besides that, I'm not the only one who feels this way. We all know those people are emotional—heathens who love to hoot and holler like their ancestors who stalked the jungle before we civilized them." The young deacon lets his tongue fly as his feelings get heated. "Now you want to make amends? Take a look at the world, they will never change. If they can't help their own people, what makes you think we can do them any good? This is not a religious issue. What the Harlem Heights community is lacking is commitment and love for themselves."

"Stop, that's enough! Your attitude is sickening. How can you love God whom you never see and not love your black brother? I don't understand it." The priest is repulsed by the deacon's attitude. "I see why we don't interact with the other denominations. It's even clearer why we can't even tolerate ourselves. There's no love in our hearts, let alone in the church," the elder admits.

The priest's eyes reflect sorrow as he lectures his associate to reconsider his wayward thinking. Resting a gentle hand on the young man's shoulder, the wiser and older one softens his tone to counsel the deacon. "I'm proud of you."

"What for? I just said things that shouldn't come from the mouth of one who is training for the ministry," the younger one admits.

"For that reason exactly. I consider it a blessing that your shortcomings were revealed before your very own eyes. You know, some of us have gone our entire lives deceived in thinking we have no flaws … or that some faults are better than others. But you're blessed because you identified an issue that is dear to your heart. Now all we have to do is deal with it."

"Wouldn't it be easier if you found someone better?" the deacon suggests.

"No, not in this case. We all have baggage. At least we know what you carry. What about those who always seem perfect? I would rather be in your position knowing my weakness than to be considered flawless and then one day slip from an esteemed position."

The young deacon is not thrilled to know his personal feelings have been exposed. "So what's your plan?"

"Do you remember in the New Testament, the book of Matthew, when Peter goes to Jesus and asks, 'Lord how often shall my brother sin against me, and I forgive him? Up to seven times?' And in the following verse Jesus replies, 'I do not say to you, up to seven times, but up to seventy times seven.'"

The junior one is familiar with the scriptures quoted by the priest. "Yeah, I've read those verses many times—chapter eighteen, verses twenty one and twenty two."

"It takes a lot of love to care for our brothers. Do you think you have forgiven them seventy times seven? I know I haven't."

"No, I haven't at all," replies the young one.

"Another question: have you considered what we have done to them?"

"What do you mean, slavery?"

"Not only that. We came to them preaching a gospel of peace and love. Some of our people demonstrated that perfectly; others of us didn't. Our government made promises to them that were broken because the agreements were not in writing. We opened the doorway for colonialism to come in, stripping the people of their right to choose their own religion and style of government. We took away their history.

I can trace my family roots back to Europe; can they trace their roots to Africa?"

The deacon seems to be getting the point. He gives his undivided attention to the priest as the elder continues.

"It's been a little over forty years since the civil rights movement. Think about it, after hundreds of years of slavery, do you expect those people to be like us? I'm not saying they don't have the same opportunities to succeed, but they're competing against people with subtle attitudes like ours. Moreover, they still bear the psychological scars of the past. I don't totally understand, yet it's a factor in the way some of them may think."

The young man is suddenly overwhelmed with shame. "You're right, please forgive me. I have sinned."

The elder is touched, "Thank you."

"Why are you thanking me?" questions the puzzled deacon. "What did I do for you?"

"You just opened my eyes."

"How?"

The senior one explains, "You've demonstrated to me how we can make things better for Harlem Heights. Just because we look and act different doesn't mean we're not the same."

"Well, that's a mindset that will take much effort to change. I'm not the only one who thinks like that," says the deacon feeling a bit better. "And what about those black congregations who want nothing to do with whites? Are they going to change because we did?"

"Son, I don't know. At least we can try by reaching out first. Correction—we won't be the ones reaching out first. That Pastor Robinson I mentioned before—he's the first who has reached out. You should have been there. Robinson called on his own people to wake up and take responsibility for their own actions. He made no excuses for the Harlem Heights community's failures. The man laid it straight."

"He didn't point fingers at the white man at all?" the younger one quizzes.

"Not at all. You can appreciate him for his honesty. He referred to the issues within his community as self-inflicted wounds, and then he offered solutions."

The deacon is still in doubt. "Is he really willing to face the backlash from his own people for the comments he made?"

"He's proven that already. After listening to Robinson, I realize we need to bridge the gap that separates our congregation from others. He's organizing his people to begin working with others. When that happens, I want our church to be ready to do its part too."

The discussion between the elder clergyman and young deacon is a conversation that replays itself all throughout the city and surrounding areas. The Protestants and Catholics began to look inward; the Baptist and Pentecostals embrace one another too.

Some churches refrain. Nothing negative is said. The saints just take the matter to prayer in hopes of seeing a change of heart regarding those congregations.

28

The March Begins

The Light House of Hope is finally getting its wish to participate in the protest. Thanks to the outcome of the town hall meeting, the church leaders have come together in an attempt to guide the protest in a positive direction. Their goal in bringing their congregations together is to mend differences between the people and local government.

Rather than for personal interests, Angela and Perez attend the rally for job-related reasons. The policeman is on bike patrol monitoring the marching route to ensure crowd safety. The reporter is there, along with the other big-time media personnel, to capture the events. Her one advantage is full access to Randy Robinson whose popularity has grown considerably since his speech at the town hall meeting.

The reporter makes a sarcastic inquiry about Perez's uniform. "What's up with the bicycle and biker shorts?"

"Squad car is too big for the mission. I gotta be close enough to monitor the crowd for suspicious activities."

Laughing to herself, she asks, "What does that mean: suspicious activity?"

"Just like it sounds; anything unusual," says the vigilant policeman who looks like a boy-cop in his biker's uniform. "You never know who may show up at one of these events."

The reporter isn't the least bit concerned. "Nothing bad will happen. Besides, who you gonna scare with that outfit?"

Sergeant Perez has no comeback for Angela's wisecracks. Being the ever-mindful officer, he simply replies, "You can never be too cautious during times like these. The enemy is always up to something."

The ambitious reporter, is more focused on the physical realm. What she sees today is an opportunity to advance her career. What she doesn't know is that there are dangers lurking about, waiting for the right time to make a move.

The radio on Perez's hip chirps, signaling a call from higher. He answers, "Sergeant Perez, over." Listening intently, he acknowledges his orders then fastens the radio to his waist band. Turning to Angela, he gives her a passionate look. "Hey, sweetie, I'll see you later."

"Gotta go now? Well, give me a call later," she says. "Bye." The reporter watches the super-cop cycle away in the direction of the gathering church leaders.

Perez scans the area as he pedals along the marching route; the streets appear to be calm. The only action so far are children running around holding helium balloons on strings as they giggle at one another's finger-painted faces. Hotdog and drink vendors are setting up shop for the public's convenience. It's a great day for a march—and even a barbecue.

Hell's warriors observe the activities from the city hall building. Seething with anger, they watch the saints attempt to unite the body of Christ. The march is an insult; a slap in the face and even more irritating is the sight of Randy Robinson. "There he is now," one warrior observes, "the troublesome pastor who hasn't learned to mind his own business yet."

Drooling from the thought of inflicting harm upon the saints, another warrior replies, "Yes, these dirtbag humans are in for a surprise. I can't wait to stomp these two-legged maggots back into the mud from whence they crawled."

As the demons fantasize about wreaking chaos, a messenger appears. "It's starting now, master. Shall we summon the forces to action?"

"No, we will wait a while," says the first warrior. "The big one wants these fools to build momentum and think all is well. When they are confident, we'll strike. Besides, I know the sons of Heaven are slithering somewhere among those Christian vermin."

Just as hellions suggested, Solomon and Lee have stationed themselves in the public library, which is located near city hall. Other Empyrean forces remain hidden between the rows of bookshelves that provide excellent cover. This is not the only hiding place. The street gutters and garbage dumpsters are filled with angels too. They stand on guard ready to confront any attacks the enemy may bring their way.

"I know Fratricide and Molder's warriors are somewhere on the prowl," says Solomon. "Surely they won't let us march freely about the city proclaiming the gospel. It's just a matter of knowing when the attack is going to occur."

Lee makes his own prediction. "If I were the enemy, I would strike at the leadership. The best time is when the leaders separate from the people, making for an easier target."

"Yes, that's most logical," agrees Solomon. "There's one more thing that concerns me though. Is the enemy willing to make one of these ministers a martyr? Such a blow could possibly drive the people into the arms of Christ."

Before the people begin the march, silence falls upon the crowd, and they all bow their heads in prayer. With a megaphone in hand, a Lutheran minister begins. Being a wise clergyman, he offers praise to the Lord for making the special event possible. He continues by asking the Lord for protection, knowing unseen danger could be lurking about. As the prayer ends, a song breaks out among the people, and the march begins.

On cue, quite a few imps deploy alongside the mortals with the intent to stir up trouble. "Their savior cannot save them from the hand of Fratricide," says one devil as he rides the back of his mortal host. "You see this one here? He only came to see the show. He's no saint; I can prove it, just watch." The imp stands upon his human's head with talon feet dug deep into the man's mind. Pointing at a vendor, the mortal instinctively departs from the crowd to buy a hotdog.

Feeling cocky, the imp proudly claims, "No one can stop me. I have a legal right to this man here, he's mine." The devious spirit draws the attention of the unseen angels, but nothing is done to shut his mouth. The rascal is correct in stating he has a legal right to the man. "I told you he's mine, look at him. See how he devours the filth I spill upon his soul. Notice his lack of devotion for their Savior. He's here to see this movement fail."

As the imp pours on the accusations, the bound mortal makes true of the claims. While the people sing, taking delight in the unity of Christ, the man nudges another to make comments. "To tell the truth, I expected more than this. What's a march going to do for the community?"

His buddy replies, "We'll see. Perhaps they'll unveil a plan to bring more jobs to the city."

"I don't care how much god you put into a speech, it's not gonna change these people. Jesus ain't gonna reach down from the sky and do that for anybody," says the pessimist with the gremlin on his back.

The fun is contagious. Other little sniveling monsters join the festivities; the rascals jump for joy bouncing from one human to another.

The demons' contact with the mortals has an effect on the humans' souls, which causes complaints to surface: "It's hot out here; they should have chosen a better day."

"I hope the route isn't too long … my feet hurt."

"What about food?"

Just as it seems the worst is about to take place, a fervent praise to the Lord erupts among the people. The troublesome gremlins are surprised by the outbreak of worship that overwhelms the troublemakers. Like mosquitoes in smoke, they buzz in all direction trying to escape the cloud of holy reverence.

Out from among the crowd of believers flies a beautiful messenger angel who bears a scroll in hand. Unfurling the scroll, he reads aloud for all to hear: "This is the day the Lord hath made. Let us rejoice and be glad in it. This is the day!"

At the same time, the crowd breaks out in song with lyrics that echo the divine message.

The inspiring angel, knowing he just dealt a blow to the imps' ploy, catches a rogue's attention and gives the creature a Heavenly smile.

The ugly spirit responds with an obscene hand gesture and a few choice words.

Watching from afar are Solomon and Lee. They aren't deceived a bit by the simple win of that battle. This is the start of a long day that will bring many struggles—anything could happen next. Lee confirms the notion. "Be sure the messengers bring good news to keep the saints motivated. Positive words keep the people focused on the purpose of the march," advises the guardian who wants to squash the enemy's effort to hinder the saints.

The Empyreans have their plans ready. Still, their faces bear looks of concern for the saints for whom they battle. The enemy has proven to be resilient and capable of maintaining a strangling grip on the city.

The number of marchers increases as the day goes along. The sudden success is temporary though. Just when the rally achieves a good, positive momentum, storm clouds roll in on the saints. "That's funny," Pastor Robinson suddenly realizes, "the weatherman said nothing about rain today."

Louise, who walks alongside Randy, is not surprised. "Who can predict the weather anyway?"

"It's strange, though. All this week, there's been sunshine ... no rain. Now, all of sudden, we hear thunder rolling in the distance."

"Perhaps it's a coincidence—or maybe an attack. Who can tell?" Louise concludes.

"I don't know, but I pray it doesn't get in the way of today's event," Randy hopes.

Back at the library, Heaven's sons examine the sky as the rainstorm settles in for a torrential down pour. Lee questions the source of the storm. "This is not the season for such weather. This has to be the hand of Fratricide at work. He thinks this bad weather will make the saints quit the march."

Solomon, who's determined to succeed, turns to his brother with a look of resolve in his eyes. "The big one wants to play," he challenges, "so let's give him a game now."

"What's your plan, brother?"

"It's simple. I'll convey to the messengers to continue ministering to the saints," says Solomon. "It's time for the people to show how much they love the Lord by weathering this storm."

Lee agrees. "Yes, let the rain come. We'll petition the Father to hold back the lightening."

Quickly, Solomon summons his subordinates, issues orders, and sends them on their way. The messengers disperse among the people spreading words of encouragement. As they weave in and out of soaking wet mortals who flinch from the clapping thunder, the angels break out in unison with a song. It brings a spontaneous response from the saints who burst out in song too.

A burly man with a long beard and big hair jumps for joy. "Hey, you people with your heads down, what's the problem?" he yells. "Don't you know this is the day that the Lord has made?" With his flowing hair and joyful exuberance, he resembles the Biblical prophets—maybe even John the Baptist. Seeming to be immune from the cold, the wild man strips off his shirt to run about in the rain. "Can't you all see this is a test of our faith? I don't know about you all, but I'm not going out like some sucker. The devil can't beat me with a storm. My God is greater!"

The people find the crazy man to be amusing. His enthusiasm spreads throughout the crowd as he encourages them with a reference to the book of Mark, Chapter 4; verse 35–41. "Our savior is the one who quieted the storm. Don't you all remember when Jesus fell asleep in the boat during the storm? The disciples became frightened as the waves rushed aboard flooding the ship," the wild man recalls. The crowd is tuned in on the man as speaks with animation. "Just when the boat was about to sink, our Savior woke up and told the elements, 'peace be still.' And the Lord said to his disciples, 'where is your faith?' And now I say to you all, where is your faith?"

"My faith is right here," yells one man.

"I got mine over here too," shouts a woman.

Claims of faith start sprouting everywhere as momentum begins to swing in favor of the marching saints. As shouts of joy erupt from the crowd, the lightning and thunder become more intense, flashing and rumbling overhead, but no one is frightened. Watching the brilliant display of electricity dancing in the sky, the people stand in awe as nature puts on a spectacular fireworks show. The marchers are compelled to offer up praise for the dazzling display.

Sheol's warriors are angry. The lightening was supposed to scare the saints, not entertain them. Frustrated, the big one shakes a filthy fist toward Heaven while cursing. "It's not fair," cries Fratricide. "He protects these trash-bag humans from harm."

"These walking mud sacks deserve punishment—why must He interfere?" cries another foul spirit whose wishes to assault the saints have been denied.

Confident, but still aware of how resilient the enemy can be, the angels realize they have been victorious with only a few of the many battles to come. The sons of Empyreal know God may tie the opposition's hand in one way yet allow the enemy free reign in another.

29

The Sacrificial Lamb

The march is approaching its final destination—city hall. As the building comes into the marchers' view, the people cheer wildly. It's a beautiful sight to see citizens of various denominations and racial groups walking hand in hand.

Hovering in the sky like the Goodyear Blimp, the big one observes the activities below. Molder and Wrath are present too. It's the common cause that brings them together. All three spirits wait eagerly for the *surprise* to occur. Becoming impatient, Fratricide makes his feelings known. "Hmm, nothing you've done so far has impressed me. When is this surprise going to happen?"

The statement is an unwanted comment. Already irritated by the large one's presence, Molder lets his sharp tongue fly. "That rain storm of yours did little to wash away these two-legged bugs. Now watch how a real attack is executed."

The behemoth is losing his patience. "For someone who has yet to join the fight, you talk a good game. We don't have eternity to wait—make it happen now!"

Pointing at a moving vehicle that is a few blocks from the rally, Wrath interjects, "Our man is here."

The rally area is blocked off by barriers, so the sedan pulls aside to park along the curb. The driver remains inside the car for several minutes.

Fratricide is still impatient. "What is he doing down there?" the big one hollers.

Molder is unsure and doesn't want to give a stupid answer. "Be patient and watch."

The response doesn't sit well with the big one, who becomes aggressive. "Must I repeat myself?" the mammoth yells as he reaches out to place a strangling grip on Molder's neck.

"The mortal …," says the gasping demon who can barely breathe "… is preparing himself to make the strike."

Wrath considers attacking Fratricide, but the big one has his warriors, and they are abundant in numbers.

"That's more like it," says the behemoth. "I don't understand why you couldn't say that in the first place. I've ruled this city for decades and never had any trouble such as this. Hmm, if anything else goes wrong, I will have plenty of heads to decorate the halls of Hades with." The big one eases his grip while keeping a meaty hand resting on Molder's neck. If needed, the mammoth can always retighten the clenching grip.

The lone figure sits behind the wheel of the parked car. In the CD player is a disc playing the mortal's favorite song, "Pour Out a Little Liquor." JT reaches down on the passenger side floor to grab a bottle he's been chugging all day. He unscrews the cap, throws his head back, and takes a long, hard swallow. Buzzing about the mortal's head are his spiritual companions, Insanity, Murder, and Alcoholism. Of the three spirits, Murder is in the most serious mood—he has work to do. The other two scoundrels are tagging along for the ride.

Taking a place in the pit of JT's body, Murder speaks to his mind. *"Check the gun for bullets."*

The gangster is clumsy with the pistol. Already intoxicated, he struggles to place the tip of his thumb on the ejection button that releases the ammo magazine. Finally it slides out revealing a cartridge full of bullets. Now the drunkard slaps the cartridge upwards into the hollow end of the gun handle to chamber a round.

"Take off the safety, get out of the car, and join the crowd," orders the killing spirit. JT does as told, making his way to the crowd. The gangster halfway staggers and struts toward the crowd seeking a human target that is mixed in among the thousands of people attending the march. Either the alcohol or the large crowd—or a combination of the two—makes JT dizzy. The feeling is so discomforting that Murder even steps outside the mortal's body to get his demon senses stabilized.

I gotta sit down … get it together, the gangster says to himself. Searching for a place to sit, JT heads for an empty park bench.

Murder waits until JT is comfortably situated before he reenters his body. Talking aloud to himself, the crazed devil says, *There's too much alcohol in his system; some of this has to go.* Reaching his reptilian hand into the pit of JT's stomach, the spirit stirs the man's belly. *Yeah, that ought to do the trick.* And it does. Vomit hits the pavement splattering on JT's pants and speckling the sidewalk too. The gross sight of pink gelatin dotted with brown gravy compels the people passing by to walk around the mess. A couple of nice strangers ask JT if he's all right, but the drunkard mumbles aloud waving off any help. Putting his head between his knees, the gangster tries to get himself together.

The voice over the loudspeakers indicates the church leaders are gathering and there's not much time to waste. "Brothers and sisters, the march has been a success for us all and for the city of Harlem Heights. This is what the spirit of God is all about: People of different backgrounds getting together to worship the one almighty God," says the speaker, who happens to be a Methodist preacher.

Just hearing that short speech causes Murder to burn with anger. He hates the Christians for trying to clean up the city. Nothing would please him more than ruining this rally. With revenge hot on his mind, Murder beckons JT to proceed with the mission. *"Stand up; it's time to take care of business."* The Pharaoh rises to carry out the sinister plan. Though Jermaine is still intoxicated, Murder helps him to think and operate soberly.

The Methodist man continues speaking. "Before we bring this march to a close, there is one more important thing we must do. For the sake of our city and the welfare of our people, we should now come together—all of us as one—and pray to the Lord that Harlem Heights becomes a holy city. Please join hands as we ask for the deliverance of our city."

Fratricide can't believe his ears. How dare the saints defy the behemoth by bringing the people together for prayer? Before the mortals go any further, Fratricide orders an attack. "Summon the forces and stop the prayer!"

The hellions take immediate action. Priority being communication, the evil forces seek to snuff out the sound system. Just before the damage can be done, however, the imps evaporate into dust. Angelic warriors are there in time to send them to the abyss. Lee shouts a war cry signaling all of his forces to take defensive action. The Empyreans surround the stage to protect the sound system and the generator from harm.

Fratricide's forces are well prepared and show no surprise at the sudden appearance of the holy guardians. Assuming an attack formation, the behemoth's fighters gather openly and face the opposition, eager to initiate battle. Before the sparks fly, the leader of the dark forces makes a proposition. "You can make it easy for us all. Cut the prayer, send these mortals home, or we'll do it for you. These dirtbags are not worth the trouble."

Lee has a counter offer. "We will never surrender the glory of the Most High; we shall fight for the honor of our Savior."

"Have it your way, then. It's your skin," the hellions commence to attack.

The enemy is strong; they outnumber the sons of Heaven. Though the battle is going their way, the microphone and speakers have yet to be taken out. "Take out the communication," is the command given to any devil who can manage such a task. Several try. Though it seems to be a simple task, the demons are finding it increasingly difficult to make progress.

As the battle takes place in the spiritual realm, the Methodist minister hands the microphone off to a church mother to lead the prayer. As she raises her hands toward Empyreal, a splitting headache ravages her head, causing the woman's mind to draw blank. The prolonged silence puzzles the audience.

Being nearby, pastor Robinson senses something is wrong. He feels an urge to go onstage to assist the church mother. Hurrying to her side, Robinson puts an arm around the elder's shoulder hoping to comfort her. Since he's on stage, the pastor might as well do the prayer—shouldn't be any harm in helping.

What Robinson can't see in the spiritual realm is the arrow of the enemy that has been shot through the church mother's head. It doesn't crush her spirit, but it temporarily renders her ineffective.

The opportunity for prayer quickly draws thin as more saints are struck by the arrows. Before matters become drastically worse, Lee looks to make a counterattack. Meanwhile, Pastor Robinson grabs the microphone to pray. As he begins, guardians surround him to prevent any harm from coming his way. The people, still waiting on a cue, join in with Randy. The prayer is effective enough to slow the demonic attack.

Fratricide is hot. "I will not be defeated," shouts the blimp from above. Being a wise general, he beckons a servant. A secret order is whispered quietly and then the underling is sent to pass on a message. The spirit descends freely to the ground without hindrance—Fratricide's forces still own the air. The message is relayed and ready to execute.

Deceiver, sent out a while ago to poison the ministry, is given a special task. Making his way toward the so-called Reverend Brown, he enters the man's soul. So encumbered, Rev Brown now makes his way onto the stage. Somehow he acquires a microphone and interrupts Pastor Robinson in mid sentence. The spirit uses Brown's voice to speak: *"Enough of this prayer. It's time for us to realize our power as people united together. We have the ability to make things happen on our own,"* claims the speaker.

Pastor Robinson takes a puzzled look at Brown, who refuses to look in his direction. The so-called reverend continues, *"For so long, we Christians have waited on some big hand to come from the sky and deliver us from our troubles. Such a thing will never happen. God helps those who help themselves, so let's come together to make our city better—c'mon brothers and sisters we can do it."*

With so much emphasis placed on tolerance and diversity, pulling Brown from the stage would only undermine the accomplishments of the march. Unsure of what to do, and not wanting to defy the reverend publicly, the audience gives a courteous applause.

Deceiver makes another rally call: *"C'mon, brother, do it. There's nothing holding you back from making a difference for your community."*

For some reason, JT believes the speaker is talking directly to him. Murder speaks to his mind to ensure JT knows he's being called out.

Wanting the gangster to move faster, Brown utters another command. *"C'mon man, it's your time now. If there was ever a time to make it happen, now is that time, take your best shot!"*

It's more than obvious now. JT realizes he's being called to action. Moving a hand toward his front pocket, the gangster reaches for the gun, which is tucked away in his pants. Securing the pistol handle, JT eases the gun out in a discreet manner. Not sure if he has a good sight, he relies on instinct to work for him. Murder takes over from there. JT aims the gun at Robinson. The wicked devil whispers, *"Squeeze the trigger slowly."* JT follows the order.

On stage lies Randy Robinson in a pool of his own blood. Reverend Brown rushes off the stage without rendering aid to the downed man. The people scatter to safety.

Sergeant Perez reports the incident to his command. "There's been a shooting; a man is down on stage. Send paramedics. Suspect shooter is a dark-skinned black male approximately six feet, two inches tall. Suspect is wearing baggy jeans and a red sports jersey. Suspect is still in the stage area. Send backup."

Fratricide and his minions rejoice from above. "We got him! We've struck the big-mouth pastor!"

Unsure of what to do, JT runs about in a stupor. Murder steps outside his body leaving the mortal drunk again. His companions are there too. Insanity and Alcoholism giggle, buzzing about with glee. *"You got him, you crazy fool,"* exclaims Insanity.

Murder chimes in, *"It's all over now. You ought to kill yourself."*

"No, no, no," shouts JT. Dropping the gun, he swats the air about his head as if something is bothering him. "Leave me alone; go away," he yells to the imaginary flies buzzing about his head. It appears that JT has lost his mind. As he yearns for another drink, the shooter doesn't notice the crowd of men encircling him. The killer's world is spinning, and he wants everything to stop.

Spotting the gun he dropped moments ago, JT falls to his knees and scrambles for the weapon. He manages to grasp the pistol and points the handgun to his temple. Before he can pull the trigger, however, his arm is yanked down, bent behind his back, and his head slammed to the concrete causing his lights to go out. Bound with handcuffs, the shooter is taken away.

Attention is brought back to Pastor Robinson who remains unconscious on the stage. While the medics make every effort to save Randy's life, photographers capture images of the crisis on camera.

High above the city, Fratricide grins with pleasure at the turn of events. His minions cackle and howl along with him. The celebration reaches the ears of the angels below who sullenly mourn the attack of the pastor. Knowing this has happened for a reason, Solomon immediately instructs his subordinates to keep the people encouraged. Looking for a ray of hope at such a cloudy time, the messenger seeks counsel from the Lord above. "Oh, Father, a child of yours has been harmed. I know everything happens according to your will. So please see fit to make good of this situation," prays Solomon.

Still meditating to the Lord, Solomon is gently distracted by his scout, who brings news. "My brother, I believe your prayers have been answered already, look at the people."

As Solomon observes the people standing before city hall, swollen teardrops fall from his eyes. The saints have regrouped. They stand hand in hand offering praise to the Lord. It's not the superficial kind of worship that people give just so they don't look out of place. The saints are sincerely pouring their hearts out to the Lord. It's a compelling sight that forces the enemy to retreat in fear.

Turning to his companion, Solomon tells Lee, "The Lord never ceases to amaze me. A tragedy has turned out to be a blessing."

"Yes, it's so, my brother. Now turn on the television and see the people of Harlem Heights witness the event for themselves."

On TV is a reporter broadcasting live from city hall. She informs the public of the shooting that just occurred. People throughout the city view the event from their homes and places of business. The television broadcasts images of thousands of praying saints who have put aside their differences for one common cause: Jesus Christ. The diversity of the people and the sadness of the event draws sympathy from the hearts of all viewers. The reporter, speaking in the true spirit of the rally, challenges all viewers throughout the city to make a difference in their community.

Since the shooting of Robinson, the atmosphere in Fratricide's lair is light; the actual celebration has passed, yet a festive mood still lingers. Though he has reason to be jolly, the mammoth is rather quiet. He sits pensively on his throne ignoring the chatter to consider something that eats away at his mind.

Informer attempts to engage Fratricide with a frivolous comment, but the effort backfires by pushing the big one's pensive mood to anger. The behemoth slaps the runt aside, and his violent action brings the room to silence. "Stop it all," Fratricide hollers. "Stop the foolishness. Deceiver, come forth."

Up slithers the serpent with his head bent low in reverence. His long body weaves between the spirits that make up the crowd, bumping the smaller demons out of the way. An imp, displeased with the serpent's rudeness, subtly draws his sword and stabs its point underneath the reptile's belly scales. A sudden jolt of pain causes the snake's tail to stiffen. Before the giggling devil can hide his hand, he quickly finds himself wrapped in the serpent's suffocating coils. The other spirits clear a path to avoid becoming the next victim.

Pleased with his latest accomplishment at the city hall march and a fresh new victim in his coils, Deceiver proudly reports to the overlord, "What does my master request of me?"

Seeming to be unaware of the choking imp, Fratricide compliments his servant. "That was good work out there today. Finally, someone was able to take care of that meddling pastor. Now to my concern: What are you going to do with the shooter, hmm?"

A bewildered look crosses Deceiver's face. "The matter is now in the hands of Herod. What concern of that is mine, my Baal?" The serpent's humble words are laced with subtle hint of disrespect.

Fratricide snatches the snake by the neck, causing Deceiver to wriggle and hiss as his long body thrashes about the crowd like a hooked fish. Quickly the spirits move to avoid the flying coils. As for the choking imp, the rascal falls free to scamper away to safety.

Fratricide poses his questions again. "What about the man at the jail? What are you going to do about his mouth?"

The behemoth loosens his grip just enough to allow the anaconda to speak. The reptile gasps, "Master, I will be sure that man tells no one about us ..." Deceiver stills looks as though he has more to say. "Master ... please let me go, I can't breathe."

"Let you go? Why should I do so? Isn't this the mercy you showed the imp? What's good for him is certainly good for you," says Fratricide with smoke puffing from his nostrils. The look of concern that covered his face moments ago has given way to anger.

"I hear and will obey," coughs the serpent hoping to persuade the large one to let him go. "The man will be destroyed. Your kingdom will reign."

Those magic words set the reptile free. "Flattery doesn't get you anywhere with me, you wretched belly crawler. I'm letting you go on one condition. You will kill that man, JT. Failure will not be tolerated, understand?"

"Yes, master. Consider the mortal dead."

Now free, the serpent slumps to the floor like a wet bag of trash. Slithering through the crowd, he curses while demanding all onlookers to clear a path. On the way out, the serpent spies the imp who poked him, and whom he choked for the favor. Pretending not to notice, the snake slithers by hoping to catch the sneering gremlin off guard. Snatched in a coil before realizing it, the imp attempts to sound some type of alarm, but the effort is useless. Hands, arms, and mouth are all bound; the rascal disappears for good.

Though he was publicly reprimanded, Deceiver is feeling a bit better after taking his revenge. The next task at hand is for him to rid the world of JT before his mouth becomes a serious issue.

The snake sprouts his wings, taking to the air like a swan. He is such an ugly creature, but flying never looked so graceful. The serpent's long body slithers smoothly on the wind like a silk ribbon in a brisk breeze.

30

The Conversation of Life and Death

Pastor Robinson lies in the hospital still unconscious. A bullet wound to the chest has caused a great amount of blood loss. Randy is fortunate that paramedics were already on location when the shooting occurred. Had rescue efforts taken a few moments more, the pastor could have lost his life.

Louise is at Randy's bedside holding her husband's hand. Her attention is on the equipment that monitors Randy's heart rate. Nervously, she listens to the beeping machine trying to detect an irregular heartbeat. Louise's imagination is starting to get the best of her; she is startled by the slightest change in rhythm that might indicate the possibility of cardiac arrest.

Realizing she has no control over life or death, the pastor's wife does the next best thing for a situation like this—pray. "Lord, if there is ever a time that I need you most, this would be it. Please intervene in this situation to spare my husband's life. Father, I love him and want nothing more than to enjoy many more years with the man you blessed me with." Louise is overwhelmed with grief, which causes her sorrow to become anger. "He's mine, and this isn't how it's supposed to end! Randy has always done as you directed without question. Is this his reward? Jesus, it's not fair if you allow this to happen—he doesn't deserve this." Louise pauses for a moment to rethink what she just prayed. Not wanting to offend the Lord, she questions whether she's being selfish and bossy.

Many times Mrs. Robinson has counseled others in situations like this, having to remind them that God doesn't always save loved ones from death. Now how receptive is Louise of her own advice? Personal tragedy is a big pill to swallow.

After an internal examination of her attitude, the gloomy wife gets things into perspective. She remembers saying it so many times: No one is promised tomorrow.

Looking at her husband causes memories of the times they have spent together to flood her mind. Bible study at college is where it all began. The relationship evolved into a deep love, and she felt the need to bring Randy home to meet her parents. If he could pass the test of meeting her parents, then he could possibly be "the one." Things hadn't gone as well as she had planned; the meeting became a test for her parents more than for Randy.

Now here she sits staring at a man with one foot in the grave and the other slipping from the world. Whichever path the Lord chooses for Randy remains to be known. Regardless of the choice, Louise is preparing her mind to deal with either decision. "Lord, please pardon me for not thinking clearly. I want more than anything to spend the rest of my life with Randy, but this is not a decision I can make; it's all in your hands. Please consider the desires of my heart, yet have your way in this situation. Heavenly Father, with your help, it's my intentions to be at peace with the decision you make concerning Randy."

The angels stand nearby observing her dilemma. They are caught between the sorrow of a wife about to lose her husband and the thought of knowing Pastor Robinson could be going on to a better place than the physical realm.

"It never ceases to amaze me when they cry so much for their loved ones who are leaving for a better place. This is a time to rejoice," Lee comments.

Solomon, too, is oftentimes puzzled by the way humans respond to death. He gives his best response to Lee regarding the lost of human life. "I guess they feel as we did when the King laid down His life on the cross. It was something we all did not like to see, but it had to happen."

"At least we knew victory was near when they crucified our Lord. Death was defeated; the opportunity for eternal life was made available to all mankind. Why can't they understand that as we do?" replies Lee.

Understanding the warrior's concern, the messenger tells Lee something he already knows. "They don't have the luxury of knowing the Father as we do. Their relationship with the King is based more on faith than experience. This brings a more challenging task. Those who can overcome their struggle to see by relying on faith will be greatly rewarded."

Lee is content with Solomon's explanation. His attention goes back to the woman who weeps for her man. The angelic warrior knows the loss of a righteous man is a heartfelt setback, yet it's a time for all of Empyreal to rejoice when a saint is called home. It all depends on which side one sits when viewing the issue.

Louise is unaware of the conversation between the angels in the hospital room. She meditates on the Lord knowing the best will happen to her husband regardless of the outcome.

31

JT in the Jailhouse

At the police department, JT lies on a cold metal bed sleeping off his drunkenness. Alone in a holding cell, he's separated from the other inmates who are crowded into a larger cell with a telephone on the wall. From this large cell, they can look across the corridor to JT in his smaller cell.

The humans hardly notice JT at all; he's just another face in the crowd. What's important to them is being next in line to make a phone call. But, in the spiritual realm, a buzz is beginning to stir. Up from the souls of the mortals rise several evil spirits. They all look, pointing and asking one another, "Is that the one?"

Murder sits proudly like a native chief at a rain dance, soaking in the attention of his admirers. JT's actions have made him a celebrity spirit for the moment. Suicide and Insanity, proud to be associated with the killer, beckon the other jailhouse spirits closer. They come to see for themselves the one who finally struck the loudmouth preacher. "Are you the one who finally took down Pastor Robinson? How were you ever allowed? He was covered by a hedge."

Feeling proud, Murder makes a gesture allowing Suicide to answer the question. "We were designated by Fratricide, himself, to take out the pastor. No one else was capable of the task—that's why we were chosen."

The lizard, Murder, puffs with pride as the demonic crowd gathers to hear the story of the great killer. His basking in glory is short-lived when a sudden shadow darkens the cell where JT dwells. Murder's mouth drops wide open when he sees a giant serpent. The majority of his body is coiled, but his head is up, and he is swaying back and forth high over JT.

Of all the rogue spirits there, Deceiver appears to be the largest. There are a few devils as large as the serpent, but they recognize the visitor's rank and power.

Still silent, Deceiver sits high on his belly swaying, hissing, and flicking his forked tongue. He is relishing the fact that he has just stolen the show from Murder. "Where is he?" the serpent asks as if he doesn't see the mortal sleeping on the steel bed.

Attempting to play dumb too, Murder answers the serpent with a question. "Whom do you seek?"

Deceiver, caught off guard by the killer's flippant response, is suddenly angered. After dealing with Fratricide, the serpent has no tolerance for a lowly underling's bad attitude. With a snap of his tail, the snake lashes out and wraps a coil quickly around Murder's neck. "This is the last time that I will ask. Where is the man who did the shooting?"

"Here, with me, my lord," says Murder with respect in his voice this time. He no longer looks like the proud chief who bravely leads warriors on the warpath.

Feeling that he has established dominance over the scene in the jail, Deceiver loosens the coils to inquire a bit more. "Why is he still alive? Don't you know this man is a liability?"

Murder's been around long enough to know a dead-end question when he hears one. Saying yes would implicate him as a foolish imbecile without the foresight to take care of issues before they become problems. On the other hand, admitting ignorance would only subject Murder to punishment he doesn't want—especially after his great accomplishment of taking down Pastor Robinson. What's a demon to do? Considering the choices, Murder opts for the obvious. "I'll take care of him; consider the man dead."

The neutral answer leaves Deceiver without the motivation to further punish the killer. "Well, get on it with it then," demands the snake. "Should this man's tongue get loose, he could cause a lot of damage. He knows too much to be trusted at a time like this."

An eerie silence bombards the sober mind of JT as he sits alone in the interrogation room. Besides a splitting headache, Jermaine has a lot of issues pounding in his mind. The shooter thinks to himself, *Why hasn't Mo' come to bail me out yet?* JT is snatched back to reality when he hears the door slam loudly. Two men he recognizes very well have come to pay a visit.

Hughes and Diggs strut into the room like two roosters walking among a barnyard full of hens. Wasting no time in getting down to business, the detectives quickly take their seats. One sits directly in front of JT, while the other takes a seat by his side. Whether it's intentional or not, the seating arrangement makes JT nervous.

Hughes is devious as usual. "To get you out of this mess, it's really gonna cost you big-time, sport." He slaps JT on the back of the shoulder like an old chum would. If the situation were different, the Pharaoh would have tried to break the detective's arm for that move. Instead, he must tolerate the visitors' antics.

"I don't know why you shot that Bible thumper in broad daylight. How are we supposed to help you now, man?" inquires Diggs.

"Maybe he can plead insanity in court," laughs Hughes. "The judge might give 'im a lighter sentence."

Diggs is not amused by his partner's humor. His mind is on more serious things. Shifting to the edge of his chair, he leans in close to get the shooter's attention. "Listen, man, we got some serious issues to discuss. There's more at stake than just your case. You understand that, right?"

No response from JT.

"Certain people have made it clear that you shouldn't say anything that could possibly jeopardize their ..." Diggs stops to search his mind for the appropriate word. "Operations." Sitting back, the detectives give JT a moment to digest the advice. It's a delicate situation. Pushing JT too much could make him crack; being too easy may lead to a plea deal that ruins the cops. The reality of situation is this: If JT could somehow disappear, a lot of people would be happy.

"Look here, buddy, you have a lot to think about. Remember what we discussed; don't forget. We already set up a lawyer for you who understands the situation. Just follow his guidance," instructs Diggs.

JT gives them the same treatment as before—silence.

As usual, Hughes gets the last word as he exits the room. "Should you forget our agreement, you'll definitely pay the price for running your mouth." The door closes and JT is alone.

Sitting cross-legged on the mortal's shoulder is the mischievous Insanity. With sword in hand, the evil spirit pokes at JT's brain creating a severe migraine headache. The spirit is amused to see the big bad gangster cringing with pain. When JT clasps a big hand on one throbbing spot of his head, the crazy spirit quickly pokes at another. This cat-and-mouse game goes on for several minutes.

Not able to stand it any longer, JT grabs his head with both hands and ducks his face between his knees. He sways back and forth yelling, "Stop, stop, stop!" He slumps from the chair to the floor and assumes the fetal position.

Insanity enjoys his dirty work. He dances a jig, leaping circles around the suffering mortal while singing a blasphemous song. The revelry catches the attention of other imps in the jail who eagerly join the frolicking fun. Like children playing ring-around-the-rosy, the spirits form a circle and hold hands. They kick their legs in unison like demon Rockettes on Broadway. Oh how they relish tormenting horrible humans.

The angels at the precinct watch with sorrow at the sad state of affairs. Heaven's servants wish to reach out to JT, but the Lord is a fair God, which means the doorway must have been opened for this torment to exist. If only JT would repent of his wicked ways and embrace the gospel of Jesus Christ, he then could be free of this torture. The holy guardians dare not to openly intervene; yet they always have a trick up their sleeves.

The Pharaoh is still on the floor when Lieutenant Boyer enters the interrogation room. Finding a grown man lying on the floor like a child surprises the officer. His first impulse is to rush over to help JT up, but lessons from the past serve his memory well. Standing at a distance, he decides that calling the detainee's name is the best option. "Hey, Jermaine Trotter, are you all right?" inquires the officer with a tone of concern. There's still no response, so Boyer inches closer, taking little steps as if approaching the edge of a steep cliff; he's prepared for any tricks. "Mr. Trotter, can you hear me? If so, beware, I'm coming toward you. I won't hurt you. I just need to know that you're all right."

The attempt to get JT's attention seems to work. The shooter stirs a bit then he mumbles. Looking up, the Pharaoh reveals his blood-shot eyes.

"You look like bad," exclaims Boyer with surprise in his voice. "That's okay though, I've seen worse. Besides, we can overcome what you did out there yesterday." The officer's words sound like hope to JT. Life springs back into Jermaine's eyes as he sits up and seems to show more interest in Boyer than he showed the previous two visitors.

Seeing an opportunity to reach out, Boyer offers a hand to the depressed criminal, helping him to stand. The officer directs him to have a seat in the same chair from which he recently slipped.

"Well, I'm here to make sure all your needs are being met," begins Boyer. "Normally, the precinct doesn't devote so much attention to an offender unless he's somewhat of a high-visibility figure. Your case falls into this category. What you did—pardon me, allegedly did—requires us to treat this matter as a high-profile case. So let's get straight to business." Lieutenant Boyer pulls out a checklist in preparation for asking questions. Usually it's an easy routine, but JT's reluctance to speak makes the process a bit slow to get started. "Look, buddy," continues Boyer, "if you don't answer these questions, there will be no way for us to help you out. I'll be honest … what I'm asking you for will not incriminate you in any way. See, here's the disclaimer." And Boyer shows JT a paper. "So c'mon, lighten up."

JT is somehow convinced to cooperate. Clearing his voice in effort to speak, the gangster takes a long hard swallow. It seems like years have passed since he last used his very own voice. "Something's not right with me," he tells the officer. "The voices in my head won't go away. Can you make 'em go away?" pleads a desperate JT.

Boyer looks puzzled. "What voices are you talking about?"

"I keep hearing these voices that talk really loud to me. I can hear 'em just as good as I can hear you."

Lieutenant Boyer jots down a reminder to recommend a mental evaluation. *"Inmate seems to be on the edge and losing it fast."* Looking back up to focus on JT, the officer has questions of his own to ask. "I would like to know more about these voices you're hearing. Describe them."

The thug feels comfortable enough to talk now. "I can hear people talkin' inside my head. Sometimes they talk to me, and sometimes they argue with each other. I can usually block 'em out, but lately, I can't do nothin' to stop 'em from takin' over my mind. All they ever do is talk and stuff like that. They only quiet down when I drink."

"How many voices do you hear—two or three … maybe more?"

"Yeah man, it's three of 'em in here." Jermaine Trotter holds his hand to the side of his forehead indicating where the voices dwell.

"Well …" Lieutenant Boyer pauses a few seconds while fishing in his mind for the next question to ask. "Who are they? Can you describe them?"

JT is surprisingly compliant. "It's three of them, like I said. One talks more than the others. I think he's the boss. He always tells the other two what to do."

"Does he have a name?"

JT appears to be lost in his thoughts.

Boyer asks his question again, a bit louder this time. "Mr. Trotter, does the dominant one have a name?"

Still, no results. The detainee continues staring with a blank look on his face.

Knowing nothing else to do, the officer says a quick prayer under his breath. *"Father, in the name of Jesus, I call upon you now to touch JT's mind and mouth. Help him speak without hindrance from the enemy."* With the prayer done, Boyer takes a long, hard look at JT to see what his reaction will be. The officer is on the brink of giving up when the Pharaoh seems to snap out of the trance. Eager to seize the moment, Boyer asks his question again, "Does the dominant one have a name?"

This time JT attempts a response. "Yeah, but it ain't no ordinary name like yours or mine; I can't exactly say it. The others refer to him as … " Frustrated, JT smacks a flat hand loudly on the desk causing the policemen standing guard outside the room to barge through the door to rescue Boyer from a possible attack. Surprised to see it's nothing, the guards stop cold in their tracks and look about the room for signs of a struggle.

"Go back, it's nothing," shouts Boyer in a calm but demanding tone. "Everything is under control."

The guards leave. Right away, the officer gets back to the business of asking questions. "Well, JT, you still haven't told me his name."

"He doesn't have one, but I do know what he does."

"What is that?"

"He kills."

"How do you know?"

"That's all he ever talks about is killing. He threatens to kill the others whenever they disobey him. All he ever wants me to do is just kill."

"When you say others, are you referring to the other voices?"

"Yeah, man."

Lieutenant Boyer is content with that answer. Now he must find out the names of the other two culprits. "Okay, we have the first one figured out; what about the others? Who are they?"

JT thinks hard trying to recall their names; he can't. The gangster can only describe what the voices talk about most of the time. "All I can say is that one jokes around a lot. He's the part of me that likes to do crazy things."

"Like what?"

"I don't know. Whatever I do, he makes it fun for me. He's not serious all the time like the killer."

The information is not enough. The officer needs more details on what exactly the fun one does. Boyer crosses his arms, placing his chin in the palm of his hand like a thinking man. *Lord, what can I ask this man to help reveal the character of this spirit that we're dealing with?* the officer thinks to himself. Instantly a thought pops into his mind. "The fun things you do with this voice, are they dangerous things? You know, things that endanger your life or someone else's?"

"Yeah, now that you mentioned it, it's always dangerous," JT confirms.

Inching closer to the edge of his seat, the officer wants to know more. "Well, tell me, what are the crazy things you do?"

JT's mind goes into overload causing him to squirm a bit. Part of him is eager to answer the questions while another part doesn't want him to comply at all. The more Boyer attempts to get into his life, the more difficult it becomes for JT to sit still. "Man, we do all kinds of crazy things."

"Give me examples, Jermaine Trotter."

"I don't know, man. I can't tell you anything specific."

"Well, let me help you out. Have you ever played roulette with a gun?"

That question causes a flood of memories to rush into JT's mind. He recalls many times when he, along with friends, would put a single bullet in a revolver, spin the chamber and take turns placing the gun to their heads and pulling the trigger. It was suspenseful to see who would blow out his brains first. Cheating is how JT survived the deadly game. It wasn't that his slight-of-hand-trick was quick enough to avoid detection, but, rather, everyone else would do the same thing too. "Yeah, that voice was there when I played that game."

The gangster is talking more easily now. Boyer might as well continue with more questions. "What else, Mr. Trotter? What other things did you do?"

"Besides roulette, I love shoot-outs. Whenever there's trouble, I'm always right there in the middle ready for the showdown; I never run away. I've been shot several times … still stood my ground. On the streets, I'm a true soldier who fears nothin' at all. That's how me and Mo' operate."

Boyer thinks to himself, *I've heard that name before.* Curious to know JT's relationship with that person, the officer makes a few more inquiries about Mo'. "I understand there's a lot of competition out there on the streets; you have to be strong in order to survive. How did you and Mo' make it so much further than those wanna-be hustlers?"

The question appeals to JT's ego and alter ego as well. As he responds to the question, Murder helps him along. "If you're gonna run the streets, you gotta have a higher power. See, most cats don't understand that. They think a little money and a gun will get them everything they need. That's where the average hustler goes wrong."

JT is getting philosophical and Officer Boyle finds it interesting.

"Since we don't have the law or the justice system on our side, we found a source that works for us," says JT with a proud smile on his face. The killer takes over JT's conversation: *"We went beyond the power of man by tapping into the spiritual plane where there's no allegiance to man's color or race. In this realm, there is a being who gives opportunity to any individual who is willing to prove his potential value."* JT points to himself. *"And I decided to use him for a higher calling."*

Boyer is a bit confused about the conversation. "JT, what do you mean by the spiritual plane? Do you believe in a higher power?" When JT doesn't respond, the officer tries another subtle tactic. "Do you mean a higher power like Jesus Christ, who died on the cross for our sins?"

"That's none of your concern," screams Murder through JT's voice. *"What I do with him is none of your business. Finish your job and leave us alone."*

"You haven't answered my question. What is this spiritual plane? Is it a Christian thing?"

"If you persist in being flippant, I'll kill you. Don't mention that name again."

The officer suddenly realizes he's not speaking with JT. "Who am I talking to?"

A wry smile creases the corners of JT's mouth as he speaks in a voice that's not his own. *"You think you're smart, but it's not going to work. This man is doomed. He's mine, and I'm gonna kill 'im before you ever get a thing from him. Our little meeting is now over,"* says the killing spirit.

Lieutenant Boyer retreats to his desk, so he can conduct a mental review of his conversation with JT. One minute he'd been talking with a man, he realizes; and the next minute, he'd been speaking with an alter ego. He figures a doorway must have opened sometime in JT's life as a youth allowing the alter personality to form. While time permits, the officer hopes to find the source of the gangster's mental trouble.

Boyer is good friends with Sergeant Perez; they go back a long way. Boyer, being the older and wiser one, mentored Perez when he first came to the police force. Perez was the scrappy young kid with the mentality that he would save the world from all trouble. His desires to be the best cop oftentimes led him into conflicts with his peers. On a number of occasions, Boyer had to rescue Perez from situations a seasoned policeman would have been able to foresee and avoid. Boyer had to teach the younger one that teamwork was far more effective than one man's intelligence and physical prowess. Yet his greatest accomplishment with Perez had been leading the youngster to Christ.

It was duty that separated Perez and Boyer. Their career goals had led them to differing paths. Still, they remain close. Picking up the phone, Boyer gives Perez a call. "Hey, Hector, how's it going? It's me, Boyer."

"I know who this is. What's up, brother?"

Boyer gets straight to the point. "Things are all right. I got an issue for you. Provide me some insight on this guy you arrested a few days ago."

"I arrested a lot of people a few days ago. Which one in particular?"

"The shooter, man. Tell me about the banger who shot the pastor."

All jokes aside, Perez gets serious. "That was the first time I ever dealt with the guy. From what I heard, he's an untouchable figure. If so, it doesn't explain why he did the shooting instead of someone else. What did he have to say?"

"We talked a lot, but not about the shooting. From what I gathered, I don't think he's solely responsible for the incident. As a matter of fact, he's not in his right mind."

"Boyer, I see where you're headed with this. I'm not buying it though."

"No, Perez, just hear me out." The older officer is eager to explain his point of view. "Of course, he did the shooting. You saw that with your very own eyes. What concerns me is the motivation. Who's in control behind the scene? If you could see what I've been dealing with, you'd realize there's an unseen power behind this shooting."

Boyer's statement makes Perez think deeply. Are there really such things as angels and demons? If so, what part do they play in the lives of mankind? Perez is not sure he understands his former partner. "Are you saying what I think you're saying? You believe JT might be influenced by some kind of power? You can't prove that in court."

Boyer is reluctant to openly say the word *possession*. "I think the man is suffering from some type of … uh … mental illness. Second of all, I don't want to prove anything in court. It's more than obvious that he's guilty of the shooting, and he should pay for his actions. I'm concerned about the man's soul. Where is JT headed if he doesn't get the chance to make Jesus Christ his Lord and Savior?"

Perez disagrees. "Okay, I see your point, but I still think JT should be fully punished—and Hell would be a good place to start. There's no excuse for his action."

"My brother, have you forgotten where we all came from? We were all like JT at some point in our lives. Fortunately, we never took things as far as he has, yet we were sinners who fell short of the glory."

"Well, I have to pray about it because I still have a heavy heart. It's hard to love a gangbanger who attempts to kill a pastor. I'm tired of 'em all. They shoot, rob, and destroy everything that crosses their paths. They never accept responsibility for their own actions, and no one's willing to hold them accountable," says an angry Perez.

"I agree with you one hundred percent. I hope JT will be an example for the youth of our city to see. He should be punished, but also afforded an opportunity for repentance just as we all were."

The younger officer surrenders to the idea of helping his buddy. "Okay, Boyer, I get it. So where are we going from here?"

"I'm scheduled to sit down with JT a few more times. Hopefully, I can make a breakthrough with the man before he gets sentenced and sent away. What you can do in the meantime is talk with your congregation without going into detail—you know this is a confidential matter—concerning JT's spiritual welfare. With a prayer cover, we should be able to reach the Pharaoh before someone else does."

If Perez had been reluctant to help JT before, he seems to be willing now.

32

Robinson on the Road to Recovery

Since Randy Robinson's condition has stabilized, he has regained consciousness, yet the pastor remains in the intensive care unit. If he continues to improve, Robinson will be moved to another unit to begin rehabilitation. Ever since the shooting that nearly caused his death, hundreds of cards and letters have poured in wishing the pastor a speedy recovery.

"The doctors say you're fortunate to be alive. Had that bullet gone just a fraction of an inch closer to your aorta, you would have died instantly," says Louise with relief in her voice.

Feeling groggy from the medication, Randy makes a feeble attempt to clear his voice. Coughing even lightly causes pain to streak throughout the pastor's body, and he makes a physical effort to hold his upper body with his arms. The sudden movement of his arms, however, causes more pain in his chest. Instinctively, the pastor surrenders all movement to spare himself the agony.

"Relax, baby," advises his wife, "you're weak right now; give yourself time to recover."

Randy closes his eyes, savoring the sound of his wife's nurturing voice. Always putting others before himself, Randy wishes he could do more to comfort Louise. Until he's stronger, the pastor must settle for sleeping.

Mrs. Robinson is grateful to know there will be more years to share with her husband. Lost in thoughts of happiness, Louise's blissful thinking is interrupted by a vibration she feels on her hip; her cell phone on silent mode.

"Hi, Louise, how's Randy doing?"

"Oh, Angela, he's conscious now but sleeping."

"Thank God. I'm so glad to hear the good news. When's he coming home?"

"Soon, I hope. The doctors can't give a definite time. It all depends on his recovery."

Angela is optimistic. "Well, I have some good news that may speed his recovery."

"What is it?"

"There's been a positive response to the shooting incident throughout the city. Church attendance has skyrocketed since we held the march. Gang leaders have gotten together to talk about a truce, and the police department is cleaning the streets with fervor. As much as I hate to say it, the shooting has made the city a better place."

Louise sighs as silent tears slide down her face. "Considering all that we've been through, I'm glad to hear our efforts are finally paying off," she tells her friend. "Now I just wish Randy were awake to hear the good news."

"Don't worry, Louise, he'll have plenty of opportunity to hear about it. Expect to see an article in Sunday's paper detailing the benefits of the march."

Both parties hang up the phone to carry on with their personal matters. Louise goes back tending to her husband's needs while Angela concerns herself with the newspaper column that's due by the end of the day.

Louise is overjoyed and embraces her recovered husband. "Honey, it's so good to have you back home. I was so worried we would never share this house together again."

Smiling but grimacing at the same time, Randy tries to hug his wife without causing much pain. "Baby, I haven't been gone forever," is his manly reply.

A quick hug is enough for Randy, but his attempt to let go is met with resistance; Louise is not having it. So they remain in their embrace a bit longer until their hearts are content.

The angels accompany the Robinsons. Enjoying the happy reunion, the sons of Heaven take a moment to watch the couple reunite. The joyful moment is but a brief recess from the upcoming battle that seems a long way off.

"So, how's the congregation coming along, Louise?"

Mrs. Robinson can't resist hugging her husband some more. "The church is doing all right. They have been praying for you, and I'm so glad they did—now you're back home with me."

Again he grimaces from the pain, but he returns the affection. Still curious, Randy questions her more about the shooting. "So what's the status on JT?"

Not seeming to hear the question—or perhaps ignoring it—Louise clings to Randy with a warm embrace. She lets go to answer the irksome question. "I haven't heard much about his case. I've been concerned about you." Before she resumes to holding Randy, a thought pops into her mind. "Oh, there was one thing Perez told me about JT. He says the guy is going through some mental struggles since the shooting."

At a time when he should be enjoying the reunion with his wife, the pastor is suddenly concerned about the spiritual welfare of the man who shot him. "I wonder if I could go see him?"

Solomon's wings sprout to attention upon hearing that statement. What a great accomplishment it would be if Empyreal won JT's soul. It would be even more of accomplishment to cause the forces of Hades a great loss.

"Oh, no you don't! Don't go getting those wild ideas in your mind. You have orders from the doctor to stay home and relax. The law will take care of JT."

"Well, what about his soul, baby?"

"That's what prayer is for," Louise reprimands. "You can do just as much for that man right here in this house as you can at the police station."

"Yeah, I understand that, but sometimes a face-to-face visit has a better effect on a person, you know what I mean?"

"Randy, I don't want to hear it. You've done enough for that man and this community. You need time to take care of yourself."

Robinson surrenders for now. "I suppose you're right. If it's meant to happen, the Lord will make a way for me to see JT."

The wheels in Solomon's mind are already turning. He will find a way to arrange a visit. The chief messenger agrees with Randy: A personal visit would have a greater effect on the gangster.

Boyer walks through the door accompanied by two warrior angels with their swords drawn.

"What's the meaning of this?" hisses Murder. The two companions of Murder take refuge behind his back, leaving the killing spirit to confront Heaven's warriors. "Guards, we have intruders," yells the desperate demon, not wanting to face this trouble alone.

"Silence, you filthy lizard," says the guardian. "Not another word from your mouth. This officer is going to minister to JT, and there will be no interference."

Murder attempts a few more words, "Who let you—?" A sword pointing in his face compels the killing spirit to close his mouth. Another slip of the tongue and the lizard is gone.

It may be a coincidence, but Murder notices that the light in the jailhouse is a bit brighter than usual. Looking about the room, he realizes why. It's the army of the Lord. Empyrean forces hover above the jail with drawn swords gleaming in the sunlight. The long, sharp blades magnify the brightness of the sun. The guardians make no attempt to attack, but they definitely didn't come to the police department to be run off either—another benefit of the saints' prayers.

Lieutenant Boyer sits at the table across from JT. He pulls paperwork from a folder. Not knowing exactly how to start the conversation, he resorts to a quick and silent prayer. *God, please help me to reach out to this man. I don't know exactly how to begin, but I do want JT to have an opportunity to hear the gospel. Jesus, I'm depending on you to somehow work this out. Let this man's eyes and ears be opened to receive—*

Before Boyer can finish the prayer, he's suddenly interrupted by a strong grip on his wrist. Looking up, he sees JT's face full of tears. With his arms stretched across the table, hands still gripping Boyer's wrist, JT declares to the officer, "Man, I'm going to die!"

Thank you, Lord, for this opportunity, Boyer thinks to himself, feeling more than confident to share the gospel with the gangster.

JT makes the task even easier by coming clean with his personal grief. "Man, I've been tryin' to shake the feelin', but I believe I'm going to die soon. I just know it."

"C'mon, don't talk that way. You don't know for sure what's going to happen. If you put your faith is Jesus Christ, things will work out for the better."

"I've heard that talk before. What can Jesus do for a man like me at a time like this? When they put me in general population with the rest of the gangbangers, my life is done," claims JT.

Lieutenant Boyer has been in law enforcement long enough to know JT is correct about his fate. Not one lawyer has come to the man's rescue. Even his best friend, Tommy, has been a no-show. Most of all, Willie Mo' has been silent. No use in pretending everything is going all right, so Boyer keeps its real. "JT, I'm gonna be honest with you. Things don't look so good. Unless a miracle happens, you will pay a heavy price for your actions."

The gangster's facial expression indicates he's well aware of the pending legal outcome.

"However," continues Boyer, "all is not lost. Whether it's here on Earth or in Heaven, you can win the final battle. Confessing your sins and believing Jesus Christ to be your Lord and Savior is the path to victory."

Still not convinced, JT sits back in his chair frustrated. He takes a moment before speaking. "You know, I've seen some pretty weird things hangin' out with Mo'. He's always been into that voodoo stuff that gives him special powers. I don't know exactly how it works, but I do know Mo' always had the hookup. Do you have the same connections?"

"Yeah, I got a connection, but it's different from what you've seen. You wanna hear about it?" Boyer waits to see if JT wants to hear more. The thug responds with silence which the officer takes as an indication to continue. "To be more exact, JT, I believe there are two powers in this world. One is loving, honest, and merciful; the other is demanding, deceitful, and harmful."

The detainee clearly understands. "Yeah man, it's all about good versus evil."

Boyer nods his agreement. "The good power is the love of Jesus Christ. He is the Son of God who came to Earth just to save the souls of mankind. Jesus doesn't impose His will onto others, and He doesn't use intimidation as a weapon. Christ wants you to freely accept His gift of eternal life by believing in Him and living according to His will."

Boyer gives the detainee a moment to let the words settle in his mind. The Pharaoh understands well and is eager to hear more.

The lieutenant carries on with the conversation. "Then we have the dark side, the realm in which evil dwells. Wherever wickedness goes, death and destruction is sure to follow. Instead of love, fear and intimidation rule in this dark world. Nothing is ever good enough; Satan can never be satisfied. He always wants more money, more power, more grief, and more destruction. You've been a part of that lifestyle and know firsthand how it works."

JT is compelled to acknowledge that life on the street is always busy. There's hardly any time to relax and enjoy the day. It's always a rush to pick up a package or to drop off a delivery. People are constantly getting hurt, if not killed. Conflicts exist on almost every street corner. He's heard the cliché many times: busy as the devil's workshop. Not until now has he realized how busy his life's been.

Just when the Pharaoh begins to sink deeper into to despair, Boyer says something to raise his spirit. "Perhaps the man you shot can explain it better than I can."

A fire ignites in Jermaine Trotter's eye. The gangster has never sat face-to-face with someone he attempted to kill. "Is he still alive, the man I shot?" asks the anxious inmate.

"I believe so, why do you ask?"

JT gives a simple answer. "I gotta know that everything is not lost."

The idea of meeting Robinson intrigues the Pharaoh. He's in such deep thought that Murder and the other spirits are unable to connect with him. Trying desperately to claw into his mind, Murder attempts to sink his talon fingertips into JT's skull, but they hardly scrape the surface. "Curse you," screams Murder from the top of his lungs. "What is this? They put a hedge around this fool, he doesn't deserve this. How are we supposed to do our jobs when *he* has a hedge around him?" says the desperate killing spirit who takes to pacing about the room in frustration. "Why me? How come this happens to me?" he thinks aloud. Suddenly, he realizes why it has happened. It's a brilliant idea because now it places blame somewhere other than himself. "It's the *prayer*," he shouts in glee. "The saints are praying again because Fratricide has failed to stop the movement. Now where is that snake when I need him the most?"

Deceiver is nowhere in sight. He has a knack of disappearing when trouble comes. The snake is hidden in a safe place where trouble will have a difficult time finding him.

Like Murder, Deceiver will be looking for an excuse if matters don't go well.

Pastor Robinson and Perez are having a casual conversation about JT. "Every opportunity is being taking to share the gospel with the gangbanger," says Perez, "yet he's still reluctant to give his heart to Christ. I hope a breakthrough happens soon."

It may be a mystery to the men why JT is reluctant to give his life to Christ; however, someone close to them knows the reason.

"I have a confession to make," says Louise.

The men ignore her, taking her statement for granted … seeming to think her claim is a minor issue. The pastor picks up the morning paper and flips the pages to his favorite section while Perez heads for the door to start his duty day at work.

"I'll see ya later, pastor," says Hector.

"Stay safe out there, man."

Louise intends to be heard. "Honey, did you hear what I just said?"

"Oh … no, baby, what did you say?"

Exhaling deeply, Mrs. Robinson tries one more time. "I know what's hindering JT's progress."

Laying the paper aside, Randy now gives Louise his full attention. "Well, go on and tell me what you think the problem is."

"Forgiveness, Randy."

"Forgiveness?"

"Yes, forgiveness. I haven't let go of the fact that he almost killed you."

"So what have you been praying for all this time?"

Sighing again, Louise admits the truth. "I haven't been praying for the welfare of his soul."

Pastor Robinson remains silent to consider his wife's confession. It comes as no surprise his spouse may have bitter feelings toward JT—at least she admits it. There's another question running through his mind: *what in the world could she have been praying for then?* Feeling disappointed, Randy asks her directly, "Do you hate him?" Realizing the question is confrontational, he rephrases his words. "Forget I asked that question. I meant to say do you forgive him now?"

"I don't know about that; I'm not sure I'm ready to let it go. I may be wrong, yet I really believe he should rot in Hell for all the wrong he's done to innocent people in this city. Why should he be forgiven?"

"You can answer that question just as well as I can."

Now Louise is frustrated. "Don't play that game!"

"Why ask me a question that you already know the answer to?"

"Randy, I *hate* it when you do this."

"There goes that word again. If Jesus can love his enemies, why can't we?"

Louise remains quiet.

"No, JT isn't a good person. There's no excuse that can justify his actions. Still, we have the moral responsibility to understand where that gangster comes from and how we can influence him to be a better person by showing him the love of Christ. That's all we should want to do, honey."

Randy's comments are persuasive. Louise's facial expression seems to indicate she understands. Not willing to concede yet, Mrs. Robinson vents a bit more. "A bad childhood is no excuse to do wrong. These street thugs, JT and Willie Mo'—what kind of name is that?—can't blame the past for their behavior today."

Randy remains cool as Louise releases her anger. "Both men are old enough to know the difference between right and wrong; they both chose to do bad. Why should any of them be pardoned for their actions? These men should suffer like all the people they have victimized."

This angry woman can't be my wife, Randy thinks. Is this his loving woman who always sees the good in everyone she meets? Randy doesn't like Louise's hard feelings and must bite his tongue to keep the conversation from escalating to an argument. Just when he's about to give up, Randy has an idea. "Baby, here's a question I have for you as a believer in Christ: Knowing that Jesus laid down his life for your sins and for a world that mistreated him for no legitimate reason at all, are you saying that forgiveness is not in your heart for one man who apologized for his mistakes? Don't answer that question out loud for me to hear. You must be alone to do some soul searching. I will love you regardless of the decision you make. But this issue is between you and God."

With that said, Randy picks up his paper to resume reading. There's no conflict between the husband and wife; it's between Louise and God now.

33

The Confrontation

Fratricide has a concern. "Why is it the saints have free access to the inmate? Don't we control the jails in this city?"

A servant standing before the mammoth has an explanation. "My lord, the prayers of the saints give them access to the mortal, JT."

"Why hasn't anyone put a stop to the prayer, hmm? Must I do everything myself in order to make things work as they should?"

Carefully the servant explains. "The attempt to assassinate the pastor served to bring the saints closer together. We must acknowledge the competence of their leadership, my lord."

"I don't *like* it," the mammoth yells.

The servant, accustomed to being hollered at, graciously remains bowed in the presence of the big one as he throws his temper tantrum. The wind from Fratricide's hot-air-balloon lungs fills the room with stinking sulfur and humidity. Not wanting to be the object of Fratricide's anger, the servant uses the foul wind as a ploy to back out of the behemoth's reach. Feeling safer now, the servant makes a suggestion. "My lord, shall we call for reinforcements?"

The big one has little tolerance for silly ideas. "And where should these reinforcements come from?"

The servant is now worried. He can see the overlord is insulted by his suggestion. If he doesn't give a good answer, the flat side of the Fratricide's sword may be his punishment.

"My lord, perhaps our allies within the city will devote their efforts to destroying the prayer cover?" the servant suggests.

It's a wise response, which Fratricide considers. The servant relaxes a bit but still remains tense. Now he's in fear of being tasked to do the impossible.

"Okay, out of my sight. I have work to do."

The underling quickly leaves, feeling relieved that all his body parts are still in place. As the big one contemplates a plan to somehow stop the Christians, matters at the jailhouse are starting to heat up.

Hughes and Diggs are highly upset with Lieutenant Boyer. He's getting too close with JT and there's a lot to lose should the gangster start talking.

While Boyer sits at his desk reading through e-mail, the two detectives suddenly appear in his office. The lieutenant doesn't notice their presence until his door is slammed hard enough to make the blinds in the window shake violently. The rude entrance does little to draw the officer's attention from the monitor. Still clicking away on his keyboard and mouse, Boyer reads his e-mail without acknowledging the detectives.

"Excuse us, we really hate to interrupt, but we have some questions for you," says Hughes with sarcasm in his voice.

Boyer doesn't bother to look at either one of them. He keeps his eyes on the monitor as if more interested in e-mail than personal visitors.

Patience worn thin, Hughes reaches a hand around the monitor and shuts the screen off. "I take it that we have your attention now?"

"Well, at this moment you do," replies Boyer with pleasantness. "What do you want?"

Diggs jumps in the conversation, "I'm so glad you asked. We hear that you're in charge of JT, right?"

"He's one of many that I'm accountable for."

"We have reason to be concerned about Jermaine Trotter's welfare. Rumor has it that you've been evangelizing the detainee. You know it's not ethical to impose your religious views on any flunky that lands into this jail. You can't *save* anybody—that is how you Christians say it, right?" Diggs chuckles as he elbows his partner.

Boyer laughs right along with the detectives, and surprisingly, it pisses the two off. The laughter ceases as their faces suddenly take on a serious look. "No more jokes!" Hughes pounds a fist on the desk to emphasize his point. "We have reason to believe you're evangelizing in the workplace, and it's interfering with our case."

The detectives can't be serious. "You gotta be kidding, what case? The case is closed. Trotter is guilty of shooting Pastor Randy Robinson—everyone knows that. So what is that you fear to lose?" insinuates Boyer.

"We have evidence that suggests JT also shot the little kid, Kenny."

The situation doesn't feel right to the lieutenant. "Why are you telling me this? If what you say is true, you have the right to question him without my permission. No need to be here in my office."

"The punk's mind has been poisoned, and he won't talk to anyone but you. That's why we're here."

Boyer calls their bluff. "I think it's more than what you're telling."

Diggs gets the last word this time. "We're here to pass along a message—stop trying to save that bum's soul. It ain't gonna work. JT's a killer … a drug dealer who deserves what he has coming to him. Leave JT alone."

The meeting ends as the detectives exit the office. Boyer sinks back into his chair. Whatever they came by for, it wasn't necessarily about the shooting of Kenny.

For being in confinement, the last few days in jail have been rather peaceful for JT. He's had time to think deeply about the past. Recalling the atrocities he's committed over the years eats away at the thug's mind. The senseless killings, beatings, and everything else associated with gangbanging tugs away at his conscience. How can God forgive him for the wrongs he's done? Even if the Lord forgave him, why should JT be shown such mercy? These are the questions that Jermaine Trotter asks himself.

A man in JT's situation is never alone. Hanging close by are the three companions who scheme of ways to torture the mortal. The prayers of the saints shield the Pharaoh from an outright attack, but the tormentors still badger the human with discouragement hoping he'll give up on life.

As the demons curse and spit at the fallen gangster, a sudden bright light flashes causing the devils to scatter. Solomon has arrived to the cell with a word to share with JT. A host of guardians accompany the messenger ready to fend off any intrusions. "Son of man, if you would only humble yourself before the Lord, everlasting life will be granted to you."

JT cannot hear the words, but he is suddenly feeling a bit better about himself; there's a sense of hope flickering within his dark soul.

"Word from the Father says there will be a burden you must bear for a short while before your troubles come to an end. He understands you and knows the pain you are going through. The Lord laid down his life so a person such as yourself can be saved. He's willing to forgive if you would only confess and ask for forgiveness," declares Solomon. "Won't you at this time give your life to the Lord?"

JT doesn't know why he feels an overwhelming urge to pray. The idea of sliding from his bed to kneel before the Lord appeals to his mind. Does he dare to pray?

Jermaine's heart is willing, but his knees will not budge. Something inside of the gangbanger fights the mortal's desire to submit unto God. Deciding to compromise, the Pharaoh, still sitting upon the bed, leans forward with his elbows resting on his knees. Attempting the first prayer, Jermaine places his face within his hands and begins. "Hey man, I've never prayed to anyone before in my life..." *Wait a minute, I just called God a man,* JT says to himself.

Though Jermaine is determined to have his little talk with the Lord, he realizes prayer is not as easy as he thought it would be.

The gangster tries again. "If there is a god, please hear me out. I can feel my life coming to an end because I hurt so many people. There's no reason for you to fix the mess I've made. But, if it's true what them Christians say about forgiveness, then I'm asking you to forgive me," pleads JT.

Prayer completed, Jermaine quickly stands to his feet as if he doesn't want anyone to know what he has just done. He paces back and forth within the cell with a million thoughts running through his mind. Grabbing the bars on the cell door, he sighs, lowers his head and shakes it. What should he do next?

Solomon witnesses the scene and is pleased with what he sees so far. This could be the beginning of a beautiful ending.

Mayor Hurt has been a bit stressed out after learning that a significant portion of his campaign contributions has been donated by gang members. Hurt is not the only one guilty of accepting money from shady organizations. There have been judges, district attorneys, lawyers, and even policemen themselves who have accepted kickbacks from certain people of questionable character.

If word gets out that Mo' and his gang of hoodlums have political ties with the mayor, his political career will be in jeopardy.

Thomas Hurt picks up the phone to contact his loyal aide, Dudley. The assistant answers on the first ring. "This is—"

Hurt barely gives Dudley a chance to answer the phone, "What's the latest news?"

"Well, sir, as of now, nothing significant has occurred. JT hasn't leaked any sensitive info."

"How much longer must we wait until the punk is sentenced and sent away?"

"Not much longer now, sir. He should receive a long sentence sometime next week when his trial takes place."

"Okay, that's real good news," replies the mayor.

That's what he needed to hear for reassurance. Now he can relax for at least another day until his worries get the best of him again.

34

JT Makes a Breakthrough

The fact that more FBI agents are visiting the police department is beginning to bother some of the policemen—especially Hughes and Diggs. The feds are on to something, which no one knows for sure what it is. If only JT and that Lieutenant Boyer would go away.

"His trial will take place in a few days, and then JT should be gone for good," says Hughes.

Diggs is feeling desperate. "As long as that joker doesn't get so much religion that he spills his guts, we'll be all right."

JT is not the only one the detectives should be worried about. Sergeant Perez and Pastor Robinson have been doing some digging of their own. They want to know why a gang of wild, young kids has access to a building such as the warehouse without being considered trespassers.

As Perez and Robinson continue their investigation, they begin to learn that a number of businesses—funeral parlors, liquor stores, and even that strip club owned by Tommy—are used as fronts to launder money. Maybe they'll hit the jackpot and find that all these businesses made large campaign donations to several key figures in city politics.

Perez is thrilled to have discovered the underhanded business dealings. "All of this is very interesting. I never knew there was a connection between these gangs and the politicians," he tells Robinson.

The pastor has his map on display. "Take a look at the areas where these questionable businesses operate. The building locations are sitting on prime real estate where the city redevelopment plans will take place. It's clear to see that some people are going to get paid off as soon as for-sale signs are posted. The gang members and politicians may act like strangers in public, but they're all in bed together in private."

Solomon and Lee are present with the mortals who do their best to figure out Fratricide's puzzle. They both know a plan is needed to smoke the moles from underneath the ground. "We have a new angle to work. It's time to redirect our attack at the big one's political goons. Hitting him where it hurts will loosen his grip on the city even more," declares Lee.

Solomon responds with enthusiasm. "Take out the bottom, and the top will fall down."

The saints now have a better perspective on how the enemy operates within Harlem Heights, and knowing so is half the battle. It's almost time to pull off the cover and expose the mammoth's schemes.

"JT, we know that you were second in charge when it came to operations. Surely you have an idea of what these businesses are here for, don't you?" the FBI agent questions. "If we can get some information, we may be able to strike a deal that could get you a lighter sentence."

If the offer tempts JT at all, he doesn't show the slightest bit of interest. Sitting quiet as ever, he drums his fingers on the table. He's fully convinced about giving his life to Christ, but he hasn't decided to be a rat. Besides, he's more focused on life after death—if there is a Heaven or Hades, where will his soul go? JT could care less about money trails and plea deals.

Nevertheless, the agent is determined to get something from the Pharaoh. "JT, man, you have to work with me here. I'm trying to solve some cases that are years old. I want to get you a nice deal and depending on how well you cooperate, we may be able to avoid the courtroom by settling matters behind closed doors. Like I said, you gotta give us something good."

The lonesome Pharaoh seems to be paying attention now. "Yeah, I know a lot. I might be willing to tell some things, but you ain't offering anything I want."

"Mr. Trotter, what do you want?"

"I wanna see that preacher, Robinson. You know, I haven't been the best man in my life. I wanna make sure things are right before I go."

The task is too easy for the federal agent. "C'mon, sign this affidavit promising to comply with the FBI and we'll get the man you want. Now, if you don't mind me asking, why of all people do you only want to see a pastor?"

JT smiles to himself. "Like I said, I gotta make everything right before I go."

The agent settles for the answer. "Fine with me. Boyer, can you get Robinson down here as soon as possible?"

The lieutenant will make it happen.

Directing his attention back to the detainee, the agent says, "JT, you talk with the man all you want—just remember to hold up your side of the bargain when it's all over."

Boyer, grinning ear to ear, follows the agent out of the interrogation room. The prayer is making a breakthrough. Of all things JT could have asked for, he wants to speak with Pastor Robinson. This could be a double victory. The law can get the justice it seeks, and Empyreal can gain another soul.

Hell's underlings maintain their presence among the inmate hoping the time to attack will come soon. If the evil spirits have their way, JT will never taste freedom again. Not only will he die in prison, his soul will rot in Sheol as well. To ensure the mortal meets his demise, the evil spirits must have access to his body. When will that protective hedge be removed?

"We must wait patiently for the prayer to subside," says Murder.

"How much longer must we wait?" declares Insanity as he shakes a fist toward Heaven. "Look at him lounging about the place like he's royalty, he doesn't deserve this. The Tyrant is not fair."

Under normal circumstances, Murder would have put a swift kick to Insanity's rear end. On this occasion, the killing spirit feels the same way as the crazy one, so the outburst is tolerated. Murder grabs Insanity by the shoulders, and says in a hushed tone, "Remember, the Tyrant up there plays by the rules. This hedge that protects JT is only for a season. When it's lifted, we'll seize the moment and make him suffer like never before."

Slithering around corner is Deceiver. He's heard everything that has been said and realizes Murder is correct in his assessment of the situation. Yet a wretched creature such as he must still impose his authority to demonstrate his power. Slipping his coils around the necks of Murder and Insanity, Deceiver makes his entrance known. "Interesting topic that we are discussing, isn't it?"

Neither one of the subordinate spirits respond. Disappointed by the silence, the serpent tightens his coils.

Gasping for air, Murder makes an attempt to speak. "Of course … it's interesting."

"That's more like it. Now how are we going to solve this problem, fellows?" quizzes the serpent with a look of amusement on his face.

Murder replies with sarcasm, "I don't know, but I'm sure you will tell us, thou slithery one."

"You dimwitted, worthless killer—bite your tongue. It's your fault for this mess we have now. And I'll tell you what we're going to do since you don't have a plan other than waiting for a hedge to be removed." The snake draws the two spirits in closer with his coils to spew his venomous plan. With their differences aside, Molder and Insanity brighten when they hear the devious plot.

The meeting of minds is suddenly disrupted by the sounds of a lonely man praying to the enemy. All three spirits are knocked to the floor when the detainee utters that awful name. The turncoat thug has officially switched sides.

JT is praying aloud to the Tyrant, begging for mercy—and he's on his knees doing it. The demons are furious.

"Jesus Christ, I've never prayed to anyone like this before. I'm doing so to make up for the bad things I've done. I know I gotta pay the price for my sins, so I ask that justice be swift. And then, when it's all said and done, please remember me in that place you call Heaven," prays JT.

It's a small prayer but a good one for starters. Jermaine rises from his knees and takes a seat upon his bed, content as he imagines the wonders of Heavens.

The foul spirits boil with anger. They feel insulted that the repentant Pharaoh would dare pray to the Tyrant. After all he's been given, the Pharaoh dares to switch sides like a traitor? JT must be dealt with quickly now.

"That man must die before it's too late," declares the serpent.

Murder is frustrated. "How can we get to him when he's covered?"

"Very carefully," hisses the snake. "We may not be able to touch him, but somebody else in here can. We shall work around the system as we just discussed, idiots."

Insanity has his doubts. "And how will we do that?"

"You fool, take a look around here—don't you see all of these mortals who would gladly do our dirty work? That man has done much wrong to the other inmates in this jail."

The crazy demon has a revelation. "Yes, these dirt-bag mortals are worse than us demons, they'll take him out."

"Now you see the light," exclaims Deceiver.

Eager to find someone with a claim to make, Murder scrambles to start his search. His companions follow closely in his wake. They, too, are eager to find someone who can strike JT without hindrance from the Tyrant above.

The serpent remains in the cell with Jermaine, ever watchful, observing JT through a crevice of his coils. When the time is right, the snake will have his way with Mr. Trotter.

Just as Deceiver closes his eyes to retreat for a nap, a familiar figure approaches the cell provoking the snake to greater anger. "What does he want now," hisses the serpent.

35

The Setup

Pastor Robinson's visit comes earlier than expected. Jermaine had figured it may be at least a day or two before he would see the pastor. Nevertheless, the surprise is a pleasant one. With so much on his mind, how can he start the conversation? JT draws a blank, so Robinson starts the conversation in an awkward way. "Well, how's it feel to meet the man you shot?"

Trotter is thrown off guard with that question, but he does manage a response. "I don't know … I just don't know where to start."

Robinson helps him out. "I hear you made a big change in your life. Was it a hard decision?"

"It was difficult, man. You know, no one ever told me about the true love of Christ. I always thought God was for old people."

"As you can see, Jesus is for everybody. Sometimes we have to make big mistakes before realizing Christ is available to us at all times."

The Pharaoh comes clean with his feelings. "Pastor Robinson, I need to know if I'm saved, man. I gotta know somethin' before it all ends. Am I saved?"

"JT, the Bible says confess your sins and repent. Did you confess to all the wrong you've done?"

Jermaine nods his head.

"As for repenting, have you sincerely committed yourself to not doing any of those sinful things again?"

"Yeah, I have," JT confirms.

"Do you believe Jesus Christ died on the cross for the sins of the world only to rise three days later from the dead?"

"I do."

"My brother, if you have answered truthfully to those questions, then you are saved. It's that easy."

JT is not convinced. "See, that's the problem: It can't be that easy—you gotta pay somethin'. Why would He want to forgive and accept someone like me after all I've done?"

"Too good to be true, right? Okay, there's something I didn't mention. There will be some sacrificing on your part; you should no longer live for yourself, but rather, for Jesus Christ. In other words, you must develop a new way of living your life. Then you must love others as the Lord loves you."

"That's not asking much. I believe I can do all of that stuff," says the redeemed thug.

Robinson gives a warning. "Changing your lifestyle will be a difficult challenge because you must abandon old friends and destructive habits. Next of all, you gotta practice unconditional love which is not as easy as it sounds. Some people will do things making it nearly impossible for you to love them." The pastor allows his words to sink in. JT seems to understand him well. "When you give your life to Christ, the enemy will use your friends to throw the past back in your face; your faith will be tested—and if those circumstances cause the old JT to resurface in your life, you'll find yourself slipping down a slope of destruction again. Starting right now, you will have to develop a close relationship with the Lord, trusting He will provide you with patience and understanding for every situation."

"I can do that, and I will do that. When trouble comes my way, I will pray to the Lord for help," JT pledges.

"Very good, my brother, but remember, the challenge is greater than you realize. I want to leave something with you. Take this Bible and read it. Read whatever you like in this book. However, I recommend you read the New Testament." Robinson flips through the pages showing JT.

The detainee is receptive to the pastor's guidance.

"This is where you'll learn of Jesus Christ's character. You'll also see how His disciples struggled and succeeded with the common everyday issues in life. Your situation is not too different from theirs. Paul, Peter, and Stephen have walked the path you're about to take. Read about them, and you'll learn more about yourself."

The FBI agents are true to their words in allowing JT plenty of time to speak with Pastor Robinson. As the two men talk of God and other spiritual things, the serpent remains in his coils listening ... seething. Deceiver knows the hedge will come down sooner or later. When it does, JT will pay the price.

The pastor is gone, and now JT is alone. Down the corridor, he can hear the sound of jingling keys. The noise indicates someone is headed toward JT's location. A correctional officer whom Trotter has never seen before opens the cell. "Get dressed," he sternly commands.

"Where are you takin' me?"

"Shut up," snaps the unknown guard. "I ask the questions around here. Just do as you're told, and there won't be any problems—yet."

JT can sense that the guard is up to something devious. Getting dressed, he makes his way out of the cell ready to walk as directed.

"Stop," the guard shouts, "you know better than that. Since when do we walk about this place without handcuffs? Turn around. Place your hands behind your back. Try anything funny, we'll crack your jug head."

Two other guards stand in the corridor grinning, wishing JT would try something foolish.

Slowly, JT turns around and assumes the position. When the handcuffs are fastened, he feels a shove in his back signaling him to walk. "Hey, officer, where y'all takin' me?"

"Shut up, boy, we gotcha now; gonna take good care of you too."

Slithering behind JT and the guards are Deceiver, Murder, and a small host of other malevolent spirits. They cackle fiendishly as the prisoner is led down the corridor like a lamb to the slaughter.

As they approach the main holding cells, JT can hear catcalls from the inmates as his presence is made known by the guards. "Look here, boys, at what we got," the officer announces loudly to the whole jailhouse population. "We got a special one here. I think everybody knows Jermaine 'JT' Trotter, king of the Pharaohs? If there's something you need, just give ol' JT a holler."

The celebrity inmate is shown a cell that he must share with a brute like himself from a rival gang. Looking about the place, all JT sees is the enemy. The guards deliberately put the Pharaoh among rival gangbangers, knowing full well the probable consequences of such a move.

The officers head back to the corridor where they join two lone figures. JT can't see for sure whom the guards are talking with, but they sure resemble the two detectives, Hughes and Diggs.

While things are not looking too good for JT, the opposite can be said for the Christians in the Harlem Heights community. The recent turn of events, which first appeared to be a tragedy, have led to wonderful opportunities. It's amazing how the Lord can make a bad situation good.

Sharing the good news with one another are Louise and Angela. Both are pleased with the sudden progress of the Light of Hope church group. "I'm working on a story that details the church's struggle to meet the spiritual needs of the community," the reporter tells Louise. "It will take a whole series of articles just to explain it all."

Louise is impressed. "Sounds like you have a lot work to do."

"Yeah, I do. This is the kind of work I like, though. It's work with a mission."

"So what's so special about this article?"

The reporter corrects Mrs. Robinson. "Series of articles."

"Okay, this *series* of articles," Louise says with a smile. "What's so special about them?"

"My plan is to structure these articles like journal entries—basically, present them as a log of your experiences here with the church. It will start at the beginning, from when you all first came to Harlem Heights and then document your activities thereafter."

"Sounds interesting," Louise comments.

"It should make for a good story, and I believe a lot of people will be interested in knowing what you all went through."

"You know, your writing can help others who are going through a similar experience to ours. There's no telling where it could lead to."

As the women talk, a car pulls up into the driveway unnoticed. Not until Louise hears a key in the door does she realize her husband is home. Behind Randy comes Sergeant Perez. Both women are pleased to see their men.

Greetings quickly exchanged, the journalist reveals her idea about the articles. Randy and Perez take the time to listen.

"Definitely a good idea," the pastor comments, "and it will be even better once we take care of one more thing."

"What might that be, honey?" inquires Louise.

"It's JT; we have reason believe that his life is in great danger."

His wife doesn't share the same concern. "Why are you so worried about a man who almost killed you? What more can you do for him?"

"Sweetheart, you have to see the whole picture. JT has given his life to Christ, and we should make sure he remains steadfast in his faith."

Louise gives her husband a cynical look as if she's heard that lame excuse before.

Paying the gesture no mind, Randy continues his explanation. "Yes, he did a bad thing, but please understand where he comes from," the pastor implores. He wasn't born in the best of circumstances. Its taken all the unfortunate things—like my shooting—to get this man to see the light. If the rest of these gang members can see the change in JT, we can then turn this city around quickly."

Mrs. Robinson surrenders. "All right, Randy, stop preaching at me."

"Baby, I'm just trying to make you see where I'm coming from."

"Honey, I understand and fully accept the idea of you helping him out."

"Are you sure?" he asks emphatically.

"Yes, Angela and I have already talked about it. How can I love Christ who laid down His life for those who despised Him and not accept JT?"

"Good, because I'm going to need your help with one more issue."

"What now, Randy?"

"I need you to make phone calls to the people on this list." Pastor Robinson hands his wife a list of names. "Ask if they'll join us for a special prayer service."

Angela chimes in, "When were you going to tell us about this prayer service? Are we invited too?"

"Of course—everybody is invited. More importantly, we need to get the community church leaders involved in this prayer service to make it work."

Sergeant Perez is eager to know more details. "When will this prayer service take place?"

"In due time … don't worry. We'll all be there if the good Lord is willing—gotta win this city back."

Solomon and Lee stand among the mortals listening. The reinforcements needed to make the plan work have been arriving by the hour. Heaven's warriors will be ready for the great battle.

Fratricide sits on his throne questioning the reports he's received from his subordinates. There's been a noticeable increase of angelic activity, which indicates the enemy is prepping for battle. Still, things have been quiet in the city … too quiet. "Hmm, what is the enemy doing? Has anything of significance happened in my kingdom?" the big one demands to know.

The minions standing before him respond with silence until one of them, fidgeting, catches the attention of Fratricide, who yells, "Politician, answer me, what's going on in my city?"

The demon responsible for government affairs responds like a true politician. "All is fair, my lord. The mayor is still our puppet to dangle as we see fit. His constituents are loyal, and there's no threat that they might attempt betrayal. They all share a common flaw—guilty of corruption."

Content with politics, Fratricide carries on to another spirit. "Education, how are the schools coming along?"

The scoundrel beams with pride. "The schools are worse than ever. Most children have no respect for authority, and the parents have no interest in their children's lives. We've convinced society that kids sometimes have a chemical imbalance in their brains, which makes students misbehave. As parents feed their children a steady diet of Ritalin and Prozac, we undermine the ability of these kids to deal with the stress of everyday life. Master, as these kids become adults, Hell is harvesting a generation of losers."

"Splendid, keep up the *bad* work, Education," says Fratricide, amused by his own pun. The behemoth directs his attention farther down the line, making inquiries of his demons of racism, sickness, substance abuse—and of other spirits who plague mortals with vices. All have good reports to make except for one—Law Enforcer.

"Enforcer, what's the meaning of your report?"

"My lord, as I told you earlier, the FBI has been snooping about the police department."

"What is the purpose of their presence?"

"They have questions for the man who shot the loud-mouth preacher. I assure you, my lord, no sensitive information has been told."

As Enforcer speaks, Deceiver subtly draws the attention of Informer. Like the sneaky imp he is, the runt eases over to the serpent to hear some juicy gossip—he hopes. The snake doesn't disappoint. Informer gets an ear full of dirt that will put Enforcer in hot water. Sneaking back to Fratricide, the runt eagerly baits the overlord with questions to ask Enforcer. "Master, ask him who are the angels at the precinct protecting?"

Knowing full well how the game is played, Fratricide obliges Informer in his folly. "What is the status of this mortal, JT?"

Enforcer is caught off guard with this question, yet his quick wit takes over and enables him to answer wisely. "JT has been put into general population among rival gang members who will take his life at the first opportunity."

Informer is just getting started. He whispers another concern for Fratricide to ask about.

The behemoth takes the bait. "And what about the hedge that's been placed about the mortal? How can you get to a man when the enemy has him protected, hmm?"

"It is only temporary, my lord," says Enforcer. "This man has committed great sins, which opened the doorway for us to intervene. When the hedge is lifted, his life will be taken."

Informer doesn't stop. He tells Fratricide about the agreement that JT has made with the FBI to meet with Pastor Robinson in exchange for a plea deal.

Enforcer responds with a lie. "Master, no such thing has happened under my watch. JT has told nothing. Neither has he inquired about giving his soul to the enemy."

Deceiver snickers as he watches Enforcer squirm on the hot seat. As the snake relishes the idea of putting another fool in the spotlight, the table is suddenly turned on him as Enforcer addresses Fratricide. "My lord, there is one issue we must discuss: The spirit responsible for running interference against the saints is slacking. The saints are praying again which makes my job more difficult. Why, my lord?"

Blindsided by Enforcer's question, Deceiver quickly stops the snickering to muster an explanation. He's already envisioning the mammoth's meaty hand wrapped around his neck.

"You slimy imbecile," shouts Fratricide, whirling to face Deceiver. "Why are the saints praying, hmm? It's your job to block prayers to the Tyrant."

The serpent is squirming now. "As Enforcer mentioned, my lord, we are going to kill the mortal."

"He has a hedge about him, remember, fool?" the behemoth yells. "Shall you undo the work of the Carpenter?"

"My lord, it's just a matter of time. He is not an innocent man. We all know the Tyrant is fair; He will lift that hedge in due time. When he does, we'll take JT's life."

"Of course, you'll kill the man—who cares? But, back to the original question—why are the saints praying?"

Deceiver, far from being a dummy, realizes the consequences of any answer he may give the overlord. Claiming to be busy with JT will make him appear negligent of his main duties. Professing to be overwhelmed by the power of the saints will make the serpent look weak. The thick anaconda answers wisely. "My lord, the Tyrant has used our victory against us by rallying the mortals around the pastor's shooting. He plays on the emotions of these gut-bag humans whose hearts are drawn toward gloom. Had we foreseen this move, we could have taken different measures. This is why the saints pray."

Seeing an opportunity to speak, Enforcer chimes in with his belief. "These mud-sack humans are all the same. They cry to the enemy when in trouble. Where are their voices when things are going good? We'll make JT quite comfortable and see how much salvation he requires when there's no need for him to struggle."

"For your own sakes, you two better hope that Hades wins this man's soul," Fratricide threatens. "Your failure to destroy that mortal will only seal your fate for an early arrival to the abyss."

Deceiver and Enforcer are now bound together more out of obligation than camaraderie. The two must cooperate or bust Sheol wide open in the near future.

36

The War Room

Randy is ready to meet with the various church leaders throughout the city. Everyone will gather at the downtown protestant chapel, which is centrally located and big enough to accommodate a large crowd. Randy grabs his book bag and a rolled-up map. Now he and Louise are ready to make their way downtown.

Louise is concerned. "Are you sure this is going work?"

"Honey, I have faith this will work. I've prayed and meditated on it; I feel this is the right thing to do. If it be His will, tonight's meeting will be a success."

Mrs. Robinson finds her husband's words encouraging.

The minivan rolls into the church parking lot. It's early and the parking spaces closest to the building are still available. Robinson parks the vehicle, grabs the map along with other personal belongings and exits the van. Louise slings her purse over her shoulder, closes the passenger side door and falls in beside Randy as they head toward the church.

A middle-aged lady wearing glasses greets the couple as they reach the front door. "Hello, I'm the pastor's wife, Lorraine, and you two must be the Robinsons." All three exchange hugs and smiles. "Come right on in and get situated. We've been waiting for this meeting all week. Our media room is just down the hallway. You'll see we have everything to accommodate your needs."

"Wow, the resources here are wonderful," comments Randy.

The hostess, Lorraine, is flattered. "I'm glad that you like it. I'm sure you'll find everything to your liking."

Inside the media room, Randy unrolls his map and pins it to a bulletin board. Then he begins to put the colored thumbtacks back in their respective places. Meanwhile, Louise prepares the projector for the slide show. The presentation itself will be a simple task. Getting the church leaders to buy the idea of strategic prayer warfare may be the challenge.

As the starting time draws near, church leaders begin filling the room. Pastor Robinson had been hoping that at least half the people invited would show up. Surprisingly, the majority of the leaders are there. Feeling optimistic, the pastor perceives the attendance as a good sign.

Randy begins the meeting by inviting a Baptist minister to lead the group in prayer. Following the prayer, all attendees are asked to introduce themselves and the church they represent. This serves as an icebreaker that enables the ministers to put down their guard and relax.

Lee is impressed with his brother's work. "Solomon, the atmosphere in here is light. You all did a good job ensuring no one brought any issues with them."

The messenger is pleased. "Praise to the Most High, things are going well. The guardians are on their job now encouraging these mortals to be accepting of one another. The quicker we develop a bond among these humans, the sooner we can begin our attack on Fratricide."

"We just have to be sure the enemy does not get a foothold in here," says Lee as he spots a few imps sneaking about the room like rats. "If they did not have the right to be here, I would send them hurling to the pit of Hell."

Solomon acknowledges the concerns. "The presence of those devils sickens me too. Someday there will be a time when all of our church leaders are righteous ... without sin."

"Well, redemption starts at the top. These people will carry back to their churches lessons they will learn here. May the Father above equip these mortals with the knowledge they need to win back their city," declares Lee.

The brothers grip hands and embrace each other before going their separate ways to execute their missions. Lee is responsible for keeping outside intruders from interfering with the meeting. He has dispatched warriors to monitor the perimeter of the church. There will be no electric power failures; neither shall any imp start an argument to distract the people. Solomon is responsible for the message. He will make sure the saints properly execute the game plan. There will be no misunderstanding to cause strife among the leaders; the divide-and-conquer tactic will not work here.

Pastor Robinson reveals the city map to the church leaders, explaining the problems that have plagued each area of Harlem Heights. In the minority neighborhoods, the problems are obvious: substance abuse, violence, and poverty are the main culprits afflicting the people of color. The issues in the more affluent areas of the city are not so easily seen. Government policies and corrupt business practices are the underlying problems.

As the church leaders receive their assignments, they break into groups to discuss their tasks in detail. Like artillery units, they identify specific targets so they know where to aim their prayers. If their efforts are sincere, conditions will change in the targeted areas. If all the leaders can attack their areas at the same time, then all of Harlem Heights will undergo an immediate change. Humans and spirits alike hope the mortals can see the plan through to the end.

The church leaders will return at the end of the week to wage a real battle with Hades' forces. A showdown is brewing.

JT's move to general population is a surprise. More surprising is the fact that no one attempted to harm him. The rival gang members, also having issues with the police, know exactly why the guards placed JT among their kind. They refused to give the police the satisfaction of seeing the Pharaoh get a beat-down. Fate seems to be on Jermaine's side until he is moved again to be among his own gang.

"Hey, JT, what's up man?" says a fellow gang member.

"I'm all right, what's up, bro?"

A brief exchange of greetings, a few seconds of an uncomfortable silence, and a conversation evolves.

"Hey man, word has it that you lost your mind. They say you shot that preacher in broad daylight then stood around just watching. Is that true?"

JT gives a one-word answer, "Partially."

"Then we hear you found religion since you've been locked up. The guards say they seen you on your knees praying to that cat called Jesus. You ain't going out like that, are you?"

A true change must have occurred in JT. There was once a time when he would have lashed out if someone dared to question him in such a manner. Now he sits calmly, taking little offense to the questions.

"JT, I see they tried to put you with the enemy on the other side. Man, we gonna make the guards pay for that move. We also got a plan to take out some of those Reds over there, you down with us?"

"Naw, man. Y'all got it; I don't want any part of it. Gotta lot on my mind, need to sort a few things out."

JT's spiritual hecklers stand by listening to the conversation. They cannot afflict JT as they wish, but they do their best to work through the other mortals. As a group of Pharaohs gathers about their notorious leader, spiritual whispers start to bubble among them. Within their midst are imps determined to start trouble. "*I can't believe this joker is not willing to represent the set. This can't be the JT I know,*" whispers a spirit in the mind of a doubting hooligan.

Disbelief spreads among the group causing the mumbling to get louder. "The word is already out—this punk is a sell-out. If he ain't with us, then he must be against us. This sucker has to go," declares a demonically inspired inmate.

Many of the Pharaohs echo the imp's thoughts; however, there's one sympathizer who makes an attempt to save the reluctant leader. "Hold up, that's JT, we can't do him like that."

"Why not? This man is a turncoat punk. He turned his back on Mo', and you heard for yourself, he's praying to a white man's god. He ain't down with us," says a thugged-out gangbanger.

The lone defendant doesn't agree with the comment. "Listen to how you sound. Everybody knows Jesus was a black man. The Bible says He had skin like copper and hair like wool."

"Stop lying! Every picture I saw of Jesus had blue eyes and long straight, blonde hair. I ain't never saw a dark-skinned Jesus sportin' an afro," the laughing gangster quips. "And I don't care what color Jesus was, JT's still a sellout."

"So why you gotta say things about Jesus being a white man's god?"

The accuser reveals his bogus answer. "'Cause JT's tryin' to use religion to get out of jail, so he can hang out with that white boy at the club sellin' dope. Who's gonna get us out of jail?"

"Man, you just a player-hater."

The side-bar conversation is over and the gang's attention is refocused on JT. Most of the crowd is still uncertain, and none moves too hastily. If by chance this is all a mistake, they don't want to suffer the consequences.

Yet one person is bold enough to approach JT. Young Shelton—aka Shel-Rock—is an aspiring thug who's eager to assert himself as a true gangster. The two stand face-to-face exchanging mad-dog stares. Shel-Rock does his best to provoke JT, but the elder Pharaoh has seen this act many times before, and he is not intimidated. However, Jermaine knows the young gangster is committed which means Shel-Rock must follow through with his actions or suffer ridicule from his peers. The hot-tempered young one gives JT a violent shove that causes a Bible to flutter from Trotter's hand like a wounded bird before the eyes of the inmates.

"You a sucker for readin' a book like that. Ol' punk, whatcha gonna do now?" Shel-Rock quips.

The sharks smell blood. A frenzy of violence begins to simmer among the gang members as they surround JT. If they were waiting on the green light to start a fight, Shelton's aggression is the only signal they need to begin the assault. And just when a beat-down is about to take place, all action stops. Holy guardians hover above with swords drawn, a fierce look in their eyes and a strong desire for a fight.

An order is given. "Hold your peace, it is not time yet!"

Reluctantly complying, the rogue spirits slink away spewing blasphemous curses.

JT's attention is drawn from the angry mob to the swat team that has just entered the jail, taking their respective places on the second-floor corridor. The guards aim weapons at the crowd below while a voice on the loud speaker shouts commands: "Everyone, face-down on the floor, now! You have ten seconds!"

JT gives praise to the Lord as he assumes the proper position. Moments later the Pharaoh is taken back to an isolated cell where no inmates can have access to him.

Deceiver, already beyond frustration, is further heated by the sudden turn of events... The spirit is on a tirade. "Look at this despicable human," he shrieks. "I can't believe the Tyrant kicked us out of Empyreal for the sake of these walking trash sacks. Enjoy the moment while it lasts. Thou shall suffer greatly when that hedge is lifted."

Out of anger and frustration, the serpent whips his tail at Murder, Insanity, and Suicide causing them to scramble out of reach of those choking coils.

"It repulses me how this bag of vomit pretends to be holier than thou," continues the serpent. "This maggot human never needed a savior when things were going good. What name did this dog call upon when he ran wild with the pack scratching his fleas and chasing the desires of his heart?" The snake is so obsessed with anger, he slobbers bile from his reptile mouth.

"Nothing held him back, not even the Tyrant himself," hisses the spirit. "Now he does one thing to get in a bit of trouble, and he feels justified in crying to the Carpenter for help—you ungrateful idiot." Deceiver is all in JT's face hissing and spitting his venomous accusations at the repentant Pharaoh. "We blessed him with money and turf to call his own kingdom, and this is how he shows his gratitude? To Hell with his soul. We shall condemn this fool to Hades with the rest of the wormwood mortals," vows Deceiver as he consoles his subordinates after lashing out at them.

Meanwhile, JT sits alone in his cell reading that book which demons consider wretched. Free from any hindrances, the former gangbanger reads a segment of the New Testament. The life of Jesus is imprinted on his mind. Repeatedly he reads about Christ laying down his life for mankind because all have sinned and fallen short of glory. This means to JT that there's a place for him too in Heaven.

Still engrossed in the Bible, Jermaine is surprised by a visitor—Pastor Robinson makes an unannounced appearance. Pleased nonetheless, Jermaine joyfully receives his newfound friend.

Robinson is eager to learn about JT's progress. "Have you read the scriptures I recommended?"

"Yeah, man, I've been thinkin' deeply about 'em."

The pastor is impressed. "Well, how's your relationship with Christ coming along?"

"Since your last visit, a lot of strange things have been happenin' around here. Twice I've been in trouble, and both times I was saved from harm," JT reveals.

A sense of urgency stirs the pastor's soul. "You really seem convinced it was divine intervention that saved you from trouble."

"Man, it had to be the hand of God."

"Is this proof enough for you that Jesus Christ is real and His love is beyond measure?"

"Yeah, the Lord is real to me; there's no doubtin' that."

The sissy talk makes Deceiver sick to his wicked stomach. The wretched mortals' conversation compels the snake to intervene, but a sudden iron grip around the neck jolts the serpent's body into tight coils. Lee has the serpent in a death grip. The angel also has a sword that he is gliding back and forth over the scales of the snake causing his belly to quiver. "I would think twice about that if I were you," Lee warns.

The conversation continues in the physical realm between the two humans uninterrupted.

JT has a request to ask of Pastor Robinson. "You know, I've already prayed to be a Christian, but I would like it better if we could do it together. Please pray with me that God will accept me as his own."

Robinson is more than happy to do so. "Okay, brother, just repeat after me: Lord, I believe you came to Earth in the form of Jesus Christ to die for my sins. You laid down your life only to rise three days later. This you did to pay the cost for my sins."

JT repeats every word that Robinson speaks.

"So, Jesus, now I confess that I have sinned. I have faith that you now forgive me, and I believe with my heart that I am now saved. No matter what happens from this moment on, I will trust in you," the pastor says.

Empyreal rejoices as another name is written in the Lamb's Book of Life. The Heavenly laughter causes the devils in the jail to cover their ears as if the rejoicing is torture.

The pastor takes a few moments to give thanks to the Lord for saving the Pharaoh's soul. Overwhelmed by the magnitude of this victory, Robinson wants to ensure Jermaine remains encouraged. "JT, remember that this change you just experienced is an ever-evolving process. You must take this journey one day at a time. You still have some old habits that will take time to break. Also, don't rely totally on your emotions as an indicator of where you stand with Christ. The enemy can easily manipulate your feelings to mislead you with emotions."

JT chimes in, "Yeah, man, you're right about that."

"Just continue to read about the life of Jesus. Study his character closely, taking heed to the situations in which He found Himself and also the disciples. The word of God will benefit you greatly in here. Get it into your heart and don't turn from it."

Before Robinson can end the meeting, a guard signals to the pastor it's time to leave. Not wanting to jeopardize the chance of a future visit, Randy departs immediately. But he offers one last bit of guidance as he goes. "If you have any questions, you can always talk with Officer B."

Officer B, who is Officer B? JT thinks to himself. No sooner than he can finish the thought does Lieutenant Boyer appear before him smiling. "I'll help you as much as I can."

Still agonized by the rejoicing in Heaven, Deceiver seethes with anger and can hardly wait for the hedge to be lifted. JT will be tested. If the snake has its way, the mortal's punishment will serve as an example for all others who dare to leave the game.

37

Saints Up, Fratricide Down

Pastor Robinson and the group meet again. This time the meeting takes place in the streets of Harlem Heights. Members from the black churches stand alongside the congregations from the white churches. A leader from each group takes the forefront, facing one another. Both figures have issues they want to address publicly.

The white minister begins first. "I would like to take this opportunity to apologize for the racist practice of my forefathers in this city. Though it was long ago, I admit that blacks were overlooked by our society and dealt a substandard level of living. We discriminated against them, physically abused them, and now implement government policies that perpetuate the problems that eat away at black society."

A dark-skinned woman in the audience weeps aloud in typical soul fashion. Her passion for change causes others in the audience to quietly cry. Both groups can feel the burdens lift from their souls. Angels surrounding the crowd give praise to the Lord as the people pray for forgiveness. A few moments of rejoicing then another confession is made.

The black minister quiets the crowd to begin his speech. "I would like to confess the shortcomings of my people—how we turned our backs on the virtues of the Bible to embrace the bittersweet sins of the city. Please forgive us for surrendering our dedication to honest work for the quick dollar hustled on the streets. We now admit the white man alone is not the sole cause of our problems. For oftentimes our greatest enemy has been the black man himself. Failure to take responsibility for our own problems has led mostly to our demise. Please forgive us for burdening society with our problems."

Waving her hands in the air, the big soulful woman expresses herself again. "Oh, thank you, Jesus, this is what our city needs."

As the ministers complete their remarks, the two racial groups come together as a single mass to exchange hugs. They also introduce themselves to one another while apologizing for past sins. This is just one portion of the city in Harlem Heights. In other sections of the city, Heaven's servants are reuniting the people too.

The results of all these demonstrations of love are having a negative effect on Fratricide's kingdom. Sheol's messengers come by the minute to inform the big one of the saints' activity. "My lord," says a messenger, "I have word from Prince Zelub of the east side."

"Speak."

"Master, the white and black mortals on the east side have gathered to forgive one another for past transgressions," says the messenger with his head bowed low.

Fratricide is not pleased but remains silent. However, his patience draws thin as another messenger appears before him with bad news. It doesn't stop there; more and more arrivals come with reports of the saints gathering together to repent of past sins. The trickle of bad news has become a monsoon of trouble that overwhelms Fratricide. More so than ever, the big one can feel his grip on the city slipping. Suddenly, he emits a deafening roar. "Why am I just hearing about this, hmm? Somebody had to know this was coming. Heads around here are going to roll if no one puts a stop to this foolishness—summon my warriors now."

Before the warriors are called, another messenger comes before Fratricide. This imp flutters in on one wing, for the other is torn to shreds and its body bears multiple cuts and bruises. The gremlin carries the remaining fragments of a sword that has somehow been broken off in battle.

Like an airplane preparing for an emergency crash landing, the imp buzzes about in looping circles. Finally, he attempts to touch softly to the ground. His balance is off—probably due to his missing foot. At the last second, he flutters out of control and spills forward causing his ugly rodent face to drag along the ground as he skids toward the throne.

Squealing from pain, the wretched rascal gathers his bearing. "Master..." the haggardly looking spirit struggles to catch his breath, "We are under attack! A host of enemy forces have staged a surprise assault. They have destroyed our stronghold on the west side. It is awful," cries the imp. "I am one of the few who managed to survive."

"What is this I hear, hmm? The saints are not only praying, but enemy forces have engaged us in combat? This cannot be so—summon my warriors now."

Standing before the mammoth are war-mongering hellions who crave a fight with a formable foe. Swords already in hand, they wait eagerly for the command to attack.

Alongside the mammoth is an advisor. He kneels before his master begging a moment of consideration. "Let's not be so hasty, my lord. We don't know what awaits us. We still have the stronghold here and also the government. The saints may have confessed their sins and shaken hands, but it's only for a moment. Maintaining freedom is harder than getting it. Let's wait, master," the servant pleads with the big one.

Fratricide considers the idea and after a moment's time agrees with the advice. "Let's wait. We shall take this opportunity to lay down snares to entrap those who dare to rob me of my kingdom."

The big one's warriors sheath their swords. Their directive to attack is postponed for now.

"Let the saints have their confessions," declares the behemoth. "We still possess the curse on this entire city. Our loyal mortals pay tribute to us on a weekly basis. This is no threat; just a desperate move by worms to make us slip our grip of dominance. The enemy's attack will not thwart my plans."

As for the remainder of his kingdom, it remains safe and unhindered. Still, Fratricide sends reinforcements to maintain their security. He's determined to keep a grip on the business district, night clubs, bars, porno stores, and pawnshops that line the streets like trophy cases. This is the fruit of the big one's labor. It will take an all-out war to rip this from the overlord's hand.

"How did Fratricide's forces react?" inquires Solomon.

"We caught him off guard. With the reinforcements we received, it was easy work taking ground from the enemy within the neighborhoods—as a matter fact, too easy," remarks Lee. "One would think the mammoth would have a contingency plan in place to maintain a foothold."

"The big one's long-term success has made him complacent," Solomon speculates. "But what's the lost of a few neighborhoods? His power source is the government and the business district."

Lee agrees with his brother. "Why not forsake the people when they know very little about the city's secret pact hidden deep within the pages of history? Yet there is one danger in neglecting the people."

"What's that?" queries a sly Solomon.

"When the people come together to pray, the saints can wreak havoc beyond one's wildest imagination," proclaims the angelic warrior.

"Yes, let him hide in city hall; let his demons hide among the filthy shops. The prayers will undermine their power base."

The two captains give glory to the Lord, thanking Jesus Christ for the battle they believe already won.

Solomon leads the ministering spirits to the air for their follow-up mission. Their duty is to spread the gospel in the newly claimed territories. The mortals must be encouraged to pray to the Lord, making it easier to tear down Fratricide's kingdom.

Business on the streets has come to a near standstill; there's plenty of product, but no demand. Mo' is putting pressure on his Pharaohs to make sells, but they can't force the customers to buy.

Making matters worse is the division settling in among members of Willie Mo's gang. Some of the Pharaohs question why Mo' hasn't bailed JT out from jail, and they have trouble with some of Mo's orders.

"C'mon, man," complains one member, "what's up with all these orders? We can't go past Palm Beach Boulevard, that's the forbidden zone. Not even the Reds go that far pushin' dope."

"Hey, you gotta problem with it, talk with Mo'," says another member. "He wants those kids at the high school to have easier access."

The youngster is angry. "Oh yeah, who's gonna bail us out if we get flipped? Mo' gonna leave us hangin' like he did JT if we get caught sellin' near school grounds?"

"Better watch yo' mouth before you get caught up. You sell where Mo' tells you to. If you don't, you'll be on your own—and don't say I didn't warn you."

The situation is becoming difficult. Getting rid of his second-hand man has proven to be Mo's first major mistake. Though JT's abuse of alcohol was more an irritation than a hindrance, Willie is feeling the absence of his muscle to make things happen on the streets.

Molder and Wrath are getting worried too. Willie is not aware of it, but his spiritual companions can see the changes taking place in Harlem Heights. If matters were to worsen, the saints could possibly ruin the demons' operations.

The spirit guide voices his concern. "I sense uneasiness in the streets."

Wrath's assessment confirms the notion. "The enemy has taken ground from Fratricide; some of the neighborhoods reflect the Tyrant's glow."

"We must ensure no harm comes to this mortal vessel. Willie Mo' is too precious to lose right now," Molder admits. "The dirtbag may not be a Roman emperor, but we've done all right under his rule—living here ain't bad at all. We can get one or two more decades out of this worm if we use him the right way."

"I've been promised his offspring; the first-born male shall be mine. I will groom a warrior in my own fashion to rule these streets. So yes, let us see to it that no harm comes to our precious chattel. Work this slave until we need him no more," says Wrath with gratification.

They stand behind the mortal, Mo', watching him as he stares at the people socializing throughout the club. The man's eyes are drawn toward the strippers dancing on stage. Though dancers come and go all the time, the routine remains the same. Willie is not aroused.

Looking elsewhere, he watches men in business suits enter the club. Immediately Mo' thinks, *more money.* He gazes onward to where Tommy is sitting at his usual spot at the bar. The mayor's son is sipping a drink he's been nursing for the past hour. Willie Mo' keeps his eyes steadfast on Tommy for a good minute. Something's changed about the mayor's son. Willie can't place his finger on it, yet something is different.

If Hades' minions could see all, they would notice a business card in Tommy's back pocket. Somehow Boyer got word to Perez and the FBI agents to established contact with Tommy. He's another key to the dark world of Mo'. If Willie can't be caught on drug charges, the law will find him guilty of something else—anything to get a person like him off the streets.

38

It Fades Away

Back at the jail, Jermaine Trotter and Lieutenant Boyer talk with one another. JT has been going through some trying times, yet the more trouble he endures the more encouraged he feels about Christ.

The former thug is disappointed. "Mr. Boyer, I can't believe my very own friends in here have turned against me," he confesses. "Man, it's not like I quit the gang to join the enemy. I'm still JT. I just believe in Jesus Christ—that's all. How bad can that be?"

"Well, my friend, I'm not surprised to hear this. It happened to Jesus; it's only natural for it to happen to you. Remember, you may be *in* this world, but you are no longer *of* this world. Funny as it may sound, this is a big deal."

JT is puzzled. "What's so bad about living for Christ?"

"You gotta understand there's a war going on in the spiritual realm where there is no such thing as a neutral side. You just made a decision to fight against the very same enemy that employs your so-called friends. As I said before, you've upset certain individuals who can't stand to see you live your life for Christ. If they could have their way, you would suffer greatly for your decision to embrace Jesus."

Jermaine continues to vent his frustrations. "Talk about player hatin'—I've never felt so much pressure. I wish I could share the message with the fellas in here, but no one wants to listen. After all the dirt I did, I can't really blame them."

Of all the statements JT has made, his spirit tormentors finally agree with him on that one issue. Deceiver takes the lead. "That's right, Judas, you have no right to talk about salvation after all the wrong you have done. Who's going to listen to a hypocrite? You are no better than the rest of these vermin mortals in here … in fact, you're worse. You taught most of these criminals how to live the thug life. This place is your handiwork, and now you want to run to the Carpenter King for refuge. No, you trash bag. You will rot in Hades with the rest of the maggots in here."

As the Deceiver ends his tirade, the other scoundrels continue to the badger the human. They spew curses at the man as he stands in his cell talking with Lieutenant Boyer.

The angels that guard JT's life stand at a distance. They have orders to intervene only if the mortal's life is in danger; otherwise, the man is free game. As JT gains knowledge and strength in his Christian faith, the protective hedge is gradually removed. Now he must learn to fight in the spiritual realm.

"JT, there's something I need to tell you about the Christian fight," says Lieutenant Boyer. "It's not like any other conflict you've been in before. We don't fight in the flesh; our battle is in the spiritual realm where prayer is the most effective weapon."

Boyer shows JT a passage in the Bible that teaches how to put on the full armor of God. "In the New Testament, there's the book of Ephesians." The lieutenant directs JT to chapter six, verses eleven through eighteen. "This is where you find instructions on how to protect yourself from the enemy's assault. Read this passage each morning and go through the motions of putting on each individual piece of armor."

Jermaine takes a moment to read the scriptures.

"And don't step out of this cell unless you're fully strapped —understand what I'm saying?"

"Yeah, man, I hear ya."

"I've got one last bit of advice for you. When you've done all that you can and nothing seems to work, you should praise the Heavenly Father. There's something special about the power of praise and worship that can't be totally explained. Do it anytime, but especially when times get rough."

That's what those church folks were doing when we ..." another painful memory floods JT's mind. "... when we burnt down that church a few months ago."

How could he have burned down a church with people inside because they spoke against selling drugs? Then he had tried to take the life of Mattie Moore as she recovered in the hospital. How shameful. JT's eyes become watery and one single drop is about to roll down his face, but a knuckle-scarred hand quickly wipes it away.

Deceiver rips into him again. "You are not worthy of forgiveness. Curse the Lord and die, worm. That's the best you can do for yourself. There is no place in Paradise for a wretch like you."

Taking his cue from the serpent, Insanity ridicules the mortal by pounding his mind with accusations. The crazy one is trying to convince JT that he cannot be forgiven for his sins; to believe so is lunacy.

Lieutenant Boyer can't see the battle taking place in JT's head, but he senses the struggle.

Taking extra effort to concentrate, JT struggles to stay focused on the topic at hand. The hedge is starting to fade. With the grace of God, Jermaine Trotter will have to bear his own burden.

Deceiver is relentless. "Yes, the tide is heading back out to sea. Once this hedge is fully gone, we will have full access to this fool. Ride him until he collapses; grind that entire gospel out of him. Those saints think they will harvest his soul. Never! We shall press his soul and drink his blood like wine. He is the fruit of our labor, not the saints'. Let us prepare him to meet his doom."

Dinner is being served at the jailhouse. JT stands in the receiving line waiting his turn for food. Chowtime is the most nerve-racking part of the day. This is when all inmates have full access to one another. Since the last altercation, JT doesn't feel so safe standing alone in the chow line with no one to watch his back.

The jailhouse guards do a good job of keeping rival gang members separated from one another, but the issue for JT is staying safe among his own kind. He can feel the stares of others burning his back. Something's up, and the redeemed thug senses it.

The old serpent is among the mortals in the cafeteria. He and his underlings slither about the place stirring up trouble.

More than usual, the inmates are rowdy and restless; there's a lot of pushing and crowding in the lines. JT tries to keep his distance, but the criminals standing behind him demand that Jermaine close the gap in the line.

Now the imps get busy. They fill the humans' minds with gossip, burn their ears with rumors. All the talk is about the traitor who turned his back on the gang to become a Christian.

For those who don't fall for that propaganda, there's another story that suggests JT agreed to a plea deal to shorten his sentence at the expense of Willie Mo'. One of those stories should do the trick. At the least, it's enough to get a shoving match going among a couple of inmates.

Standing nearby is Shel-Rock and a partner in crime, a conspirator. Pretending to be in a heated argument, Shel-Rock violently shoves the conspiring thug. In retaliation, the goon returns the push, and, of course, another person jumps in to break it up. Now there are three individuals tangled up in a squabble.

The imps, too, are involved. They tussle with one another being sure to steer the mortals in the direction of JT. As the conflict makes it way to the Christian, more men jump into the fight. The scuffle becomes a riot that swallows up JT and brings him to the ground.

Punches and kicks fly everywhere. Though many men are struck, JT receives the majority of the blows, and he is unable to defend himself. Hit after hit makes contact with his head and ribs. He can't tell for sure, but his sides feel warm and wet. A thought goes through his mind that he may have been stabbed. Making a conscious effort to concentrate on his body, JT can feel a deep cut on his side as the pain starts to register. The inmates are cutting Jermaine's body with shanks. All one can see are elbows and arms flying—ripping and stabbing JT's belly.

As quickly as the riot started, it ends. The fighters slink away to hide among the innocent onlookers standing in the chow line or sitting at the tables.

JT is left alone squirming along the floor like an injured rat struggling to get back to a hole.

An inmate yells, "Where you goin', man?" Laughter erupts from the mob.

The lone victim ceases to move, seeming to succumb to the drowsy feeling of death.

Though the mortals have stopped the physical assault, the imps still pounce upon JT in celebration, hoping to torture him for the brief remainder of his life. The serpent, pleased with the outcome, joyfully hisses, "Yes, kill him; make him suffer!"

As the devils torture Jermaine's soul, the mortal, in a feeble effort, reaches his hands toward Empyreal. What he sees is a surprise. There's no Jacob's ladder, but the guardians are coming down; the sons of Heaven descend to the jailhouse cafeteria just to comfort one ragged soul.

The demons, following JT's line of sight, discover what the man sees, which compels them to scramble for cover.

"*Enough!*" booms the voice of a burly looking guardian. Bearing a sword in hand, he has come to escort JT home. Angelic warriors form a perimeter around the dying mortal to protect him from further attack.

"Your work here is done," declares a Heavenly warrior. "No more harm will befall this man. He has paid the price for his sins and now must go home to be with the Savior."

The inmates in the cafeteria have no clue as to what's going on. All they see is the outstretched hand of Jermaine Trotter reaching up to something unseen.

The unseen being—a beautiful servant of Heaven—descends toward JT to grasp the outstretched hand of the fading Pharaoh. As their hands secure a grip, the man's soul is whisked away to Paradise. JT is dead. Yet his spirit will live forever, hallelujah!

Hell's minions scream with anger.

39

The Battle Begins

Solomon and Lee evaluate their situation. A battle is about to erupt, and the angels are biding their time, waiting for the right moment to initiate the attack.

"My brother," says Lee, "the saints have come together and have provided us with an adequate prayer base. While the opportunity exists, I suggest we attack Fratricide while his forces are in disarray."

Solomon agrees, "Confirmation from the Lord says the time is right for battle; the big one's grip on the city can be broken. Tonight will be the ideal time—the saints throughout the city are having a city-wide prayer service."

Indeed the guardians have grown bolder. Their movements, once done in secret, are now carried out in the open for the enemy to see. A confrontation with Sheol's forces, something Empyreal's warriors have been hoping for, is about to happen.

Again, reports are coming in about a massive buildup of the guardians throughout the city. Fratricide feels threatened, so he readies himself for the battle that will take place soon.

The mammoth is a worthy adversary who is not easily conquered. Though the angels are highly capable of unleashing a good dose of Heaven's fury, the saints will determine whether the battle is won or lost, not the sons of Empyreal.

Pastor Robinson and the church leaders gather for prayer. Forming a circle, they hold hands and focus their minds on the map. As the prayer assault begins, Pastor Robinson first prays that no outside interference will hinder the meeting. This serves to bind the imps who are running loose in the room and the enemy forces hovering above. The pastor then confesses to the Lord that he and the ministers gathered together are sinners who are saved by the grace of God. "So, Lord," prays Robinson, "be with us and have mercy as the assault begins."

While standing on guard, Fratricide and his minions suddenly see a bright light swelling in the distance. It resembles a giant tidal wave forming in a distant sea. The hellions stand puzzled trying to figure out what it may be. Moments later, imps and other minor spirits come flocking in with panicked looks on their faces. "Master, they're coming! They're coming!" yell the thousands of wicked spirits seeking safety in Fratricide's lair.

The big one seems confused as he keeps his eyes fixed on the typhoon headed to the shores of his kingdom. Finally, having seen enough, Fratricide quickly reaches up to snatch an imp from the air. The bugged-eye rascal screams with fright, fluttering like a fish caught on a hook. The overlord gives the spirit a good shaking to bring the wretched gremlin to his senses. "What is the meaning of all this panic, hmm?"

"They're coming our way, we must flee," cries the imp.

Fratricide already knows who *they* are, but he seeks clarification. "Calm down, fool, tell me exactly who you are referring to."

Under normal circumstances, an inferior spirit would harness his tongue when addressing a superior. But, this situation is not normal. Frustrated that he can't flee as he wishes, the imp speaks his true mind. "Are you a fool? There's only one thing we demons fear, and it's getting closer. Let me go before He destroys us all."

The mammoth is still not convinced.

"Yes—*He; it's* the *Son!* He's bringing legions of warriors with Him. We will be destroyed if you don't do something quick," cries the desperate imp.

The bad news, along with the imp's flippant tongue, angers Fratricide. He lets off a mad roar that compels his guards to assume a defensive position. The large one still holds in his fist a gasping spirit who is suffocating from the choking grip about its neck. "Let me go," the imp manages to gasp.

A devious thought comes to Fratricide's mind. "I'll let you go indeed." The behemoth rips the rascal's head from its neck then watches while the body evaporates into thin air.

Feeling a bit better, the overseer redirects his attention back to the tidal wave that has grown brighter since he last seen it moments ago.

The presence of angelic forces in Harlem Heights is greater than ever before, which Solomon and Lee find encouraging. The increased number of warriors will be needed during the heat of the battle when Fratricide deploys his forces into combat. No matter how many guardians join the fight, it is still the prayers of the saints that will determine the outcome.

Never before has the mammoth experienced an attack on his own turf; all throughout his kingdom is chaos. Now that old feeling is back again. Fratricide hasn't forgotten, however, it's been a while since he last felt fear … since he last felt himself a victim.

In an effort to feel more secure, the big one assembles a crew of his mightiest warriors. They take refuge in the bowels of city hall where Heaven's sons will be reluctant to go.

Platoons of angelic forces sack the city, seizing control of the streets. As they penetrate the enemy's defenses, most of the devils scatter like roaches rather than standing their ground. The stronger of the evil spirits attempt to remain steadfast, yet it's hard to be courageous when standing alone. Having no choice but to flee, the remaining ones abandon post seeking safety at Fratricide's lair just as their underlings did.

As Lee makes his way to city hall, the battle intensifies. Enemy forces are everywhere and not as easily intimidated as the spirits in the streets.

Hell's warriors attack from all direction, slowing the progress of the guardians who seek a confrontation with Fratricide. Being confident in their skills, the evil combatants taunt their holy adversaries, inspiring some of the imps to return to battle to sneak in a few blows whenever possible. Lee makes adjustments by signaling the reserves to the fight. Again, the cowardly imps scatter for safety when they see reinforcements on the way.

From a distance, city hall looks like an upset beehive. Blades and sparks light the atmosphere. Fighting can be seen from miles away.

As the reserves come with overwhelming force, Lee is free to make a deeper move down into the bowels of city hall. He brings with him a select group of guardians that seek a showdown with the big one, Fratricide.

While Lee hunts for the large one, Solomon is busy managing the prayer meeting. His subordinates are stationed throughout the room guiding each minister to stay the course with prayer.

The wicked spirits within the room are doing their best to afflict the humans with fatigue or to distract their minds with personal problems.

It's a seesaw battle between the forces of good and evil to sway the minds of the mortals. So far, Solomon has maintained control of the prayer meeting, but the number of saints dropping out of the battle increases. If the humans lose sight of the objective, Lee's forces may suffer a setback. The prayer cover is a critical need.

As the guardians venture deeper into city hall, the battle becomes more fierce. Spirits from both sides clash in combat, hacking limbs from one another. It's a gruesome but awesome sight to see Heaven's fury and Hades' rage lighting up the skies.

On a regular basis, Empyrean scouts return to the church to inform Solomon of the progress at city hall. Reports indicate that Lee is taking ground. However, each victorious battle leads to a greater challenge, so it's crucial for the prayer cover to remain in place—a task easier said than done.

Approximately two hours of prayer have passed, and the church leaders are getting weary. Never before have they experienced such labor-intensive prayer. Something must be done to keep the mortals motivated.

Pastor Robinson has a word of encouragement to share, so he takes a moment to address the saints. "Brother and sisters, there's something special going on in the spiritual realm. I don't know exactly what it is, but we all can feel it. Right now, the burden in this place is heavy, which means we're doing something right. We must carry on just a bit longer until we reach a breakthrough."

As Randy Robinson speaks, lightning flashes and thunder cracks in the sky. A few of the saints are startled by the clapping thunder as it reverberates through the church roof. Others are spooked by the peculiar sounds they hear. Could it be their imagination? That strange noise sounds like clashing armor.

At this stage of the fight, Lee notices that Sheol's warriors are bigger and stronger than the spirits he faced earlier in the battle—an obvious clue that Fratricide is somewhere nearby. Suddenly, the fighting ceases, causing the atmosphere to become eerily quiet. Out from among the shadows step the most menacing warriors the guardians have encountered thus far. The dark spirits, exuding arrogance and bearing swords in hand, approach the angels like cowboys at a showdown.

As Heaven's fighters situate themselves for the battle, their attention is directed to a moving shadow. What they first perceive to be a wall is really a silhouette of something grotesquely large. There's no doubting now, the angels have found exactly what they're looking for. The shadow is none other than the behemoth, Fratricide, who appears to be a mountain towering over hills. This will not be an easy fight. No wonder the evil warriors act with such confidence.

For the first time since the battle ensued, Lee and his fighters must take the defensive.

Meanwhile, the big one uses the opportunity to speak. "Michael, Empyreal's greatest warrior, I know, and the *Son*, I know, but who do you think you are confronting *me*, hmm?" inquires Fratricide with a crazed look in his eyes.

The large one has tangled with Heaven's greatest warriors. He was even there when Christ laid down His life on the cross. More so, the

Harlem Heights overseer was there and suffered miserably when Jesus conquered Hell after rising from the dead three days later—what a horrible day that was. And now this no-name guardian dares to stand before him in battle?

Fratricide declares, "I shall crush you and your feeble warrior fairies."

40

Prayer Cover

The city of Harlem Heights seems to know exactly what's happening in the spiritual realm. It moans and groans as the fight for her life takes place.

Having grown weary of the tug-of-war battle between good and evil, some of the saints have taken to the sidelines to watch the game from the bench. When the saints take a neutral position, the evil spirits perceive the mortals' actions as a sign of victory.

But the loyal servant, Robinson, is not quick to give up. Randy stops to address the crowd again. "People, we must continue the fight. I know we are tired, and it may seem pointless to some of us, but please let's continue the prayer. The battle is almost won. We can assure victory if we can just carry on a bit longer."

Solomon, in total agreement, gives orders to the ministering spirits to help the saints renew their strength. The angels' faith never wavers as they go about their task with great determination. If only mankind was as dedicated to the Savior's cause, the fight would be easier.

"Everybody, let's take a break with some praise and worship. I'll play the piano while we sing songs to the Lord," pleads Robinson. "For when praises go up, blessings will come back down. This is one way for us to maintain the prayer cover … one way for the Lord to have his will in our city."

Lee takes the first step forward beckoning Fratricide to a duel. Amused by the angel's courage, the big one grins a wicked smile while paying his adversary a snide compliment for such bravery. "Hmm, I see the Tyrant is still in the sacrifice business. You gladly give your life for the cause … how nice." The mammoth has a comment for Lee's warriors too. "And these sheep that follow you, are they for the slaughter as well?" The large one chuckles while slabs of blubber ripple up and down his belly like waves.

Suddenly, without warning, the big one snatches his sword from its sheath. He takes a swooping slice at Lee's neck. With cat-like quickness, the guardian ducks the sword and returns the strike with one of his own. Fratricide easily blocks the blow and is impressed by Lee's strength despite the angel's lack of size.

The other spirits, both good and evil, are compelled to watch as the dueling chiefs steal the show.

Lee, the smaller but swifter one, moves about with quickness. Fratricide, standing in place, moves nothing but his swollen arm and the sword it bears. He's like a cat at play with a mouse.

The Empyrean seeks an opening to attack the body; Sheol's behemoth looks for an opportunity to deal a crushing blow. Neither one is able to overcome the other—that is until several demons run interference. Lurking in the shadows are more of Hell's minions. They ambush the guardians. The odds are now stacked in Hades' favor; there are at least two devils fighting against every one angel.

Heaven's warriors fight valiantly, yet their efforts do little to hold the dark forces at bay. Fratricide and his cronies hack and chop off angelic limbs, causing the body parts to dissolve into thin air.

As the demonic onslaught becomes too fierce to defend, Lee and his warriors find themselves standing back to back, surrounded by the enemy. Hades' wicked warriors close in for the kill.

Surprisingly, the evil horde is in no rush to deal the final deathblows; rather, they relish the moment while Fratricide says a few words. "Where art thy Savior now, hmm? Shall He descend from His throne to save ye worthless servants? I thinketh not. As I have grown tired of thy meddling hand in the midst of my affairs, thou hast been a thorn in my side. I shall now smite thee, ridding the Earth of thy Heavenly stench."

Drool drips from the big one's foul mouth as he spews more curses. He stands triumphantly with a clenched fist in the air while his other hand hangs downward, gripping a sword. Just as the mammoth gives the order to slay the guardians, time abruptly stands still...

A shaft of light, from an unseen source suddenly appears, moving slowly from one spot to another as if searching for something lost. The hellions feel uncertain about the light; they watch it suspiciously trying to figure out if it's friend or foe.

The desperate angels are equally curious to know the source of the light too. Lee hopes it's the prayer, something inside his heart believes it *is* the prayer. If Solomon has fulfilled his side of the deal, then the prayer cover is taking affect.

The light from the unseen source circles in closer to the spirits. Moving slower, it intensifies in brightness and radiates more heat. The rogues are no longer concerned about the guardians, and they turn their backs to the enemy. Like mischievous kittens mesmerized by a dangling string of yarn, the evil spirits watch every move the mysterious light makes. As the diameter of the light widens, the demons crowd in among the angels.

Lee welcomes the light by giving praise to God above. The evil spirits howl, panic, and suddenly flee the area.

"Where are you cowards going? Stay and fight like real warriors," yells the big one while his minions abandon him. "This is not fair that He intervenes. This is *my* city and it belongs to *me*!" whines the overlord. "I will finish this myself."

Lunging toward Lee, Fratricides attempts to sever the angel's head from his shoulders. Just as the blade comes within inches of Lee's neck, it abruptly stops. Everything stops.

Fratricide hangs suspended in mid air paralyzed. He can move nothing but his eyes. And now his hearing begins to fade in and out like the fluctuating reception of a shortwave radio as the prayers of the saints' tune into his ears. The behemoth is tormented by the broadcast of praise and worship.

Sensing the presence of the Lord, the angels let down their guard. They watch the big enemy float through the ceiling to the top floors and out of the city hall building like a hot air balloon. The rain still showers down on the city as lightening rips back the evening's darkness in quick flashes. All spirits can see the fallen ruler of Harlem Heights.

The shaft of light that once appeared as a narrow beam in the bowels of city hall now illuminates the evening sky. It compels every wicked creature in Harlem Heights to scramble for cover in some dark corner or hole.

Angels throughout Harlem Heights flock to the light to bask in the glory of the Lord. The joy spills over to the mortals at the prayer meeting. "Praise the Lord," shouts one of the saints. "A breakthrough is happening," exclaims another.

Fratricide is swelling to an enormous size. Just when it appears that he can get no bigger, his size increases dramatically. His arms and legs are no longer visible. The large one is just a big ball of demonic blubber.

Lee, talking to no one in particular makes a prediction. "I don't know for sure, but it seems like the mammoth is about to burst."

The crescendo of praise is punctuated by a bolt of lightning that rips the sky, causing Fratricide to suddenly explode like an atomic bomb. The combustion is loud enough to set off car alarms in the physical realm. The sight and sound of the explosion causes every foul creature to dig even deeper for cover.

The big one's grip on the city is finally broken—Harlem Heights is free!

41

After the Battle

"**D**id you hear the sound of that thunder?" asks a minister.

"I think it means our work is done; I feel a sense of closure," Robinson concludes. "We certainly achieved something."

Solomon and his angels gather about the saints to confirm the feeling. "This part of the job is done, my friends. Now we can continue on with the healing process."

Dismissing the saints, Robinson takes a seat to relax a bit. Though everyone is free to go home, no one leaves. They prefer to hang around for a while meditating on the wonders of the Lord. A calm silence falls upon the church leaders as all individuals pray within their hearts, giving thanks to Jesus.

The storm subsides as quickly as it appeared. The clouds part, revealing a full moon shining brightly. To human eyes, the clear evening sky is a treasure chest of stars opened for the world to admire. To the guardians, the light is glory emanating from the throne room of Empyreal.

Solomon and Lee observe their comrades basking in the splendid radiance of the Lord. The light is an open freeway for Heaven's servants to access the city of Harlem Heights with no more interference from Fratricide's minions. This is what the angels have always desired.

Getting back to business, Solomon addresses his brothers, "Praise to the Highest."

"Praise be to the Lord," they respond in unison.

"The Savior has blessed us to overcome the forces of Sheol. Though we accomplished much, we still have much work to do. The seeds we planted throughout the city must be cultivated. May the Lord bless our efforts to make the gospel flourish in Harlem Heights."

The moment of celebration is short lived. Heaven's sons slip away into the night; some go alone while others travel in pairs or in small groups of three or four. They instinctively go about their individual tasks to make the city a place for the gospel to flourish.

Just two angels remain—Solomon and Lee. At the moment, they are concerned about the whereabouts of Molder and Wrath. Surely they witnessed what happened in the city tonight. Are they the ones looking to occupy the throne where Fratricide once sat?

"Have we received word on Molder and Wrath?" asks Solomon.

Lee responds, "I gave Siron the mission of keeping an eye on Willie Mo'. I expect to hear from him soon."

"Yes, Willie James Moore," Solomon says quietly to himself, "what has he been up to lately?" Then, to Lee, he says, "Speaking of Willie, what about the police department and the mayor? I'm curious to see what has become of the government officials."

"I've got a feeling Mo' will resurface once the smoke clears. In addition to the prayers, I believe Molder and Wrath had something to do with undermining Fratricide's power base."

"That's the nature of the enemy. They're always scrambling for power," Solomon concludes.

As expected, Siron comes with news. "It's confirmed, Fratricide has been banished to the abyss. The remaining enemy forces are scrambling to pledge their allegiance to the leaders they believe can establish dominion over Harlem Heights."

"Are there many candidates?" inquires Lee.

"Yes, there are many, but these wicked spirits are no fools. The majority will follow Molder the guide and Wrath the warrior. These two occupy the mortal, Willie Mo'."

Solomon is curious. "What are the odds that Molder and Wrath will replace the big one?"

"I say the odds weigh in their favor," Siron predicts. "They control most of the human resources."

"We must prevent them from establishing a foothold within this city again," declares Lee.

"And we must make them atone for JT's death," says Solomon.

Siron is uncertain about the fate of Jermaine Trotter. "What was the final outcome for that man; tell me he made it?"

The messenger places a gentle hand upon the scout's shoulder to inform him of the good news. "Yes, my brother, he did."

"Hallelujah!" Siron is pleased.

The prayer warfare of the saints is over, yet the effect of last night's prayer meeting is still wreaking havoc at the police department. The precinct is infested with FBI agents who have emptied file cabinets and seized computers.

The dirty detectives, Hughes and Diggs, sit in separate rooms being interrogated by federal agents. It feels weird to be on the receiving end of a loaded interrogation; no cop likes to be the target of a grilling session.

"Let's get this straight," says the agent, "you have no idea as to where Willie James Moore is?"

Diggs responds in a cool demeanor, "That's correct."

The agent isn't convinced. "All the time you spent on this case—years of undercover work—and you have no clue where this drug lord could be hiding?"

The interrogated cop nods his head in agreement.

"I got a bad feeling about you and Hughes. I think you two are in bed with this thug. If I find out you had something to do with this criminal, I'll be sure to put you in a cell underneath the prison."

Diggs plays cool, but, if the agents could see his heart, they would see a twist of muscle pumping like a piston. If the agents could read his mind, they would know Diggs is concerned about his partner. Hopefully Hughes can hold his tongue. If he doesn't, everyone is going down.

The same situation is taking place in the other room where Hughes finds himself thinking, *What all do these federal agents know? Has Diggs told anything at all?*

Seeming to cooperate, Hughes tells enough to convince the agents of his innocence—or so he thinks. The detective's body language remains consistent; he wills himself not to make an awkward movement that may indicate he is telling a lie. Despite his worries, he performs well.

The interrogation is finally over and both detectives sit at their desks in relative silence. Drops of suspicion drip in the back of their minds as both consider the possibility of a plea deal. They make small talk, pretending not to be concerned—that is until Mingo walks by with an agent.

Hughes springs from his chair with a look of astonishment on his face. He can't believe what his eyes just saw: Mingo and an agent walking together can't be good. Just when he's about to say something, another FBI agent walks by with a sheepish smile on her face. It's as if she arranged the situation on purpose.

"Sit down, control yourself!" Diggs advises. "You're making us look guilty."

The female agent sticks her head through the door to make a comment. "I see you guys don't like what you just saw." She winks an eye, "Gotcha."

Hughes gives her the middle finger.

"Control that hot head of yours," Diggs insists. "You're drawing negative attention, and that's the last thing we want at this time."

Hughes isn't in the mood for corrective guidance. A swelling urge to attack surges throughout his body, yet he heeds his partner's advice. If he can ever get out of this mess, ol' Hank will deal with Diggs when the time is right. Division has taken root among the detectives.

Just when matters begin to cool down, Mingo and an agent walk by again talking together. They stop in front of the detectives' office where both men can see them. The agent presents a business card to Mingo. The two shake hands. If the FBI is trying to make a statement, the message is quite clear—and threatening.

Pastor Robinson and church leaders throughout the community take advantage of the opportunity to bring Christ to the streets. They understand religion is a touchy matter for most people, so a decision is made to demonstrate the love of Christ rather than preach it.

The church has helped to renew the community's interest in maintaining safe neighborhoods, which has led to a truce between all gang members. Not everyone agrees with the truce, but none dares to defy the majority. The peace is a welcome break from the bitter strife of the past.

Even Tommy Hurt, the mayor's son, turns his life around. The death of his best friend JT, together with the arrest of several government officials, has scared Tommy straight.

The angels enjoy the change of scenery as well. No longer are the streets dominated by evil. Hell's minions still lurk about the clubs and other shady places, yet they no longer run rampant as they did before; Heaven is the dominant force now.

Things are looking good for the city of Harlem Heights.

42

The Mayor and Pharaoh Meet

Willie Mo' and Mayor Hurt meet privately at city hall to discuss a few matters in secrecy. Molder, Wrath, and other evil spirits accompany the two mortals. The meeting is short, and Willie does most of the speaking. "I must go underground for a while," he says. "It's going to take some time for this whole ordeal to blow over. Our connections with the FBI will do what's necessary to ensure this case goes no further than it has."

"What are we going to do with detectives Hughes and Diggs?" asks Hurt.

"Diggs has been taken care of, Hughes is next."

"What about Mingo and the rest of the gangs?"

Mo' replies, "That punk thinks he's hiding in the witness protection program. When we need him, we know where to find him. As for the gangs, no truce is safe when money is involved. A promise of one big payoff will plunge these gangs back into war."

"JT?" the mayor questions.

"He's history. He crossed me—something no one should do if he values his very own life."

"You took out your best friend?" inquires Mayor Hurt with his mouth hanging open in disbelief.

A wry smile comes to Mo's face. "Yeah, I put out the order to have him snuffed. I'll do the same to you if things ever get out of hand the way they did in the recent past. The warehouse, the operation in the projects, and the strip club are gone. I'll get it all back and more—you'll make sure of that."

Mayor Hurt understands the consequences of failure should it happen again. He seems not the least bit worried by Willie's threat. Besides, what does he have to worry about? Hurt won the reelection. The city is being renovated, and the people believe it's all for a good cause.

43

Willie Mo's Last Words

Like I said before, I had it all. The money and power was all mine until it was taken from me. Now I have to start over again—hustling like a starving pimp. I'm not accustomed to losing. All my life, I've always been a winner. I had to fail for the first time to realize I've been losing all along—it's ironic isn't it? This life isn't what I expected ... they lied to me. Every promise they made was a lie. I no longer pledge my allegiance to them. Molder and Wrath are not what they proclaim to be. For the time being, I have no choice but to play their game. But when the time comes, I'll slip off just like old man Levy did. If those Christians can protect that old man from harm, surely they can keep me safe ... we'll see.